Julieanne Howells loves the romance of a stormy day—which is just as well because she lives in the rainy north-east of England. On inclement days, if she's not writing and reading, she has a fondness for cooking. Sometimes her efforts are even edible. She compensates for her lack of domestic skills by being an expert daydreamer, always imagining ways for plucky heroines to upend the world of handsome, provoking heroes. For Julieanne, writing for Mills & Boon is just about the perfect job.

Bella Mason has been a bookworm from an early age. She has been regaling people with stories from the time she discovered she could hold the dinner table hostage with her reimagined fairy tales. After earning a degree in journalism, she rekindled her love of writing and now writes full time. When she isn't imagining dashing heroes and strong heroines, she can be found exploring Melbourne, with her nose in a book, or lusting after fast cars.

STRANDED
WITH HIS
RUNAWAY BRIDE

JULIEANNE HOWELLS

AWAKENED BY THE
WILD BILLIONAIRE

BELLA MASON

MILLS & BOON

First published in Great Britain 2022
by Mills & Boon, an imprint of HarperCollins*Publishers* Ltd,
1 London Bridge Street, London, SE1 9GF

www.harpercollins.co.uk

HarperCollins*Publishers*
1st Floor, Watermarque Building,
Ringsend Road, Dublin 4, Ireland

Stranded with His Runaway Bride © 2022 Julieanne Howells

Awakened by the Wild Billionaire © 2022 Bella Mason

ISBN: 978-0-263-30100-7

09/22

MIX
Paper from
responsible sources
FSC C007454

This book is produced from independently certified FSC™ paper
to ensure responsible forest management.
For more information visit www.harpercollins.co.uk/green.

Printed and Bound in Spain using 100% Renewable Electricity
at CPI Black Print, Barcelona

STRANDED
WITH HIS
RUNAWAY BRIDE

JULIEANNE HOWELLS

MILLS & BOON

CHAPTER ONE

THE CATHEDRAL OF St Peter's was looking its baroque best. Decked out in floral displays so spectacular they were upstaged only by the guests in all their wedding finery. Half the crowned heads of Europe were sitting in the congregation. Joined by presidents, prime ministers and, of course, all the senior officials of the principality of Grimentz. There to see its ruler wed.

So for His Serene Highness Prince Leopold Friedrich von Frohburg, waiting in the sacristy for proceedings to begin, his cousin's whispered message was not what he wanted to hear.

'It appears your blushing bride has fled.'

Leo swirled from the mirror where he'd been submitting to the last adjustments of his perfectionist valet.

'Although—' Seb added casually, and entirely at odds with the gravity of the situation '—it would be more accurate to say disappeared. Because one minute Princess Violetta was in her room at the castle and then, *poof...*' He snapped his fingers in the air for effect. 'Gone.'

Leo glared at his cousin. Prince Sebastien von Frohburg was the only person on the planet he truly trusted, which meant he allowed him informalities he'd tolerate from no one else. But this was definitely not the time for any of them.

'A young woman in her wedding dress, and wearing

our priceless Elisabetha tiara, I might add, has simply vanished?'

Seb shrugged. 'That about sums it up, yes.'

'Who the hell allowed that to happen?'

His cousin slanted him a look. 'Er…well, that would be you, Leo, wouldn't it?'

Leo ignored the implication.

Get to know this one, Seb had begged him. *Woo her… don't take the chance.*

But he'd been reassured that this Della Torre sister was different. Biddable. Willing. Decorous. And certainly, at the few joint functions they'd attended, her hand had been cool and steady in his while she'd played the part of consort-to-be flawlessly.

Better than the last. The elder sister who'd run off with her bodyguard—a bodyguard!—a month before she was due to fulfil her decade-long engagement to marry him, a prince, and monarch of the oldest and richest principality in Europe. Where was the comparison?

The shame, of course, had all been attached to her family. He and his father had made sure of it. No woman could be allowed to sully the great name of von Frohburg. Especially not a Della Torre one. They'd been a thorn in the side of the von Frohburgs for four hundred years.

Their grand duchy sat opposite Grimentz, separated by only a thin stretch of water. With no males to inherit, once Leo wed the female about to become the next grand duchess, her little state would rejoin his.

A bloodless reunification after centuries of bitter waiting.

For that prize Leo was ambitious enough to risk another go at marrying into the family. Despite the elder sister's rebellious streak.

Violetta, the younger daughter, her uncle and regent, had

assured him, had been carefully raised and would never do such a thing.

No female had ever been allowed to rule the duchy in her own right, and none of the officials were keen to try that now. The Della Torres had approached his father fifteen years ago. Once it became clear the grand duke and his wife would have no male heir.

Leo hadn't seen the need to get to know the second daughter any better, other than at the handful of official functions they'd attended together as a betrothed couple. He'd gone through all the relevant groundwork when he'd been engaged to her sister. He knew the key players, the role she had in her duchy. Her uncle had been involved in the first negotiations anyway and he was still in place. It was essentially just a matter of replacing one sister with the other in the existing arrangements. All the requisite background checks revealed a female who'd led a quiet and blameless life.

Leo liked the fact she'd appeared bland and undemanding at their few meetings. It boded well for a businesslike union with no complications: like romantic expectations on the girl's part. Or, heaven help him, emotions. Life had long since taught him to be done with all that. While she wasn't a beauty like her sister, he was confident he'd be able to do his duty in bed and get the son and heir he needed. The future of his country and his people depended on him.

But could it be happening again? Was this girl eloping too? Anger and humiliation sliced through his gut.

'Was she alone?' Leo growled.

'As far as we know. It seems to be a spur-of-the-moment thing. There were less than ten minutes between her maids leaving and her uncle showing up to escort her here—' Seb paused to fish his phone from a pocket. 'Interesting. One of the businesses supplying flowers for the reception has reported a van stolen from the castle courtyard.'

'So now she has transport?'

'Looks that way. But where could she go? She's hardly been here. How well could she know Grimentz?'

Barely at all. Historically, the two families had kept their distance since the treacherous Della Torres, then a vassal family, had stolen the grand duchy for themselves from his ancestors four centuries ago.

Unless she'd bribed a Grimentzian boatman to take her back across the water, there was only really one place she *could* go. The one place Leo knew for certain the girl had visited in Grimentz. Unfortunately, this was the last place he'd ever wanted to set eyes on again.

He began striding towards the private side entrance of the cathedral, the one shielded from the press and the crowds lining almost every other inch of the capital, calling for a car—a fast one—and issuing a rash of orders as he went. For his security chief. And for Seb, his best man, who, with the abrupt cessation of his other duties, was now in charge of damage limitation.

'The official line will be that she's taken ill,' Leo said as he strode 'The wedding is postponed. No bride wants her special day spoiled by a bout of the runs.'

Seb winced. 'You want everyone to think your absent bride is stuck in her bathroom? The press will have a field day.'

'Not my problem. That's hers. She ran away. My protection is no longer a given,' Leo said, arriving at the doorway as a red Ferrari pulled up.

Seb's beloved car. Leo had indulged his cousin, who'd insisted he should surrender his bachelorhood in true playboy style, and allowed him to drive them both to the cathedral in it. The crowds had lapped it up. Cheering like maniacs as the groom and his best man climbed out.

Something more anonymous would have been his preference now, but at least the thing would eat up the miles between him and his missing bride. She'd had maybe a twenty-minute head start and if she was heading where he believed this would get him there before anyone else.

He climbed in.

'What do you want me to do with that lot back there?' Seb waved a hand in the direction of the cathedral behind them.

'You're supposed to be the charming one. I'm sure you'll work something out. And tell the staff in the castle they get a bonus for their silence. Any who do decide to talk to the press will not only lose their job, but get themselves and their family kicked out of the principality. Permanently.'

Seb looked shocked. 'Can we even do that?'

'We can now. Blame the woman. The shame all goes one way, remember.'

'So where precisely are you going?' Seb asked, leaning on the open door.

'Grandmother's chateau. Violetta went there every summer. Right up to Grand-Mère's death four years ago.'

'But you had it closed up.'

'Which makes it even more perfect as a bolt-hole, don't you think?'

Seb's brow knotted. 'Wait, isn't that where—'

'Yes.' Leo cut him off. 'And I won't let that happen again.'

Leo lowered the car window to give some last-minute instructions. 'Give the archbishop the blue suite at the castle. He's fond of the bed in those rooms. I'll have the girl back here before midnight and he can marry us in the chapel. You can be a witness. No need for anything grander. Get a press release ready so we can announce the marriage in the morning.'

'You're that confident about persuading her to come back?'

'She's not her sister. It's probably just nerves. There are

numerous benefits to being married to me. She just needs to see the sense of it.'

'Oh, I'd definitely open with that. She'll be putty in your hands.'

'Seb, we're so close to getting the grand duchy back I can almost taste it. I won't be denied that by some unreliable girl who can't see what's good for her.'

None of his ancestors had ever come this close to regaining the duchy. Not even his father. Leo would wed the Devil's mistress to prove to that cold-hearted bastard he was better than him and all their mutual ancestors put together.

He gunned the engine and sped out of the cathedral close, into the streets that had been closed for the duration of the wedding celebrations and kept clear for service vehicles. Heading north, out of the capital. Twenty miles to the very edge of his realm. Where Grimentz finally succumbed to the mountains and its neighbours beyond.

As he drove Lake Sérénité glittered below him. How ironic. A lake called serenity dividing two ruling families who'd battled each other to a stand then maintained a belligerent silence of deep mistrust for four centuries. This wedding was supposed to have put an end to all that.

Beyond Sérénité's calm waters sat the grand duchy of San Nicolo, lush and green with its superb vineyards and rolling pastures. It wasn't rich like Grimentz. It hadn't embraced the financial services that had given his principality unimaginable wealth and global influence. But it was soft and welcoming in a way that Grimentz, with its dour medieval castle and looming mountains, could never be.

His ancestors had struggled over their peaks finding a rocky outcrop on the western edge of the lake, where they'd built their castle. As forbidding and unforgiving as the mountains that soared behind, it rose from the shoreline to dominate everything for miles around. Previous princes had tried to pretty it up with fairy-tale turrets and terraced pleasure gardens, but at its heart it remained what it was: a fortress.

But there was no castle hewn from cold rock for the Della Torres. They lived in Palladian elegance. Princess Violetta's forebears had fallen in love with the Renaissance and remade San Nicolo in its image, gracious and refined. Tourists flocked to its chocolate-box capital and pretty villages to quaff the wine and gorge themselves on the cheese and pastries it was famed for. Its subjects were comfortable, though perhaps not content. Since the death of Violetta's parents in a plane crash three years ago, just months after the elopement of her elder sister, there had been rumblings that the Della Torre family were no longer fit to rule. Her uncle, the regent while Violetta was not yet of age, was unpopular and fuelling the dissent with his rigid and old-fashioned governance. The sooner Leo could step in and take power—in the name of his wife, of course—the better.

He only had approximately thirteen hours to do that. After that, things became more complicated.

On the stroke of midnight, in the reverse of a Cinderella tale, his flighty bride turned twenty-one and would no longer be just Princess Violetta of San Nicolo, subject to her uncle's rule, but would be transformed into Her Serene Highness the Grand Duchess Violetta Della Torre, absolute monarch.

Some weird twist in the San Nicolo succession meant her husband couldn't take power until she was twenty-one. But take power he would. San Nicolo was old-fashioned that way. Never before allowing a woman to rule in her own right, and her uncle was determined that wouldn't happen now. Though if they'd married before now Leo would have had months of deferring to him. Obliged to be involved in the country's affairs but with no actual power.

Leo had solved the problem by arranging the marriage for the eve of the princess's birthday. No frustrating wait, forced to watch as her uncle wielded power—badly, he might add—and no legal complications. Because if they *weren't* married by the time the girl reached her majority there'd be a tortuous legal process to have him recognised as Head of State in place of his wife.

He gritted his teeth as he drove. All that stood between him and achieving his lifelong goal was an unsteady girl. What was she running away from? A life of privilege, and of ease. He'd shoulder all the responsibilities of monarch. She'd never have to raise a finger. Never have to make difficult choices.

'The girl has no aptitude for the work,' her uncle had told him. 'Better to have you at the helm.'

Leo was fine with that. Glad to have no interference from the Della Torres. What had they achieved with their picture-postcard duchy? Cheese, wine and tourism. That was the extent of their ambition. Leaving the people trapped in an agrarian living museum. He'd be bringing them up to date.

Once he'd made Violetta his wife.

Briefly he pitied the girl. Her father was happy to give away the first daughter to an enemy. The uncle even happier to hand over the second. No chance for her to be Grand Duchess in her own right. Her father and uncle preferring to relinquish the duchy's sovereignty rather than have a female at the helm. What a family to have!

Then he recalled the packed cathedral, the spoiled banquet, the bunting, drooping in the July heat, and his sympathy deserted him.

He slammed the car into a higher gear and screamed down the road.

He hoped he'd guessed her destination correctly. This was his way. React swiftly. It had been drummed into him since birth.

'Never dither. Better to act, and act decisively. Inde-

cision is for commoners, boy.' His father's mantra. He'd learned it well. Along with several others.

'Kindness is a weakness you cannot afford.'

'Compassion is for fools.'

'Love is a lie.'

'Women are for bed sport and offspring and otherwise not to be trusted.'

Pity his father hadn't had one for dealing with being jilted, twice. By the same damn family. But Leo knew what he would have said.

Marry her, get a son by her and we finally have the duchy back.

Oh, I intend to, Papa.

In his life he'd never wanted anything more than to be the von Frohburg to finally regain the grand duchy. To prove to his father, even though he was long gone, that he deserved to be the prince he'd been born to be.

Once he had secured her, he'd paint it as wedding jitters, all eased and soothed by her handsome groom. He'd have photos released. Preferably of her gazing up at him, doe-eyed and adoring. The least she could do under the circumstances.

If he failed, not only would he lose the chance of regaining the duchy but, should he die without siring a son, Grimentz would suffer the rule of Max, Seb's older half-brother.

It was hard to imagine a man less suited to the task.

Devoid of his sibling's intelligence and loyalty, Max cared for only two things: himself and his pleasures. That was it. He was dedicated to a life of indolence and excess. The principality had not risen to the heights it had under the guidance of such men.

Leo wouldn't let that happen. He was thirty years old. The time had definitely come for him to wed.

And reclaim San Nicolo at last.

He met no one on the road. The entire population would be watching the wedding. Either at home or in the streets of the capital. In just twenty minutes he passed the gate-house and entered the grounds of the estate of his grand-mother's chateau. The very last place he'd thought to visit again. After she'd left it to him in her will, he'd ordered it be practically closed up. Except for authorising a monthly visit by a housekeeper, maid and groundsman to see to any repairs and keep the place watertight, he'd wanted nothing more to do with it.

Damn and blast the girl. Why did she have to go there of all places? With all of its bitter memories and mountains of regret. A place he'd vowed to never set foot in again.

Where he'd taken the elder Della Torre girl, his first fiancée.

Francesca was the beauty of the family. She'd inherited her mother's blue eyes and golden hair. Her mother's height and lithesome figure too. She'd charmed and flattered him and given no inkling she'd been using him to plot her escape.

'Let's go to your grandmother's chateau,' she'd said. 'The two of us, for a night away from everyone and their prying eyes.' He'd believed her. When she'd asked if they could wait so she'd come to him a virgin on their wedding night, he'd agreed and they'd gone to their separate beds.

Only for him to discover the next morning that she'd run off. A month later she was married to her ex-bodyguard. Going to the chateau with him had simply been a way for her to escape the watchful eyes of her father and the San Nicolo security team.

Leo's humiliation had been complete, and his father's rage and censure had been blistering. But he'd learned his lesson well. He'd never trust a woman again.

The last section of road climbed upwards to the chateau itself. The road had become rutted, the winters having taken their toll. So intent was he on his destination he missed the deep pothole. Sadly, the car did not. On a shudder and with a sickening grinding noise he came to an abrupt halt.

Leo flung the door wide and climbed out into the July heat. He'd be completing his journey on foot. With a curse he set off, sweating already in his wedding regalia.

The woman had better be at the end of this track.

Then the chateau appeared from behind the trees. Somewhere Grand-Mère had laughingly called the summer house but Chateau Elisabetha had three floors, nine guest bedrooms and a ballroom lined with mirrors and finely painted figures of dancing couples. An elegant white limestone chateau, nestled in its own valley with lush green foothills behind, extensive gardens on all sides and its own boathouse and jetty on the lake. His grandmother's summer residence. She and her husband had originally bought the place when their daughter had married the ruling prince and when she was widowed, his grandmother had spent every summer there to be close to her.

Leo hadn't expected the rush of memories as he approached. That it would look pretty much just as he'd remembered. Before he'd turned fourteen, and fate had taken a different turn and holidays with his grandmother had instantly ceased.

The gardens were a little more overgrown than Grand-Mère used to keep them, but even there she was a lover of nature, letting every kind of lost, loveless creature find a home—including him once—so she might have approved of the meadow of wildflowers that had taken over the lawns.

He could see her now. On that terrace, overlooking the lake. Drinking schnapps by candlelight and listening to Buena Vista Social Club. With her beloved rescue dogs by her side. Various mutts missing a leg or an ear, or with a broken doggy heart that she somehow fixed. All once unloved creatures, given the best of homes in this chateau.

Sometimes other guests had joined them. Like that last summer he'd spent there, when the grandchildren of her best friend had been invited to the house for two weeks.

Girls. One so young and tiny he and Seb had dubbed her *la fée*, the fairy. He remembered she'd followed him around like a puppy. To a thirteen-year-old boy a small girl had been beneath his dignity, and he'd found a way to chase her off.

Then came that last visit, three years ago. When the chateau was his. Left to him in his grandmother's will.

The night he'd spent here with Francesca, the elder of those two girls.

What a debacle that had turned out to be.

But despite all that, it was still a house that held a touch of magic. It wound its way around him now.

He fought it off. Now was not the time for pointless sentiment. It had never served him well in the past and he didn't need it for what he was about to do.

The florist's van sat abandoned at the side of the building. A large sunhat, gauzy scarf and sunglasses stuffed on the dash. Probably also stolen from the florist. That would explain how his bride had driven from the castle unchallenged. She'd disguised herself.

Leo strode on. His determination building with each step. He'd caught up with her. Now to put a stop to this nonsense and persuade her to return with him.

CHAPTER TWO

VIOLETTA HEARD THE roar of the high-powered engine, cutting through the quiet, then the abrupt, grinding stop followed by the slam of a car door.

She dropped the receiver back into its cradle. No time to wait for Luisa to pick up the phone now.

From the window she saw a glossy red sports car hunkered under the trees. But whoever had climbed out of it had already disappeared into a dip in the drive and was lost from view.

How had they found her so quickly?

She hurried to throw back a dust sheet and perched in the middle of a long, high-backed chaise. Hoping she looked thoroughly regal and unassailable. Knowing if she stood, her trembling would show her to be the exact opposite.

Her heart pounding, she waited.

First came the crunch of booted feet on gravel.

Then the heavy strike of leather soles on the flagstones of the hallway.

She straightened her spine and stared resolutely ahead. Whoever had come for her, she was determined she would not be going back with them. Then in *he* walked, and she fought to hide her shock. Never expecting that her forbidding groom would bother to come after her himself.

Violetta stared at the man filling the doorway. The man her sister had exiled herself to avoid marrying. How had

Francesca described him? Like a half-tamed wolf: prowling, watchful and ever hungry. That was exactly the man who stood there now.

He was tall. He certainly always towered over her. Six feet two, she'd been told, when they'd determined what height heels she'd be permitted to wear at joint functions. At least three inches. Elevating her diminutive five feet two to the optimum height. The delicate bride to his alpha male prince, making the photos of the two of them together look perfect.

Unlike the match itself.

His dark hair, cut short at the sides, fell thick and lustrous across his forehead. There was a long, straight imperious nose—of course, what other kind would he have?—and deep-set blue eyes that women the world over swooned for.

Those eyes watched her now. His mouth might be smiling but, oh, those stunning eyes…they were scorching the flesh from her bones.

Feeling a sharp pull of attraction was deeply inconvenient though she should have expected it. She'd not been immune to him on those few occasions they'd met. But the pulse of heat and longing had lasted only while she was in his company and any after-effects had been bested.

Eventually.

Violetta decided that right now her best defence against that was attack.

'Oh, it's you,' she said, as nonchalantly as she could, and in her native Italian, not his French that they'd always conversed in before. Hoping to insult him. That the man accustomed to a lifetime of deference had rarely been greeted with less.

But he countered all that with a gracious smile, and said, in the most perfect Italian accent that shivered over skin, 'You were expecting someone else?'

'My money was on it being the prime minister. When

I heard the sports car, of course, I knew it wasn't him. Far too flashy and undignified.'

A strong male jaw tightened. He wasn't smiling quite so hard now.

'But I really wasn't expecting you. I thought you'd have been too busy.'

'My other appointments for the day were all cancelled. At rather short notice,' he added pleasantly enough. But she wasn't fooled. She could see the anger in the set of his shoulders and the fists bunched at his sides.

'Yeah, sorry about that...' She peered past him to the empty hallway.

'I'm here alone, if you're wondering. I took off so fast my security team didn't have time to follow. I told them I'd call them en route but, sadly, I forgot I'd left the valet in charge of my phone so they've no idea where I am.'

His crack security team did not have a clue where their prince was? That sounded unlikely. 'Won't they be out scouring the countryside for you?'

'Of course. But I doubt anyone will think to come here just yet.'

'You did.'

'But I know you have history with the place. As far as anyone else will recollect, you do not. Unless your uncle or your people consider it.'

She snorted. '*My* people have all been replaced and my uncle will hardly have cared about any holidays his niece once took.'

His brow knotted. 'Your people were replaced?' His surprise almost sounded genuine. But he'd had a hand in the changes to her team. She'd bet her life on it.

The man who stood before her now was palpably angry. Gone was the smoothly charming prince. Here was a creature of hard angles and bunched muscle. Was he bigger than she remembered? Surely not? It had only been two weeks since she'd last been in his company. Heat coursed through her belly.

She looked away to gaze straight ahead. Feigning aloofness, because inside she quailed. It gave her a moment to gather her wits. To push back the clamour of need.

Finally she steeled herself to it. Straightened her spine and met his eye.

His hard gaze burned into her. Not as a man wanted a woman but as a man wanted a thing, because to him she meant nothing more than a conduit to San Nicolo. Like every man in her life. Her only value to them was in the possessions she held. That was why it was him that followed her. She'd denied him the duchy and he was here to collect.

'I won't go back with you if that's why you're here?' she said, using French now.

She'd known this moment was coming but she hadn't expected to be completely alone with him when it did. And with him looking like *that*.

Stunning in full military uniform as Colonel-in-Chief of the Grimentzian Guards. With the addition of a blue sash denoting his royalty and his chest bristling with honours, her every soft feminine instinct wanted to simply drink in the sight.

Foolish woman. Think of something else.

Her gaze flickered over the bar of medals he wore. Apart from being born into privilege, the only child of a very important man, what single useful or arduous thing had he done to earn even one? By contrast she'd been denied every one of her own San Nicolo royal honours.

'It will be a mark of respect for your new position as Crown Princess of Grimentz,' her uncle had said. Brushing aside her concerns, just as he had her team of faithful retainers, fired, moved on, or replaced over the last six months. Her chauffeur and Rolfe, her secretary, even Luisa, her dresser, her confidante, her friend. The one per-

son she'd truly had to talk to. She'd been removed a week before this sham of a wedding. All with the agreement of her future husband, she had no doubt.

She couldn't think of any of that right now. She had to get through the next thirteen hours without succumbing to the faux charms of her groom and remain unwed. At one minute past midnight, she'd become Grand Duchess and no man would have any say in her life again.

'May I sit?'

She started. How could she have become so lost in her thoughts with him standing there?

The palm he ran over his face was the first sign of vulnerability she'd ever witnessed in his company, and now she noticed the sheen of sweat on his forehead. He'd marched the last five hundred metres up that bank, in heavy military uniform and full summer heat. It was tempting to leave him where he stood but she was not a vindictive woman. She shuffled sideways, making room for him on her chaise.

As he prowled towards her Violetta wondered had she just invited a stalking tiger to come closer.

For heaven's sake, Violetta, make up your mind. Is he a wolf or a tiger?

With a click of his heels and a brief bow he sank down beside her. As his large frame lowered and his long legs folded beneath him, she decided he was a mix of both and all of him dangerous.

This close up he smelled amazing. But then he always did. It had taken at last twenty-four hours each time they'd met to expunge the effects of him from her consciousness.

A large and rather beautiful hand rested on his knee. The gleam of the ruby in his signet ring reminding her of another ring she should be wearing about now.

But here they were instead. Decked out in all their wedding regalia, perched together in this abandoned house of dust covers and long-ago laughter. The image, a stylist's dream. And a publicist's nightmare.

But as a portrait of a couple, it was quite fitting. The space between them a physical reminder of emotional ties between them. As in, there weren't any.

Violetta shot her former groom a sideways glance. There was an uncharacteristic weariness to the set of his shoulders and, she noted, a tiny nick on his jaw. As if the hand usually adept at the task had not been so steady shaving this morning.

She sent her gaze front and centre.

It really wouldn't do to dwell on anything so intimate as this man's toilette, or that he might have been nervous and that he had any vulnerabilities. That could lead to a host of other, less innocent and more dangerous thoughts.

What was he really but another in a series of powerful men who saw her as a commodity to be bartered? No different from her father or uncle. She despised each of them and this prince most of all because he was ready to marry a woman he barely knew, the sister of a woman who'd very publicly jilted him, to get his hands on the grand duchy. What a mercenary act.

And yet he called to her in some deep, dark, sensuous way. His presence throbbing through her like a heartbeat.

Needing to put some space between them again, Violetta stood and walked to the window. Beyond the gravel driveway the once immaculate lawns were lost beneath a riot of wildflowers. Uninvited, still they'd made it a refuge. Rather like her, fleeing to one of the few places she'd ever been happy, shown any genuine love. Her grandmother and Leo's had been bosom friends and every summer, even though their grandmother had been long gone, she and her sister had visited for a holiday. The only place in Grimentz she'd been permitted to see.

Grimentz. It had loomed over her, physically and emotionally, throughout her life. Every San Nicoloan knew that Grimentzian eyes turned covetously towards their lush pastures and elegant architecture.

But her uncle had decided that the time for the old animosities was over.

And her marriage was to be the means to that end.

Leo watched as his bride paced restlessly, as if even in this empty house she felt confined. Her trailing skirt sent up blooms of dust from the neglected floor.

She was small and slender with the dark hair and the brown eyes of her people. Certainly no beauty, but she had a warmth to her that could draw the eye; if you had the time or inclination to look.

She turned to him, instantly spoiling the effect. Her delicate heart-shaped chin had a mulish turn to it. It angered him. He had every right to expect nervous and abject apologies, not this hostility.

'Do you know when Marie Antoinette arrived in France for her wedding, they'd erected a tent that exactly straggled the border,' she said. 'They took her in there, stripped her of everything she wore and replaced each item so when she stepped onto French soil, she was dressed head to toe with French-made items. Even down to her underwear. As if they were trying to expunge what she was, as if it wasn't good enough.'

He experienced a faint sense of alarm. Had his people done something similar without his knowledge? No, surely not! He'd had approval of everything, including that dress.

The closely fitted, high-necked bodice and long sleeves were made of the finest ivory lace. A silk cummerbund circled her slender waist and beneath that a full skirt of plain ivory silk fell to the floor to cover her toes.

It pleased him, as it might any man in his position. The

perfect, virginal bride in a gown fit for the princess consort she was meant to be.

'The dress, I think, is rather beautiful,' he said. Adding, for good measure, 'You look very lovely in it.'

'You don't have to wear it. And it's not me. It's not close to being me.'

His brow knotted. 'Then why, may I ask, did you choose it?'

'I didn't. You did.'

When he looked blankly at her she added, 'The photographs? The ones they sent for your approval. I quote.' She dropped her voice into a parody of his. '"Very nice, although of course she'll be wearing the Elisabetha tiara."'

He wasn't flattered by her impression. He assumed he wasn't meant to be. His anger spiked.

'You ran away because you don't like your dress?'

She shot him an angry look. 'If I'd been allowed the privilege of wearing a watch, I'd mark the time for posterity. Because that, Your Serene Highness, is the very first time you've asked me anything about how I'm feeling about our marriage.'

'Surely not. We've spoken numerous times.'

She gazed steadily at him and gave him the time to mentally run through their half-dozen encounters. All official functions. All surrounded by others. Okay, barely a genuine private moment.

'You asked me about the duchy's wine harvest,' she said. 'You asked me if I preferred the operas of Beethoven or Mozart.'

'Mozart.' He distinctly remembered that.

'Actually, I loathe opera. My parents were forever dragging me to it. So I lied.'

'You could have told me the truth.'

'What was the point? Would anything have made you

change your mind about our marriage? Not with the grand duchy at stake.

'And you never gave the impression you cared either way about me. When you took my hand you could have been picking up a sock you were about to put on. You were that disengaged. It felt like you never really saw me. Do you know how demeaning that is? To be so…so…' she grappled for the word '…inconsequential.'

'But I remember a number of interesting conversations,' he said with a placating smile.

'Oh, yes, our…' she made quotation marks in the air '…"*conversations*". The first time we met, you granted me twenty minutes. We walked on the terrace at the castle. You pointed out the architecture and the modifications various forebears had made and those you were planning. Then you told me what would be expected of me as your wife. I forget the details but quiet compliance seemed to be the main requirement. And an heir or two, of course.

'After that we met ten minutes before appearing in public. Always in Grimentz. I was given details of where to stand, where to sit, when to sit. Definitely never before you were seated. Your staff had already sent over details of whom I might speak to, and what I should say, whom I would not be permitted to speak to. You were very clear on the topics of conversation. The wine harvest and cheese production of the principality. Any charities I was involved with, though nothing controversial, which precluded discussing the teenage mothers I support and get through school. You held my hand only when there were others around to see. By others, I mean other dignitaries or the press, not our own people. You never once called me by my given name or invited me to call you by yours. And after all that, you thought I'd relish the prospect of being married to you and be expected to have…to do…' she waved a hand through the air '…*that*. Should I go on?'

She made it all sound pretty damning. 'The walk on the terrace wasn't the first time we met,' Leo pointed out, trying to defend the indefensible.

She snorted. 'You behaved even worse on that holiday we shared here. Because mostly you ignored me. When you did notice me, it was only to chase me with a handful of spiders. And I hate spiders,' she said, darkly.

He glanced to the shrouded light above her head where several cobwebs hung. She'd fled to the wrong house, then.

'I was thirteen. Perhaps you could allow I've matured since then.'

'Maturity and charm are not the same thing.'

Ouch.

'Then I beg your pardon, firstly for chasing you with spiders and latterly for apparently being a dolt of a fiancé.'

Her eyes widened. Perhaps she was not expecting the self-recrimination. But then her face crumpled. 'And what if we are physically incompatible? What if the sex were terrible? What if I didn't like it?' She sounded lost.

'Then I'd definitely be doing something wrong and I'm not known for that.'

She scowled at him. 'Of course, you've been allowed to have lots of experience. While I've had none. How is that fair? I've been protected so much I wouldn't know an erect penis from a bedpost. Not literally, of course. I've seen the pictures.'

Pictures? What sort of pictures? Arty ones? Erotic ones? His mind reeled.

'They didn't tell me you were so forthright.'

'I'm not. I'm normally very well behaved and ladylike. You must bring out the worst in me.'

She was pacing and muttering to herself. 'How did I let this happen? What was I thinking? Oh, and he just had to find me here, didn't he?'

His involvement in the conversation no longer seemed

to be required. Much like his involvement as groom. At his own wedding.

The clock was ticking. He needed to control the situation. Calm her, charm her, persuade her back to the castle with him and get them married. Before midnight.

It was time to take a different tack.

'What were you going to do when you got here?' he asked.

Violetta stopped pacing.

Call Luisa from the house phone and have a boat sent along Lake Sérénité to collect her from the chateau's private jetty. But Luisa hadn't picked up the call and then the Ferrari had arrived.

'I don't know. I hadn't thought that far ahead. I suppose I'd hoped there would be a housekeeper or someone.' Lies, of course. She wasn't going to tell him, a powerful, self-interested man, what she ultimately hoped to do. She'd learned long ago to hold all her opinions close to her chest.

'You'd be lucky. The place has been closed up since my grandmother died.'

She looked around at the dust covers shrouding all the furniture.

'I can see that now. I was very sorry about her, by the way. I loved your grandmother.'

He didn't answer. Just stared at the floor between his knees. It was well known that grandmother and grandson had been estranged since he'd been a teenager. She wondered if Leo the man regretted that.

He looked up but made no comment. Apparently unmoved.

'We might be here for a while. This won't be the first place they'll think to look for us,' he said. 'In the meantime I think we should get more comfortable.'

Violetta's hand fluttered to her throat. He couldn't mean…

He raised a brow. 'I'd like to take off all this paraphernalia.' He gestured to his jacket and sash. 'This house may have many charms, but air conditioning isn't one of them.'

He stood, his fingers going to the bar of medals adorning his chest, but he struggled with the pin holding the rack in place. 'My apologies, but this appears to be stuck. I may need your help.'

Even though removing his jacket was a sign that he meant them to stay at least for a while—eating up a few more hours to midnight—could she risk getting closer to him? Actually touch him? Violetta's heart pounded at the thought.

'I won't bite, if that's what's concerning you,' he said, with a lopsided smile that made her heart beat even faster.

No, but she was concerned she might *want* him to. Why did her body have to react to him like this every time?

She stayed exactly where she was. 'Can't you just rip it off?' she said.

He looked appalled.

'One does not simply rip items from a Grimentzian Guards uniform. Besides, have you met my valet? If this goes back to Matteo anything less than pristine, he'll torment me for a month at least. Sending me off to official functions in a straw boater and lederhosen, or some such, and his reputation be damned.'

That made her smile despite herself.

She had met the valet. A trim, fifty-year-old. Half Scottish, half Italian and one hundred per cent forged in the grand houses of Europe. A gentleman's gentleman of such impeccable credentials and exacting standards it was he that chose his employer, not the other way round. The prince was not even the most elevated he'd served. Only one man met with his sartorial approval. The second most infamous playboy in Europe, Prince Sebastien von Frohburg.

The most infamous stood before her now. At least he used to be. Until his father died and, abruptly, he switched from party animal to serious and stern ruling prince. Up to then there'd been a stream of glamorous women in his past. All tall and blond and beautiful. Like her sister.

Quite the opposite of her.

Violetta's smile faded. Well, what did that matter? She didn't need to match up to any of them. She and the prince would be nothing to each other after today. She only had to get through the next few hours in his company.

She couldn't really say no to his request. Leaving him trussed up in that heavy, braided thing when indeed it was hot in here.

She swished her skirts, straightened her back then approached him. That seemed to amuse him. A distracting, crooked smile made an appearance.

This close up, her eyes were level with his broad chest, made still more impressive by the medals and starburst honours pinned to it.

Violetta's hand floated up to the medal bar that held the jingling rack of honours. Suspiciously, the pin came away easily. She carefully placed the bar on the chaise behind them. His intense blue eyes watched her every move.

'Don't do that.'

'Do what?' he asked, all innocence.

'Stare at me like that.' It was making her hot, much hotter than she already was in this tight-fitting, heavy-skirted dress.

'You said I'd never properly seen you before. I'm making up for it. I'll stop if it's making you uncomfortable.' His gaze lifted to fix on the room behind her. 'Is that better?'

She missed those blue eyes on her, but hell would freeze over before she'd admit to it. She reached for the sash traversing his chest, her hands caught the edge then lifted upwards. He dipped his head allowing her to lift it from him. Her wrist brushed the top of his hair. Soft and silken and feeling so ridiculously intimate.

She was being foolish. It was just hair, but her fingers trembled as she carefully placed the sash with the medals.

He sighed in relief as he slipped the jacket from his shoulders. The scent of his cologne and sweat filled the air. Violetta dipped her head, but still it invaded her senses.

'Thank you,' he said, undoing the top buttons on his collarless white shirt, rolling back his shirt sleeves.

Violetta blinked.

In full uniform he'd looked dashing, too handsome. Now, in braces and black trousers with the narrow scarlet stripe down the side, with rolled-back sleeves and part-unbuttoned shirt, he was gorgeous.

A flicker of movement from the gardens snapped her attention away.

'There's someone out there.'

Leo was instantly on guard, swinging round to place himself between her and the window.

Oh, chivalry!

Protected only by those paid to do so, and never truly valued by her family. Genuine chivalry had been in short supply in Violetta's life. How nice to experience it from this big, vital, handsome man. Her heart gave a most annoying squeeze.

'Where?' he demanded.

'In the treeline. Just beyond the wildflowers on the lawn.'

His eyes narrowed. 'I see nothing.'

'Maybe you were followed here after all.'

'Unlikely. Only my team saw me leave the cathedral and if anyone else had spotted me in the city they'd have assumed I was simply a guardsman tasked with returning the Ferrari to the castle.'

'Maybe there was someone already here when we arrived? A burglar or someone. Shouldn't we at least go and investigate?'

'If it makes you feel better I'll go and check. Wait here.'
He started for the door. Violetta followed him.

'I'm not staying in here by myself. What if there's an accomplice already in the house?'

He looked down at her. 'Was the place locked when you arrived?'

'Yes, I retrieved the spare keys from the key safe where your grandmother kept them.'

'And all the shutters were still closed?'

'Yes, I opened this one so I had light in the room.'

'Well, then. How did this mysterious accomplice get into the house? Down the chimney?'

But she stared stubbornly back.

He sighed. 'Very well, Grand Duchessa, we'll go and check together.'

Leo exited the front door with Violetta trotting at his heels. As they approached the tangle of wildflowers on the lawn he hoped whichever of his security team she'd seen had made themselves scarce. If they hadn't, and she spotted them, they'd worked their last day for him. If it was paparazzi and they'd been allowed to penetrate the tight ring of security he'd ordered thrown around this place, years of loyal service or not, his head of security would also find himself out of a job.

He wanted her to believe they were entirely alone. He didn't want her thinking she could just march out of here and request help from one of his men. Not until he'd had time to talk her round and persuade her to marry him after all.

'Wait here,' he ordered as they reached the edge of the overgrown lawns.

Of course she ignored him. She hitched up her dress and clambered onto the lawn. Instantly struggling to wade through the tussocks of grass in heels and all those petticoats. She nearly tumbled and made a grab for his hand.

Irritated, he took it, his own progress slowed by having to assist her with almost every step. Eventually they reached the treeline.

The tall grass swayed in the breeze. The boughs creaked in the heat. A startled bird shot for the safety of the skies. Otherwise, silence.

'See,' he said, 'no one here at all.'

She peered around him. 'The grass is battered down and there is a trail leading away from it.'

Damn it, she was smarter than he'd been told. Willing and decorous—the penis and bedpost remark came back to mind—neither of those had been true so far.

'A deer, most probably. Basking. It took off when it heard us,' he said.

She snorted. 'Sharks bask. Deer maybe sun themselves. But that…' she pointed at the bowl of flattened grass '…is far too big to have been made by a deer.'

He pretended to assess the terrain, squinting at the mountains behind them. 'I suppose we're high enough up for it to have been a wolf.'

'A wolf?' She shrieked, flattening herself against his back.

'Relax, it'll be long gone. It would have run off the moment we stepped outside.' He looked down at her. 'Satisfied?'

She sent one last piercing glance to the trees but there was nothing to see. 'I suppose it could have been a bird.'

She struggled to turn to walk back to the house. In frustration Leo scooped her up and hefted her over the grass to the gravel drive.

As he picked his way back through the tussocks of flowers she clung to his neck. Her hips and thighs were swathed by all her petticoats. But her waist was slender and her arms supple. Small breasts pressed against his chest.

What would she do if he carried his prim bride right over the threshold back into the house? With all the connotations that had.

His foot landed on the first of the gravel.

'Put me down. I can walk from here.'

'It's only a few more paces to the house.'

'You are not carrying me over the threshold. Put me down. Now!'

Biddable? Strike that too.

'As you command, Grand Duchessa,' he purred.

'Stop calling me that. I'm not the grand duchess until midnight.'

Wasn't he acutely aware of that?

The second her dainty feet hit the ground she scooted away from him, making a production of shaking out her petticoats and smoothing down the skirt. Beautifying the dress that she apparently loathed. She gave a little sniff of derision and stalked off towards the house, voluminous skirt dragging through the gravel. Her maids would never get the dirt out of it, he thought.

Leo strolled in her wake. Oddly fascinated by the angry sway of her hips in that full gown. What were her legs like beneath all that fabric? Long? Slender? Would there be a supple curve to her thighs? He'd never wondered before and during their previous meetings they'd both been in evening wear, which had meant full-length gowns for her.

Her sister too had been lithe. She'd been a keen rider. Did Violetta share that passion? He was beginning to realise how little he actually knew of his intended. And that it might be useful to know more if he was going to change her mind about marriage.

The midday sunshine glinted in her hair as she walked away. He'd only ever seen her hair styled in an elaborate chignon. Much as it was now. Were those rich brown locks as plentiful as they appeared or was the bounty of intricate coils helped along by a hairpiece? If it was all her own, would it spill to her waist? Long enough for a man to wind his hands through?

Leo frowned. Surprised by the direction of his thoughts, he dismissed them. It was probably the novelty of finding his chaste bride was not as meek as he'd thought.

A nearby bush interrupted his musings.

'Sorry, sir,' it hissed.

Leo halted. 'I think we got away with it,' he answered, his voice low as Violetta disappeared into the house.

He squinted at the horizon in earnest. An ominous cloud had appeared over the mountains to the north. Bad weather had been forecast but not until later in the day. Contingency plans had been made to take the wedding reception from the gardens and inside the castle when necessary.

'That storm front is moving pretty fast. Head to the gatehouse with the team. Anyone coming to the valley will have to come past you there anyway, so we should be safe enough. I'll call on the house phone when I need you. Give me an hour or two and then be ready to collect us.'

'Very well, sir.'

The bush rustled as the guard began crawling away.

'Wait. Check on something, find out what happened to the princess's people. She said they'd been dismissed. Find out where they are and have them brought to the castle'

'We'll get on it straight away. Would you like us to inform her uncle where she is?'

'Yes. Tell him she's safe with me. That it was last-minute nerves and that we'll be returning to the castle by nightfall and we'll be married then.'

He hoped.

'Very well, sir. And…er…good luck with the princess.'

Luck? That would have nothing to do with this. With

San Nicolo at stake, he was prepared to use all the powers of persuasion he had to convince his little runaway that marriage to him would be all to her benefit.

A flurry of wind snatched up clouds of wildflower petals and swirled them at his feet, like so much confetti.

He recrossed the threshold—still brideless.

For now, Leo thought.

CHAPTER THREE

THE SALON WAS DESERTED, so Leo paused only to collect his discarded jacket, sash and medals bar.

At the rear of the hallway, tucked beneath the grand staircase, the door to the service areas stood ajar.

He found her in the vast kitchen.

The staff who visited the chateau every four weeks kept them spotless. It smelled of beeswax, much as it always had. The long table and rustic chairs gleamed with it, as did the enormous oak dresser that still sat against the wall facing the large window. The granite worktop and the old range cooker were polished to a shine.

He knew this kitchen well. His grandmother loved to cook and often he and Seb would sit with her while she chopped this, stirred that.

It was a house where a royal heir had got to live a life as close to normal as possible. He and Seb were allowed to play outside all day, coming home filthy and starving, to plates piled with fresh pasta and the best tomato sauce he'd tasted to this day. Allowed to bathe after eating with no one nagging him about correct manners. Allowed to get up from the table and collect whatever he wanted from the pantry. To wind his arms around Grand-Mère's neck and listen to her tell fascinating tales of her youth with her best friend, Violetta's grandmother. To go to bed when he was tired and to speak when he had something to say and be listened to.

He glanced around.

His grandmother's battered old CD-player still sat on the oak dresser and beside it a small stack of CDs. Perhaps when the staff had cleared the house, they hadn't realised it was a personal item of the former and kept it to use themselves.

Violetta had found a glass and filled it with water from the tap. She gulped it down in one go then wiped her mouth with the back of her hand.

In that grand dress, fit for the princess she was, and with the emerald-strewn Elisabetha tiara on her head, it was yet another incongruous picture from today.

She shook the empty glass at him. 'Would you like one?'

'Please.'

He hung his jacket and sash on a chair back and placed the medal bar on the table while she hunted out a second glass and filled it from the tap. Before she could set it on the table, he reached out to take it from her hand, making a point of brushing her fingers. Her little shudder pleased him.

She stepped back and folded her arms across her chest.

'What do you think is happening back in the capital?'

'They've been told the wedding is postponed because the bride is indisposed. Stuck in her bathroom.'

Her eyes flew wide. 'You told them *what*? I'll never live that down!'

'Whereas jilting your groom will cover you in glory?'

She lifted her chin. 'There's something romantic and noble about fleeing from an unwanted wedding.'

'Not when you're the one left dealing with the fallout.'

'So what happens now?' she asked.

He sat. Draped an arm along the back of the seat next to him, crossed one long leg over the other. Relaxed and apparently unconcerned that a congregation packed with high-born guests and dignitaries waited on his pleasure in St Peter's cathedral.

He took a long, slow drink of his water and watched as Violetta swallowed convulsively.

'What would you like to happen?' he said.

'You expect me to believe that what I want will really matter in the long run? No man has ever cared about what I want.'

'I assure you, *this* man has the most acute interest in what you want right now.'

She studied him. Saying nothing as she collected his empty glass, rinsed and dried it and returned it to the cupboard.

She squared her shoulders, a gesture he was coming to recognise as her plucking up her courage, and turned to face him.

'Perhaps this wouldn't have happened if we'd got to know each other a little better. Maybe we could do that now? What I've really wanted is the chance to get to know you better.'

Uh-oh. He'd heard that before. Usually from a woman when she wanted to cling and he didn't do clingy. He didn't do getting to know anyone better. That wasn't his way, not any more.

Once they were safely wed, he'd make it clear that a cosy intimacy wouldn't be high on his list of priorities.

Certain she wasn't being honest with him and wanting to probe for the truth, he asked, 'Would there be any point if we're not getting married?'

'Maybe you could, you know…change my mind?'

Another lie. Why didn't she just ask to be taken home? It was obvious she was stalling, but to what end?

For now, he'd go along with her. He studied the small

pert breasts, the neat waist, and the maidenly flush creeping across her cheeks.

'You won't do it like that.' Her hand was back at her throat. 'I'm not about to be seduced by your charms. Because so far, I've yet to see any.'

He shouldn't have been insulted but her blunt dismissal of him as an adult, sexual being was offensive.

'You haven't seen any because I've yet to use them. Once I do, you'll be thinking differently.'

Her mouth tightened. 'So sure of your own worth. But you forget, unlike all your other conquests I'm not impressed by your title and your wealth. I have enough of those of my own. And on those few occasions we did meet, you were so self-absorbed how could I believe you'd really mean any of it now?'

His gut twisted on a rare moment of shame. Hadn't he been on the receiving end of just that kind of behaviour himself in the past? From his father. He shared the man's genes but that was where he wanted all similarities to end.

She'd drifted to his jacket hanging over the chair back and was studying the insignia still attached. She reached out to stroke the gold badge, shaped in a pair of wings, that had been pinned to his right breast.

'What's this?'

'A French Army Parachute qualification.'

She glanced up. 'An honorary award, I presume?'

'Certainly not.'

'You actually took the course? Isn't it extremely tough?'

'Yes. Achieving that nearly broke me.'

She flashed him a look that suggested she wished it had.

'And this?' She trailed a finger across a second badge that had sat just left of his heart, and a frisson of something skittered through him. He shifted his shoulders.

'Helicopter pilot's badge.'

He waited for her to be impressed.

She tapped at the pilot's badge. 'I wonder how good you are at this…' her fingers turned back to the parachute wings '…if you also need these.'

The little madam.

'The altitude is often too low for a parachute to have worked.'

That wasn't true but she wouldn't know that and for some reason he wanted her to be impressed with him.

She wasn't.

'So you don't have a head for heights?'

'Flinging myself from a perfectly good aeroplane with essentially a large tablecloth strapped to my back would suggest otherwise.'

But he noticed her lips curling into a smile. She'd been teasing him and suddenly he wasn't half as annoyed about that as he might have been.

Flirting? This was progress.

If his little *grand duchessa* wanted to play, bring it on. He was a master.

'And what, might I ask, have you ever done to drive terror into your bones?' he teased right back.

Instantly her face fell and the good humour evaporated. 'Allow myself to be put in this dress with no idea how I was going to get out of it. Out of any of it.'

He cursed himself. Not so masterful after all.

'Well, then, let's at least get you out of the dress.'

Her brow rose.

'And put on what? A dust sheet? I'm not parading around in front of you in nothing but my underwear.'

'While that is an enticing thought, I was assuming there'd be something in this house for you to wear.'

'Apart from the furniture the house looks pretty empty.'

When he'd inherited this place he'd ordered it cleared of all his grandmother's personal effects. He'd wanted nothing to do with any of them, the memories were too painful.

Everything was in storage now. But there might be something they could use, and it would give them something to do and distract her, while he tried her to persuade her to change her mind about the marriage.

He sent her a smile. 'We'll find something for you, Violetta, I promise,' he said, in his most seductive Italian.

He didn't want to look at her in that dress for much longer either. He'd find her something to wear if he had to fashion a dust sheet into something appropriate himself.

Violetta tried to concentrate.

Tried to stop melting every time he spoke in that silky accent. Tried to stop staring at the man and focus on getting to midnight unwed and un-seduced.

It was the collarless shirt, or maybe those braces, or just something about the suggestion of being scantly clothed that was so alluring. When had she seen him as anything other than impeccably turned out? This off-duty Leo was thoroughly tempting. Each time he moved the shirt shifted and allowed a glimpse of a broad, muscled breastplate beneath. Why did he have to be such a stunning example of masculine beauty?

'But before I go hunting for a change of clothes, why don't you tell me the real reason you ran away? So far you've revealed you don't like your dress and that no man, including me, has ever paid sufficient attention to you.'

'You make that sound so childish,' she grumbled. 'That's not quite how I meant it. I just want to be seen as an equal, an adult who is perfectly capable of making her sensible decisions.'

'Unfortunately running away from your wedding paints you as immature.'

'Or someone who had no other choice.'

'No choice? All you had to say was, "Leo, I don't want to marry you." See? That easy.'

'You know nothing,' she muttered. 'I would never have been allowed to do that.'

His expression darkened. 'You were being forced into this marriage?'

'No, not exactly.'

'Then what? Why was it so impossible for you to simply say nothing before this point?'

'If I'd told my uncle I didn't want to marry you he would have found some pretence, or argument, to try and persuade me.'

'Point out the many benefits of a match with me, perhaps?' Leo said, sweetly.

Violetta rolled her eyes. 'Probably.'

Leo studied her, eyes narrowed. He shook his head. 'No. I still don't believe you…it feels like you're hiding something.'

Why did he have to be so insistent?

Because he wants the duchy, Violetta. While you're ogling his chest and melting to a puddle every time he speaks Italian, he's probably plotting and planning to get you in front of a priest before nightfall. Does he really care about your objections to the match? No, he believes he knows better and that there are so many advantages to being married to him. Never forget that. He's the enemy, a powerful, self-interested man.

But there was absolutely no way she was telling him the truth. He'd laugh at her, or, worse, insist on marching her back to her uncle. What if the result of that was her uncle just taking power in his own right after all and simply cutting her out of the succession? Maybe he could if she didn't marry and she'd lose everything anyway. Where else could she have run to at the last minute? She'd known the chateau was empty. At one of their joint functions Leo had told her in passing that it was closed up, and she didn't know anywhere else in Grimentz that would be a safe place to hide.

Why did his *grand-mère* have to tell him about those holidays in her cards to him? No one else knew or would have cared. Her mother had never told her uncle where her daughters went for two weeks every summer. He would have considered it beneath his notice and by the time he did notice his niece those holidays had already ceased. So he had no knowledge of Violetta's visits.

She and Luisa had had it all planned. They would hide away in a safe house in the city until midnight. Then go to the cathedral, where she was going to take the flag and swear her allegiance. They were going to film it on their phone and then post it on the Internet for all the world to see. It wasn't much, but it was all she had. She was going to invoke the ancient ritual of swearing allegiance and hope that the people would come with her. But to do that, she had to get back to San Nicolo tonight! Without this man knowing anything of her plans because he'd surely try to stop her. He wanted San Nicolo for himself, as had every Prince of Grimentz for the last four centuries.

She couldn't afford to tell the truth, but she couldn't tell half-truths any more either. He wasn't easily fooled. She'd have to tell a substantial lie and something so profound he'd finally back off.

Violetta turned from him, fixed her attention very deliberately on the dark clouds swirling down from the mountains above, and told perhaps the biggest lie of her young life.

'I'd hoped to spare you this, but the truth is I don't find you at all attractive, quite the opposite in fact.'

At that precise moment, as if the heavens themselves rebelled at that appalling falsehood, a blinding lightning flash illuminated the room, followed by a nerve-jangling thunderclap.

Violetta leapt from her skin. But the man seated behind remained still and silent. There was a long and testing pause until…

'I see.'

That softly spoken response danced across her skin like the brush of warm fingertips.

'In fact…' she said, shivering to hide her real response to him, 'I'm sorry but I couldn't imagine anything less appealing than going to bed with you.'

She couldn't look at him. Those blue eyes would find her out at once.

'Well, then.' He was on his feet behind her.

Was she mistaken or did she just hear a thread of sorrow running through that simple statement? She wondered belatedly if he'd loved Francesca, if her sister's elopement had genuinely wounded him and if she'd hurt him now too.

He came to stand beside her but instead of looking at her he stared up at the skies. Dark roiling clouds chased one another over the valley towards the lake, blocking out the sun and shrouding the gardens and this room in shadows. The man beside her became darker, bigger. Despite the grand dress and priceless tiara, she felt smaller and more insignificant than ever. Because he seemed to have forgotten she was even there. He was studying the lines of trees that ran around the edge of the lawns. They writhed helplessly in the rising wind.

She'd been mistaken. There wasn't a hint of heartbreak in those stern features. He was concerned with something entirely different, and she understood at last.

'It wasn't wolves or basking deer out there before,' she said, gazing up at him. 'It was one of your men, wasn't it?'

Leo exhaled heavily. 'Yes.'

An angry splatter of rain landed on the windows. 'Will they be safe?'

'I ordered them to the gatehouse. They should be there by now.'

Her heart plummeted. How would a car or boat get past Leo's security, now he had them in place? They could only get as far as the gatehouse, but if she could find a way to call Luisa without this man knowing, she could have her send a car to collect her from the gatehouse. They couldn't stop her then.

'Should we think about joining them? If I take off my petticoats I'll fit into the Ferrari.'

'It wouldn't matter if you were in nothing but your underwear,' he said. 'The Ferrari hit a pothole and is out of action.'

'What about the florist's van?' She peered out to the driveway where it sat, lurching back and forth in the wind.

Leo looked at it and back at her. 'No.'

He leant against the counter, his arms folded, head bowed, deep in thought. He wasn't about to demand she tell him the truth, was he? She didn't have another grand lie left in her. She fidgeted, waiting for what he might say next.

'I'm getting hungry,' he announced, and pushed away from the counter.

What?

'I wonder what there is in this kitchen.' He began opening doors, peering in cupboards.

She watched him in disbelief. 'You're worrying about your stomach at a time like this?'

'A man can't think when he's starving.'

'You can't actually be starving. Surely you had breakfast.'

'That was all of…' he glanced at his watch '…six hours ago. If things had gone to plan this morning I should have been fed by now. I burn off a lot of energy, even more so when I'm hungry.'

There was nothing at all in that mundane remark to make her blush. So why were her cheeks turning pink? It was the heat, she decided, and this blasted dress. Maybe she'd calm down if she removed his disquieting presence for a while. Plus, it would give her the chance to try calling Luisa again.

'Why don't you go and look for that change of clothes you promised me, and I'll see if there is anything to eat? Then we can think about how to get to the gatehouse,' she said.

The kitchen door burst open on a violent gust of wind. A flurry of rain, twigs and leaves flew in. Leo leapt to the door and slammed it shut.

'I don't think either of us are going anywhere any time soon,' he said as a crash outside heralded the toppling of plant pots next from the kitchen window.

That declaration that she didn't find him attractive was so obviously a lie. He'd seen the way she looked at him. But he'd respect it. It would just make persuading her to marry him that bit harder.

Right now they had other priorities. The wind had picked up significantly and the florist's van looked in serious danger of turning over. Despite the kitchen being sheltered, at the angle the van was parked, should it start rolling they'd be directly in its path. If they were truly going to be marooned here, they needed this room intact, where there was running water, heat, and hopefully food.

There was no choice. He'd have to move it to safety.

'You can't, it's too dangerous out there.' Violetta placed an anxious hand on his forearm, her small fingers warm against his skin.

'Only for the first ten metres or so. It would be bad for us if we lose the use of this room. I'll move it to the central courtyard. It will be safer there.'

'Then please be careful.' Her brown eyes looked up at him awash with genuine concern. Something warm and needy kicked in his chest. He quashed it. 'I'll be fine.

Unlock the courtyard door for me and I'll come back in that way.'

Then he wrenched open the kitchen door, fighting with the wind to pull it shut behind him. Violetta watched him from the kitchen window as he pelted across the gravel and leapt into the driver's seat. As soon as he started moving she also took off, to run through the corridors to the back of the house. Hopefully getting that courtyard door unlocked.

The buffeting of the wind rocked the vehicle back and forth on its chassis. Twigs, leaves, uprooted plants, all were flung at the windscreen as he drove the fifty metres to the U-shaped courtyard that was formed by the wings at the back of the house. As he turned into it the strength of the wind dropped considerably. He could see Violetta wrestling with the key of the door at the end of the courtyard. He parked the van in the most sheltered spot but as he stepped out the heavens opened on another mighty thunderclap. He raced for the door but was soaked through in seconds.

Her anxious face turned up to him, she was shouting but he could barely hear her over the whine of the wind.

'Won't budge…lock stiff…key not turning.'

Leo grasped the handle and tried twisting it from his side. Nothing.

'Stand back,' he yelled and, once she was clear, threw his weight against the door. Still nothing budged. The rain streamed down his face. He could barely see for it. He swept it away with a palm and gave one more almighty yank at the handle.

No movement.

She was frantically searching for another way in, but there was nothing. He was going to have to get back to the kitchen door he'd come out through.

He yelled to Violetta who nodded furiously and took off again. Ready to let him in. He hugged the house as much as he could, but once he'd left the shelter of the courtyard the force of the gale nearly took his feet from under him. He put up a hand to protect his face from all the swirling debris. A branch whipped by and a tangle of twigs wrapped round his ankles, nearly tripping him. He gasped, fighting to breathe as the wind rammed air into his lungs.

His progress back was painfully slow but eventually he reached the kitchen door. Violetta was waiting anxiously at the window and as soon as she saw him, she flew to the door and hauled it open. He staggered in and together they rammed the door shut again. Then both sagged against it, exhausted.

Leo looked down on Violetta. She'd taken a dousing when she opened the door for him. Water dripped down her hair and the front of her dress was drenched. All the perfect silk and lace was stained and smeared with wet leaves. 'That blasted lock. I'm so sorry. It just wouldn't budge.'

'Some wedding day I'm having,' he said and she spluttered, looking up at him with surprised eyes. But her expression changed instantly.

'You're hurt.'

He put his hand up to his forehead. It came back spotted with blood. He frowned at it. 'It's nothing.'

'Sit,' she said, pulling out a chair.

'It's just a cut.'

'Sit,' she ordered and took his arm, pushing him into it. 'There used to be a first aid kit.'

'In the last cupboard by the door.'

He'd sat here before in this kitchen, with cuts or bruises, while Grand-Mère fixed him up, tutting over him and Seb and their fondness for getting into scrapes. One of those rare occasions in his life when he'd known what it was like to have someone care for you who wasn't paid to do so.

Armed with plasters, a towel and antiseptic wipes, she hurried back to him.

She was focused on inspecting the cut above his brow, so he took the opportunity to study her.

Her eyes, he decided, were actually rather fine. Warm and dark. Like the best and bitterest chocolate. They kindled when she was angry with him, or, better still, when she was laughing up at him. He liked how her whole face transformed then.

'You're doing it again.' Violetta had paused in her work. He raised a brow in question.

'Staring at me.'

'I was just admiring the colour of your eyes,' he said, not looking away. 'I hadn't noticed them before.'

She made a little harrumph in the back of her throat, but he could tell he'd pleased her. She quickly distracted him in an entirely different way.

He hissed as she dabbed at the cut with a wipe, but she was gentle. Nimble fingers working quickly, cleaning the cut and carefully applying a plaster.

'There, all done.'

'It's not fatal, then?'

'It was a scratch. I thought you were supposed to be some rough tough airborne warrior?' She tutted at him. 'What would your ex-comrades say?' She slanted a saucy look at his parachute badge and the jacket still draped on the chair back. Then set about gathering up the supplies.

'If I'd perished out there it would have saved you a lot of trouble.'

'I'm not going to marry you, so whether you're alive or dead it makes no difference.'

'Your concern for me is heart-warming.'

Interesting that despite her claims to be repelled by the thought of their being intimate together, she'd had no problems touching him.

He'd try an experiment.

As she gathered up the first-aid supplies from the table,

he rose to his feet beside her and began unbuttoning his shirt. Her eyes went as big as saucers as he peeled the damp fabric from his shoulders and tugged the sleeves down his arms. Her gaze slewed to his chest and lingered there.

Until she caught his wry expression and went back to tidying away the supplies. She made three goes as one item after another slipped through her fingers.

'Here.' He picked up the bandage that had rolled for the third time from her grasp. He dropped it on top of the pile she carried.

She turned away. Her ears pink.

The look she'd given him just now was not that of a woman repelled by a man. It was the opposite. He might even say it was hungry for him.

How much did he prefer this blushing, but determined Violetta to the bland, bloodless creature who'd stood meekly by his side at the events they'd attended together?

It felt like the real Violetta, so why had she adopted that fake persona on the other occasions? And what was her real reason for running away from their wedding?

There were still several hours to midnight. The storm might pass in time for them to get back to the castle and wed. *If* he could persuade her to change her mind.

He wasn't giving up on San Nicolo. That was all that mattered here.

CHAPTER FOUR

SHE'D KNOWN HE was a strong, lean god of a man, but that wasn't the same as seeing his muscled chest just inches away...*naked*.

Violetta swallowed and cursed her flaming face. She buried her head in the cupboard and took longer than necessary to put away the medical supplies.

His skin was tanned to a deep gold, as if he spent a good deal of time outdoors with his shirt off. When did he find the time?

The lines of muscle she glimpsed were deeply fascinating. She wanted to run her fingers along them, or her lips. She made a strange little sound of shock and stood up abruptly.

He was shrugging back into his jacket, and she couldn't decide which emotion had the upper hand.

Relief or disappointment.

He didn't button the jacket up so as he moved there were more glimpses of that muscled breastplate. The silky skin and the line of dark hair running down his abdomen and disappearing into his waistband.

'We can't stay in these wet things.' Violetta was patting at her hair with a towel. 'I'm bad enough but you're absolutely soaked through. We need dry clothes.'

Costumes? Of course.

'I wonder if Grand-Mère's costume gallery is still there,' Leo mused.

Violetta brightened. 'From her parties? Will it still be there?'

'I ordered all her personal effects be placed in storage when she died. But the costumes may have been left with the other fixtures and fittings.'

Throughout their marriage his maternal grandparents had held a masked ball every year, one of the most sought-after invites on the European social calendar. Grand-Mère had continued the tradition even after her husband's death and after every ball she'd kept a selection of the costumes worn. Her own and her husband's, and many donated by guests.

'I'll go and see if it's still here and you can check the pantries for food.'

Leo headed for the grand staircase. Time alone to think.

All those things she'd said of him earlier. How he'd behaved towards her when they'd met at official functions. Had he really become that man? As cold and unfeeling as his father? It shocked him.

The empty house echoed to the sound of his footsteps as he crossed the marble tiles of the hallway. Chateau Elisa-betha had never felt so forlorn, because his grandmother had always been there. Seb too and a handful of servants. It bothered him that the place felt so lonely now. It didn't seem right somehow. After it had always felt so alive with his *grand-mère* in residence.

Most of her things had gone, but the staff who'd cleared the house had missed the odd item, such as the CD player in the kitchen.

On the landing were several portraits that over the years Grand-Mère had commissioned of her beloved dogs. They watched him as he passed, shaming him with their patient, unconditional devotion. One-eyed, one-eared, balanced on three legs, whatever their imperfection, each had been painted to make the viewer see them as perfect and as well beloved as they'd been to their owner.

Leo went by, ignoring the reproachful eyes.

He passed the family and guest bedrooms and up the stairs to the final floor.

Under the eaves of this wing ran an attic. Its entire length had been fitted with wardrobes. Leo opened the first.

Bingo.

Carefully wrapped in linen covers sat line after line of his grandmother's beloved costumes. He checked out the first. An extravagant blue dress with hopped petticoats and an elaborate white wig: Marie Antoinette had once graced the ball. The next, in sharp contrast, was a cheerleader outfit, in burgundy and gold with Grimentz High emblazoned across the front and complete with a set of matching pom-poms.

Unbidden came lustful thoughts of Violetta, ministering to some of his baser needs while dressed in it. Well, well, looked as if his prim runaway was stirring his blood after all.

'What are you grinning about?'

He looked up to find Violetta in the doorway.

'I was imagining you in this,' he said, holding up the short dress and giving the pom-poms a cheery shake.

'Well, I'm about to wipe that smile from your face. I've searched the kitchen and the larder. Apart from tinned stuff there isn't a single fresh, edible thing in this house.'

Leo allowed his gaze to wander in a slow appraisal from the tips of her toes, past that slender waist, the subtle swell of her breasts and her small, currently belligerent mouth. Eventually he met her eye.

'Oh, I wouldn't say that.'

She rolled her eyes, pretending outrage but he noted the flush of red across her cheeks.

She marched over to the closet where the female out-fits were stored and riffled through them. Opening the first to check the contents, finding the elaborate wig and blue gown.

'Marie Antoinette? Not a chance, I'm not enjoying the similarities.'

More bags were unzipped. A mermaid. A gladiatrix. A ballerina ready for the starring role in *Swan Lake*. On that one she paused. Stroking the snowy white feathers adorning the tutu.

Leo watched as she gave a little sigh and moved on. Suddenly, he hoped she'd already discounted the cheer-leader outfit, thinking it might be better for him if she didn't choose it.

But back she came.

'As you were so taken with the idea of me in this, per-haps I'll wear it,' she said, taking it from his hands with a challenge in her eyes that sent a sharp kick of lust straight to his groin.

There was the rapid clatter of heels on the stairs, then the opening and closing of a door as she entered one of the bedrooms on the floor below.

Leo blew out a long breath. Feeling unaccountably… *rattled.*

The gale outside buffeted the rafters and a draught chilled his skin through his damp shirt. He needed to find something dry to wear.

He crossed the attic to the other set of cupboards where he thought to find all the male costumes his grandmother had saved.

But the first wasn't male at all, and, sadly for him, the woman who'd worn it was well known to him. It had be-longed to his mother.

Prince Friedrich had been strict about what costumes his wife had been allowed to wear. He'd had final approval on her choice and it had always had to be something exalted and dignified. A heroine from mythology or a celebrated monarch or leader. No mermaids or gladiators were allowed for Giovanna von Frohburg.

Leo drew the lapis-blue headdress of Queen Nefertiti from its protective covering. He vividly remembered the year she'd worn it.

He'd been accustomed to seeing his mother dressed for grand occasions, but this costume had so suited her fine-boned beauty that from his hiding place on the landing outside his rooms he'd been transfixed watching her descend the stairs on her husband's arm.

His beautiful mother, whom he'd adored.

And who'd abandoned him.

Prince Friedrich had had his choice from the cream of European aristocracy from which to take a wife. He'd chosen badly.

Giovanna had loved her status but not the expectations and restrictions that went with it. Nor had she loved the man who'd elevated her to her lofty position by making her his wife. He had been too serious and strict, too obsessed with regaining the grand duchy. And too averse to anything that might constitute fun. No one had been surprised when his beautiful young wife had sought her entertainment and then male affection elsewhere. The only real surprise was how long she'd actually stayed with her husband. When she'd finally departed Leo was a teenager.

At fourteen, with all the swagger of youth, he'd imagined himself a man. But not on the day his mother had left. That day he'd wept like the child he still was.

Seb had burst into his room.

'You'd better come. Your parents have had an enormous row and now Aunt Giovanna is leaving.'

Leo had found her rooms in uproar. Servants hurriedly packing clothes into trunks. Footmen hefting them to the hallways. His mother sweeping make-up and pots of lotions into a vanity case.

'Don't go,' he'd begged her.

'I've found a wonderful man to love me,' she'd answered, snapping the case closed. 'Not like your father.'

'But I love you,' Leo had cried.

She'd patted his cheek absently. 'I know, darling. I'll see you soon. I promise.'

He'd followed her to the castle forecourt, all the while pleading with her not to leave him. When that had no effect, he'd flung himself at her. There had followed an unseemly tussle, where his mother's security team had been forced to physically prise his arms from about her neck.

As her car had borne her away his cousin had tried to comfort him, but Seb had been younger, smaller and Leo, wild with grief, had been having none of it. He'd shoved him away.

Servants had averted their eyes. Tight-jawed castle guards had stared straight ahead. Seb, on his backside on the cobbles where Leo had pushed him, had sobbed openly.

At a first-floor window a lone, impassive figure had stared down on the scene. The only one to witness his teenage son's humiliation and remain unmoved.

All Leo's pain and rage had coalesced on him. He'd stormed up the stairs and barged into his father's study.

'You did this,' he'd yelled. 'You drove her away.'

His father had advanced towards him, arms outstretched, and Leo remembered feeling stunned that his father might be about to change a habit of a lifetime and embrace his only child.

How wrong he had been. With one hand he had grasped Leo's shoulder, with the other he had slapped him hard across the cheek.

'Stop making a spectacle and control yourself, boy. You're a prince, not a commoner.'

Leo had folded inwards. His own hand against his stinging cheek. Shocked by the sudden eruption of violence that had disappeared as quickly. His father had been in command of himself.

'I gave your mother a choice. She could have her lover, but she'd never be permitted to see you again. She chose him.'

The anguish of that simple truth had sliced through Leo's heart. The mother he adored had abandoned him to a father she knew was heartless and cold. It had been the defining moment of his life as he'd vowed there and then never to let anyone close again.

He'd stood and showed no emotion while his father had poured a storm of recrimination over his head.

She left because of you. You were too demanding, too clingy. What kind of monarch will you be if you can't control yourself? You shame the great name of von Frohburg.'

As something had broken for good inside him, Leo had stared at a blank strip of wall between two portraits of his most illustrious and pompous-looking forebears. He'd hated those portraits ever after and they were the first things he had consigned to some backwater of the palace the moment that study had become his.

Leo had never again tried to do anything to please his father. Quite the opposite. He'd embraced disobedience, courted disrepute. He would have been expelled from school but for the cachet his title had brought to the place. As the years had passed, and Leo had matured into a man, observers had been hard pressed to say who had cut the most scandalous swathe through the opposite sex. He or his mother. She was on husband number four. Leo had scores of conquests, most of whom he barely remembered. For a while he had been the undisputed wild child of Europe. Even Sebastien, with his title, good looks and easy charm, had been in second place. The aloof heir to the Grimentzian throne had been too much of a draw.

But Leo had never forgotten the scorn and the blame of

his father's verbal thrashing. Since that day he'd never allowed a moment's true emotion to be on display. Perhaps that was why Francesca had eloped. Had he become too like his father?

Exploring that now wouldn't help. He had the other girl to persuade to the altar instead.

Leo held the Nefertiti crown up to the light. His grandmother had kept her daughter's most celebrated costume.

Giovanna's departure had hurt Grand-Mère too. She'd become a pariah overnight. She had been denied all access to her only grandchild. He'd believed it when it was revealed she'd helped her daughter by allowing the lovers to meet in secret in Chateau Elisabetha. Leo had felt so betrayed he'd never forgiven her, even as an adult, when she'd written to him, explaining herself. She knew her daughter was selfish and spoiled but she loved her and wanted her to be happy, and she hoped maybe one day he would understand sacrificing something for love.

Never. He would never understand that. Love was such a fleeting unreliable emotion to hitch anything to. He'd never made the mistake of loving anything again.

Every summer an invite had arrived for him to visit her. He'd never even replied. She'd spent the rest of her year in France, close to the capital. All those times he'd been in Paris, he'd never once gone to see her, and she would have known he'd been there. He and Seb always made the headlines—for all the wrong reasons.

Still, a handwritten card and carefully chosen gift had arrived every birthday and Christmas, and when she'd died she'd left him this house.

With the bequest had come a brief message.

You were happy here once. Perhaps you could be again, if you try, my darling boy.

The old woman hadn't deserved his treatment of her. She'd loved her daughter. Selfish, shallow, dazzling Giovanna.

But how did you punish a mother who didn't care if you lived or died? You punished her kin.

'I'm going to need your help getting out of my dress.'

Framed in the doorway stood another woman determined to get what she wanted no matter the cost to him.

His mother. Francesca. Now Violetta.

He shoved the Nefertiti headdress back with the rest of the costume and closed the door on it.

'I thought we'd established you'd find my touch repellent?' he drawled.

'I'm only asking you to cut me out of my dress. I think I can cope with that.'

'Cut you out? You're sewn into it? Women still do that?' he asked, surprised.

'Women like me still have that done to them, I think you mean. What woman in her right mind wants to be stuck in something she can't get out of without help? Why do you think I ran away in it?'

She turned on her heel.

Leo sighed and set off after her. He was going to be damp for a little longer.

Violetta felt those cool blue eyes burning a hole in her back as he followed her down the stairs to the room she had chosen to change in.

What had possessed her to challenge him in that way before? She'd chosen that cheerleader dress because she'd liked something in his expression, flirting? She was supposed to be repelled by him.

Now they struck another problem.

'I thought it would just tear once I tugged at it. I didn't even try back at the castle—there was no time. But I can't even get the two tiny buttons on the neck undone, never mind the rest of it.' She reached up to fiddle with the tiny silk-covered buttons. 'See, nothing budges.'

She peered over her shoulder at him. 'Have you anything to cut it with?'

'On me? No, of course not.'

'Don't you have a Swiss army knife or something? I thought the Grimentzian Guard were famously prepared for anything.'

'Normally, I never leave the castle without one,' he said, tartly. 'But curiously, I hadn't imagined I'd need it on my wedding day.'

'I've looked through the drawers and in the en-suite bathroom, but all personal effects have indeed been removed from the rooms, just as you'd said. There isn't so much as a pair of nail scissors to be had.'

Her teeth chattered.

'I can go hunting for a knife but you're shivering in that wet dress. You need to get out of it quickly. I'll try tearing it.'

His fingers landed on the back of her dress. Exploring what she assumed was a neatly sewn seam. He gave an exploratory tug, but nothing budged. He tugged again, harder. It rocked her on her feet.

His fingers brushed the nape of her neck. Violetta swallowed hard. Heat poured through her.

'Forgive me. I'm going to have to touch you.'

Wasn't that what he'd already been—?

Oh...

When he said touch, she didn't know he meant with his mouth.

Warm lips brushed the back of her neck. Then bared teeth as he used them to tear at the threads. The faintest scrape of stubble as his jaw moved against her skin. Violetta clutched the cheerleader dress harder, willing the torture to end, or wanting it never to stop. She wasn't sure which. Every nerve ending at the back of her neck was on fire.

Then, mercifully, a ripping sound and cool air hitting her spine. He ripped some more, until the dress flapped open to the base of her spine.

'Will that do?' He sounded hoarse.

She wriggled out of the lace sleeves and bodice. But she wore so many petticoats there was no way she could simply step out of the dress. She needed to lift it over her head, and she was going to need his help.

She peeked back at him. He was staring at her spine.

'Um, I need your help to get this off.'

His gaze lifted back to her face.

'Yes, of course.' He was behind her. Grabbing the skirt of the dress to lift it upwards. It caught in the tiara, and it took a moment of struggling to release it again.

Her hands went across her breasts. She heard the moment Leo saw his next challenge. An odd, strangled sound in his throat. The petticoats were fixed with a drawstring and bow at the back. It needed loosening.

His fingers were at her back again. She felt a little tug and the petticoat fell with a whoosh to puddle at her feet.

'I'm not looking,' he said, sounding even more strangled.

She quickly shimmied into the sleeveless mini-dress and glanced over her shoulder. Her former groom hadn't lied, he didn't so much as peek. Instead, he was wrestling manfully with her gown, trying to lay it carefully over the bed, looking a little hot and bothered. Not his usual composed self.

She reached around for the zip, discovering she had a new difficulty.

'I need you to fasten this one up.'

Would this torture ever end?

Leo had peeked. He'd pretended not to, of course, but he saw the shapely bottom, the limber thighs, the frou-frou of bridal underwear. He masked his reaction by focusing all his attention on dealing with the mountain of a dress. Hell, how had the woman managed to run even a metre in it? Despite the inconvenience she'd caused by fleeing, he had a new grudging respect for her.

Yards of silk. Acres of petticoats. Had this genuinely been their wedding night all his ardour might have been dampened by the sheer bloody effort of getting her out of it.

Until he saw what was beneath. Tearing all those neat, tiny stitches keeping her in had given him ample opportunity to study the delicate bone structure of her spine and the perfection of her skin.

What was wrong with him? She wasn't his type, nothing like it, but his heart still racketed about in his chest as he drew closer.

Because every inch of her spine was on show, and he itched to place his fingers back on her exposed skin and not cover it all up.

Perhaps it was because she'd said he repelled her.

He knew that was a lie. He wasn't blind, he could see how he affected her. But whatever her reason for not being truthful, he would respect her choice and not touch her unless absolutely necessary.

He stood behind her, grasped the zip in the cheerleader outfit and tugged it closed, then stepped back.

'How does it look?' she asked, turning to face him.

Too short. Showing too much leg. Too cute…

He shoved his hands in his pockets. 'Fine. Except for…' He nodded towards her head.

'What?' She froze. 'It's not a spider, is it?'

'No. It's an irreplaceable tiara.'

'Oh.' Her hand shot to her hair. 'I completely forgot. Poor Elisabetha. I doubt she'd ever thought it would be used like this. Could this be the most expensive cheerleader outfit in history?' She giggled.

It was a simple female laugh.

Nothing to get all bothered about.

So why had the effect of it shot straight to his groin?

He cleared his throat. 'I'm going to see what else there is up here that we could use, in case the weather gets worse.'

The house phone ringing in the hallway halted him. Violetta hovered close by as Leo answered.

'Okay, we'll sit tight here, then.'

He replaced the receiver.

'What is it? What's happened?'

'Sadly, you will be stuck with me for a while. That was my head of security. The road between here and the gatehouse is blocked by a fallen tree.'

'Don't they have four by fours? Can't they just drive round it?'

'If they could don't you think they'd have said that?'

She flew to the window. 'But I have to get back to San Nicolo tonight.'

'Perhaps you should have fled there, then,' he said. When she looked stricken, he added more gently, 'Look, this weather is already much worse than predicted so who knows? But it will be tomorrow now at the earliest.'

'Tomorrow? I have to be back in San Nicolo before then. My uncle might…oh, never mind.'

'Trust me, I've no more desire to be trapped alone here together than you. But we've no choice, so we need to make the best of it.'

'I wouldn't be in this mess at all if it weren't for you,' she railed at him. 'You planned all of this. I just know it,' she muttered.

'Yes, that's me.' He flourished a hand through the air. 'At my command tempests blow and storms rage.'

'Why don't you use your powers to make me disappear

and then you can have the grand duchy without the need to marry anyone at all?'

'Why don't you stop behaving like a spoiled child and do something useful, like help me search the house for things we might need now we're stuck here for the night?'

A spoiled child?

Who'd ever spoilt her? Who in her family had treated her as if she mattered at all?

No one.

Ever.

That blistering injustice sent her rage soaring.

'It's your damn house. You can do it yourself,' she shouted and slammed the bedroom door in his face.

CHAPTER FIVE

VIOLETTA PACED THE ROOM. What was she going to do now? How was she going to get back to the duchy in time to claim the throne?

The simple answer was she couldn't, and she feared her uncle might snatch it out from beneath her by claiming it for himself. Would he dare do that? Legally he wouldn't have that right but, since she'd run away, could he portray her as being unfit to rule and persuade the duchy's ministers to back him as Grand Duke?

None of her careful planning with Luisa had imagined this scenario. Being trapped in Grimentz and with the one man she'd hoped to get away from.

Footsteps sounded overhead. Her tormentor was back in the attics.

She scowled up at the ceiling. If she were really lucky, he might encounter a few rotten floorboards to fall through and be stuck up there, out of her way, until this was all over.

When he was near, she found it too hard to focus.

She rubbed the back of her neck, remembering those perfect white teeth nibbling at the nape of her neck, the searing heat of his lips. She'd felt the effect everywhere.

She shook herself. There was no time for thinking of that. She had to work out what to do next.

Could she risk trying to phone Luisa again while he was prowling about upstairs? What if he heard her and came down demanding to know who she was talking to? Would his team at the gatehouse be able to intercept her call? Her mobile had been taken away from her last night. At least, it wasn't in her rooms when her possessions had been unpacked. They'd told her it was with her other luggage. She'd asked for it, but no one had brought it to her.

There went those footsteps overhead again. She scowled up at the ceiling. This was his doing, she was certain. He'd deliberately isolated her in his chateau.

He was coming back downstairs now. Violetta stopped pacing; it wasn't helping. What could she do? No one was getting anywhere near the chateau until the storm had passed anyway.

She regretted that silly remark about him causing the storm. It made her sound like the witless female her uncle thought she was.

She didn't entirely trust Leo, but she'd jilted him, not the other way round. A second Della Torre sister to humiliate him in the most public of ways and, so far, he'd been rather forgiving and decent to her.

But beneath all that he was still the enemy. A powerful man who'd in the end expect her to do as he wanted.

She stepped out of her high-heeled wedding shoes. She was wearing a different costume now and she'd be a different Violetta to match. Plus, she knew where there was footwear that suited her much more.

She left her tiara where it was. She liked how it flashed and glittered in the low light. It reminded her that she was not only a princess but about to be a grand duchess too. She wouldn't let any man stop her, however powerful—or divinely attractive—he was.

Elisabetha's tiara was staying put.

They both had a job to do. And no matter how fast he made her heart beat, Leo von Frohburg had no part in it.

In a foul temper, Leo stalked off down the landing.

How dared she blame him for their predicament when

it was she who'd chosen to flee to this God-forsaken valley and its cursed chateau with all the conflicting memories it held for him?

He reached the attic stairs and took them three at a time. Pretending it was solely anger that drove him upwards, and nothing to do with the temptation of a delicate spine, of warm skin the colour of honey and a telling shudder of desire when he placed his mouth to a sensitive neck.

Whatever her real reason for fleeing their wedding was, it certainly wasn't due to a lack of attraction.

In the line of wardrobes, Leo found some dry clothes and quickly changed.

As he dressed, he considered how to deal with Violetta. His belief that he'd easily persuade her to marry had quickly foundered on his bride's hostility. He was going to have to dig deeper if he was ever to win her over.

Leo wasn't accustomed to dealing with females beyond a date or two—he always ended things before they got messy and never stayed to deal with the fallout. He was a charming dinner companion and a generous lover but that was the extent of his interactions. He simply didn't do protracted relationships with women. He'd learned the impact of that the hard way.

In fact, he barely did personal relationships at all. Only Seb was allowed close and even he was often kept at arm's length.

His easy path to the grand duchy had been blocked by the weather, but it was still in his sights.

For now, they were trapped here and there was nothing he could do about it, so he focused instead on what he could control. He made a mental tally of precisely where they stood.

They had shelter and basic foodstuffs. They had extra clothing, of sorts.

While he was obliged to keep his hands off her, that

cheerleader outfit was proving to be too distracting for comfort.

He wandered the house, checking the guest suites and family bedrooms first, looking for anything they could use for an overnight stay, but beneath the dust sheets they'd all been stripped of their linens.

In the servants' quarters he had more luck, finding two small rooms with a made-up single bed and en-suite bathroom each. He found a supply of unopened toiletries, including toothbrushes and shampoos.

The rooms also faced away from the worst of the weather. At least they might be able to sleep despite the gale blowing outside. The storm was getting worse, and the old house creaked and groaned as the wind tore round it.

On the ground floor the storerooms yielded up torches and storm lanterns. A pantry held a stash of candles and matches. Yet there was no radio and no TV in any of the rooms. If they were to have any entertainment tonight it would be coming from his *grand-mère*'s battered CD-player or themselves.

Under other circumstances there would be some pleasant ways for them to while away a few hours together.

He thought again of Violetta's slender spine. The perfect legs and buttocks in those sheer panties.

Perhaps they didn't have to sleep separately. Perhaps he could persuade her to join him in his bed. Perhaps they could return to the palace tomorrow and actually wed.

Once he'd discovered the real reason she ran away.

There wasn't another man in the equation, he was certain of that. She would have said so. It would have been the easiest way to extricate herself from the wedding. Instead, she'd chosen to make up some lie about finding him repellent.

Leo gathered up his supplies and headed back to the kitchens.

Why was it so imperative that she get back to San Nicolo tonight?

Unless…

Could she be honestly thinking of trying to take power in her own right? A woman who'd been carefully trained only to be the perfect wife to the monarch, not the monarch herself.

Her uncle had said she had no aptitude for the work, but perhaps she'd concealed her true identity from him as well.

She wasn't in the kitchen when he returned with his finds. He dumped everything on the table and went off searching for her.

He called to her, but the servants' quarters remained silent.

The door back to the hallway stood open and beyond that he heard sounds coming from the ballroom.

In the hall the door to the ballroom stood ajar. The shutters in there were closed and the room was filled with shadows. Then Leo saw a flicker of movement.

Violetta was there, in the centre of the room.

His gaze slid inexorably down those slender legs. She'd returned to the costume cupboards in the attics and filched the ballet shoes. Their ribbon ties criss-crossed her ankles. As he watched she rose up en pointe and sketched out a few steps.

Ballet.

There'd always been a certain gracefulness to how she moved, a pleasing fluidity. Now he understood why.

She wove unhurried, elegant moves through the half-light. A series of pirouettes, an arabesque, a leap, as graceful as a gazelle, where she appeared to almost hover in mid-air.

Unnoticed Leo watched, transfixed by the heart-stopping grace on show as Violetta danced. Lucky would be the man who held the heart of a girl who had the passion to dance like that.

In the dim hallway Leo scowled at nothing in particular. When had he become so fanciful?

She saw him and stopped abruptly, mid-move. She marched towards the doorway to exit the room and shut the door firmly behind her, as if she could expunge the memory of what he'd seen.

Certain it was seared on his memory for ever, Leo ached to see more.

'I'm sorry,' she said. 'I suppose I should have been looking for useful things, but it's just—'

'That you dance,' he said, almost in wonder.

She shot him a wary glance. 'Something like that.'

'And that open space called to you?' Leo tipped his chin in the direction of the ballroom.

'Well, yes.' Her expression was guarded but her eyes glittered through the gloom.

'I'm the same when the wind is fair and the lake calls to me. I just want to be out there sailing.' He smiled down on her. 'It feels like flying.'

She studied him, and he could tell he'd surprised her. She apparently knew as little about him as he knew of her.

With a swift move she slipped round him to start off across the hallway. 'Let's hope you're better at that than you are flying for real,' she said, perhaps trying to deflect the attention from her. He ignored her teasing.

'It was very beautiful,' he said to her back.

She flung a glance over her shoulder. The tiara glinted at him, the gaudy cheerleader dress with its pleated skirt revealing so much leg. She was a tiny punk ballerina and he wanted to watch her move again.

'Will you dance for me later?'

'Absolutely not. Apart from my tutors, I don't dance for anyone else.'

That struck him as tragic because he'd glimpsed something that was beyond simple beauty.

She'd disappeared back through the service entrance.

On a sigh Leo set off after her. This woman was drawing more from him than he'd ever expected.

Violetta's heart raced. No one had ever seen her dance. No one.

When Leo arrived in the kitchen, he looked at her as if she were a conundrum he'd just solved, and with a warmth in his gaze that sent an answering heat coiling in her belly.

'So why do you never dance for an audience?' he asked, continuing a conversation she'd hoped they'd ended. 'You're a gifted dancer.'

'It's not about that. It's…'

He'd thrown the light switch in the kitchen and now they were out of the shadows she could see what he was wearing.

She stared at him. 'Out of everything up there, that's what you chose?'

His choice of 'costume' was a white collarless shirt and formal black trousers. Identical to what he'd been wearing before they were both drenched.

'So I'm dressed as a cheerleader with a ballet addiction and you're dressed as what? Yourself?'

'It's appropriate,' he said.

'There's no one else here to see you but me. Can't you let your hair down a little?'

He looked as if she'd suggested he prance naked along his castle battlements. Violetta shook her head at him. 'It's all true, isn't it? You really don't have a fun side.'

'There isn't much time for fun when you're the leader of a country.'

'You're not a leader here. We're just two people stuck in this house together. Surely you could relax a bit.'

'In the same way that you could let me see you dance?' he said.

She scowled at him. 'It's not the same at all.'

His gaze grew warm, his expression softened.

'Allora, dimmi perché?' he asked. Then tell me why. Said too gently and in Italian.

She wished he wouldn't do that. Again it whispered over her skin. Why couldn't he stay the uninterested creature he'd been before?

'It's just for me. It's always been just for me.'

'So you've said but that still doesn't explain why. Please, I'd like to know.'

She shuffled a foot en pointe back and forth, wondering how much to share. Wondering how it was he made her *want* to share.

'It's because it feels like a rebellion against all the strictures placed on my life.'

'Go on.'

Outside a poplar tree swayed back and forth in the gale. Despite the forces at work, it still looked graceful and strong.

'When my sister ran away and I became heir to the duchy, any small freedoms I'd been allowed were instantly curtailed. My father had always been strict, but it became even worse after Francesca left. He took everything but ballet. That he allowed me to keep. He said it would keep me slender and give me poise, so I'd look good for you and be a credit to you. As if that was all I could ever be. An addendum to you.'

His brow knotted. 'I'm sorry. That's not what I would have wanted.'

'Isn't it?' She speared him with an angry glare. 'Isn't that precisely what you wanted from me? You'd have taken the time to get to know me better otherwise.'

His mouth opened but he closed it again. He remained silent. She was right.

'Despite that, they didn't drive the joy of dance out of me. I love it,' she said. 'The creativity. The hidden strength behind the beautiful, sinuous shapes I can make with my body. But I won't share that. My family never cared about what I could achieve.'

And neither would Leo, she thought, despite his apparent interest now. He just wanted to persuade her to marry him.

'That's why, apart from my dancing tutors and a few classmates, no one has ever seen me perform.'

When required she danced with partners at social occasions with the staid gliding around the floor, but, while she was graceful, she'd never once set free her dancing heart.

She'd learned long ago to conceal her true self. It was so easy to be dismissed and ridiculed. She remembered her mother, forever deferring to her husband, undermined and excluded. Gradually losing all faith that she could make a decision herself. Becoming precisely the kind of creature her menfolk imagined she was all along. Francesca had eloped to save herself, but that was not going to be Violetta's fate. She would have her independence. She'd learned to bide her time. She would achieve her dreams and she'd have them on her terms.

Leo was the only thing standing in the way of that. However charming he was being right now.

She must remember he'd had her staff removed. It must have been him because why would her uncle have done that? The regent had little interest in her, yes, but cruel? No. She doubted he actually gave his niece a moment's thought once she'd left her weekly, perfunctory meetings with him. He was too busy running the duchy, so why would he have arranged for her staff to be dismissed?

It all pointed to her future husband, making sure his

bride was only surrounded by those loyal to him, so he could do exactly what he wanted in the grand duchy.

Well, he wasn't getting his hands on it.

Even if those hands were beautiful. Her neck tingled at the memory of his fingers moving across her skin.

She moved away from him, putting the kitchen table between them. He narrowed his eyes on her, sensing the shift in her mood perhaps.

'Now you're being so frank, why don't you tell me the real reason you won't marry me?' It was quietly spoken but a steely certainty ran through it. It said, I know you're lying. 'When I touched you before your shudder had nothing to do with revulsion. As you so charmingly mentioned earlier, I've had enough experience to know the difference.'

He came round the table towards her, removing the only barrier between them. He was lean and powerful. A prowling wolf on the hunt and she had nowhere to run. She gripped a chair back so hard her knuckles turned white.

What could he do if she told him now? Nothing. They were trapped here until tomorrow at least. Her instinct was to get this over with, be honest with him. After what she'd done today, perhaps she owed him that after all. She released her grip on the chair, turned and lifted her chin to stare right into those fierce eyes.

Facing him down.

'All right, I'll tell you. I won't marry you because I plan to be Grand Duchess in my own right. As soon as I get home, I'll claim the throne as the rightful heir. Then I'm going to give San Nicolo its freedom and make it a democracy.'

As if all the dark fates in the world had aligned for a second time that day the room was filled by the dazzling white light of a lightning flash.

Leo's face was stark with shock in the split second of eerie light.

Then another mighty, foundation-rattling thunderclap crashed directly overhead.

The power went out and Violetta shrieked.

In the gloom she saw Leo's shadowy figure head to the phone. He picked it up then slammed it back into the cradle with a curse.

'The line's gone dead.'

He grabbed a torch from the stash on the table. 'I'll check the fuse box.'

When he came back the kitchen light remained off.

'The power is out too.'

'What do we do now?' She looked about her helplessly.

'Same as before. We wait it out. We have candles and a gas cooker. We'll manage.'

Violetta wrapped her arms about her, suddenly feeling chilled. Not just trapped with this man, but now in the dark too.

'Okay.' She pulled herself together. 'We have to make the best of it. I'll find something to eat.'

She rummaged around in the pantry, found two tins.

She held them aloft. 'Coq au vin or beef bourguignon?'

'*Canned* coq au vin?' Leo said, eyeing both with distaste.

'Or we could push the boat out and have baked lentils and sausage.'

Leo grimaced. 'What a shame you hadn't fled in a catering van. We might have had something better to eat.'

'You can talk.' Violetta grabbed a can opener and a saucepan. 'You drove our only other transport straight into a ditch.'

'I did not drive into a ditch. It was an unavoidable pothole, which I would have never encountered had I not been out searching for you.'

'And yet I managed to avoid it.' She opened the tin and tipped the contents into the pan.

'You were not driving a million euros' worth of Ferrari.'

'No, the florist's van is much more practical and useful.' She sat the pan on the stove.

'Ah, yes,' he said. 'Just what one needs when stranded miles from civilisation with no power and little food, floral arrangements.'

He came closer and bent to take a tentative sniff at the contents of the saucepan. When he looked up at her his expression was pained.

'That's the beef bourguignon,' Violetta explained.

'It smells utterly delightful. One can only imagine the taste.'

'At least we have something to eat. What about your men at the gatehouse? Aren't they just as stranded as we are?'

Leo stared out at the pelting rain and the trees writhing in the wind.

'They should count themselves fortunate if they've been spared the horrors of canned beef bourguignon. Though I suspect the gatehouse will be similarly stocked.'

Then his face brightened. 'But they won't have a wine cellar. With any luck there might be a bottle or two still there.' He disappeared with the torch again and when he returned a few minutes later he clutched two bottles of wine.

'These might mask the taste of what you are about to serve from that pan.' He dug a bottle opener out of a drawer. 'It may be the only way I can bring myself to eat it.'

'I thought you were starving?'

'Sadly I haven't lost my taste buds.'

She busied herself finding cutlery, bowls and two glasses for the wine.

'You seem very at home in this kitchen,' Leo said.

'Your *grand-mère* loved to cook. We spent a lot of time together here.'

'It was the same when Seb and I came to stay. She'd set us to work. Shelling peas, chopping herbs. We did it because we knew the food would be good. She was an excellent cook,' he said with a doleful look at the empty can by the stove.

'She taught me, too. I'd often cook for Luisa and sometimes Rolfe.'

When he looked blank, she added, 'My dresser and my personal secretary. At least they were until you had them removed.'

His gaze turned icy. 'You think I did that? To what purpose? If they were removed without your consent, it was your uncle's doing!'

She didn't want to believe that. Her uncle wasn't affectionate—much like her father, he saw her only as a commodity to serve the duchy—but he'd not been deliberately cruel.

'Why would he do that?' She couldn't keep the hurt from her voice.

His expression softened. 'I'm sorry, but my guess would be to isolate you by removing your support network. Do you think he had any inkling you weren't going to go through with the marriage?'

She shook her head. 'I was so careful to appear willing.'

'You certainly fooled me.'

She sent him a glance from beneath her lashes. 'I had to. I'd planned to disappear the night before the wedding and hide in a safe house in the city. But then my uncle said that the arrangements had changed. I was going to spend my last night in Grimentz not San Nicolo. I thought that was your doing too.'

He raised a brow.

'Okay, I get it, that wasn't you either.'

She spooned the contents of the pan into bowls and put them down in the two places she'd set at the table. Leo filled their glasses and then sat.

He took a tentative spoonful of the beef dish.

Violetta watched the muscles of his jaw as he chewed.

Such a mundane act shouldn't be so fascinating. He swallowed, took a quick swig of wine.

'And?' she asked.

'Not the worst dish I've ever tasted, but the bar is pretty low. In the survival course of my army training, a sergeant once served up a worm omelette.'

She laughed and started on her own bowl of food.

'So why do you want to give San Nicolo its democracy so badly?' he asked.

'Because I've lived a life with so little chance to determine my fate. I understand the position my people are in. I've seen first-hand how their chances have been limited by the offices of the grand duke and now the regent. Unlike my family the people have shown me nothing but love and I want to give back to them.'

Leo nodded. 'You saw something first-hand? Something in particular?'

'I think it all began with one person. Being dismissed yourself is one thing, but seeing it happen to a boy who didn't have the compensation of the privileged life I had sowed a seed in me. From then it just grew and grew.'

'What boy? Was he a sweetheart of yours?'

An odd gruffness to his voice made her look up. Those blue eyes were unreadable in the low light, but his expression was curiously intense.

'No, nothing like that. I actually only met him on one occasion but the memory of it has stayed with me for years.

'I was only eleven, I'd accompanied my parents on an official visit to a food festival. We're big on those in San Nicolo. Food and wine make up our biggest exports. A teenage boy had entered his farm's cheese in one of the competitions and he should have won. It was the best there that day, but my parents gave the prize to one of their cronies. I tried to argue with my mother about it, but she told me, in no uncertain terms, to be quiet and remember my place.' She shrugged. 'I know it probably sounds insignificant to you.'

'Not at all. It's those small moments that shape who we are.'

'I don't know why I even tried to make a difference. My parents never listened to me. I was a second daughter when what they wanted was a son. My mother used to look at me as if it were my fault. She tried to raise us in the way she thought appropriate to our futures but there was no love in it.'

'Did you love her?' Leo asked.

'Who doesn't try to love their parents? Until it becomes obvious you're a big fat disappointment to them. Is it terrible to say that I didn't miss them much after they were gone? Uncle Guido at least showed some minor interest in me, even if it was only to get me ready to be a wife to you.'

'And we know how successful he was doing that!' Leo said. But this time she couldn't feel any humour in it.

'My parents poured all their efforts into getting Francesca ready to be your grand duchess, but in the end she hadn't even wanted it. How could she have forgotten? The duchy is everything, our people needed her.'

Leo's eyes glittered. 'So you hatched a plan to take power yourself?'

She'd come to terms with how Leo affected her physically, she hadn't reckoned on her prospective husband being so emotionally attentive and that he would take the time to listen and even take her seriously.

'Yes. I did. I was about to be married and that would mean losing the thing I wanted most. I had to act. If I want to truly serve the people, I have to be free.'

'Freedom,' Leo said, almost wistfully. 'That's a rare commodity indeed.'

'But you're a man and a powerful one at that. You're telling me you don't have freedom to choose?'

'The only son of a monarch, my future was mapped out for me from birth. I had no choice in the matter. How different is that from your situation?'

'Seriously? You think there's a comparison? You chose to marry Francesca and at any time you could have said no without any consequences. What choice did she or I have?'

He took her left hand and ran his thumb gently across her ringless fingers. 'And yet here you sit, having said an emphatic no. That looks like a choice to me.'

She should have tugged her fingers free but the warmth and strength of his were so comforting.

'I may have said no but you still came after me. You plan to change my mind, don't you?'

'You've already stated what you want is freedom to run the duchy yourself. I doubt you'll be persuadable.' He watched her from hooded eyes.

Her stomach did a flip. If he kept looking at her like that she might be persuaded to do anything.

But it was just a ploy to get her back on side. He might not have been responsible for the dismissal of Luisa and Rolfe, or that sudden decision for her to spend last night in Grimentz, but that didn't mean he wasn't still to be avoided. As soon as this storm cleared, he'd want her to go back to Grimentz with him and be married, she was sure of it.

She snatched her hand free and pushed to her feet.

'It's been a trying day and I'm tired. I'd like to rest for a while.'

He lounged back in his seat.

'There are two rooms in the servants' quarters we can use. Take whichever you prefer. Though if you want to bathe, now that we are without power, sadly the water will be cold in both.'

He smouldered up at her, with an added wicked curve to the corner of his mouth as he saw the blush spreading across her cheek. 'Though perhaps you'd welcome the effects of a cold shower, Grand Duchessa?'

CHAPTER SIX

LEO SAT NURSING his glass of wine.

Thinking.

Running through his various options and feeling unprepared. Because of all the reasons Violetta might have chosen to run, this was the last thing he'd expected.

A democratic duchy right on the doorstep of Grimentz? Meaning San Nicolo would be lost to the von Frohburgs for good.

His father would have been apoplectic.

Yet curiously Leo was able to summon little outrage at the prospect. A few hours ago, he'd come up here all guns blazing determined to reclaim his runaway bride. And now?

Now he was no longer sure what he wanted.

His people had their own elected bodies, with a say in how Grimentz was run. The Della Torres had not been so liberal-minded, they'd held onto power with a fierce grip. The current regent being more rigid than most. Why shouldn't San Nicolo have the same freedoms Grimentz enjoyed? He'd planned to introduce something similar once he'd become Grand Duke.

Yes, but a full-blown democracy, with potentially all power stripped from its former ruling family? That should give him pause, surely?

Again, Leo felt nothing beyond a curiosity about how that might work for the duchy.

Perhaps a pair of melting brown eyes had temporarily bewitched him?

Was that it? A woman making him think twice about what he wanted? When he'd had little cause to trust one before.

He left the kitchen and walked back through the grand hallway. With its marble pillars and elaborate chandeliers and frivolous ballroom. All symbols of the power and wealth and status of a well-connected family.

The wind had moaned and rattled at the window of her little room, but, snuggled beneath the counterpane of her single bed, Violetta had actually slept. She'd felt safe knowing that Leo was somewhere in the house, which was a revelation, because wasn't he supposed to be the last person she should trust?

The night before she'd been so tense, she'd barely closed her eyes, but now she woke feeling refreshed.

She washed her face, smoothed her elaborate chignon and, on impulse, put the tiara back on. For some reason it gave her confidence.

On the window ledge outside her room sat a torch. Leo must have placed it there for her and she was touched by the thoughtful gesture.

The roiling clouds lashed rain against the windows, but Leo's torch lit the way as she descended the stairs of the servants' quarters.

The kitchen was cosy with its blinds drawn and storm lanterns sat on the table and dresser. The man who'd set them emerged from the pantry.

'Ah, you're up. I thought I was going to have to beat on your door to wake you.'

She rubbed her eyes. 'How long have I been asleep?'

'Several hours. It's past seven now.' He held up another of the tins from their small pantry. 'Dinner?'

'You can't already be hungry?'

'After the delights of that gruel you fed me for lunch, you mean?'

He moved around the kitchen with the same grace as he moved through his royal duties. In that collarless shirt, with his sleeves rolled back, he had such a relaxed allure about him. The dim light caught on the slash of his cheekbones, the strong jaw, those broad shoulders and lean hips.

Such a dangerous charm. She must not forget he could still so easily derail her plans for the duchy if she let him. Violetta took a steadying breath, trying to control the effect he had on her.

She watched him collect plates and cutlery and set two places at the table.

'You're actually quite domesticated,' she said, slipping into a seat.

He grasped a bottle of wine. 'You make it sound like I'm half wild.'

She watched the muscles on his forearms flex as he worked a corkscrew into its top. The strong grip of his hands as he pulled the cork clear.

How had Francesca described him? A part-tame wolf. He was all lean strength and barely contained energy. Despite their everyday surroundings, it was there, a distinct aura of danger. Violetta crushed her fingers together in her lap.

'I meant you seem at home in a kitchen.'

'Only this one. Grand-Mère insisted that Seb and I did our share of the chores here.'

'I used to love that. I felt like I was a regular person. Maybe like one of the servants. Able to leave all my parents' expectations behind at the end of the day.'

'We're servants too though, aren't we?' he said. 'Just not the kind who can easily choose alternative employment.'

Had she imagined that hint of regret? She thought he cared for nothing but power.

'Would you have liked a different career?'

He shook his head. 'My earliest memories are of my father, standing me on the castle battlements. Pointing out San Nicolo, saying that it had been stolen from us and that essentially my only reason for existing was to get it back. A different career was never an option.' He poured two glasses of wine and set one in front of her. 'Although perhaps that's where my head for heights comes from,' he said casually, as if there weren't a dark reason for that.

Violetta thought of a little boy, too tiny to see the duchy over the hulking stonework without being lifted onto it. There'd been no protective hug of a father holding a beloved son, helping him see the wonder of the world below.

More a prince drilling his obsessions into the heir. She was beginning to understand why Leo had come charging after her when she ran from the wedding.

He took a slug of his wine.

'Let's eat. I hope you're ready for the culinary adventure that is canned coq au vin?'

The table had been cleared, the dishes put away and Leo let the evening settle in over him. The violence of the storm outside forgotten, muted by the magic of this house and this night.

No one demanding his attention. Nowhere to be. Nothing to do but sit here with this woman and watch the candlelight play in her hair and glint through the emeralds of that absurdly out of place tiara.

The true magic of this house, of course, was that it made him ordinary. Just a man sharing dinner. Not thinking about tomorrow and all its implications but for the moment content to be with Violetta and enjoy her surprisingly refreshing company.

'Do you know what your castle is missing?' she asked.

'I know you're going to say a dog.'

'Yes! A big lolloping hound. I remember you and Seb tearing about the place with a dog always at your heels.'

'Yes, Grand-Mère always cared for rescue dogs.'

'You must have looked forward to seeing them every time you came.'

He shook his head. 'You know, I never came back after that summer you were here.'

'Never?' Her eyes widened. 'Why?'

'My mother left,' he said.

'And?'

He looked at her sharply. 'Surely you know the story?'

'Only the bare facts. I'd like to hear it from you.'

He almost reverted to classic Leo, sharing nothing, but those disarming liquid eyes were hard to resist.

'My mother didn't just leave, she abandoned me and my father.' And the hurt of that still had the power to take his breath way.

'So he became both parents to you?'

Leo snorted in derision. 'No. He became even less of a parent to me than he was before. He blamed me for my mother's departure. First I'd been too clingy, then not dutiful enough. It depended on the day and the mood he was in. It was always worse when news of my mother's latest affair hit the headlines. When she imagined herself in love yet again. What a futile emotion. Who needs it? So fleeting and unreliable.'

Violetta regarded him sadly, but she was in no position to offer sympathy.

'You can't pretend you've had much of it in your life either,' he scoffed.

Her gaze softened on him. 'Except for here. We were both loved here.'

'Not after I cut Grand-Mère out of my life.'

'That's not true. Right up to that last year she spoke of you with pride and affection. You were loved unconditionally by her. She even left you her beloved chateau.'

Leo recalled the regular cards and the gifts and was assailed by guilt. 'I couldn't forgive her for allowing my mother to meet her lover here and I tried to punish her for it,' he said quietly.

'You were in pain. You lashed out at the only person you could hurt because she was the only one who cared about you. She would have understood that. She was a wise woman.'

Those beguiling eyes watched him, ablaze with certainty. It wrapped around him and warmed the cold, dead place where his heart used to be.

It was startling to realise Violetta was the first person he'd spoken to in this way. He hadn't even shared this much with Seb, but with her for some reason it felt right.

He stared at a candle guttering in one of the lanterns. 'Love is hardly top of the list for people like us.'

'Despite all the wealth and privilege, and responsibility, we are still people though, aren't we? Surely, deep down you'd want to be loved by your wife, to be happy?'

'Based on the choices I'd made about our marriage, you know the answer to that question already. In my experience it's safer to have a business arrangement with a woman from the outset, then I'm unlikely to be disappointed. A fruitless quest for happiness would only get in the way.'

She regarded him, sadly. 'But what about taking her to bed?'

'Grand Duchessa, love is not necessary for good sex, or even adequate sex that gets the job done.'

'Pregnancy, you mean? What a cold life that would be.'

'But producing an heir is vital for people like us.'

'Only if you don't believe in democracy.'

'Even then, the family won't end because it's no longer

in power. There will be properties and possessions to pass down. A title to preserve.'

She huffed. 'What use is a title if you can't *do* anything with it? I know a title can draw attention to good causes, but influence can only go so far if you haven't any real power.'

He laughed at her. 'Grand Duchessa, you haven't thought this through, have you? How does that work in your world where democracy is king?'

She glanced up at him. Delighted by the sound of his laughter. 'Yes, of course, you're right.'

And why was she sharing so much? He shouldn't be this easy to talk to, he was supposed to be the enemy, but her heart ached for the boy he'd been. Trying so hard to be the man his father would be proud of and desperately hurt by his mother's rejection.

Still, she really shouldn't tell him another thing.

'I hated that I was never taken seriously.'

Oh, Violetta!

'Well, things are about to get very serious.' He checked his watch. 'In two hours, you reach your majority. You could take control as soon as you get back to San Nicolo.'

It was ten p.m.? The hours had flown in this man's company.

'Now it's nearly here I'm rather scared.' Since she became the heir to the duchy, she'd dreamed of the moment she turned twenty-one.

'When my father died, I remember feeling a combination of exhilaration and blind terror, but I had so much work to do, there wasn't really time to think about anything but the job.'

'I was so sure before, but now suddenly I feel like I've no idea how to begin.'

'What's important to you?' he asked.

'That's easy—that people get to choose their own destiny.'

He took a lazy sip of wine. 'Well, begin there, then. Gather good people around you. People you trust, who share the same values, but who won't be afraid to tell you the truth if you're getting things wrong. Then once you have that support network in place, ask San Nicolo precisely what it wants to do.'

'You make it sound so easy.'

'It isn't, but it will be worth it.'

He was talking to her as if he believed what she wanted was possible.

'You think I can do it? Actually introduce democracy to a four-hundred-year-old absolute monarchy? Me? The girl who didn't have the guts to stand up to her uncle and say no to a marriage she didn't want.'

'Running away ten minutes before you were due to leave for the cathedral took courage. You grabbed the only opportunity you'd had at that point. Apply that to introducing democracy and you'll get there.'

'What? Run away a lot?'

'No.' He laughed. 'Grasp the opportunities as they present themselves.'

Getting naked with you and hang the consequences. That's the opportunity I want to grasp right now.

She took a gulp of her wine at that shocking thought.

Leo watched the soft blush spreading over her cheeks and wondered what had caused that. And wondered too about her ambition for herself and her duchy.

Hers was a noble aspiration. All she wanted was for her country to flourish. It had nothing to do with her needs.

How short of that did Leo's ambitions for San Nicolo come?

They were about him. His wants and his proving something to a dead man who'd never given a damn about his only son. Except for how he could benefit Grimentz. Prince

Friedrich had certainly never cared about San Nicolo in the way this young woman did.

He'd let his father poison his mind and drive him in the wrong direction.

Here sat a petite woman with a big heart, caring only how she could use her position of privilege to serve others.

'What is it?' she asked, concern in those brown eyes.

What had she seen? The moment when his shame had obliterated his ambitions? San Nicolo wasn't his, it belonged to her and her people. He had no right to it.

'I was imagining you running amok in the palace of San Nicolo. Your uncle has a shock coming.'

'Uncle Guido isn't going to like this at all, is he?'

'I think that's a given.'

'Will he try to stop me?'

'Almost certainly, but you have the right of succession on your side. There is nothing in the constitution that says you can't rule. Just that you can't if you marry. Then you'd have to surrender power to your husband. But if you believe in it you should go after what you think is right.'

She smiled.

'What?'

'For a moment there you sounded just like your grandmother. She was for ever telling me to go after my dreams.'

That wasn't quite what he'd said. His comment was more cynical, less emotional. But he heard Grand-Mère's voice, too. Telling him to stop being so rigid and controlled like his father, and to lead with the heart, at least try to be happy.

She sighed. 'Imagine if my dream allowed me a husband too and it could be like this. Just two people getting to know one another, enjoying each other's company.'

Yes, he thought wistfully, just imagine…

Then dialled back. He never wanted that. That was how you got hurt.

'There are other advantages we have that others don't, which compensate,' he said.

'Like what? So far I've only experienced crushing expectation and little chance to do anything I actually want or believe in.'

'That will change tomorrow when you take power.'

'You truly believe I can do it?'

Her gaze fixed expectantly on him and he realised with some surprise that, yes, he thought she could.

'You said before that everything changed for you when Francesca ran away,' he said. 'Did you miss her? Were you close?'

'Not really. Even though we were sisters our worlds were very different. We were raised separately. She was going to marry you and be the next grand duchess. Whereas I was destined to be married off to a European aristocrat. My father said I couldn't expect the state to keep me, and that I had no other usefulness to it apart from marrying well and providing the Della Torres with wealthy, well-connected in-laws.'

Leo's anger rose at that. Another child who'd been told they had no value in themselves.

'Did it hurt you? When she ran away?' She peeked up at him, concern in her gaze. It warmed and comforted him.

'Only my pride. I didn't have any tender feelings for her, if that's what you're asking. I don't really blame her any more either. I genuinely wish her well and hope she's happy with the choices she made.'

'I hope so too. She may have been the heir but to my parents she was still just a girl. Do monarchs only love princes?' she said bitterly.

'Not in my experience.' Who'd loved him because he was the prince and heir? Definitely neither of his parents.

'Leo, I'm sorry for that,' she said, placing her hand over his. The intimacy took him by surprise and before he could control it, all the hurt and humiliation came flooding back. Tightening his throat. He withdrew his hand from beneath hers.

'It's in the past, it no longer matters.'

'Being hurt by those who should love us always matters.'

Despite his best efforts that reverberated through him, the pain danced close to the surface again. He slammed his mind shut on it.

He didn't want this. Allowing someone close was how you got…*hurt*.

And yet this woman, with her gentle eyes and gentler hands, was creeping into the heart he'd thought was shut away for ever.

He got to his feet. 'Let's change the music.'

'Or change the subject, you mean. I get it. Talking about your feelings is painful.'

'Not at all.' With his back to her he shuffled through the collection of CDs. 'It just doesn't serve any purpose for me.'

Seb would have rolled his eyes at that one.

'Here we go again. Leo the untouchable. The man without a heart. The only person you're fooling is yourself. You're flesh and blood like the rest of us.'

Leo slammed his mind shut on that too. He found one of Grand-Mère's favourite bands and the strains of samba filled the air.

'Dance with me?' he said, stretching out his hand.

Violetta hadn't missed that haunted expression in his eyes. Despite those broad, straight shoulders, the determined chin, she'd spied it—a sudden air of vulnerability. He was briefly that teenage boy again, who'd been betrayed by both parents and had his heart broken.

She looked at that outstretched hand but couldn't trust herself to take it.

'Your grandmother used to love listening to this.' She stood and started moving by herself, swinging her hips.

'What's that you're doing?' he asked.

'It's salsa.'

'You do it well.'

'I'm a dancer, remember.'

'That's sultrier than any ballet I've ever seen.'

She swirled her hips again. 'Perhaps.'

'Teach me?'

'You can already dance.'

'Enough to twirl a visiting royal around the dance floor when required, but not like that.'

She studied him, frowning. 'How ever did you seduce all those women?'

'That's an entirely different kind of dance.' He was trying to copy what she'd just done.

Badly.

Had she found a chink in this spectacular man's arsenal? Could he really not dance?

Wooden hips. Rhythm all wrong.

Oh, Lord, badly wrong.

'Stop.' She held up a hand. 'Watch.'

She traced out a few easy steps. 'See what I'm doing. Lift your heel and your hips will move on their own.'

'What's the step called?' he asked, absolutely murdering whatever he thought it was.

'It's a cucaracha.' Her brow knotted as she watched. She took his hands in hers. 'Follow what I do,' she said. 'Yes, that's much better.' And didn't notice he'd edged closer until he gathered her up, brought their hips almost together and executed a perfectly beautiful cucaracha.

She'd have extracted herself from his arms but he'd taken her by surprise and being able to touch and feel all that strength moving beneath her fingers was intoxicating.

'*This* is how I had all that success with the ladies,' he purred.

Not with this one.

'That's enough dancing,' she said just as a slow, mellow number began.

'Come now.' He tucked her hand to his chest. 'This was supposed to be our wedding day. At least grant me our first dance. You owe me that, surely.'

A sultry songstress was crooning about losing herself to love, that it felt like home, as Leo swirled her round the room.

Oh, the man was devious. He danced beautifully. Violetta couldn't help herself, she started to enjoy it.

He twirled her out and back, and again, and this time as she danced back to him he turned her beneath his arm and then into a perfect dip. As she tipped backwards her hand flew up, grabbing his biceps in alarm, but he held her easily. She was perfectly safe, and a moment later she was upright again, being moved effortlessly round the room.

'Ready to try another dip, *la mia piccolo ballerina*?'

His little ballerina.

She shouldn't be so charmed but her giddy little ballerina heart skipped a beat. Italian spoken in that deep baritone was lethal.

So out she went, spinning beneath his arm and then back into a perfect dip. She laughed up at him, her hand resting lightly on his biceps this time, his other arm strong beneath her back.

She was expecting to come back up, but he held her there, his gaze on her mouth. Then suddenly he tightened his grip, lifted her towards him and pressed his lips to hers.

They were soft and warm and Violetta, caught off guard, let them move over hers. Her hand slid up his arm to curl about his shoulder.

He pulled her closer, deepened their kiss, and a pulse throbbed hard between her thighs.

A soft noise rolled in her throat. Her fingers on his shoulder dug in. She pressed closer so more of her body connected to his. He was all hard muscle and heat and she wanted more.

Reason, common sense, dreams and determination were forgotten…or were they? What about her people? What about San Nicolo?

Her eyes fluttered open.

It might all be lost if she allowed herself to be seduced. Distracted from the course she knew she must take.

From somewhere she found the strength to break the kiss and push him away.

Leo leant forward wanting to taste those lips again, but his met thin air. She'd lurched back in his arms and planted a hand firmly against his chest.

'That's enough of that. I know what you're planning and it won't work.'

Planning?

He'd *planned* to kiss her again, to savour the delight of her mouth and hadn't thought of a thing beyond.

She pushed at him, wriggling to get free. Reluctantly he let go.

Looking thoroughly flustered, she instantly rounded the table to put it between them. She scooped up her wine glass and knocked back its contents.

'I won't be falling for your seduction technique.' She sloshed another measure of wine into her glass and gulped that down too.

'You might want to slow down,' Leo cautioned.

'Don't tell me what to do.' She slashed an angry hand through air. 'I've had enough of men like you telling me what to do.'

Leo shrugged. 'Okay, but you may regret that in the morning.'

She sank down into a seat. 'The morning,' she said, almost wondrously. 'I'll be free. I'll be Grand Duchess, and no one will ever tell me what to do again.'

He didn't have the heart to remind her that her life was about to get a lot more complicated. Being the sole decision maker wasn't going to be the easy route.

CHAPTER SEVEN

IN ONE RESPECT Leo's wedding night was much as he might have expected. He'd barely slept.

However, that was where all of the similarities ended. He'd spent the night entirely alone, listening to the ravages of the storm outside and the restless pacing of the woman in the room next door.

More than once he'd been on the verge of leaving his room to hammer on her door and pick up where they'd left off, but he knew it wasn't the answer.

He checked his watch, seven o'clock on the day of Violetta's twenty-first birthday. She was now officially Grand Duchess and his chance at easily claiming San Nicolo had passed. Oddly, that didn't bother him as much as he'd have expected, and today was another day. If yesterday was anything to go by, who knew what it might bring? With the woman next door anything could happen and while the storm raged there was nothing anyone could do to move things along.

Despite their circumstances Leo had enjoyed his evening. Unexpected in the scheme of things. He hadn't imagined they'd have been doing quite so much talking, expecting to be engaged in something less cerebral and more physical. But he'd liked it.

She was an excellent dinner companion, entertaining,

energising. He couldn't remember the last time he'd enjoyed an evening so much.

Of course there'd be no repeat. He needed a wife. She'd declined that position and he had neither the want nor desire for a woman in any other capacity. Why would he?

A twig, torn from a tree somewhere and still bearing its lush, fresh leaves, landed with a splat against the window then was wrenched away again.

Grimentz was still in the grip of a storm. Here, in this sheltered valley, it was bad enough but what was the rest of his country suffering? While he was trapped here and powerless to do anything but wait it out.

He threw back the sheets.

He needed coffee and something to eat from their meagre pantry. Then he could put his thoughts back in order.

Who knew what time she'd finally slept? Not till the early hours at least, because she remembered a faint light creeping beneath the curtains.

Kept awake by the storm, which if anything had got worse.

But also kept awake by thoughts of the man she'd pushed away and fled from. Twice in one day.

She'd tossed and turned, she'd climbed out of bed and paced the room just to burn off some of the restless energy that coursed through her body.

She couldn't get that kiss out of her mind. Her lips burned with it and the promise of so much more from the man who was sleeping just on the other side of that wall.

Violetta grimaced. How could she have let that happen? How could she have allowed herself to…to…*want* Leo?

She ducked back beneath the covers and screwed her eyes shut for good measure. It made no difference to the fact.

She wanted Leo. His hands on her. His mouth on hers. She wanted everything he was and more.

She had not expected to like him.

Prince Sebastien, with his lazy smile and easy charm, was the likeable von Frohburg. Not stern, aloof Leo. Yet last night she'd spied a different man behind the mask, she'd caught a glimpse of his vulnerabilities. She saw his aching loss, his mistrust of women and what the bitter experience of growing up with his father had instilled in him. Along with the biting need to reclaim the grand duchy that his forebears had bred into him.

But that wasn't who he was, not at his heart. Beneath that dark facade, there was warmth and fun and kindness, if only he could allow himself to show it.

Violetta flung herself over in bed. All that should matter to her was San Nicolo and its people. Leo might have talked reasonably about her plans for radical change in her country but when it came down to it, he'd stand against it. Just as her uncle and father had. Powerful men always thought they knew better.

If she let him in then she'd be betraying all the people of San Nicolo who, like her, dreamed of a different future. Brighter, bolder, freer. Where you got to choose your own destiny. Getting tangled up with the Prince of Grimentz was a sure-fire way to lose all hope of that.

There was movement next door. The sound of the shower cranking on, followed by a muffled, but expressive curse as cold water hit warm skin.

Violetta couldn't help but smile.

Then the smile faded.

On the other side of the wall, in the small en-suite bathroom, His Serene Highness would be naked. Those beautiful hands working soap across his torso. That strong body sluiced with water and suds.

She'd been chilled in the night and, not wanting to explore the costume attic with its groaning timbers and in the pitch dark and moaning wind, she'd returned to the kitchen and grabbed Leo's wedding shirt from the back of a chair where he'd left it to dry.

Now she tugged the fabric closer to her nose and inhaled. It smelled of him, of his cologne. She imagined touching him, running her hands across that broad chest.

Her hands slid over her own body, along her arms, across her breasts, her belly contracted. Instinctively she clenched her thighs together. She drew the hem of the shirt higher, baring her hips, and let her fingers wander downwards over her belly, to between her thighs.

There was the rude clatter of the shower turning off, the rattle of curtain rings as it was swept back.

Violetta snatched her hand away and lay still until she heard footsteps along the landing and a heavy male tread on the stairs.

She let out a long slow breath. Time to get up herself and face him, and whatever the day would bring. But first she'd also take a bracing cold shower. It might be just what she needed to snap out of this nonsense.

Leo collected the cafetière and coffee from the pantry. Thankful the staff who visited felt fresh coffee was an essential. He was filling the pot from the tap when there was an ear-piercing scream from above.

Good God! Had someone found their way here and broken into the chateau despite the foul weather?

He pelted up the stairs, yelling for her.

'Here! Oh, come quickly.'

With fists raised he burst through the door to her bathroom. Skidding to a halt when he discovered she was alone.

Or apparently not.

'There,' she wailed, pointing to a small spider sitting in the bath.

'For God's sake, woman, I thought you were being attacked.'

'Never mind that now,' she said, hopping from foot to foot. 'Do something, please. I hate spiders!'

This was not how he'd imagined his honeymoon would be. He sighed heavily and bent down to take off a shoe, getting ready to flatten the offending creature.

'You're not going to kill it?'

'I thought you wanted it gone.'

'But you used to catch them in your hands.'

'I was thirteen and less fastidious than I am now.'

She snatched up a glass sitting on the washbasin and thrust it at him. 'Here. Use this.'

'And keep it in there how?'

She looked about her frantically, then shot out of the door. Leo heard her running from room to room.

Violetta's footsteps returned along the landing and she burst back in.

'There,' she said, handing over a piece of card. 'You can trap it in the glass with that.'

One glance at what she'd given him and his gaze shot back to hers.

'Seriously? *This* was all you could find?'

She shrugged. 'There was a pile of them sitting on a bedside table. I think someone must have had a bit of a crush.'

In his hand Leo held a postcard, the kind on sale in any principality gift shop. A photograph of him, this one had him in military uniform, looking his most pompous and austere.

With a deliberate flourish he flipped it over so his image would not be in contact with the spider. There followed a minute of undignified scrabbling about at as the intruder scuttled back and forth out of his reach. But a small arachnid was no match for a fully grown human and eventually it was caught.

Leo turned, with glass in hand, to see Violetta—the brave young woman who'd had the guts to flee her wedding yesterday—cowering against a wall, and something in him railed at the sight.

'You stand over there and Antonio and I will stand over here.' He smiled reassuringly at her.

'What? *Who?*'

'This is the famed Antonio.' He held the spider aloft. 'He needs to go back to his wife.'

She snorted. 'Spiders don't have wives.'

'Then where do little girl and boy spiders come from?'

Her lips twitched. 'So what's she called? This wife of the famed Antonio?'

'Hildegard.'

'Hildegard?' She laughed.

'Shh… He adores her and won't have anyone make fun of her.'

Violetta eased away from the wall. 'Well, that's an honourable thing, I suppose.'

'Yes, it is,' Leo said.

He and Antonio took a step towards the doorway and her. But though she kept her gaze fixed on the glass in his hand she didn't flinch as he drew nearer.

She followed him down the stairs, to the rear of the servants' wing, and the scullery door, which opened onto an enclosed courtyard, protected from the full force of the weather. Leo dropped to his haunches, carefully upended the glass beneath a rosemary bush and Antonio scuttled to safety.

As he stood, re-entered the house and closed the door back on the weather, Violetta held his gaze.

'Thank you,' she said. 'No one has ever tried to help me get over my fear of spiders before.'

'Antonio and Hildegard will be pleased they've helped you.'

'I know it's irrational. Being scared of such a teeny creature.' Her eyes clouded. 'At least that's what my father said when he locked me in a dark closet. Knowing there were spiders lurking in every corner. He said I must conquer my fears and I'd stay in there until I'd learnt to control myself. By that he meant stop crying. He left me in there for hours. I was four.' She hugged herself. Small and helpless again. 'Who does that to a child?'

'A monster, that's who!' Leo said, raging inside for her.

She gazed up at him. Her eyes filled with remembered hurt and he reached for her, wanting to clasp her to him, and eradicate all that pain, but she stepped back.

'Um…thanks.' She chewed her lip, looking torn. 'I should probably go and get that shower now.'

He watched as she hurried away. Toned, tanned legs on display beneath the shirt she wore.

His wedding shirt, no less.

He ran a hand through his hair. She'd rejected his marriage suit and after this storm abated they'd be going their separate ways. She'd no longer be his concern. She'd even just made it clear that while they were trapped here she'd prefer he stay at arm's length.

So why had he felt compelled to comfort her just now?

Because he knew intimately the pain he saw in her fathomless brown eyes and the failure of a father who'd helped put it there. And because he couldn't ignore the feeling that they shared a connection beyond being royal.

Somehow they were kindred spirits.

Thirty minutes later, in the small, first-floor room that had once been his *grand-père*'s study, Leo was perched on the edge of the desk. Long legs stretched out, ankles crossed, staring out at the view, still shrouded by rain clouds.

Out there his country was hunkered down beneath the pummelling of the storm. He could only hope that the damage was as limited as it appeared to be here. What else might await him when he returned to his castle? Would his people be angry that the duchy hadn't been restored to them or was it really just the objective of the von Frohburgs?

Was he really thinking of letting San Nicolo go? The dream that had obsessed his family for generations and his father most of all. The dream he had drummed endlessly into his only son.

'The duchy is your destiny, boy. The only reason you were put on this earth. Don't fail me. Don't fail Grimentz. Make amends for the shame your mother brought to this family.'

How often had Leo heard those words? Or something like them.

The door behind him creaked open.

'There you are.'

He glanced over his shoulder as Violetta appeared.

The temptation of her supple, toned limbs back on show in her little cheerleader dress. He couldn't be sorry. He was in sore need of cheering up as even beyond the grave his father still had the power to taunt him.

She padded towards him.

Barefoot, her chestnut hair hanging in damp tendrils down her back, she was nothing like the lofty grand duchess her birthday had made of her, or the apparently insipid woman he'd been engaged to marry. She was more vibrant and real to him than either of those illusory creatures. She hopped up beside him on the desk. Her legs swung back and forth.

'What are you doing in here?' She glanced about the room that contained only a desk, three empty bookcases and a solitary painting hanging on the wall.

'Thinking.'

She studied him, her head tipped to one side. 'About?'

'Your grand duchy.'

'You're not going to try and persuade me to marry you after all?'

'Are you persuadable?'

'No,' she said, flashing him an odd look, as if trying to convince herself as much as him. 'I won't lose the duchy by taking a husband.'

'Then I won't be wasting my time with that.' It surprised him to discover he meant it.

'But still you were thinking about it.'

'Actually, I was thinking more about what my father would say about the turn of events.' He'd have been incoherent with rage.

'He'd have been disappointed?'

'An understatement. He'll be cursing me from the grave. I can hear him now. If you don't regain the duchy what use can you be to Grimentz? You might as well have not existed.'

Violetta watched him sadly. 'Your father was a monster too.'

Long before his father's death, Leo had learned to expect nothing from him, but it didn't mean it couldn't still hurt. Like the swift stab of pain at the reminder he meant nothing but a way to grab the duchy.

'Indeed he was.'

She glanced around her. 'What room is this?'

'It used to be my grandfather's study. I regret I never knew him, but Grand-Mère kept everything as it was after he died and it was my and Seb's favourite room in the house.'

'Not because of the view?' She squinted out at the gardens lost beneath the mist and rain.

'Partly. It looks straight out over the mountains to the north. You feel like you are at the edge of civilisation and that hordes of barbarians could come streaming over the peaks at any moment.'

'Sounds lovely.'

'It was to two young boys. Grand-Père had a collection of medieval swords and shields.' He pointed at the lines of fading on the white plaster. 'They were mounted on the walls. We imagined all sorts of battles and heroics, of course.'

He fell silent for a moment. Remembering the very real, emotionally traumatic battles he'd endured back at the castle.

'Sometimes, when things with my father got really bad,' he said, 'I'd imagine climbing over those mountains and never coming back.'

'Was it often bad?'

'Yes.' His gut churned at the memories of his father's displeasure. 'However hard I tried, nothing I did ever pleased him. The best exam results, becoming captain of all the sport teams, trophies, accolades. Nothing was good enough. It got so much worse after my mother left though, as unfortunately for me I inherited her eyes. I don't think he could forgive me for being a daily reminder of her. He'd certainly never forgive me for losing the duchy.'

Violetta's conscience pricked her. Her defiance had stolen Leo's chance to finally prove Prince Friedrich wrong by regaining the duchy.

Leo caught her sympathetic gaze.

'Don't worry,' he said, with a quirk of his mouth. 'I'll move on.'

He would but not with her. She had to do this alone… didn't she?

Where had that niggle of doubt come from? Possibly because there was something so appealing about the man sitting beside her. Something about his vitality and his vulnerability. The warmth in those startling blue eyes. Not at all the prince she'd thought she'd fled from.

And then there were his kisses last night.

She peeked at him. Her gaze lingering on his beautiful

mouth, with lips that were so unimaginably soft. Her own tingled at the memory.

'Violetta,' he warned. 'If you stare at me like that I won't be answerable for the consequences.'

She blinked at him and hopped down from the desk, putting some space between them. She was far too interested in what those consequences might be and that was dangerous.

The room was empty as his father's heart had been. The only decoration left on the walls was a small canvas in a heavy gilt frame, of a young woman wearing a green brocade gown and a determined expression.

Violetta looked closer. Here was a nice neutral thing to discuss. Nothing at all tempting about fixtures and fittings.

'Who is this?'

'That's Elisabetha. At least how an artist in the sixteenth century imagined she may have looked.'

Elisabetha again. 'Who *was* she?'

'She saved Grimentz and its prince from destruction.'

'That's some feat. How did she achieve that?'

'Her father coveted Grimentz. He was more powerful, had a bigger army. He marched on the castle and lay siege to it, demanding the prince surrender. The Wolf of Grimentz refused.'

Violetta could hardly believe it. 'One of your forebears was called the Wolf?'

'He'd been badly disfigured in a fire as a child and he'd grown up to be fierce and guarded. Where he could he avoided company, and particularly that of women.'

Could those traits be hereditary? she wondered. 'Our lonely wolf was unmarried, then.'

'Correct. But the rival king had a daughter—'

She clapped her hands together. 'Oh, there was a romance?'

He made a face. 'No. Elisabetha simply wanted to prevent all the bloodshed. One night she crept through her father's encampment, stole a horse and rode to Grimentz castle, begging admittance. The next morning when her father came again to demand the prince surrender, the Wolf stood on the battlements. With his new wife—'

'Elisabetha.' She'd taken destiny into her own hands. I knew there was a reason I liked wearing her tiara so much.'

'You know it wasn't actually hers? It's a much more recent piece.'

'Oh, don't spoil it for me.' She studied the portrait with a new respect. 'Saving the whole of Grimentz? That's quite an act to follow. No wonder my sister ran away.'

She shot Leo a glance. 'That was insensitive of me. Especially as she ran away from you here.'

'And back I had to come when you decided it was the perfect bolt-hole. I seem cursed by the place.'

'Perhaps Elisabetha is trying to tell you something?'

He snorted. 'To stay away from Della Torre women?'

'Or that you should reopen the chateau. It's a lovely old house and it deserves to be used again.'

'I'll bear that in mind,' he said, watching her with hooded blue eyes.

A wolf, she thought on a sudden lick of heat. They conjured all manner of forbidden things.

Like the tearing of clothes and fingers allowed to roam at will over naked skin.

Like being pushed back and flattened to this very desk by his big, hard body.

Her gaze slid back to his mouth and lingered there. She licked her lips. If she took a step closer, she'd be close enough to press her mouth to his. Her tempting wolf. One step.

She mustn't.

But the decision was made for her. He leant in, slid a hand to the back of her neck and drew her close.

She could have so easily resisted but she didn't. His lips

were too warm and soft and every bit as inviting as she remembered. He tasted of coffee and storm clouds.

Leo's fingers massaged the base of her skull. His tongue traced the seam of her mouth. She opened hers with a sigh, letting him in. Heat curled low in the belly, a sweet, drugging heat. She lifted her hands to his chest and a growl rumbled in his throat. He wrapped a fist in her hair and gently tugged, pulling her head back, exposing her throat. He pressed his open mouth to the pulse throbbing beneath her ear and sucked gently.

Violetta's fingers dug into his chest, her eyes fluttered, losing focus. Dimly seeing the portrait on the wall.

Violetta's eyes flew open.

Elisabetha stared back. Disapproving. Is this what you really want? Think of what you might lose.

The duchy.

No.

Leo lifted his head.

'I can't, Leo.'

'They're just kisses, Violetta,' he said. 'There's no need to look so shocked. It's supposed to be fun.'

Fun?

She stumbled back.

'Maybe to you, because what have you got to lose if they go further? Nothing! If I let my guard down, even for a moment, you might convince me to marry you after all and then I'll lose everything I've worked towards. Everything!'

She looked up at the portrait. 'I've waited so long, put up with my father and my uncle treating me like I've no intelligence or abilities of my own. Watched them take the duchy for granted.'

How had she forgotten?

'Men! You always think you know better. You always take what you want and give nothing back.'

Now he was the one to look shocked, but she didn't care.

'I'm sorry but I'm not doing this.'

She took a last look at Elisabetha, who was gazing down on her in approval, Violetta hoped. Then she walked away, leaving all the temptations of the Wolf of Grimentz behind her.

Leo pressed the back of his hand to his mouth where the touch of her still burned. The floral smell of the shampoo she'd used in her hair was all around him, and the ghost of her in the pounding of his heart and the ache in his groin.

He'd lied when he'd said they were just kisses. They'd been so much more than that. No one had ever lit such a fire in his belly before.

But the anger and anguish in her eyes when she turned on him just now? He recognised that all too well. He'd seen that same look in the mirror, after every excoriating encounter with his father.

'You always take what you want and give nothing back.'

The men in her life had failed her too but perhaps, today at least, he could redress the balance and give a gift with no expectation of reward.

Something just for her, and he had the perfect idea how to do it.

CHAPTER EIGHT

SHE'D SPENT THE day avoiding him, in what was left of the library, to be precise. She told herself she'd gone to kill an hour or two reading. The history of the Grimentzian lace industry was utterly fascinating.

Really, truly it was.

But pretend as she might, some musty old book wouldn't keep her thoughts away from Leo, or kissing him, more precisely.

She had heard him wandering about the house, although mercifully he hadn't sought her out, though she'd have to face him again eventually. Maybe she was overreacting. Maybe they were just kisses after all.

Then why, amidst the shocking sizzle of energy, the explosion of heat and desire, had she felt such a connection, as if he'd reached inside her and forged a link between their hearts?

He was supposed to be the enemy, determined on wresting the duchy out of Della Torre hands. Yet he said he no longer planned to do that. What if she could trust that? What if having Leo at her side could actually be a good thing?

If he helped guide and support her, what might she achieve then? He talked to her as an equal and he'd listened to her, not dismissing her ideas and dreams for the future but actually giving advice. When had her family ever done that for her?

It was a long time since she'd trusted anyone enough to tell them what she was really feeling. She'd learned the hard way to keep her own counsel, and hug her dreams close to her heart. They'd have only ever been trampled on otherwise.

Now she wondered if he did the same. Perhaps all that aloofness was for protection and behind that cool facade beat a heart as full of hopes and crushed dreams as hers. It was a startling thought.

Another vulnerability, something to tug at your heart, something that could make you love him.

Love him?

That would have disaster written all over it. Leo had made it clear he wasn't interested in love and that was what she dreamed of. A man to stand at her side because he loved her.

Violetta stared out of the library window. Rain streamed down the other side, blurring her view of the real world beyond the walls of this house. But the real world was out there and after this storm had passed, she'd have to return to it.

This time with Leo, and the conflicting things he made her feel would all be back in their proper perspective.

When she retreated to her room, across the single bed lay a garment bag. On top sat a note. A postcard, to be precise. On it, written in a bold hand, was:

Meet me at the foot of the stairs. Seven p.m. sharp. Formal attire required.

Violetta unzipped the bag and gasped as the costume inside was revealed. Not so much costume but a gorgeous gown. Leo had chosen something so far removed from her wedding dress as it was possible to find. A fluid, feather-covered number, screaming old Hollywood glamour. The demure neckline ran along her collarbone, the back dipped low to reveal her shoulder blades. There was even some underwear: pale pink French knickers. A jug of hot water sat on the dresser. A fluffy towel and fresh bar of scented soap sat beside it.

She was touched by all the effort he'd made for her, but what was he up to?

At seven p.m.—sharp—she approached the top of the stairs. The faux ostrich feathers on her dress shimmered as she walked. She'd left her hair down, brushed until it shone, and swept it over one shoulder. As the note had expressly said formal attire, she was wearing Elisabetha's tiara again.

Waiting for her in the hallway below stood Leo. Her foolish heart skipped a beat.

In tails and white tie, his blue sash running across his chest beneath his tailcoat, he was every girl's fantasy prince made flesh. Staggeringly handsome. She couldn't drag her eyes from his tall figure as she descended.

He paid her in kind, his gaze sweeping her from head to toe. Lingering on her breasts, her hips. The gown slithered around her, and she felt barely dressed beneath his searing gaze.

'Stunning…' he said, in a low gravelly tone. *'Tu sembre una grand duchessa.'*

'Thank you,' she said, rather unevenly. 'But I actually feel like a fairy princess.'

'So you are. I think I'm a little bewitched. I had an idea that gown would suit you but…' He waved his hand, indicating her dress. 'It's quite perfect.'

She sent him a crooked smile. 'Not at the back.' She turned to show him. 'I had to set to work with safety pins to make it fit.'

He gave the new view she'd presented a thorough appraisal.

'No, the rear view is just as ravishing.'

She flushed at his compliment. 'So we're Fred Astaire and Ginger Rogers in *Top Hat*?'

'Despite that dress I was thinking more Fred and Rita Hayworth.' He leant closer and said with his mouth against her ear. 'Because he always said she was his favourite partner.'

As warm lips shifted over sensitive skin Violetta stifled a moan of pleasure. Somehow she managed to say, 'So what's all this about?'

'Grand Duchessa, isn't it obvious? It's your birthday.' He held out an arm. 'And your celebratory dinner is about to be served.'

He'd made *dinner*? She wanted to ask from what, but her voice wouldn't work. The dashing man beside her had robbed her of her breath. His kindness now had touched her deeply. Yesterday she'd jilted him and today he'd made all this effort for her. He led her to the dining room. Where a candelabra sat on the table set for two. There was a crisp white tablecloth, the glitter of silver cutlery, the finest wine glasses and a bottle of champagne in an ice bucket.

'You found ice?'

'Once I'd taken a hammer and chisel to what was left at the edges of the freezer.' Her wayward imagination conjured a tantalising picture of him, bent over the chest freezer in the pantry, with that taut backside of his on display.

He pulled out the chair for her and saw her seated before he crossed to the sideboard and returned with a silver platter.

'Madame, this evening the chef has created something of a delicacy.' He removed the domed cover with a flourish. 'Pan-fried bread and haricots blancs in a tomato confit.'

She looked blankly at him.

'I believe in England you'd call it beans on toast,' he said. 'But do make the most of the bread. I discovered these few slices in the freezer, but the rest are spoiled. I fear we'll have to resort to more canned coq au vin for breakfast.'

He opened the champagne and filled two crystal flutes. 'This, on the other hand, is of the finest vintage.' He lifted his glass in salute. 'Thank you, Grand-Mère, for your excellent taste in wine.'

He handed a flute to Violetta, then with a formal bow and a heel-click he raised his glass to her.

'May I wish you a very happy twenty-first birthday, Grand Duchessa?'

She took a sip. Crisp, ice-cold bubbles played deliciously over her tongue.

'Good?' Leo asked as he took a sip from his own glass.

'Very good,' she answered.

She picked up her fork and started on her 'dinner'. 'How did you do all this?'

'I had a lot of free time while you were hiding away.'

'I wasn't hiding. I was educating myself about the history of the lace industry in Grimentz.'

His lips curved in a smile. 'Like I said. Hiding. What scared you most, that you liked the kisses or that you actually like me?'

She made a little harrumph and carried on eating.

'Surprised you, hasn't it?'

'The kisses? I suppose you could call them surprising as I have nothing to compare them to,' she said, spearing a single bean and popping it delicately into her mouth.

He sent her a wicked smile. 'Oh, Violetta, you really are delightful.'

She lifted her chin, 'That's Grand Duchess to you, or Your Serene Highness. Either will suffice until I decide that I like you enough to allow you to address me by my given name.'

'Then, Your Serene Highness, are you ready to move on to the next part of the evening's entertainment?'

Her gaze shot to his. In her excitement, she forgot she was pretending to be haughty. 'There's more?'

'It's your twenty-first birthday. Of course, there's more.'

When he opened the doors to the ballroom Violetta's jaw dropped.

Dozens of candles glittered in the candelabras. Dozens more bounced back from the reflections in the mirrors lining the walls. She stared up at Leo in wonder and his mouth creased in a crooked smile.

'It's your birthday and you should have a grand ball to celebrate your accession to the throne. Naturally you should be escorted by a handsome prince,' he said with a wink that made her heart race, 'and led to the floor for a dance.'

He held out his hand. She placed her fingers in his and followed him to the centre of the room.

A waltz started up. In the mirrors she caught the reflection of Leo pocketing a small black remote, and in the corner of the room spied the CD-player they'd listened to last night.

He began to move.

He held her so effortlessly, guided her so beautifully, it was easy as breathing to follow him round the room. In the flickering candlelight, they dipped, they swayed, they flowed across the floor in absolute unison, painting a masterpiece in shadows as they went. Safe in his expert hold, seduced by the music, and seduced more by this irresistible man, Violetta finally set her dancing heart free.

Suddenly his hold tightened, his steps slowed until eventually he stopped moving altogether. His eyes glittered in the dim light. The hand at her back pulled her close.

'Leo, we aren't dancing any more.'

'No,' he breathed and stopped any further observations with his mouth.

Violetta swooned, her lips clung to his, her hands grasped his lapels.

Outside the world raged, but here, together in their little world, they were safe.

He took her to a couch with its dust sheet already thrown back, and sank down on it, drawing her between his legs. His chin lifted as he reached up for a kiss. She cupped his face, the skin smooth from a recent shave. She slid her fingers into the silk of his hair, damp from his shower, and she melted at the thought of the care he'd taken for her.

She needed to touch more of him.

His jacket went first, her fingers sliding beneath the lapels, up his chest to his shoulders. He helped her, shrugging out of it, lifting up his backside to free those elegant coat tails. It landed on the floor in a heap to be instantly forgotten. Violetta was too intent on unwrapping the next layers. She unbuttoned the waistcoat, snatched at the bow tie. The studs of his shirt followed as she pulled it open and ran her greedy palms across his chest, thrilling at the quiver of his flank when her fingers found a particularly sensitive spot.

He was back on his feet, yanking at hooks and the zip and shoved trousers and underwear down his hips. He heeled off his shoes and kicked everything away.

He was even more beautiful naked. A feast for her eyes and hands. She wanted to touch, everywhere. Her gaze dropped to his erection, growing even bigger under her scrutiny. She'd have dropped to her knees and licked that fascinating bead of moisture from the tip, but with uneven breaths and trembling hands he was pulling her close again.

His hands trembled as he tugged at the fastenings of her gown and pushed it from her shoulders.

His breath was ragged as he slid the silk knickers down

her hips and she stepped clear of them, her hands on his shoulders for support.

Watching this strong man unravel for her banished all Violetta's uncertainties. Being with him like this felt utterly right. She climbed onto his lap, her knees splayed wide over his thighs, and took his face in her hands and kissed him.

A new dance began, one of fingers and lips and tongues. The slide of skin on skin and a new, sensual music drowned out the other. Groans and sighs, hot, sultry words in French, Italian or indistinct, but speaking volumes nonetheless. Passion rode them both.

She was hot and wet and, oh, so needy. She wanted him inside her, all of him, because, heaven help her, there was already a piece of him lodged in her heart. She ground against him.

'Violetta, no.' Hunger and regret warred in the depths of his eyes. 'We don't have protection.' His hand slid over her belly and slipped downwards between them. 'But there are other things we can do.'

She gasped as his thumb found a sweet spot and circled.

'We'd be safe. I get my period soon,' she said, breathlessly, and rolled her hips against him again.

A ripple of excitement went through him. 'But not like this. It's your first time. It will be too uncomfortable.'

Of course, he knew she was a virgin. The examination to prove that was one of the many indignities heaped on her before their official engagement, but now her virginity felt precious. Something special to share only with him.

She moaned helplessly as his mouth went to her breast. She wrapped her arms about his head. How had she not known such delight existed? Because now it felt as if it were written in her flesh, in her very bones, just waiting for this man to unleash the poetry of desire in her. A sudden panic welled up—was this one night all they'd have? Because she wanted this in her life.

She wanted him.

Perhaps they could be lovers? As long as they didn't marry the duchy would still be hers. And that was what was important…wasn't it?

Leo caught her chin, and gently turned her face so she met his burning gaze.

'Violetta, whatever you are thinking, stop. Just feel.'

With a move as graceful and masterful as anything he'd executed on the dance floor, he lifted her from his lap and laid her on the couch.

His palm floated along her thigh, pushing it wider, and he moved between her legs. A wave of desire travelled over her skin.

'Just feel, Violetta,' he repeated, rising up and taking her hips in his big hands. With one leg braced on the floor and the other bent beneath him on the couch he thrust into her. The pain was swift and sharp but quickly forgotten because Leo…

Leo was inside her. Worshipping her with the reverence of his hands and his body.

He withdrew, then gently eased into her again. His groans echoed round the room drowning out the tempest outside. His expression was a study in ecstasy.

Her arms flung back, watching this man take his pleasure in her, Violetta felt like a goddess laid out for a feast. Nothing mattered any more but Leo. So she did as he'd asked, she stopped thinking, and gave herself up to passion.

For the first time in his life, Leo wasn't thinking either.

Just feeling.

The heat of this woman, the urgent clench of her muscles around him nearly drove him over the edge.

His every instinct screamed for him to thrust, but he wanted to make this last. He wanted to watch the minutiae of every emotion chasing over Violetta's face. The wonder and the bliss, and the absolute focus.

This evening had been meant as a treat for her. And for him, a light-hearted thing to douse the heat of their earlier encounter. To make it a physical thing only and calm the emotional tempest it had unleashed in him.

Absorbed by the task of setting candles in this room, searching the costume gallery for the perfect dress, he'd almost convinced himself he'd succeeded. But when she'd appeared at the top of the stairs...

He wanted her and there were so many reasons, good, honest reasons, why he could not have her.

He touched her with extreme care, as if she might break beneath him. She felt precious, a rare treasure, almost too fine for the likes of him. The world outside might be imploding but in here, tonight, with him, she would be safe.

Later, she retrieved the ballet shoes, donned his shirt and danced for him.

As candle after candle fluttered and died and the room filled with shadows, Leo watched.

His trousers back on, but still barefoot and bare-chested, he sat, his legs spread wide, his arms stretched out along the chair back, and watched his fill of her.

She held nothing back, her hair flying loose as she swirled and leapt across the space.

Every sweep of her hand was like her touch across his skin. Leo felt it to his core as if she danced through his soul. The arabesques, the leaping splits, the strength of her supple body, he wanted to cleave it all to him. He watched as she danced, then laughed and goofed around, until he couldn't stand not touching her and went to her.

He closed his hands about her waist. She sank against him, kissed him like the angel she was, and a storm of longing, wild as the chaos outside, surged through him.

A need to capture this moment and keep a piece of it with him for ever.

Because he knew these hours, as impermanent and insubstantial as the guttering candlelight, were all they could have.

CHAPTER NINE

Leo woke to a strange new sensation.

A woman in his arms, deeply asleep. Her head tucked beneath his chin, her hair across his chest, her legs tangled in his.

On the floor beside the couch the scatter of clothes told its own story. The iconic dress was a forgotten pile of feathers. His waistcoat, shirt and trousers lay in a heap, and, feet away, his bow tie, flung there by this woman's hands.

His arms were wrapped protectively around her. His sleeping self had wanted to hold her...his waking self was also loath to let go.

Leo drew her closer.

But the world beyond the ballroom was intruding, because the storm had finally blown itself out, allowing other sounds to reach him. Feet on the gravel close to the house. The voices of his security team calling instructions back and forth, a helicopter approaching.

Leo lay there, not moving, wanting to preserve this moment for a little longer. To pretend he lived in a world where he and Violetta could both have what they wanted.

He turned his cheek against her hair.

Impossible, but also for the best.

The storm had passed both inside and out and he'd weathered them both. This...whatever it was...was done. He might have taken her virginity, but he wouldn't be taking her grand duchy.

He couldn't. It would be morally wrong and, despite what his father had wanted, Leo finally understood he'd never truly be that man and he was glad of it.

Friedrich von Frohburg had been a tyrant, coveting the grand duchy for all the wrong reasons.

Leo would not be so heartless. He let go of that dream. Now there was another to let slip away.

He shook her gently. Violetta stirred, looking up at him with luminous, trusting eyes. The breath caught in his throat.

'We need to get up,' he said, eventually. 'They're coming for us.'

Through a gap in the shutters Violetta watched the helicopter touch down on the lawns, its fuselage resplendent with the scarlet and gold of the von Frohburg coat of arms. It was a great shiny beast, big enough to seat twelve in luxurious comfort. Rivalling any used by the most powerful leaders on the planet.

The Della Torres were rich, but they had only one small private jet at their disposal. Violetta knew this helicopter was only part of the von Frohburgs' royal fleet. It was a compelling physical representation of their power.

How easily they could swallow up San Nicolo, but they could also support it and help it to grow.

A new future was possible. One where a man *could* stand by her side, as her lover, as her equal. Violetta felt a surge of excitement, of confidence. Whatever difficulties her uncle was about to throw her way, if she had Leo to lean on and lend her his strength she could achieve anything.

The steps of the helicopter lowered and Seb appeared.

Violetta watched as Leo approached, crossing the gravel with his long, powerful stride. Even dressed in last night's creased shirt and crumpled black trousers he was still the quintessential alpha male.

Tender, well-loved muscles pulsed in recognition. He was her mate. Just looking at him rocked her to her toes.

A second figure emerged from the helicopter and Violetta's brow creased. San Nicolo's former prime minister was here?

Signor Carello had been dismissed when her parents died and Uncle Guido had assumed the regency. Her uncle had cited poor governance as the reason at the time, though his evidence had been flimsy at best.

If he was here now and her uncle was not, then something serious had happened.

What had Leo said? Find good people who share your values to work with. Signor Carello was one of those. He'd always taken time to listen to her, answered her questions, taken her seriously.

As far as she knew she was now Grand Duchess, which she'd claimed she'd wanted more than anything. Time to step up and take responsibility. Perhaps she could start by working with this man.

She tugged on her wedding shoes and that feathered beauty of a dress and, because it was probably the worst outfit for such an occasion, she pulled on Leo's tailcoat to add a sombre note. It swamped her but at least it made her look less frivolous.

She combed her fingers through her hair and twisted it down over one shoulder. She left the house and headed towards the men. Their expressions altering as they saw her. The one she enjoyed most was Leo's. His warm gaze rested on her until she arrived at his side.

Seb was the first to greet her.

'Grand Duchessa, may I say how very lovely you look this morning?' He took her hands and lifted each in turn to his lips.

From Leo came an odd, low growl, which seemed to amuse Seb enormously. Leo simply glared at him.

She freed her hands and offered one to Signor Carello, who bent low over it.

'Your Highness, we are most relieved that you are safe and well.'

'Thank you, Signor Carello. Forgive me, I'm confused. Where is my uncle?'

He sent a speaking glance to Leo, who gave a brief nod.

'Tell her everything,' he said. 'She's the grand duchess now. She needs to know what's happened.'

'Ma'am, I apologise for my unannounced arrival but I have some shocking news.'

First, he said, she should be reassured that, unlike Grimentz, which had suffered significant and devastating damage, San Nicolo had been spared the brunt of the storm.

Violetta's gaze flew to Leo's. His expression grim, he merely nodded for Signor Carello to continue.

In the grand duchy there was minor damage, a few flooded vineyards, power lines down, but there was more to tell. Much more and every bit as catastrophic as if the storm had done its worst.

Violetta listened in growing shock.

The moment her uncle knew her wedding to Leo wasn't going ahead he'd fled the country. He'd been counting on the marriage to refill the San Nicolo coffers that he and her father had emptied. Oh, not through any malice. While it would have increased their personal wealth, they'd thought to make the duchy as rich as their neighbour. But their investment plans had been high risk. Her father had been weak and allowed himself to be persuaded by his younger, more ambitious brother, who'd continued on the path after the grand duke's death. The investments had failed. That was why he was so keen for his younger niece to make the match with Leo.

San Nicolo was flat broke.

Marry me, Leo thought. *Marry me and I can make all those problems go away.*

He could legitimately pour funds into the grand duchy,

but then she'd be bound by her constitution, which would immediately hand all power over to him. She'd lose all chance of running the country herself. Her dreams of democracy would be over.

If they remained apart he could not fund San Nicolo's recovery without it appearing as if he were trying to take the duchy by stealth. He would be unable to offer anything but the most basic financial support.

There was no choice, he had to let her go, and could offer nothing in the way of help. A steel gauntlet clamped about his heart.

Violetta was speaking.

'I have my personal wealth. We have the family treasures. We can raise the funds we need to fund the essential services in the short term and we'll take it from there. I won't let the people suffer because of my uncle's reckless behaviour.'

Dressed in baby-pink feathers and a man's tailcoat that swamped her, dwarfed by the three men towering over her, she was still every inch the grand duchess.

It was hard to say who looked the most surprised at this new, determined Violetta: her minister or Seb, who shot his cousin a look. Who *was* this woman?

Leo's chest swelled in pride, but his moment had also passed. She'd already laid out her plans and none had any mention of him.

The shaft of pain was quickly bested. How was it any different from anything he'd been hurt by before? His own mother hadn't loved him enough to stick around. His only value to his father had been as a pawn to reclaim the duchy. With a bitter taste in his mouth, he acknowledged he'd even failed in that.

In comparison, rejection by this woman was trifling.

He'd survived before and he'd get over this…this…infatuation, surely, it was nothing more than that. A man did not fall in love in two days. It was the circumstances they'd found themselves in. None of the attraction he felt would survive being back in the real world.

She gazed up at Leo, those warm brown eyes filled with compassion. And some newly tender thing inside him cracked apart. 'But first we help Grimentz,' she said.

She was moving on, so must he.

'Then we'd better get on with it,' he said.

Leo beckoned towards the helicopter. Two more figures appeared. Matteo, Leo's valet, bearing a small suitcase and, behind him, a woman, also clutching a bag.

'Luisa…' Violetta breathed. Her dresser, her *friend*. She wanted to run to her and fling herself into her arms, but she was mindful of the men around her. She was a grand duchess now.

Leo gazed down on her, gauging her reaction, and she knew who she had to thank for the restoration of her closest confidante.

'Thank you,' she mouthed as Luisa arrived at her side with a curtsy.

Leo dipped his head in acknowledgement.

'Can you have your mistress ready to leave in ten minutes?' he asked.

'Of course, sir.'

Precisely ten minutes later Violetta, in jeans and blue shirt, was climbing into the helicopter. She'd avoided all the questions Luisa's eyes had asked but the woman had mercifully left unvoiced.

'Later,' Violetta had said, not able to tell her the truth of what had happened.

The man I ran away from is stealing my heart.

Leo joined them, in jeans and heavy boots.

As the helicopter lifted into the sky Violetta watched the chateau disappear beneath her. Apart from some missing tiles and fallen trees it was relatively undamaged. A place of magic still.

She wanted to take Leo's hand but he was on the opposite side of the cabin. Even if she could, she doubted he'd notice. His whole attention was focused on the view below.

Beneath them Grimentz lay in ruins.

Fields had become lakes, barns were flattened, mighty trees upended like saplings. In the village streets, cars bobbed like children's toys in the angry, roiling water filled with all the debris swept up in the deluge. Power lines down, bridges nothing more than archless stumps, stranded in the swollen rivers.

There was damage everywhere, even the road from the city she and Leo had both taken to the chateau just forty-eight hours ago was washed away in three places.

The devastated landscape echoed the financial catastrophe awaiting her when she returned home, but she wouldn't think of that right now. Her first priority was to help those in need in Grimentz.

They landed on the outskirts of a small town, where Grimentz had been hit the hardest. West of the capital and directly in the path of the torrents of water funnelling down the once picturesque valley. It was unrecognisable from the place it had been.

The council offices had been spared and turned into a makeshift refuge for bewildered families to gather, to get help, to enquire for loved ones.

When they saw Leo, his people fell on him, thanking the fates that he'd been spared.

They all wanted to touch him, as if to check he was real. They shook his hand, patted his back. An elderly matriarch struggled up from her seat, placing a hand to his jaw and kissing him on the cheek.

He bore it all, though Violetta could see how it moved him. He spoke with each of them, a smile for some, a handshake for others, crouched on his haunches to talk gently to a tiny girl clutching a mud-splattered teddy.

Here was another Leo. Not stern and unapproachable, but at ease amongst his people and well beloved by them in return, she realised as she watched the little girl step into his arms for a hug.

Violetta fought back a tear.

For her there were odd looks, glances at her ringless left hand, bemusement as to why she was there at all with their prince after their botched marriage attempt. Not re-crimination exactly, for who would dare with their prince standing by?

Something bumped into her back, a woman entering the building struggling with boxes piled with blankets and clothes.

Her eyes went wide when she saw who she'd walked into.

'I'd curtsy, Your Highness, but as you can see...' She adjusted her grip on the boxes. 'I'd struggle with this lot.'

'Let me help you.' Violetta took one off the pile. 'Where is this going?' The woman tipped her chin towards to the side of the hall where trestle tables had been set up and volunteers were busy sorting through piles of donated clothing and bedding.

Violetta dumped her box with the stack waiting to be sorted, then rolled back her sleeves.

'What can I do?' she asked the team working round the tables.

For a moment she thought her offer was going to be refused. All the volunteers just stared at her. Some even looked openly suspicious and she couldn't really blame them. Not only was she a reviled Della Torre but the second one to very publicly jilt their prince.

The woman who'd delivered the boxes saved her, pointed

at the line of four tables in turn. 'Children's clothes. Women's. Men's. Bedding and towels go on the last one.'

Smiling at her fellow volunteers, two of whom at least now smiled back, Violetta picked up the first box of donations and, with Luisa at her side, started sorting.

Leo had deliberately sat on the opposite side of the cabin so he couldn't reach for her, because he'd known how much he'd want to.

As the horrors had been revealed below he'd badly wanted to curl his fingers through hers and take strength from the warmth of her slender fingers in his.

Instead, Leo stood alone. That was what a leader did. Showed no weakness, no vulnerability and you certainly didn't hold a woman's hand for comfort.

So he'd stayed on the other side of the cabin so he wouldn't indulge his yearning, reveal his *weakness*, and reach for her.

She'd made no fuss when the news of her country's financial ruin had been revealed. She'd listened and then turned all her attentions to helping Grimentz, whose need right then was greater. Then she'd sat, drawn but composed, as she'd stared down on what the forces of nature had wreaked on his country. When his people had eyed her with suspicion at the relief centre, she hadn't faltered, she'd simply rolled up her sleeves and started helping.

His brave girl.

She'd grown in stature before him, bearing little similarity to the girl who'd fled their wedding.

On the other side of the room now he could see she'd started directing the deliveries of new donations. They were coming in thick and fast and their current system for processing was close to being overwhelmed. She'd seen that, stepped in and reorganised it. His people didn't appear to mind, just hurrying to do as she asked.

She was doing what she claimed she'd wanted, being a leader. Being a grand duchess.

Perhaps he had a bigger job for her than this single relief centre.

The woman taking a new box from Violetta's hands suddenly dropped into a curtsy. Leo stood beside her. He took Violetta's elbow and ushered her to a quiet corner.

'The next village needs our help,' he said. 'We're going up there with the helicopter to help in the evacuation. Would you mind if I send you back by road? It's safe from here back to the city.'

'Of course,' she told him.

His smile was all relief. 'Then can I impose on you further? In his country's hour of need my cousin, and illustrious heir, has taken to his rooms and is refusing to come out. Will you represent me at the relief efforts at the castle instead?'

She blinked up at him, moved by this mark of trust in her.

'Of course,' she said, a little unevenly. 'It's what I've been trained to do after all.'

'Thank you.' He squeezed her hands. 'Before you go, I'd like you to meet Tomasz and Pierre.' He beckoned two men over. 'They're your bodyguards until you can appoint your own. Tomasz you almost know. He's fond of basking.' Leo sent her that crooked smile of his. The kind that could make a girl agree to almost anything.

'Do I really need—?'

'This one's non-negotiable, I'm afraid, Grand Duchessa. You're our guest and I'll have you protected accordingly. These men will guard you with their lives. I would not put someone so precious in their care if I didn't know that for a certainty.'

She wanted to keep Leo at her side for longer. She

wanted to feel his strength and certainty as she took her first faltering steps into being a monarch. What a surprise to discover that having him in her life wasn't stifling at all, but freeing.

He was already moving away, taking his own entourage of security with him. She felt better seeing the muscled figures flanking their prince.

'Ma'am?' Basking Tomasz held a side door open for her and outside waited three cars and more security. Leo had already disappeared or she might have challenged him on that.

When she arrived at the castle that newfound confidence faltered as a member of the castle staff approached her.

She was grateful to have Luisa and Tomasz at her side, and Pierre at her back, as the woman arrived.

'Your Serene Highness,' she said on a quick curtsy, 'I'm Helene. Head of the Household. The prince called ahead. We will be grateful to have your help.'

Violetta stiffened her spine. She wouldn't let Leo down, or the people of Grimentz. Not in their hour of need.

This was what she'd been trained to do: to support.

She did it now.

'The press are here, I'm assuming?'

'Yes, ma'am.'

'Then I'd like to speak to them.'

CHAPTER TEN

THIRTY MINUTES AFTER her press conference the people of San Nicolo began arriving. It was a trickle at first but soon it was hundreds, who gathered up supplies as they went and packed into boats to make the short, but perilous trip across a lake swollen with flood water and storm debris. Answering the call of their new grand duchess and coming to the aid of their stricken neighbours regardless.

Doctors and emergency personnel of course, but so too had come the teachers, the pastry chefs, the vintners, and every able-bodied person in between. The castle courtyard was filled with them.

Her head of exports was soon organising the relief effort coming from the duchy and liaising with his opposite number in the principality. Helping bedraggled and shocked Grimentzians who'd fled their homes and sought shelter in the capital. Her finance minister was coordinating the supplies coming up from the lake. The mayor and his team were ferrying Grimentzians across the lake to stay in the hotels, guest houses and even private homes, and countless ordinary citizens were pitching in. Some even just handing out hot drinks from flasks they'd brought with them.

Violetta couldn't have been more proud or more moved when they saw her and fell on her in delight. No recriminations for having run away, just relieved to find her safe and well.

She liaised with the wider relief efforts and the teams out in the countryside, expediting decisions that normally would have required Leo's approval. She acted as spokesperson for the press. She buoyed up exhausted volunteers. Even scooped up small children from weary parents, giving the adults a moment to catch their breath while she entertained their little ones.

From some there were odd looks at finding themselves greeted by the grand duchess of San Nicolo, but this was what she'd been trained to do. Create order for the staff and charm the populace. And she did it well.

For hours.

Only once she knew everyone was settled, the last of the homeless found temporary accommodation, the exhausted staff sent to their own beds and a team in place to cover any stragglers, did Violetta ask Helene to show her to a room she and Luisa could use.

Violetta assumed she'd be back in the small room she'd fled from, but it was a thing of the past. Instead, she was taken to the suite designated for the crown princess.

The Elisabetha Suite, Helene told her.

Of course it was.

His mother's old apartments, and every consort that had gone before her. Perhaps even the famed Elisabetha herself—this part of the castle was old enough.

They would have been Violetta's too had she married Leo.

'I think there's been a mistake—'

'No, ma'am. The prince was most insistent.'

The rooms were stunning, in blue and gold, with elegant gilt-edged furniture and soaring ceilings. Violetta had always lived in luxurious comfort, but never such splendour. Behind her Luisa whistled softly at the vast windows where pale blue drapes hung down in voluptuous folds caught up by lavishly embroiled swags. As for the bed, it was enormous, with a crown all of its own, perched high overhead and draped with more opulent swags of blue silk.

Piled high with downy pillows and a sumptuous silk eiderdown, it was a bed made for so much more than sleeping and with more than enough room for two.

Luisa caught her eye and raised a brow.

Violetta blushed and turned her attention elsewhere.

In the centre of the room sat a table with a vase of flowers. From the mass of gorgeous yellow roses, a postcard peeked out.

One of *those* postcards.

In this photo Leo was in mid-manoeuvre, perched on the edge of dinghy racing through a choppy ocean, doused by the waves, his gaze focused intently on the horizon. On the reverse, in his now familiar hand, and anticipating precisely the objections she'd had, he'd told her he'd not hear of her staying anywhere other than this suite. He was not about to insult a fellow monarch who'd brought her entire country to the aide of his in its hour of need.

It was the postscript that really warmed her heart because that was for her, Violetta, and not the grand duchess.

I thought you'd enjoy this one. I'm looking particularly macho, don't you think?

Despite her weariness, that raised a smile.

Macho and hot. Her heart gave a flutter.

In the midst of everything he'd faced as leader of a devastated country, he'd found time to write this postcard and show such tenderness and caring.

Violetta's heart fluttered again. Did he *really* care for her?

Did he love her?

Somehow despite all his self-assurance she knew that

he was scared too. As was she, terrified that he could so easily crush her fragile heart.

Neither of them had known much love in their lives, growing up with parents who'd failed to provide even the most basic of affections. She doubted he'd be able to make that first step.

She would just have to be brave enough for both of them.

She showered, then dressed in the ivory silk nightgown and lace peignoir that Luisa had supplied with a knowing smile before disappearing for the night.

Then Violetta settled down to wait.

For every question he'd asked, 'the grand duchess' had been the answer.

Who had spoken in the numerous press conferences to ensure the help it so needed came pouring into his country?

Who had seen to it that the palace staff had been fed and replaced by her own people when they'd clearly done enough?

Who'd made decisions and kept their spirits up all day?

He could see his staff had been impressed.

In her own moment of extreme crisis, she stood by his side.

Her people and his mixed together, working side by side for the first time in four centuries. Disaster would do that to a country. Grimentz had been offered help and accepted it gratefully.

The people of San Nicolo forgetting any enmity and discovering ordinary human beings populated the towns and farms of their neighbour. All day he'd seen it. Teams of rescue workers from both nations, wading through the floodwaters, rescuing those trapped in flooded homes. Handing them over to the volunteers who'd been more fortunate and whose homes were now thrown open to those in need. San

Nicolo farmers helping their neighbours ferry terrified animals to safer pastures.

He'd been told that boats had been going back and forth all day to San Nicolo. Bringing supplies in and ferrying refugees back to the hotels and guest houses and homes of their neighbours.

The lines had been blurred. Trust and mutual respect had won the day.

His tiny grand duchess had worked wonders.

He knew he shouldn't be doing it even as his weary feet took him up the stairs and to the suite of rooms he'd insisted she have for the night. But he had to see her. One more time, before he let her go for good. He wanted her to have her duchy, to have her dream. What he felt for her was messy and emotional and he didn't do either. It had never been what he wanted. He didn't want to *feel*. It was too painful.

He made a deal with himself: he'd only knock on her door if it was obvious someone was still up.

A sliver of light spilled beneath the door.

If a servant opened the door, he'd ask for his thanks to be conveyed to her mistress, then say his goodnights and retire to his own bed and that would be the end of it.

But if Violetta answered his summons herself...?

He lifted his hand and rapped out a brief knock.

It was after one when she heard the knock on her door.

Braced with a hand on the wall, mud-splattered and bone-weary, Leo swayed on the other side.

He followed the direction of her gaze, dropping to take in his mud-stained clothes.

'I'm sorry. Perhaps I shouldn't have come.'

'Yes, you should,' she said, taking his hand. 'You are in precisely the right place.'

She drew him across the threshold, closed the door behind him, locking out the world, and brought him safe into the domain of the princess consort.

Elisabetha would have been proud of her.

'I've heard about all that you did for us today. I've come to say thank you,' he said.

'It seems paltry in light of everything the people have gone through.'

'Don't underestimate the impact you've had. My team here are full of praise.'

She hugged his praise to her. 'Then I'm glad I was here and able to help.'

He sank down on the edge of a sofa.

'How bad was that village you went to?'

'Much worse than the one you saw,' he told her. 'Every home was destroyed. We rescued a young couple and their children. They were clinging to an outhouse rooftop when we found them. That was all that was left of their farmhouse. Their family had lived in it for generations and in one night they lost everything.'

'You being there would have been a great comfort to them.'

He snorted in derision. 'What comfort could I bring in the face of all that?'

'Immeasurable' she said softly. 'I saw how your people were with you in the rescue centre. They hung on your every word…they love you.'

He sank his head into his hands.

'How do you comfort family after family who've lost their homes? Business owners whose entire life's work is gone in one night? It was a miracle that no one died.'

'Start there, then,' she said. 'Lives have been spared. The rest can be rebuilt and you'll make that happen.'

He ran a weary hand across his brow. 'I kept thinking, what would my father have done?'

'None of the things you did today. None of the things

that people really needed. Grimentz is fortunate they have you now and not him.'

He looked up at her. 'You sound so certain.'

'I am, Leo. You're a good man and a good leader.'

'Today it seemed like nothing I did was enough.'

For that moment this strong, vital man looked defeated and she couldn't bear it.

'Have you eaten?' she asked him.

'No, but don't disturb the staff.'

'There's no need to.' She pointed to a trolley with covered platters on it. 'I had something put ready for you, just in case.'

'You're a marvel,' he said.

'If I am it's my mother's doing. She may not have loved me and my sister, but she made damn sure we'd be useful.'

'I'm sorry for that. I know what it is not to be loved.'

Another truth, another vulnerability to chip away at her heart.

'Your people love you.'

He glanced up. 'You sound surprised.'

'No, I'm impressed. My father and uncle never tried to earn that love. They thought it was theirs by right. They could never have done what you did today. I saw you give so much of yourself.'

'It's just part of the royal act.'

'No. It's what you are. You cared about those people. You couldn't pretend about that. I saw that old woman touch her hand to your cheek.'

She mimicked the gesture, placing her palm against his jaw. Weary blue eyes gazed up at her.

'I'm filthy,' he warned.

She bent and pressed a soft kiss to his lips. 'Then let's get you clean.'

Heat flared in his eyes as she urged him to his feet and took his hand. He let her lead him to the bathroom and stood meekly while she turned on the shower, gathered towels. She came to stand before him. Aware of his intense blue gaze tracking every move. She unbuttoned his shirt. She reached her arms about his waist to tug it from his waistband and pushed it from his shoulders.

She knelt at his feet to untie the mud-caked laces of his boots and waited as he heeled them off and bent to remove socks.

She rose up as the steam gathered around them.

A tug at the heavy buckle of his belt drew a sharp intake of breath from him. She loosened it then wrestled with the stiff metal button of his jeans. She lowered the zip over the growing bulge at his crotch. She pushed the jeans and underwear down over his lean hips. He shoved them down the rest of the way himself, stepped clear and kicked them away.

The knot on her wrap was loosened and the whole thing fell to the floor in a whisper of silk. She tugged the nightgown over her head and dropped that too. Such a pretty thing to discard but the heat in Leo's gaze as it slid over her body was compensation enough.

She caught up her hair in a clip, then took Leo's hand and led him beneath the water. She picked up soap and a sponge and worked up a lather. She swept it across his arms and shoulders, over that broad chest, the flat abdomen.

She handed him a bottle of shampoo and waited while he washed his hair and sluiced the suds away and tried to control her breathing as she watched him, a need clawing along her spine and pooling as molten heat between her thighs.

She stepped behind him, to soap his muscled back, the deep cleft between his buttocks, the vulnerable skin of his inner thighs.

She anointed his feet with the sponge, his shins, the backs of his knees.

He turned, his erection jutting upwards. She bathed him there too, her hand massaging through the mat of hair surrounding it, before sliding along the shaft. She pressed her thumb in a circle around the tip, revelling in his fractured breath. She'd banished the defeat and weariness there had been in his eyes when he'd arrived at her door. There was only hunger and heat in their hooded depths now.

It wasn't meant to feel this way, it was just supposed to be physical. A way to ease the tension riding him. Not something that shook his heart.

Leo trembled with every touch of her fingers. They seemed so sure, so steady.

He felt as steady as a skiff tossed on a raging ocean.

Her fingers squeezed around him and he moaned. It echoed off the tiled walls and came back at him through the steam. She held him firm and he wanted it to last for ever.

As she worked him she pressed her mouth to his chest, grazed a nipple with sharp white teeth. He groaned again and wrapped his fingers in her hair and tugged to tip her face up to his, to kiss her, trying to claw back some control because he was fast losing what little he had.

Throughout all that had happened today, over and over he'd thought of this. Being with her again. He was usually a generous lover but right now there was just a raw, selfish longing to see passion kindled in her brown eyes and watch them melt to rich, dark chocolate. To feel those supple legs clamped about his waist, as her body rode his. Demanding pleasure from him and sending him into wild oblivion.

For tonight—and he knew it had to end tonight—to forget everything and just be with her.

With one step he'd pinned her against the tiled wall. Then he lifted her, thrust into her. Sank to the hilt so there was nothing but heat and lust between them.

Her gentle lover was gone.

There was no tenderness, no care, but Violetta didn't want it.

She didn't want the urbane prince, she wanted the man, stripped of his veneer of royal restraint and at his most elemental.

He'd come to her, needing her. She dismissed any notion it was because she was conveniently there. That wasn't the look in his eyes when she'd opened the door to him.

She'd drawn him in. She'd led him here, to this moment, to the lash of passion and hunger and a flaying need to prove they were alive and whole. After all they'd both seen that day, the devastation, the terrible loss, they needed to feel *alive.*

The water sluiced away the suds and the dirt, washing them both clean. Their hands on each other, their bodies joined, making them new. Blurring the edges of the pain, the images of suffering they'd witnessed.

Easing the endless pain of those deeper hurts and betrayals by those who should have loved them and hadn't.

In this moment they'd become each other's soul mate. It was them against the world.

Violetta's heart flowered opened, the last of her defences fell, and she let him in. Gave him everything, holding nothing of herself back.

'I love you,' she said. 'Oh, God, Leo, I love you.'

She came around him on a cry.

Still buried deep inside her, he stepped from the shower, grabbing towels to fling beneath them as he laid her on the tiled floor.

Before her eyes the prince was unravelling and the man he tried so hard to hide emerged. Almost savage and never more beautiful than now, when she was his sole and absolute focus. On his knees between her thighs, his hands clamped about her hips, he pounded into her. The corded muscles of his neck grew tighter and tighter, his gasping breaths more frantic.

Then on a roar of completion, he flung back his head and spilled himself inside her.

Violetta lay there, her heart pounding, briefly unable to summon any strength to move.

On his knees still, breathing hard, Leo shoved an unsteady hand through his wet hair. Rivulets of water ran down his heaving chest and abdomen and disappeared into the crisp dark hair around his sex.

He slid out of her and stood, grabbed a towel, hitching it about his waist. He took her hand, helped her to her feet, wrapped her in a bath robe. Took a fresh towel and carefully squeezed the excess water out of her hair.

He tenderly pushed a stray damp lock from her brow, pressed his lips there instead. 'Now I need that food you promised me,' he said, taking her hand.

She went with him back into the lounge and watched as he sank to one of the armchairs.

She removed the covers from the food trolley. Her fingers trembled as she scooped sliced meats and cheese onto a plate. There were olives and bread from Grimentz and a bottle of San Nicolo wine. She poured two glasses.

He waited, bare chested, bare legged. Unselfconsciously sitting there and making no comment on what she'd just declared.

She handed him the plate and a napkin. Set the wine on the small table beside him. She bit her lip.

'Did you hear me?'

'I heard you, Violetta.'

'And?'

He made her wait while he ate some of the bread and olives, sipped his wine.

'And it changes nothing. We've had this conversation before, remember. It's not possible for people like us. The sooner you accept that, the sooner all the madness and striving goes away. Be the leader your country needs. That's what you were put here to do and there's satisfaction to be had from that.'

What about the satisfaction they'd given each other just now? Wasn't that also a precious thing?

'But I want you, too.'

'That's not possible.'

'Why not? I love you,' she said. Oh, it felt so right to say that out loud. She knew it now. That was what all the conflicting emotions of the last few days had been about. 'With everything I am, I love you. How can you pretend that doesn't mean anything for us?'

There was a long pause.

'You'll love your duchy more, trust me. Nothing will come close. Certainly not me.'

How could he believe that after the way she'd just given herself to him? Was he made of stone?

'You're saying I can't have both. I'm a woman first and a princess second. San Nicolo can have my days, but my nights... They'd be for you.'

'You're being naive, Grand Duchessa. San Nicolo will swallow you whole. You'll belong to it entirely and you'll have nothing left to give.'

Her fingers tightened around her wine glass. 'You're rejecting me?'

'I'm just being realistic. You'll have to trust me on this. Accept I have more experience and know what I'm talking about. It just couldn't work, Violetta. Two monarchs with impossible workloads. Overcommitted already. What time would we have for each other?'

Why did all that feel like a lie?

'You were prepared to marry me before.'

'When you were to be my consort, with very different responsibilities.'

Or before he got to know her and developed feelings for

her. She gathered her courage. It was now or never. She took a step closer to him.

'You're scared.' His eyes flashed in warning but there was too much at stake for her to back down. 'You're scared that you'll get hurt. That your heart will be broken all over again. You must know I'd never do that.'

'It has nothing to do with my heart and everything to do with the practicalities of the situation. You have no idea what it's going to be like once you take on your responsibilities.'

Her shoulders tensed. 'A man telling me he knows better. How many times have I heard that before? I'm not stupid. I may not have had much responsibility yet, but of course I know what will be expected of me as monarch will be a stretch. But I'm strong and I'll do what it takes.' She began to pace.

'Violetta, see sense. I've been doing this for years. I know what I'm talking about.' He was still but his eyes tracked her movements back and forth.

'I won't accept that we can't follow our hearts on this.' Her own was beating hard. She had to make him see. She couldn't lose him.

'Follow *your* heart, you mean. I don't agree with your assessment of our situation.'

'Situation?' She stopped dead in front of him. 'It's love, Leo. Love! And I think you feel the same.'

He stood, wiped his hands on the napkin and dropped it beside his empty plate. 'If that's what you believe, Grand Duchessa, then you're doomed to be disappointed.'

So cynical, and she knew to the bottom of her soul he was wrong. Yes, his heart had been twisted and broken by what his parents had visited on him, but he wasn't as stone-hearted as he pretended. How could she prove that to him?

'What will it take to get past the barriers you've put up in here?' She pounded a fist on his chest.

'There's nothing in there to find.' He gazed down his nose at her. Unmoved.

'I know that's not true. I know there's a beating heart in there. I've heard it.' She pressed her body up against him. 'I've made it beat faster.'

'That's just sex,' he said. But she felt the ripple of energy go through him. He wasn't as calm as he pretended.

'Is that why you knocked on my door tonight? Just for sex.'

'Yes.'

The pause had been infinitesimal, but she'd heard it all the same.

'You're lying. Not just to me but to yourself. You feel something for me. Admit it. Let the man be free for once and not the prince.'

'Violetta,' he growled in warning. 'After all I've seen today, trust me, you don't want to unleash the man.'

'That's exactly what I want. Can't you get it into your thick skull? I never wanted the prince. But now I know the man, he's what I want.'

'He's not available. You could have had the prince, but you made your decision about that when you ran away from our wedding.'

'So that's it? You *are* rejecting me.'

'I'm making the wiser decision for both of us.' He threw a glance to the bed, then back to her, his dark gaze all heat and need. 'But we still have what's left of tonight. Let's not waste it.'

'That's all you'll give me?' She sounded desperate but she didn't care. She wouldn't hide how she felt. Let him hear what he was doing to her. Let him know how this love stripped her soul bare and laid it at his feet. Let him see the precious gift he didn't believe in. But could actually have—if he would only reach out for it.

'That's all *you* can give *me*. By morning you'll belong to the grand duchy. Tonight is we all have. Take it or leave it.'

It wasn't working. Her heart lurched. Cracked. 'Leo, surely—'

'It's all that's on offer, Violetta. Take it or I walk through that door right now.'

She stared at him, confounded by what to do next. Nothing she'd said was getting through to him. His heart was seared and scored by too many wounds. How was she to reach him if not with her love? If that wasn't enough what else did she have to give?

Time.

She had that. She could be patient. If that was what it took for him to heal and be able to take the next step, she would wait. Somehow, she'd bear it. She'd dig deep and find the strength to cherish and nurture this love for the two of them.

But first she'd show him what they could have together. She'd take this night and make it unforgettable. She'd pour passion over him like a balm and make it as difficult as she could for him to just walk away.

She was staring at him. She looked shell-shocked.

Good, he needed her to understand that he couldn't do this. That loving her was not an option for him.

She'd declared her love for him but he knew he was right that her duchy would come first. Hell, the duchy had meant more to his own father than Leo, his only son, ever had. It had that pull on people. Hadn't she run away from him in the first place so she could claim it herself?

Still she said nothing.

The ravening beast in him roared in disappointment. He wanted her again but it wasn't going to happen. She was turning him down.

'So be it,' he said and started for the door.

'Leo, no,' she blurted. 'I'll take it. I'll take tonight.'

She made a little gasping sob when he reached the door and thought she was too late and he was leaving. Then another of wild relief when he locked it and turned back and crossed the floor to her.

His own sense of relief nearly brought him to his knees.

He flung his towel away, tore the robe from her body and scooped her up, took them both down to the bed.

'Take comfort in the fact that tonight I need you,' he growled, then claimed her mouth in a savage kiss. Her hands clamped around his skull. She kissed him back. Hard. Sucked his lower lip between her teeth. Bit down. Not painful but enough to send lust surging through him.

He snatched his mouth free of hers, took her wrists and pinned them with a hand above her head. He kissed her throat, trailed his lips over her delicate collarbone, went lower to those sweet small breasts, and sucked on a distended nipple, growling in carnal satisfaction when she groaned and bucked beneath him.

Then he parted her thighs.

Desire, need, whatever the thing driving him was called, he let it take him. Wanting this scorching consummation to burn everything to the ground so by morning there'd be nothing left but dying embers and he'd be free again.

He went down on her, wrenching climax after climax from her with his mouth. Showing her no mercy.

Or himself. Would he ever forget the taste of her?

At first, she moaned into her pillow, then dug her hands into her hair. When she was drenched in sweat, her eyes unfocused and mad with lust, he crawled back up the bed and gathered her in his arms.

Violetta shuddered as he sank into her. Enough for only the merest of the most intimate contact between them. Enough to drive them both wild. He flicked his hips again and again…waiting…waiting. Until her body jackknifed against him as a final, powerful orgasm ripped through her.

Leo buried his face in her neck and thrust into her fully, allowing himself to be lost in her for this final time. Her fractured cries, the hot wet clench of her intimate muscles around him, until there was nothing left of his grip on reality but one word. Repeated over and over.

Violetta, Violetta, Violetta…

It was a perfect summer's morning. The country that the previous forty-eight hours had devastated was bathed in glorious sunshine from a cloudless sky. But for all the damage around them you could almost imagine it had been a dream.

Luisa had arrived at seven, peeking cautiously around the door. Violetta would be grateful for ever that she'd asked no questions but just quietly got on getting her mistress ready to leave the very rooms that under different circumstances would have been hers.

What if she went to him now? Told him she'd changed her mind, that she'd marry him after all. For a brief, glorious moment Violetta imagined the world where the two of them could be together. But then she saw the von Frohburg coat of arms, fluttering high over the castle, higher than anything around them. A clear signal of who was the master here. If she went to him on his terms her duchy would be his by the law of San Nicolo, and she couldn't and wouldn't give it up, not to any man.

'The cars are here,' Luisa said. The luggage had already been taken downstairs. All there was left to do was leave herself.

Violetta walked across the room. Refusing to look again at the beautiful decor, the elegant furniture, the door to the bathroom, the vast bed, now made as if no one had slept there at all. As if she hadn't shared her last night here with the owner of this castle.

He only came to her when she stood on the castle forecourt. His car was there, at his insistence, ready to take her on the short ride to the helipad to the north of the city. Where a waiting helicopter—also his—would fly her safely back to San Nicolo.

So much care but the fact remained he was letting her go, with no further discussion about it.

He looked tired and strained as he joined her. Coming straight from a meeting with foreign dignitaries before he headed back out to help with relief efforts. For now he was dressed in an immaculate charcoal suit and grey silk tie. The antithesis of the mud-splattered jeans and shirt she'd stripped from his body last night.

He was the prince again, the monarch who'd strode into Chateau Elisabetha in full royal regalia. Not the man she'd got to know once that uniform was off. Who was she saying goodbye to? It was brutal either way, but Violetta steeled herself to it.

'I have a gift for you,' he said. 'It was tucked away in the royal collection and I thought you might like it. As a remembrance from someone you met during your stay here.'

He took her hand and placed a small velvet-covered box in her palm.

'Under other circumstances I might have felt less sanguine about you putting this in my hand.' She made a joke to hide the fact that her heart was breaking. She blinked back the moisture filling her eyes and busied herself with opening the card beneath the ribbon securing the box, but glanced up when she read it.

'From Antonio and Hildegard?'

'They didn't want you to forget them. So they thought they'd give you something to remind you of our time together. All four of us, at the chateau.'

The corner of his mouth lifted but his eyes were filled with loss. She wanted to weep for the unfairness of it all.

Could she love this man any harder? Could he want her love any less?

'Very kind of them both when you think we never even got to meet Hildegard.'

'But she was there, somewhere. Willing us on. Hoping we would find our path in life.'

She looked into his eyes. Desperate to see something, anything, that could let her stay.

'I'm not sure we have,' she said, in a small voice.

'It's the right choice.'

'But we—'

'It's the right choice, Violetta.' He took her hands and squeezed them. 'Trust me.'

There it was again, that trust thing. But should she trust him on this?

Inside the box was an exquisite opal-and-emerald-encrusted brooch. In the shape of a spider.

'Oh, it's beautiful,' she said, gently stroking its little opal body. 'I love it. Thank you.'

Her farewells had been said. Notes of thanks written to the castle staff. The car stood waiting and there was really nothing else keeping her here. When she knew the thing she wanted above anything was denied her.

This man, and his heart.

Doomed to friendship and respect. She couldn't bear the thought of it.

She waved the little box at him. 'Tell them thank you for this.'

He gave her a tight smile and took her hand to lead her to the waiting car. Almost pushing her in. As it pulled away she couldn't stop herself from taking a last look back. Hoping he was at least watching her depart.

But he'd already turned away and was striding back to his castle, getting on with his life.

Trust him, he'd said. Perhaps in the end that was all there was left to do. Give him time and trust that somehow he'd overcome all the hurt and pain that had so ravaged his heart. And wait for him to come and claim the love she was offering.

Violetta clutched the box with her spider brooch and for now let Grimentz, and the man she loved, fall away behind her.

She turned her face to the future, to San Nicolo and all that awaited her there.

CHAPTER ELEVEN

THE PALACE CORRIDORS rang to the delighted shrieks of a toddler. A little boy being chased by a roaring lion, otherwise known as Aunt Violetta.

Maids patiently scrubbed sticky hand prints off antique furniture, footmen gathered up scattered toy animals and crouched to admire, for the umpteenth time, a beloved tractor held up for their inspection by a small, chubby fist.

But for a staff, starved for so long of the laughter of happy little ones, he was a priceless treasure who went a long way to restoring both his parents' reputations in the eyes of everyone in the palace.

Violetta had reached out to her estranged sister and invited her to visit. How could she blame her for running away from her wedding to Leo when she'd done the exact same thing?

Francesca had instantly accepted the invite. At their first meeting she'd crossed the room and gathered Violetta up in an unrestrained hug.

It felt as though she'd regained a sibling she'd never really had in the first place. She restored her sister's royal title, stripped from her when she'd eloped, and made a tiny princeling of her gorgeous little nephew. She patiently drew out her stern and taciturn brother-in-law, who had refused any honorary title of his own. He also refused to call her anything but 'Your Serene Highness' or 'ma'am', despite

Violetta's efforts. She understood what had made Francesca give up everything for him.

Her sister's warrior husband was a good man.

He made no effort to curry favour or forgiveness, yet he earned it all the same as soon as anyone witnessed his behaviour around his wife and young son. His devotion melted the hardest heart.

He reminded Violetta so much of another stern, guarded man.

Having her sister back in her life was bittersweet. They'd never been close. They hadn't been allowed to—raised separately for different roles. But a new bond was developing between them and Violetta cherished it. As she did her new family.

However, it only made her longing for a family of her own more acute. And her longing for the man she wanted that family with.

Her love for Leo was a constant, as was the ache in her heart whenever she thought of him, alone, in his big, brooding fortress.

It hurt. No matter what she was doing or where she was, it hurt. Every day.

Even though on that last morning he couldn't wait to get rid of her. Opening the car door himself and just about pushing her in. He cared for her. She believed it, with every fibre of her being. He was just scared that she would let him down as his parents had.

But she recognised that too, that he'd never really been allowed to make his own choices. Oh, the irony that she was the one who'd been able to forge her own destiny. Whereas he, the powerful man, was still trapped by the expectations of his birth and the damage inflicted by his parents. She just needed to give him time to work it out for himself— that it was okay for him to choose love.

In the meantime she'd show him what true love and loyalty looked like, and she'd wait until they could meet again.

However hard he made it for her.

The people of Grimentz and San Nicolo were happily mixing in ways they hadn't for generations, but so far their respective prince and grand duchess were not.

Over the last ten months there had been several functions they were both due to attend but he'd not in the end appeared at any of them. He was busy rebuilding his country so she could understand his absence. It might have nothing to do with her being there too.

Two days ago they'd both again been on the guest list for a charity dinner. This one in Cannes. Violetta had been so filled with nervous anticipation she'd barely slept the night before. Surely he'd be there this time. She was going to see him again. Her heart had soared at the thought.

But Sebastien had arrived in his place and she couldn't pretend any more. This was the fourth event in a row where he'd failed to appear. The man was actually avoiding her.

He really had meant it when he'd said they couldn't have any kind of relationship. Short of taking a boat across Sérénité, marching up to his castle and, like the famed Elisabetha, demanding admittance, there hadn't been a way to see him again.

Except she'd been invited to the principality's May Ball and she'd hatched her crazy, daring plan. Roping in Seb to help.

She'd waited long enough. She was sure Leo loved her but obviously he wasn't prepared to do a damn thing about it. The stubborn, wonderful man would just have to be saved from himself.

And she'd have to be the one to do it.

'Everything is ready for tonight, sir.' Helene closed the leatherbound folder with her notes on the final preparations for the ball. 'The San Nicolo VIPs are arriving at eight and the grand duchess herself is due to arrive at…at…'

His head of household stammered to a stop. No doubt recalling the unspoken rule amongst his staff that no one talked about Violetta in his presence. They thought he didn't know but since she'd departed the castle that day no one had made a single mention of her and too many conversations had suspiciously halted when he'd walked into a room.

'Thank you, Helene,' he said. 'You and the team have done an excellent job.'

With a hurried curtsy and a flush of colour to her cheeks, she left.

Leo checked his watch. Four p.m. In just a few hours he would see Violetta again.

An unavoidable meeting but he was glad it was nearly here after weeks of anticipation. Good to get it over with.

He was on edge, distracted, and knew he'd get no more work done this afternoon. Irritated by his lack of discipline, he swept from the room and stalked off down the corridor with such force two Meissen figurines set by the door wobbled precariously on their consoles. He didn't much care for them aesthetically, but he kept them close by because they'd belonged to his mother. It was the one sentimentality he allowed himself about her. Perhaps the time had come to remove them, consign them to a forgotten attic.

Or, like his grand duchessa, donate them to the people.

Violetta had gifted the entire Della Torre royal art collection to the state, to sell or keep as they needed. She'd donated much of her personal wealth too, trying to swell the public purse. Then she'd embarked on a series of foreign visits to promote San Nicolo's exports and generate more trade opportunities and refill the coffers bankrupted by her uncle.

His people had loved her for it, as if she were also theirs.

Loved her for everything, in fact. The press was full of her, praising every step she took with those dainty feet of hers.

As for him? He'd definitely picked up on the air of disappointment that he'd failed to make her *their* princess in reality. That there was something wanting in him that had made her turn him down.

He ignored that. What did they know? It was the other way round.

She'd declared her love for him and he'd rejected her.

Ten months since he'd virtually pushed her into that car and out of his life. Ten months since he'd turned away before she'd even left the castle forecourt and strode back into the dark maw of the castle entrance wishing it would swallow him whole.

At the time he'd told himself he'd had a lucky escape because it would inevitably have ended badly. How could their fledgling relationship have survived the rigours of running two countries facing unprecedented challenges? He told himself he was relieved.

Only the first time he walked past the empty Elisabetha suite he felt the lack of her like a gaping hole in his chest. As if all the joy had been sucked out of his world. As it had every day since. No matter how hard he tried to move on.

His anxious advisors had urged him to start searching for a new bride. Providing him with a list of eligible women. European aristocrats, poised, accomplished, perfectly qualified. Even easy on the eye.

He took the list and shoved it at the very bottom of his to-do pile.

None of them had sparked a moment's interest for him because they hadn't been her.

Leo headed towards his private gym. An hour in there might burn off the energy burning through him. It had been building ever since he'd agreed to inviting all of San

Nicolo to the May Ball, which of course included their grand duchess.

His father would have berated him for being weak. Needing anyone, especially a woman, was beyond the pale for a von Frohburg prince. Yet that last night they had been together Leo had needed Violetta as much as he needed to breathe.

He'd thought he'd extinguish all that need from his body by taking her that last time. Only he hadn't. The want, the longing, had remained.

He'd convinced himself she was too young to have made her decision for life and that at some point, like his mother, she'd find something she loved more and move on.

It was as inevitable as breathing.

He'd thrown himself into work. Into the rebuilding of Grimentz and helping his people, barely taking a day off since the storm. It meant his country was fast recovering and his people being taken care of and it suited him to keep his days full.

It was the nights that were the problem.

Because when he was alone and tired and weak, he tortured himself by trawling the Internet for news and the latest photos.

A month before their ill-fated wedding Violetta had sat for an official portrait, in tiara and blue sash and a dress encrusted with way too many beads. She was smiling but Leo had seen the discomfort behind that demure facade and knew that someone else had chosen that outfit.

A month later came the release of her first official photograph as Grand Duchess. This time the gown was breathtakingly simple and the tiara nowhere in sight. Good girl, he thought.

Then he'd looked closer and seen what had replaced the tiara. Her up-do was decorated with a jewelled brooch, doubling as a hair ornament. Almost as valuable as any state bauble. He knew for a certainty because it had come from the Frohburg royal collection.

She'd made a modern tiara of her spider brooch.

Now each time she appeared on official duties he greedily searched for any sign that she'd used it, and sure enough each time it was there. Sitting high on a one-shouldered gown for a ballet premiere, or clipped to the ribbon waistband of a chiffon skirt on a visit to San Nicolo's state hospital, or pinned to a skull cap while braving the snow during a Memorial Day parade in wool coat and leather boots. Often it was her only embellishment and Leo knew she wore it each time to send a message to him.

I'm still here and I still love you.

No matter. One day soon she'd stop wearing it and then he'd know he'd been right to let her go.

As for her political ambitions, a nation of subjects couldn't become a democracy overnight but, by God, their new grand duchess had started her people along the route.

Announcing before her ministers had time to stop her that she was calling a referendum on making San Nicolo a democratic state. With her as their head of state…or not, whatever they decided she'd stand by.

Turned out her people loved her for it. Embracing her and her ideas. They'd voted to become a democracy and keep her and her issue as titular head of state. Even her sister had been welcomed home as the lost daughter she probably was. Bringing a small son with her, who had the brown eyes of the Della Torres and the black hair of his English father.

A son that looked like him and Violetta. When he'd seen that picture it had taken Leo several minutes to be able to breathe normally again.

Of their own accord Leo's feet took him to the Elisabetha suite. As they often had since that one night when Violetta was there.

The rooms were immaculate, of course, but they felt fresh and vivid, alive somehow. As if their owner had just stepped out and left a vital shimmer of energy behind her.

What owner? Grimentz was without a crown princess. He had no mate to inhabit these rooms and fill them with a feminine warmth and welcome. They'd been no oasis when his mother had been in possession of them but that single night, when Violetta had been mistress here, he'd found solace.

And passion like he'd never known.

From the window, his gaze was drawn across the waters of Lake Sérénité to San Nicolo, sunning itself on this perfect May afternoon. The duchy palace itself wasn't quite visible from here, tucked away in a curve of the lake shore, but he could see Violetta's standard fluttering over the city rooftops and knew she was in residence. It would be a place of welcome, he knew, despite all the difficulties her duchy faced.

He might not have been able to have her in his life but he'd wanted so badly to help her and he did what he could.

That first week he'd had his own head of security recommend a good man to her ministers. Tomasz, once formally hired, had gathered a strong team around his new employer and Leo had felt some relief knowing she was at least well protected.

The research he'd ordered on her prime minister proved what he'd already believed from the conversation they'd had. She had a capable, honest and loyal man advising her.

He'd have poured money into her little, broke state but even concealing company behind company it would only take one determined journalist to uncover the truth, as inevitably someone would, and Leo would be accused of trying to annexe the duchy by stealth.

Instead he'd contacted everyone with wealth and influence that he knew. Charming, cajoling, or bluntly calling in favours so that she'd get the assistance she needed. Offers of help began landing on the desk of her finance minister. For who'd dare risk alienating the powerful Prince of Grimentz by refusing?

There was nothing official to be done about her uncle. The man had made poor choices, not illegal ones. For a time he'd caused as much fuss as possible. He'd released his autobiography filled with 'secrets' that had painted the Della Torres as grasping imbeciles and his youngest niece the worst of all, causing a storm across the world.

But she'd weathered it. His brave, beautiful girl had weathered it all. Her people had closed ranks around her, lent her their strength, and she'd emerged stronger and more popular still.

Her uncle, however, had found suddenly that he was no longer welcome in any of the grand houses of Europe. In the States his lucrative second book deal had been cancelled and across the world invites for interviews and TV appearances had gradually dried up. There didn't seem to be any connection. Who had that wide an influence?

One man perhaps. You made an enemy of the Prince of Grimentz—or hurt something he cared about—and you'd come to regret it.

The two countries had retained the new kinship that had emerged from the storm. Some that had come to help with the rescue efforts had stayed. Others invited to take temporary refuge in San Nicolo had decided not to return. There'd been numerous marriages and many babies now on the way.

Children.

He'd never imagined he'd feel the profound lack of a child in his life. Not just because he needed an heir, but because he wanted to be a father.

Leo closed his eyes, blocking out the view of San Nicolo.

No, that wasn't accurate.

He didn't just want to be a father. He wanted to be the father of Violetta's children.

But of course that couldn't happen. He wanted to have respect and admiration for his future princess but how Violetta made him feel was so much more than that. It gave her the power to hurt him and he wouldn't let anyone hurt him again.

The May Ball was tonight. This year, not only was every citizen of Grimentz invited to the city for the festivities as usual, but, by way of a thank you for all their assistance since the storm, everyone from San Nicolo was also invited.

Their grand duchess, too.

They would finally meet again in person. It was time to let go of this infatuation. The May Ball would be the perfect opportunity for that. He might even discover she no longer held the fascination for him that she had.

He turned his back on the suite and its glorious view to Violetta's standard sailing proudly in the spring breeze. Closed the door softly and vowed he wouldn't cross the threshold again until his new princess was found and installed there.

It was well past time to move on.

CHAPTER TWELVE

LEO HAD TRIED on three tuxedos and rejected them all. Even his perfectionist valet was at a loss to the objections.

Something wrong with the fit. Shoulders weren't sitting right. Not black enough, too black.

'Too black?' Matteo asked, looking at him as if he'd lost it. 'May I remind sir, it's a *black tie* event?'

'I look too austere, too unapproachable. What about my white dinner jacket?'

His valet's lips pursed in distaste.

'Sir, if you insist on wearing the white dinner jacket this evening, then expect to find my letter of resignation on your desk in the morning. I would have no other choice.'

'What sartorial faux pas has he threatened this time?' said Seb, strolling in.

Dressed in an immaculate white dinner jacket.

Leo made a face and threw up his hands.

'Yes, well, if His Serene Highness will insist on looking like a pirate...' Matteo's lip curled as he studied Leo's overlong hair and new beard '...he must accept his choices for evening wear will be limited.'

Leo suppressed a sigh. 'I just want to look right this evening.'

'In what way were the three perfectly appropriate tuxedos not accomplishing that?' his valet asked in exasperation.

Hell, Leo thought, *I am losing it.*

He'd see her. He'd smile. He'd exchange pleasantries. They'd share a dance, as would be expected of them, then he'd move on to his other guests.

He made his decision. She couldn't be in his life and he'd live with it.

Seb was helping himself to a brandy. 'I came by before I go to collect my date because I thought you'd like an update on the charity dinner.'

The one held two days ago, that Leo had been invited to but had at the last minute conjured up something or other that had absolutely required his personal attendance—as he had for every function he and Violetta had both been due to attend—and for this one sent Seb in his place.

'Thanks. No update needed.'

Seb's glass paused on the way to his lips.

'You're not going to ask how she was? Or what I discovered?'

He yearned to know.

'It's not really of interest,' he said, casually collecting a cufflink from its box. 'But as you're apparently burning to tell me, what did you discover?'

'She's working very long hours, she's losing weight, and that she seems rather attached to a certain opal and emerald spider brooch that bears a remarkable resemblance to one I remember seeing in the vaults here.'

Leo fumbled the metal bar he was sliding through his cuff.

She'd lost weight. His petite Violetta was already tiny enough.

He willed his fingers to be steady.

'I see. And you think this concerns me how?'

'Well, I was just curious who gave her that brooch and whether that same person may still be concerned for her welfare.'

Leo willed his fingers to be steady and threaded the cufflink.

Who was looking after her, making sure she ate well, got sufficient sleep? Luisa appeared competent, and obviously cared about her mistress, but Violetta was stubborn. Would she listen, do as she was told, eat properly, rest? Goddamn it, he hated being so helpless to do anything.

'You broke her heart, you know,' Seb said.

Mattco paused in brushing the tuxedos, listening intently.

Leo frowned to mask the sudden crushing pain in his chest.

'She wanted something I wasn't able to give. I did her a kindness. It would have ended badly.'

'So two people, who are meant to be together, living alone and miserable is a good ending?'

'I didn't know you could be so sentimental,' Leo drawled.

'You're in love with her. Everyone knows it, except you!' He scrutinised Leo's face. 'Or you do, which makes what you did to her even worse.'

Seb marched over to inspect one of the rejected tuxedos.

'Matteo, he'll wear this midnight-blue Armani, with the shawl lapel. Perfect for the evening's festivities, wouldn't you agree?'

'My thoughts exactly,' Matteo said, holding up the jacket for Leo to slip into. 'Come along now, sir, chop-chop. You heard Prince Sebastien. We wouldn't want you to be late for your own party.'

Leo snatched the jacket from his valet's hands and shrugged into it. 'Since when did you two become so managing?'

'Since you decided to invite the whole of San Nicolo and its grand duchess to the ball,' Seb said. 'And you've barely been able to string two sentences together.'

'That's not true. I've been… I've had… There's been lots of…'

Sebastien laughed, knocked back his brandy, dumped the empty tumbler and headed towards the door. 'Matteo, I'll leave him in your care. I'm off to collect Violetta from her hotel. Let's hope she isn't having the same trouble deciding what to wear or this party might go ahead without any of us in attendance.'

Leo looked up.

'Violetta?'

'Didn't I mention it? She asked me to be her escort for the evening. You don't mind, do you?'

The thought of it slammed into his gut like a clenched fist. Was Violetta developing feelings for his cousin? Because the man was no more available to her than Leo himself. Seb's heart was already spoken for. Not that he'd admit to it—like Leo, he had his demons—but there would only ever be one woman for Seb and Violetta wasn't her.

Was she about to get hurt all over again? Seb wouldn't pursue her, Leo knew that. But had she given up waiting and set her hopes on his cousin?

He wouldn't let that happen. Because… Because…

It was just that he didn't want her to hurt any more, not if he could help it. That was all. He didn't…he couldn't… *love* her.

As the lamplight caught in the emeralds, Violetta's precious brooch sparkled in her fingers. She was nearly ready. All that was needed was for Luisa to fix it into her hair.

Her gown was a simple, ivory silk sheath, with shoe-string straps and diaphanous chiffon layers. She adored the way it floated round her as she moved. It felt so romantic.

Perfect for the evening.

If her plans worked. The ones she'd cooked up with Seb at that gala dinner.

Her stomach lurched. What if Leo still couldn't choose happiness?

Wearing his brooch had never held such significance as tonight. Her fingers trembled as she gazed down on it.

The gift she'd treasured from the moment Leo had placed it in her hands. No one knew it came from the von Frohburg royal collection. When asked she'd simply said that it was a gift and she'd fallen in love with it.

Not with the gift giver, of course.

Violetta stroked the opal body of her beloved little spider. She knew the precise moment Leo had stolen her heart. When he'd made up that story about Antonio the spider to ease her fears.

And the moment he'd broken it? When he'd placed this brooch in her hand then turned and walked away as if he'd forgotten her already.

Seb had said he hadn't, that he was miserable without her.

Of all the challenges she'd faced in the last ten months this was the hardest. Seeing Leo again, speaking to him, taking his hand...and then all those other things she hoped for.

The knock on the door heralded Seb's arrival. Still clutching the brooch in her fingers, she entered the sitting room where he waited.

His gaze swept her from head to toe. 'Why, Grand Duchessa, you are a vision.'

She blushed a little beneath his scrutiny. 'Thank you. You look very handsome yourself.'

'Oh, I'm just the poor cousin. I leave the real glamour to Leo. He does stern and majestic aloofness so well.' He bent to kiss her cheek.

'How is he?' she asked.

'Demanding, irritable, pompous. You know, his usual charming self.'

That won him a nervous smile.

Then his brow creased. 'But where is it?'

Violetta opened her palm to reveal the brooch. 'You mean this?' She tilted her hand so the light caught in the milky opal at its centre. 'What if my plan doesn't work, Sebastien? What if I can't change his mind?'

He placed a knuckle beneath her chin. 'Well, then, the Grand Duchess of San Nicolo will hold her head up high, in this ravishing wisp of a gown and her extraordinary signature piece, and leave every other overdressed creature at the party gnashing their teeth with envy.'

'You know how to make a girl feel better.'

He grinned and waited while Luisa fixed the brooch into the unstructured bun that sat low at the back of her head.

'Perfect,' he said and held out his arm. 'Ready?'

Violetta placed her hand in the crook of his elbow, suddenly grateful to have this tall, charming man to lean on.

'As I'll ever be.' She straightened her spine. 'Okay, let's go get him.'

The peoples of Grimentz and San Nicolo had gathered in their thousands.

The principality laying on the mother of all parties to thank their neighbours. Those neighbours gladly accepting; in their entirety, judging by the crowds.

There were hog roasts in every city square with live music and dancing in every street. For the dignitaries, and the ordinary citizens honoured with special invites, the terraced gardens of the castle had been transformed into a fairyland, with thousands of tiny lights draped over every pergola, above every path, through every tree. Even the brooding fortress looming overhead had a touch of frivolity to it, with its own light show of ever-changing colours. Projected onto the very centre of the ancient ramparts were the flags of Grimentz and San Nicolo fluttering proudly together for all the world to see.

Below on the lake it looked as though every boat that either country possessed had also been pressed into service. Sérénité was filled with them. Some lashed together side by side, with partygoers mixing freely via the gangways running across the decks between them, or smaller boats coming alongside, handing up baskets laden with pastries and cheese and bottles of wine.

The sounds floated up to where Violetta was walking with Seb towards the party. The chatter of happy conversation, the flurry of groans and laughter as a basket lurched and half its contents landed in the lake.

She could see platters being passed from boat to boat. Wine from Grimentz, baskets of bread and pastries. The reverse of what had happened after the storm, Grimentz intent on saying thank you to its neighbour. San Nicolo determined that the new accord should continue.

Helene appeared through the guests, her smile of welcome genuine. As had everyone's been since Violetta had arrived in the city earlier that afternoon and taken her suite in the hotel.

'Helene, you and your team are to be congratulated,' Violetta said. 'It all looks wonderful.'

'His Highness had high expectations for this one. It's come together, of course, but it has been a challenge.'

'I'm sure he's been very complimentary.'

'I wouldn't bet on it,' Seb murmured.

Helene sent him a rueful smile as Matteo arrived beside them.

'Your Highness,' he said with a bow, 'permit me to say you are utter perfection this evening.'

'Thank you, Matteo. From you that's high praise indeed.'

'Everything you requested is in place, ma'am,' Helene said. 'We're ready to go the moment you say the word.'

Violetta shot a quick glance to the party but couldn't see Leo yet.

'We'll have to see if he agrees first,' she said.

'If he does not, I'm resigning forthwith,' Matteo said.

'You'd do no such thing.' Violetta laughed. 'You love him and wouldn't leave him.'

'Isn't that just the tragedy of it?' Matteo sighed. 'The dratted man makes it so hard to love him and yet somehow we all do.'

'Speak for yourself,' Seb said. 'These last ten months have severely tested my patience.'

'Today every single member of castle staff has received a gift and a handwritten card with a personal message of thanks for all their efforts since the storm,' Helene said. 'Ma'am, myself and the handful of castle staff who've been involved with your requests are rooting for you. We hope your plan works. The prince deserves to be happy and that's not how he's been since you left.'

Would she succeed in that? Violetta thought, with a twist to her stomach as she heard Leo's voice up ahead, greeting other new arrivals. The elderly guest he'd been greeting moved off and now Violetta could see him.

She drank in the sight. His height, his broad shoulders. Those eyes that could make you feel like the only creature in the world. The beautifully cut tuxedo that showed off his impressive physique. He looked leaner, darker. More forbidding even than she remembered, and his lustrous hair was longer. It curled over his collar. He'd even grown a beard. All in all, it was only just on the right side of untamed.

Heaven help her, it was… Oh, God, it was *hot*.

Her throat tightened. Her mouth went dry. What if she tried to greet him and nothing came out?

'Your Highness…' Seb was saying.

She tried to catch her breath. Was she hyperventilating?

Here, amongst all these people, with nowhere to run and hide. She was. She actually couldn't breathe.

Then Leo looked up. Their eyes met.

'Grand Duchessa?' Seb's voice came again.

What if she fainted? Right here. Oh, how mortifying—

'Violetta!'

She jumped, looking up to see Seb grimacing.

'If it's all the same to you I'd like to retain the use of my arm after tonight.'

He sent a pained look to where her fingers were clenched in a death grip on his sleeve.

'I'm so sorry. It's just—'

'I know. But relax!' Seb whispered as Leo began walking towards them. 'Trust me, it's all going to be fine.'

But what if it wasn't?

CHAPTER THIRTEEN

LEO HAD KNOWN the instant she'd joined the guests mingling on the terrace. Glimpsing the slight figure in floating ivory through the crowd on the arm of his cousin.

The aged princess, whose gnarled fingers he'd just taken, winced as his hand convulsed around hers. He made his apologies as she moved off.

His attention slewed straight back to Violetta. She was even more beautiful than he remembered. Her rich brown hair caught up in an unstructured knot. Her dress, a simple gossamer sheath. On any other it would have been a shapeless sack, but of her it made a goddess. Ethereal, and gorgeous. He wanted to gaze at her for ever. He wanted to fall on his knees and worship at her feet.

Leo knew he'd badly misjudged. That even seeing her with Seb was going to be too much; his cousin, who his calm, rational head knew for a certainty would never *ever* betray him. But all that mattered to the slavering, jealous beast that reared up inside him was that Seb was another male and he was standing too close to her.

For one crazed moment he actually thought about turning on his heel and just walking out of there. Quitting the party where he was host. But then he spied Helene, talking to Violetta, and whatever vestige of reason was clinging on reminded him of all the work that she and the castle team had done to put this evening together, and he knew he couldn't do it, couldn't let any of his people down by taking the coward's way out and leaving.

Instead he headed straight towards her. Aiming to get their meeting out of the way. The blood was rushing in his ears. Despite the pleasant breeze coming off the lake a trickle of sweat slid down his back.

Then there she stood.

He devoured the sight as a starved man hungered after a banquet. The sweetly pointed chin, those warm eyes, and slender limbs.

'Good evening, Your Serene Highness.'

'Good evening, Grand Duchessa.' Leo took the proffered hand and bowed over it. He made a little heel click. 'Thank you for being so gracious as to join us this evening. I trust you are well?' His voice would barely work. Could he sound any more stilted?

'Oh, yes, thank you. I'm… I'm very well.'

Violetta's glance flickered to Seb in bewilderment. When she looked back to Leo, Seb mouthed at him.

'Stop being a dick.'

To his right Leo heard Matteo make a frustrated groan.

He tried to pull himself together, to be the charming host, but while her hand sat in the crook of his cousin's elbow it was liking asking a starving wolf to sit calmly, and be petted, while a tender lamb stood nearby.

The orchestra stirred to life.

'Do you mind?' he said, not waiting for Seb's answer but taking Violetta's hand and transferring it to his arm instead.

'The dancing is about to begin and the grand duchess and I should set the example.'

He might as well have been on a tumbril, being dragged through the crowd to his execution, not walking amongst his invited guests, the man beside her looked so grim and dark.

They reached the centre of the dance floor set up on the

largest of the terraces. With only the briefest glance at her, Leo took her in hold.

She remembered the last time he'd held her like this. She'd been wearing nothing but ballet shoes and his shirt, and he hadn't been able to keep his gaze—or his hands— off her. Now it was as if he could barely stand to touch her at all.

'You clearly aren't taking proper care of yourself,' he said as the music began. 'Do you even observe mealtimes? You're practically skin and bone.'

Perhaps she'd lost a kilo or two. She might not have eaten at regular times, she often worked late into the night, there'd been so much to do, but Luisa always made sure she ate something.

'Thank you for the gracious compliment,' she said as they danced past other couples joining them on the floor, couples who were trying valiantly not to stare.

His lip curled. 'It's merely an observation from one monarch to another. You'll be no use to your duchy if you aren't fit enough to work.'

'I'm fortunate that not all the von Frohburgs have forgotten their manners this evening. Prince Sebastien was much more of a gentleman.'

That earned her a swift glare. 'A word of advice, Violetta. If you are setting your sights on my cousin you should know he won't be interested.'

Her brow creased. 'What?'

'You asked him to be your date for the evening. I assumed that you might be developing a *tendre* for him.'

Fury lit up inside her. How dared he? How *could* he?

Here she was being all misty-eyed about how alone he was, how much he must be missing her. Yet what did he do when they finally met again? Insult her, then patronise her and then accuse her, casually, of crushing on someone else. When she'd been breaking her heart every moment of the last ten months waiting for him to wake up and come and claim her love at last.

'I don't care for what you're implying.'

'I was trying to be helpful.'

'By insulting me?'

He tightened his grip on her waist as he navigated a brief congestion on the dance floor.

'By advising you.'

'I already have enough advisors.'

'In this case they would say the same, trust me.'

'There it is again. That trust thing that you're so big on. But trusting you hasn't served me that well before.'

'Take it or leave it. I'm just advising you to choose someone else instead.'

'Who, Leo? Which paragon of masculinity do you have in mind?'

He scowled as his cousin swirled past them with a voluptuous brunette in his arms. 'I don't know, someone...*else*.'

She rolled her eyes and just in case he hadn't got the message, gave an exasperated sigh too.

'It can't be me, if that's what you're angling for.'

She snatched her hand from his and stopped dead.

'Angling?' Numerous heads swivelled in their direction, but she didn't care who heard. She was too angry. Too hurt. Was he really saying these callous things to her? 'You make it sound like you're the prize. Well, I've got news for you, you're not. I am, and I'll bestow myself wherever the hell I choose.'

'Who here doesn't know that you're the prize?' Leo said, flinging out a protective arm as another couple threatened to dance straight into her. 'Which creature watching your rise over the last few months hasn't worked out you're the most extraordinary human being ever to come out of San Nicolo, or Grimentz for that matter?'

'*You*, apparently, because if you had you would have never let me go.'

She spun away from him and began weaving her way through the other dancers.

'Where are you going?' he demanded.

'Anywhere that's away from you.' The Arctic Circle. No, the Antarctic. That was further.

'I haven't finished yet.'

'Trust me. You have nothing left to say that I want to hear.'

She reached the edge of the dance floor and stepped down onto the path. The goggling crowds parted as the Grand Duchess of San Nicolo stormed past with the Prince of Grimentz in hot pursuit.

Violetta spied an arbour, tucked away in a quiet corner of the garden. Desperate to get away from Leo, from everyone, from this whole miserable evening, she hitched up her hem and ran towards it. She groaned in frustration when she discovered it was already occupied.

With those long legs of his Leo easily matched her stride.

'You will excuse us,' Leo ordered and with no attempt at politeness. He looked so fierce Violetta suspected an entire platoon of his guardsmen would have thought twice before remaining where they were.

As it was, an actual guardsman from Grimentz and a San Nicolo doctor—Violetta recognised her from a recent visit to the state hospital—swiftly unwound from their passionate clinch and shot to their feet. With a bow for Leo and a curtsy for her, they beat their retreat.

'Isn't it obvious I don't want to talk to you?'

He folded his arms across his chest. 'I need you to know that Seb's not the man for you.'

She flung up her hands. 'I have no interest in Sebastien. Even though he is infinitely more charming. Much less frustrating, pig-headed, overbearing, patronising, pompous.'

Leo's brow rose. 'Now who's dishing out insults?'

'You deserve every one of them.'

She sat down. The layers of her dress settling around her with an indignant sigh. 'I had such high hopes for this evening.'

'I hoped merely to get through it.'

She looked up at him with a frown. 'What do you mean?'

He glowered at a terracotta pot of pretty tumbling geraniums but remained stubbornly silent.

'You broke my heart, you know.'

'So I've been told.'

'Don't you even care that you hurt me?'

'It had to be done.'

'Why, Leo? Why was it so damn necessary to rip my heart to shreds?'

'I would have hurt you eventually anyway, because I can't give you want you want.'

'And what is that? What is it you think I want that you can't give me?'

'You know the answer to that already.' He shot a look at her over his shoulder. 'Love,' he said.

'Leo, you already behave like a man in love. I know you've been using your influence to help me.'

He waved a dismissive hand. 'I'd have done the same for any neighbouring monarch in difficulties.'

'Including going to great lengths to make a social pariah of her uncle so he couldn't embarrass her further?'

His jaw tightened, and his mouth compressed into a determined line of silence.

She studied him sadly. 'Thank you for that. It helped me a lot at the time.'

He half turned towards her as if drinking in that nugget of information. But then he looked straight ahead.

'It doesn't matter anyway. Love does not work well in royal marriages.'

'Nonsense. There are numerous examples where it's thrived.'

'Very well, I'll amend that. Love would not belong in *my* marriage.'

'And why is that?'

'It's not something I want.'

'That's only because you're scared.'

He kept a determined silence.

'Admit it, Leo. You're frightened.'

His jaw tightened…again.

'I'll live with it,' he said. 'It doesn't change anything.'

Oh. *Oh.*

Finally she might be getting somewhere. He'd erred, he'd revealed a tiny weakness in his hard shell of supposed indifference. He knew it too. He straightened himself, his posture even more tense.

'And how's that working for you? Being alone up there in your big old fortress? I've heard you're miserable. That you haven't been the same since I left.'

He folded his arms across his chest and transferred his glare to an entirely innocent bed of rosemary. 'You shouldn't believe everything you hear.'

'You're going to deny it? You're going to deny that you miss me?'

'I've been extremely busy.'

'How is that an answer?' She moved in front of him. Blocking his way out of the arbour. He'd have to pick her up to get past her, to touch her, and she had the sense that if he did, he wouldn't be able to stop. 'Well, that's not good enough for me any more.'

'You have no choice.'

'No? Perhaps not, but you know me. I'm big on finding alternative solutions to a problem. I'm taking charge here and I'm going to paint a picture for you, so you can truly understand the consequences of the choice you're making.'

She lifted her chin to stare right at him.

'You let me go now and this is what will happen. I want children. Your children, specifically.'

His eyes glittered.

'But if you won't do the job then I'll have to find someone who will, and I'll do it. For San Nicolo. I'm still Head of State and my people need an heir.'

He stared down his nose at her, but his eyes flashed.

'That means there'll have to be a man in my life. Allowed to put his hands on me. Imagine that for a moment, Leo. Seb just took my arm in platonic friendship and I know you couldn't handle it. You looked positively murderous back there.'

That muscle in his jaw was working overtime. 'You can even see my standard from your castle. You'll know when I'm home, with my husband, and what we'll be doing in bed together, night after night.' She pushed her face into his. 'Until I'm pregnant.'

'Violetta,' he warned. 'Stop this.'

'He'll hold me, kiss me, touch every intimate inch of me. You know how I like to be touched, don't you, Leo?' she purred.

He was utterly still, rigid but for the tic of a muscle in his jaw.

'So let me ask you. What frightens you more? How you feel now or how you'd feel then?'

'Violetta.' It was part anger, part desperation and wrenched from the depths of him as if he'd been gutted and left to bleed.

'Bothers you, doesn't it? That image.'

She reached up to stroke a lapel. His big frame shuddered beneath her touch. As if she'd run her fingers over naked skin, not finely tailored satin.

She was getting to him and she wouldn't spare him a single detail. She'd make him admit how he felt. She was done with letting him hide away.

'And when there's a baby, Leo, an heir, a little boy or girl. What will you feel then?'

'Violetta.' His voice dropped to the barest whisper. 'Please stop.'

'No, Leo. I won't. Not until you give me a damn good reason why we can't be together. We so obviously love each other, and don't even bother trying to deny it.'

He couldn't help himself. He reached out to lightly touch the brooch in her hair.

'You wear this all the time.'

Eyes dark and compelling as midnight gazed up at him, filled with all the emotions he was trying so hard to suppress in himself. 'You must know why?'

He let out a long, slow, shuddering breath. 'You're trying to tell me you still love me.'

'Yes.' So sure, so utterly certain. How he envied her that.

'But what if we can't make it work? What if our duties get in the way?'

'Leo, I've just saved my country from financial ruin. You've just rebuilt yours after Mother Nature did her worst. Compared to all that, co-ordinating two schedules will be a breeze.'

She made it sound so simple. But there was more to this than that.

'What if I can't make you happy? What if I'm too broken to love you back?' It was a dark confession.

'Are you?' Her hands settled flat against his jacket and the comfort of a honeyed warmth spread through him. 'You feel pretty whole to me.'

She placed an ear to his chest. She'd easily hear his

heartbeat. It was pounding so hard anyone within ten metres would be able to hear it.

'Yup, all sounds fine and dandy. Nothing broken in there.'

'I drove my mother away because I didn't love her enough. It was my fault she left.' He could hear Leo the boy in that statement, but it was time for honesty and there was, after all this time, a part of him that believed it.

Fierce now, Violetta reached up to take his face in her hands. 'Firstly, your mother didn't want love. She wanted adulation. Secondly, she didn't leave because of you, she left because of your father, but he was too much of a coward to admit it so he pretended it was your fault.'

'Neither of them loved me. I'm not someone that people love, Violetta.'

There.

He'd finally said it. The truth he'd buried deep, but had carried with him for years, rooted like a malign growth in his soul. 'You think you care for me now but…' his voice cracked '…you'll change your mind.'

She gently scuffed her knuckles back and forth along his bearded jaw. 'Oh, my darling man, you really won't get rid of me that easily. I love you. I'll always love you. Believe it. Despite your efforts to keep everyone at arm's length. Seb, Matteo, your people, while she was with us, your wonderful *grand-mère*. We all love you—we can't help ourselves. You're a good man.'

Leo's throat closed.

Above their heads the image of their respective flags fluttered together on his castle walls. On the garden paths and the dance floor, Grimentzians and San Nicoloans were together.

Why could he not do the same? Why could he not reach out for happiness, for love?

Because of a woman who failed her only child? A father

who was so cold-hearted all he could teach his son was to gaze with avarice at his neighbours?

But Leo wasn't either of them. He served his people well. He'd been like a brother to Seb. He'd let go of the need to grasp San Nicolo because it was morally right. He'd supported its grand duchess in every way he could and here she stood, offering him her heart.

Violetta had risen above all the limitations her family had placed on her life and surpassed them all. Leading her people into a bright, new future.

How could he think of letting such a woman slip through his fingers just because he was afraid?

How could he leave the way open for another man…?

A possessive rage reared up inside him.

He would *not*.

He gathered her up and crushed her to him.

'No other man will be the father of your children, Violetta,' he growled. She was so slight in his arms and yet she felt like his anchor, like a safe harbour in the storm. He dropped to the bench and drew her onto his lap. He dropped his forehead against hers. 'You're right. My life is nothing without you because I love you, too. Marry me. *Save* me.'

She let out a long sigh of contentment and wound her arms about his neck. 'Yes, Leo,' she said, 'I will.' Her fingers toyed with the hair that curled over his collar. A shadow fell briefly over her eyes. 'You've scolded me for not taking care of myself, but you've also worked too hard and I know why,' she said, sadly. 'You focused on fixing your country so you wouldn't have to think about fixing yourself. That stops now. We can fix you together. A day at a time. Here, or in San Nicolo. Or both. Commuting would be easy and I'd rather like riding in that fancy helicopter of yours.'

'I don't care where I live as long as it's with you,' he

said and stopped any further discussion by sealing their bargain with a kiss.

When they strolled back onto the path hand in hand, Seb was waiting for them. Helene and Matteo hovered a few paces behind.

'Well?' Seb asked, glancing down at their entwined hands.

Violetta stared up at Leo with a glorious smile. 'Yes.'

'Finally. I thought I might have to start a fight so I could beat some sense into you.'

'We're a go then, ma'am?' Helene asked.

'We're a go.'

'I'll get the chef to bring out the cake.'

'The luggage is ready, Your Highness.' Matteo popped up behind Seb. 'I'll have it taken down to the castle forecourt.' With a swift bow he spun on his heel and followed Helene.

Leo frowned. 'Cake? Luggage? What's going on?'

Violetta took both his hands and smiled up at him. 'I thought we could get married.'

'What? *Now?*'

'Yes, now! Our people are here to bear witness. As is your archbishop. And he conveniently has all the documentation we would have used last July. It's all still legal. I checked with him.'

Leo's eyes narrowed on her. 'You planned all this?'

She studied him from beneath her lashes. 'You don't mind, do you?'

No, he thought, not even a little bit. He didn't want to waste another moment of his life without her.

For answer he gathered her up and kissed her. 'If we're going to do this, there's something I need to collect from the palace first.' He was about to stride away but turned back suddenly and caught up her hands. 'You will be here when I get back, won't you?'

Violetta's face lit up in a smile that made him giddy as a schoolboy.

'Yes, I'll be here,' she said. 'I'll always be here for you, Leo.'

Guests had squeezed into every available spot around the dance floor. Royalty and subjects alike, jostling for the best view. Leo's castle staff filled the battlements or craned for a better view on the walkways, some were even tucked in cheek by jowl amongst the VIP guests.

He paced nervously at the edge of the dance floor. Behind him, beneath a flower-strewn arch placed there by four footmen under the careful direction of Helene, the archbishop waited to perform the marriage ceremony.

Then his bride appeared.

Leo's heart just about stopped as she walked towards him, all light and joy and spellbinding loveliness. She carried a bouquet of roses his gardeners had gathered for her. A gardenia was tucked behind her ear.

But her dazzling smile was all her own and all for him.

She reached the edge of the dance floor and placed her hand in his. His nerves fled; his heart swelled. He knew for certain that nothing he'd done in his life had ever been so right.

The ceremony was broadcast across both countries, on the giant screens in the squares, onto the castle ramparts. All the people of San Nicolo and Grimentz were able to bear witness to this union.

When the archbishop asked Violetta, 'Do you take this man?' her yes was answered by a great roar that went up across the city and through the flotilla gathered below.

Before Leo could answer his own question one of his footmen shouted, 'Don't do it, sir.'

A nearby butler gave him a good-natured cuff for his

pains, but laughter rippled through the guests. Violetta was helpless with giggles, her smile growing even wider.

Leo raised their clasped hands to his lips. 'I do,' he said, and this time the roar of voices was accompanied by car horns blasting across the city and then sirens, as the boats gathered on the lake joined in.

The archbishop was obliged to wait several minutes before he could continue. He beckoned to the best man. Seb stepped up and opened his palm. Where two gold bands sat. The rings that had been ordered for the wedding last year.

When Violetta looked up in surprise, Leo gave her a crooked smile.

'I kept them. For some reason I couldn't bring myself to let them go.'

After he'd placed the plain gold band on her finger, he retrieved a second ring from his pocket and slipped that too on her finger.

'Your engagement ring,' he said. Running his thumb over the exquisite rectangular-cut emerald set with a diamond on each compass point.

When they were pronounced husband and wife, the great cacophony erupted up again, joined by fireworks.

But Leo barely heard any of it. He was too busy sealing his marriage with a kiss for his bride.

There was a toast, in the finest champagne, and the cutting of a cake. Leo marvelled at the towering masterpiece his kitchen team had created. Five tiers that bore the Grimentzian and San Nicolo coats of arms wound together in royal icing. The Grimentzian guardsman from earlier, with a wry grin, presented his sword to the colonel-in-chief and his new bride so they might perform the ceremonial cut into the bottom layer.

Then came their first dance.

A waltz, of course.

Specifically the one they'd danced to at the chateau.

When his bride looked at him in surprise, Leo sent her his best angelic smile.

'I thought you'd appreciate something familiar as you're dancing in public.' He drew her close, pressed his mouth to her ear. 'I have you safe, *il mio diletto principessa*, so set free your dancing heart.'

In his arms, happier than she could ever express, his beloved princess did…

On the castle forecourt, decked out with streamers and a handwritten 'Just Married' sign, waited a red Ferrari. Seb stood beside it, the keys dangling from his fingers.

'Please don't drive it into a ditch this time,' he said.

Leo took the keys with a glare. 'It was not a ditch. It was an unavoidable pothole.'

'Don't worry, Seb,' Violetta said, climbing into the passenger seat. 'I'm with him now. I'll make sure your Ferrari is safe.'

Leo drove them out of the city. Their security following at a discreet distance.

'I have a surprise of my own,' he said. 'I did what you suggested. I've reopened Chateau Elisabetha. I haven't been there much yet, but I thought we could start our honeymoon there.'

The roads had been repaired, any storm damage cleared away and the track up to the house re-Tarmacked. Seb's car was spared any misfortunes.

As they passed the treeline and saw the chateau in all its glory, Violetta gasped. The steps up to the front door were lined with storm lanterns, filled with candles. Inside the stairs were similarly lined, candles lighting their way upstairs to the master suite. Where a bottle of champagne on ice awaited them.

'Oh, Leo. It's absolutely perfect. Who knew you were an old romantic under that gruff exterior?'

'Only with you,' he said, backing her towards the bed and finding the zip on her dress at the same time.

Later, as Violetta slept in his arms—making contented little snuffling noises that utterly delighted him—Leo scrolled through pictures already circulating from the wedding. One in particular caught his attention.

They were standing on a terrace edge, acknowledging the crowds gathered below. His hand was flung high in an unrestrained wave, the other was wrapped around Violetta's waist. He was looking at the crowd below, but she was gazing up at him. And the expression in her eyes?

It was complete devotion.

Love.

Leo's hand came up to his mouth.

'What is it? What's wrong?'

Violetta had stirred in his arms.

'Nothing.' He pressed his lips to her brow. 'It's nothing.'

'Oh, no. We're not doing that.' She reached over him to throw on the bedside light. 'Tell me.'

She was studying him anxiously, but he took her left hand and held it up so he could admire the emerald ring on her finger. 'So, you like this, then?'

'You're changing the subject.'

He let out a shaky breath. 'Humour me? Just for a moment. Please.'

Her face softened. 'Okay. Yes, of course. I love it.'

'I knew you would. You have such a fondness for emeralds.'

She rolled her eyes at him.

'This one comes from the same collection your tiara did.'

'It was inspired by the plucky Elisabetha?'

'Yes, but I didn't tell you her whole story.'

She lifted up to look into his face. 'You're not about to tell me she sacrificed herself and died a horrible death, are you? Because that's not the kind of story a bride wants to hear on her wedding night.'

'No.' His hand cupped the back of her head and drew her closer for a kiss. 'Nothing like that.' He waited until she'd settled her chin propped on his hand, which lay on his chest. 'She didn't just save Grimentz through moral duty. She gave herself to the prince for love.'

Violetta's eyes grew wide. 'For love? I like her even more now.'

'Thought you might. The story goes that they met at her father's court months before the siege, and though he was guarded and gruff she saw through that, to the man he was beneath his wounds. Beyond his pain.' Leo's hand slid to cup Violetta's cheek. 'She fell in love with him. That's why she married him, not just to save Grimentz, but because she wanted to spend her life with him.'

He paused but Violetta waited patiently. Giving him the time he needed to voice something that would have been unimaginable to him even a few hours ago.

'It was this photo of us from tonight,' he said eventually. 'The way you're looking at me. I saw it. The love in your eyes. I understand now. You love me, like Elisabetha loved her prince.'

Violetta's eyes glittered with moisture as she turned to place a kiss in his palm. 'Always, Leo. Always and for ever.'

He rolled her onto her back. 'Always,' he echoed, pressing a tender kiss to her lips. 'Always and for ever, my love.'

EPILOGUE

LEO WAS THE last to retire, putting off the lights in the kitchens as he went.

He passed the dining room, where the table was already laid with crisp linens. Crystal champagne flutes sparkled amongst all the evergreens and icy-white baubles that Francesca and Luisa had spent the afternoon gathering and arranging in displays along its centre.

Tomorrow they'd have a lavish Christmas Day dinner, with everyone dressed to the nines. But tonight his guests had shared an informal and often raucous meal, gathered round the oak table in the kitchen. The servants had been given time off to celebrate with their own families and Violetta and Matteo had stepped in as cooks, serving up homemade pasta with Grand-Mère's famous pomodoro sauce, followed by tiramisu from Matteo's closely guarded recipe.

The kitchen had echoed to the laughter and teasing of his oddball gathered family. Leo had sat at the head of the table, surveying the scene in some wonder.

Previously estranged sisters, a former fiancée and the man she'd jilted Leo for.

Max was there, with his new fiancé. A wildly handsome major from the Grimentzian Guards who'd seen something lovable in the previously unlovable Max and helped him reveal it to the rest of the family.

Believing he might now be freed of the terrifying responsibility of being the sole heir, Max had abandoned his dissolute lifestyle. His major had encouraged him to face his demons and find a new purpose in life.

Leo knew they'd never be close as he and Seb were, but Max was still family and Violetta had taught him how important it was to cherish those bonds. He'd witnessed how she'd pulled her sister close and how much that relationship meant to her now.

So Leo had made the first move by asking his cousin if he could take on the patronage of a new charity that helped young people with mental health issues and Max had actually agreed.

Inviting him to spend Christmas here at the chateau had also felt right and seeing him that evening talking with Seb, almost like the brothers they were, had pleased Leo beyond all measure.

Earlier that day the brothers, the major and Francesca's husband had been tasked by Violetta with dressing the enormous tree that occupied a corner of the hallway.

The men had discharged their duties with gusto. Hardly an inch was bare of decoration. Grand-Mère would have loved how ostentatious it was.

She would have loved even more how Leo had gathered his new family around him for Christmas.

You were happy here once, she'd written. *You could be again.*

She was right. He was…almost. Something niggled at him. Something about Violetta this evening that he couldn't quite put his finger on.

Because his happiness was, of course, inextricably linked with hers.

A toy tractor dangled from a branch just above his head. Violetta's little nephew had been transfixed by it. Importuning 'Unca Lo' again and again to lift him up on his shoulders so he could inspect it more closely.

Leo wondered when he might do the same with a son—
or daughter—of his own. He knew he just needed to be patient. He and Violetta would have children in time. They
certainly weren't childless for want of trying.

His sigh was answered by the tap of four paws trotting
close and a wet snout shoved into his hand.

Leo fussed at soft ears then crossed the hallway to climb
the stairs to join his wife in their bedroom.

The hound had joined the family some months back.
Carrying on Grand-Mère's tradition, he was a rescue dog.

A three-year-old Newfoundland-Malamute cross called
Hektor.

Leo reached the landing. But the big dog was no longer following.

Hektor had halted next to the room occupied by the
chateau's smallest guest. Torn between loyalty to Leo and
his new-found adoration of Francesca's tiny son, he gave
a frustrated whine.

'It's okay, boy,' Leo said and Hektor sank to the rug. As
if to cement his decision, he lay down blocking the way.
To reach any of the rooms along the corridor an intruder
would now have to go past him first.

'That's a good compromise,' Leo said. Hektor's tail
thumped against the floor in agreement.

Francesca's son was to be well protected tonight.

Leo carried on, past the room that had temporarily become a nursery.

Any child of theirs would potentially become Head of
State for both countries, but no child of his would suffer
the emotional neglect and cruelty that he and Violetta had.
There'd be no expectations other than they be themselves
and if a younger child wanted the role and the eldest did
not, then that would be up for discussion also.

Their offspring would never suffer the loveless lives their

parents had. He and his wife had a loving family around them now, as would their children.

Wife.

Leo still couldn't get used to how wondrous that was to him.

She was wife and lover first, his consort second. How she'd helped him in those last stages of rebuilding Grimentz.

When he entered their room Violetta was at the window with the curtains drawn back.

'Look,' she said, 'it's snowing.' She came towards him, her eyes alight with excitement.

In the distance the bells of St Peter's cathedral and all the churches of Grimentz rang out for midnight.

'It's Christmas,' Violetta said. In her ivory nightgown she looked like his bride all over again. His breath caught in his throat. He still hadn't got used to the physical impact she could have on him. He doubted he ever would and he didn't want to.

However much it scared him, how much his love for her filled his soul, he wouldn't trade even a moment of it for what he'd had before.

A grey, cold and loveless half-life.

At first there had been days when the old fears had come crashing back and he'd faltered and hidden away. But Violetta had always found him, wound her arms about his neck, held him, kissed him, reassured him.

It was okay to be scared, she'd told him, she was too. Then she'd remind him they'd get through this together and each day it got easier and better and loving her became the most natural and important thing he could do.

Because she was his love.

Right now, with her slender body pressed against him, her eyes bright with excitement, she was up to something. He knew that look well.

'I know we're supposed to be exchanging gifts in the morning, but now it's officially Christmas I want to give you something tonight.'

He glanced around for a surprise parcel, wrapped in festive paper, adorned with a bow perhaps. But there was nothing.

Instead she took his hand, gently spreading his fingers to open his palm. She pressed a kiss to it, turned it and carried it downwards to lay flat against her belly.

His long fingers easily encompassed her and…and…

Leo's heart stuttered. Now he knew what he'd missed at dinner. She'd passed on the wine and drunk water all evening.

His gaze shot to hers to find it brimming with love.

'Yes, Leo.' She smiled at him then. 'I'm pregnant. You're going to be a father.'

As his family slumbered and the snow softly fell and the church bells rang out for a bright, new Christmas morning, Leo gathered his wife and unborn child to him.

Happiness, he thought. *This is how it feels.*

* * * * *

AWAKENED BY THE WILD BILLIONAIRE

BELLA MASON

MILLS & BOON

To my three cheerleaders for your endless support, and my wonderful husband without whom this book wouldn't exist.

CHAPTER ONE

DEEP BREATHS.

Emma Brown ascended the stairs to the party venue, and as she entered the ballroom looked around the dimly lit, extravagantly decorated space hoping to find her best friend. She wanted to adjust her mask and flatten her cobalt dress for the hundredth time, but silently instructed herself to stop fidgeting.

She walked through the entrance, eyes searching for her friend's tall frame amongst the sea of ballgown-clad women. There were masks of every colour, style and shape wherever she looked. Everyone seemed to be glittering in their adornments, and every hand was accessorised with an elegant glass of champagne.

Crystal chandeliers hung from the draped ceiling, reflecting light in all directions. Emma looked out at the wall of glass, a small smile playing on her lips as she walked, admiring the thousands of golden fairy lights as their glow danced on the surface of a pool. This hotel was always beautiful. She loved how the city rose up around it. There were very few places she loved as much as Melbourne.

She was so completely bewitched by her surroundings that she paid no attention to where she was walking until she hit a very solid wall that knocked the breath out of her. A strong arm wrapped around her waist, steadying her.

'Oh! Ex-excuse me,' she stuttered.

'Are you okay?' a deep, resonating voice asked.

She was mesmerised, both by the crisp English accent and the piercing sky-blue eyes that bore down into hers, and her stomach was doing somersaults. Emma could feel pure heat radiating from the hand on her back, but she wasn't sure of anything in that moment apart from the fact her heart was going at a million miles an hour.

'Um…yeah… Sorry about that.' She laughed nervously as she righted herself. 'Enjoy your evening,' she murmured as she walked away from him, blushing furiously.

Emma looked back over her shoulder at the tuxedo-clad man in his simple black mask and was delighted to see he was still watching her. She turned around and spotted her sisters, who had already started mingling and were nodding to her to join them, but Emma was immensely thankful that Hannah was nearby, waving her over.

Hannah, her best friend, roommate and eternal saviour, was the only reason Emma had agreed to attend this charity masquerade. It had been Emma's twenty-eighth birthday the day before, and Hannah had thought they could extend the celebration. And right now, as she once again stole a glance at the handsome stranger, she was very happy she had agreed.

'Hey! You look amazing!' Hannah gushed as she hugged her.

'Thanks…' Emma mumbled, fiddling with the fine silver filigree mask she wore. 'You're going to turn heads tonight.'

'And beds.' Hannah chuckled darkly, twirling a lock of red hair around her finger.

'You're terrible.'

'Probably.' Hannah handed her a tall flute of bubbly. 'I

think you're going to need that in you before your sisters come over here.'

'Got anything stronger?'

'Left the poison in my other bag,' Hannah deadpanned. 'So, who's the dreamboat that keeps looking at you?'

'I'm pretty sure that's Lord Alexander Hastings,' Emma whispered.

'Pretty sure?'

'The mask adds some doubt.'

'Why don't you go over there and introduce yourself and eliminate the doubt? Seriously, he looks like he'd be interested.'

'I very much doubt that—especially after I nearly bowled him over.'

Hannah laughed. 'You're an idiot. And speaking of idiots… Lauren incoming.'

'Great.'

Emma and Hannah fixed polite smiles in place as the woman approached. Lauren, the eldest of her sisters, and by most accounts the most beautiful, was blessed in many ways. Tall, blonde, with hazel eyes with flecks of gold that could bewitch most. Eyes that her younger sister Maddison shared. Lauren had always made Emma feel plain. But perhaps her biggest blessing of all, was the unequivocal favour she enjoyed from their father.

'Hey, sis,' Emma greeted her. 'Where's Maddie?'

'Somewhere around here. You've made an effort, I see,' Lauren said haughtily.

But Emma wasn't listening. Her gaze was fixed on the man who seemed to be pulling at her on a primal level. He stood with one hand in his pocket as he spoke to the group of people around him. She could see the smirk on his face despite the dim lighting, and knew he was watching her as much as she watched him. Or maybe that was just wishful thinking.

Emma tried to ignore the waspish conversation between her best friend and her sister. And she was so absorbed in watching him she didn't notice when Maddison had joined them.

'Emma!' Lauren said impatiently.

That tore her attention back to her present company. 'I'm sorry—what?'

'Honestly! I asked you what made you come tonight? I thought you were staying home with the furball.' Lauren pinned an accusatory glare on Emma.

'I changed my mind. I had an invitation—just like you, Lauren.' Emma could feel the night plunging into a nightmare. Clearly it was a mistake to have come.

'Yes, well…just remember *I'm* here representing the company.'

Emma let out a breath of a laugh. 'I know that, Lauren. I'd never dream of stealing your thunder—especially when I can enjoy my Friday night while you have to work the room.'

'Guys, maybe we should go somewhere quieter,' Maddison interrupted, casting an apologetic gaze at Emma.

'There's no need, Maddie. We're just talking.' Lauren flicked her hair back, raising her flute of champagne to her lips.

The vast room was still humming with the sound of conversation. People everywhere were chatting and laughing and smiling. It seemed no one had even noticed her. Except one person, and he frowned as he watched the beaming smile vanish from Emma's face. She thought she caught his eye as she watched him walk away from the group of people he had been talking to.

'I think we should go and mingle,' Emma suggested,

trying to defuse the tension. All she needed was time with Hannah and her mood would lift once again.

Unfortunately Lauren took Emma's arm and dragged her away. She must have noticed Emma staring at Alexander Hastings and decided she was going to do something about it.

'I couldn't agree more,' she said.

CHAPTER TWO

ALEX SAW THE two women approach out of the corner of his eye as he nursed his whisky, and had to swallow down his disappointment that the intriguing brunette was not alone. He silently chastised himself for feeling anything,—after all, he'd barely interacted with her. It was ridiculous to feel anything.

But feel something he did. Whenever she set those blue-grey eyes on him. And every time he caught her staring… every time he'd seen her fidget. She was beguiling him and he had no idea why. Why should she hold any more appeal than the other mask-adorned women present?

When the two women finally reached him, he was rather put out that it wasn't she who spoke first.

'Mind if we join you?' the stunning blonde asked, in an overly flirtatious manner that set his teeth on edge. He had dealt with too many women like her in the past.

'Feel free.' He gestured to the single free chair which she sank onto, the slit in her dress falling open seductively. He fought the urge to roll his eyes. Instead, he offered up his own seat to the brunette, but before she could thank him the blonde interrupted.

'Lauren Brown,' she said, extending her hand. 'And this is my sister Emma.'

'Pleasure to meet you both.'

'Mmm…an English accent.' Lauren touched his arm. 'Are you new in town?' she continued.

'Fairly,' Alex replied with a forced smile.

'Well, why don't you ask me to dance and we can get better acquainted?'

Alex saw a muscle twitch in Emma's jaw and watched with fascination as she closed her eyes and took a deep breath. When she opened them he could tell she was visibly calmer. That was interesting.

'I think a dance is a lovely idea,' Alex replied. 'Emma, would you like to join me?' He fixed her with his penetrating stare, his hand outstretched, waiting.

Appearing to be completely shocked, she placed her hand in his. 'I would love to.'

Emma linked her arm with his as he led her to the dance floor. The last thing she noticed was the very sour look on her sister's face. There was nothing Emma could want that Lauren wouldn't have first.

She had no idea what music played as he swept her into his arms—she still could not believe that anyone would choose her over Lauren. That was definitely a first.

As his warm hand came to rest on her back she couldn't hold back the shiver that ran through her body. She moved effortlessly with him, almost as if she was magnetised to move with him. This was certainly an attraction she had never experienced before.

'I'm Alexander Hastings, by the way,' he said softly.

'I know. I think everyone in Melbourne knows. You've caused quite a stir.'

'Have I?'

He had. And it wasn't just because of his company. There were many pages and groups on social media dedicated to the appreciation of the thirty-two-year-old playboy billionaire, the son of an English Earl, and his good looks. In almost every picture he appeared with a different date. Every one of them tall, leggy. Polished. Now, being so close to him, she could see why.

She wanted to run her fingers over the stubble on his face, to kiss the sharpness of his jaw, to tug on the soft black hair cut in a short quiff. The look in the sky-blue eyes rimmed by thick dark lashes could set her aflame. It was both intense and predatory.

'I think you know you have.' She smiled.

'I do like the attention.'

He smirked, sliding his hand down to rest on the small of her back, pulling her closer and trapping her in his gaze. Never in her life had she wanted to be kissed so badly.

Alex watched as Emma bit her lip, and it made him want to take her right there in the middle of this ballroom. He valued control and she was making that slip.

'I think we should get a drink,' he said, breaking the spell.

Even to his own ears he could hear how low his voice had become. He plucked two flutes of champagne off a tray as a waiter walked by and led Emma out onto the pool terrace. She made a beeline for the railing, looking out at the city bathed in light against an inky sky.

'Isn't it beautiful?' There was a faraway look in her eyes.

'Unbelievably,' he said, looking down at her, and handed her a glass of the golden liquid.

A chill breeze blew, causing her to shiver slightly. He placed his own glass down and shrugged out of his jacket, draping it over her shoulders.

'Thank you.' She smiled.

That smile did things to him. How could he find her so mesmerising when he hadn't even seen all of her face yet?

Alex wanted to kiss her right then. It didn't matter that they were at a public event. It didn't matter that he had only known her for the better part of an hour. He would be gone by morning anyway.

'I love this city. Have you seen much of it?'

Emma's voice cut through his thoughts and he had to force himself back to reality.

'Not nearly enough,' he answered.

'Well, Alexander, maybe I'll show you around sometime.'

The promise caused a stirring in him. He joined her at the railing and never before had he so desperately wanted to leave a party with someone. The sparkle in her eye when she looked at him made him think that maybe she felt the same.

'Would you like to get a drink?' he asked.

'I thought we were having one right now.' She laughed— a musical chime.

'I was thinking about somewhere quieter with even better views.'

He bathed her in a crooked smile and Emma's stomach flipped. She wanted to taste that smile.

She had to bite down a giggle at the errant thought. She was usually cautious. She was never impulsive. But with his scent all around her, she was overwhelmed by his presence. Maybe it was time for a little fun.

'You know what? I'd love to.'

And there was that smile again.

They placed their glasses down on a nearby cocktail table and he led her out with his warm hand on the small of her back again. She felt the heat radiate through her.

On her way out, Emma caught the murderous look on Lauren's face and had to stifle an urge to laugh, feeling a crazy level of excitement.

Alex held open the door for her when they got down to the lobby, and they stepped out into the night air. Holding Emma's hand in his, he approached the valet and in no time at all a luxury black sedan pulled up in front of them. One of the sponsors for the night was a ride-share company, which had had all the guests driven to the venue. Emma was grateful. It allowed Alex to sit beside her after helping her in.

He gave the driver his address and Emma made to remove her mask. But he stopped her. 'Keep it on.'

Staring into his eyes, and seeing all the carnal promise they held, she let go of the ribbons keeping it in place. That smile was back as he gave her hand a squeeze and looked out of the window as the city lights flashed by on the way to his Port Melbourne penthouse. It gave her an opportunity to study his features without being seen.

Emma fought an urge to place her lips below his jaw. They were still in public, and she was nothing if not proper.

The car pulled up in front of his building and he held his hand out for her before shutting the door and leading her inside. Her heart thrummed in her chest when the doors to the elevator slid closed. Alex's arm wrapped around her waist, pulling her against his side, and his lips travelled along her neck. A sigh escaped her, and she felt as much as heard his chuckle.

A *ding* interrupted them, making her curse at how fast the elevator had ascended. With a cleared throat, and as much poise as she could muster, Emma followed him into his apartment.

CHAPTER THREE

THE WIND WAS knocked out of her. He really had been telling the truth. Emma didn't even notice the rest of the apartment. The floor-to-ceiling windows called to her.

The view was magnificent. She slipped off his jacket, draping it over a large couch she didn't even look at as she made her way to appreciate it. She could see the silver and gold lights of the ferry alongside the pier, all the way out to sea. Then she realised just how *much* she could see, and figured the glass panes must wrap all the way around the two-storey apartment.

The ceilings were high, and she could only imagine how much light filled the space during the day. She was surrounded by glass and steel. It was such an immaculately neat, modern space, but still warm and inviting, and for whatever reason, she felt this could not be a more perfect home for Alex.

Emma felt his presence behind her and turned around to see him pull off his black mask, which he placed on the large coffee table.

Seeing his face, she instantly thought none of the pictures she had seen did him a shred of justice. He was undoubtedly the most beautiful man she had ever seen.

Before she'd even registered the pull his eyes had on her he was already standing before her, his hands going to her hair. With a gentle tug on the ribbons, the bow fell away and the silver mask came loose.

'I wanted to do that all night,' Alex said.

He placed it beside his, and when he turned back to her a slow, delicious smile curved his mouth.

The thought that it should be criminal to look so good occurred to her. And right then all she wanted to do was to run her fingers along his lips.

Alex watched her gaze travel to his mouth, followed by the soft touch of her fingers. It was heaven. He caught her hand, pressing a kiss to the pads of her fingers before drawing one into his mouth. Her breath left her in a sigh and she closed her eyes, shutting away her blue-grey gaze. He realised he wanted them back on him. He playfully nipped at her finger and her eyes flew open as she tried to pull back. But he gripped her finger between his exposed teeth.

The look on her face was caught somewhere between amusement and arousal, but he was about to tip that balance.

His hand went to her waist, drawing her against his body, while the other travelled up her arm, settling on the nape of her neck. He let her fingers fall from his mouth and instantly her hands were on his chest. Feeling the hard muscle beneath his shirt.

Their gazes caught. A moment passed eternally between them, before he leaned down, brushing his lips over hers and pulling away. But she wouldn't let him. She closed the space between their bodies, pressing her lips to his, and he instantly tightened his grip around her.

The moment was incendiary. The kiss deep and passionate. His apartment was silent, but they could both hear the thunder of their heartbeats. The air between them was almost crackling with electricity.

And then they were moving.

He pushed her against the wall of glass, pressing his body to hers, entwining his tongue with hers. Setting her aflame. His hand left her waist and travelled up her arm to cradle her face. She kissed him as if he was all the air she needed. He felt her hands run down his body and she tore his shirt out of his trousers, plunging her hands under it, feeling his skin and the ripples of muscle.

His low groan at her touch surprised them both and he slowed his lips. Then pulled away.

The ferocity of what he felt surprised him. Alex had had many conquests in his life, but this was the first that had affected him so strongly from the first touch. He needed to create just a little space.

'I offered you a drink,' he said slowly, still holding her in place.

He couldn't seem to let go. The way the light caught her eyes and made them sparkle was arresting. He reached up and pulled the silver pins from her hair, sending locks of brunette hair tumbling around her shoulders. She was breathtaking.

She smiled coquettishly. 'I don't mind skipping that.'

Emma wondered who this person was wearing her skin tonight. She wasn't normally this brazen. She was a quiet, usually shy copywriter. But this new side of herself made her feel alive.

Alex chuckled and planted a quick kiss on her lips, but before she could respond he was walking away. 'What can I get you?' he asked as he pulled off his bowtie and tossed it on to one of the large couches.

'Surprise me.' She took a seat at the kitchen counter, watching him prepare their drinks. 'You're good. Ever been a barman?'

He laughed openly. 'No such luck. I've just learned how to make things I like.'

'Does that mean you can cook?' Emma watched him pour an amber drink into two crystal glasses filled with ice.

'Yes, but nothing terribly fancy.' He handed a glass to her before taking a sip from his own. 'Now, I think I promised you a view.'

He laced his fingers in hers, pulling her into an indoor elevator that ascended to a private rooftop terrace. If Emma had been captivated by the view from the inside, it was nothing compared to being up here. The Melbourne skyline sat twinkling behind her while the sea stretched before her.

'Wow,' she breathed. 'If I had this, I would never be inside. How are you not out here all the time?' Her eyes didn't leave the darkened horizon.

'Because I don't work where I play,' he replied easily.

She eyed the pool, casting a blue glow over the space, and somehow understood. 'You're all about rules, aren't you?' she asked.

'They keep life simple.'

Emma couldn't disagree with that. She took a sip of her drink. It was sweet and minty, and utterly delicious. 'I would never have had you pegged as a Stinger man.'

'You want to know a secret?' he asked.

She nodded her head.

'I prefer whisky, but it's always useful to try to impress a beautiful woman.'

Emma laughed. She didn't think he would need any tricks. He was perfectly capable of being impressive all by himself. 'I don't think you need to try very hard. That accent is sexy enough.'

'Is it?' A smile played on his lips.

'You know it is.'

It was turning out to be a much better night than she could have imagined. She felt so much lighter away from the masquerade. And even though she stood there drinking a delicious drink, still admiring an amazing view, nothing could take away the awareness of her body to Alex's proximity.

As if he had a direct line to her thoughts, he suggested they retreat indoors. He invited her to get comfortable on the large plush couch that was devoid of his tie. The crystal glass in his hand was tipped back, and he was draining the last of his drink and placing it on the glass coffee table with a clink. Then he undid the button at his throat and joined Emma on the couch.

He pulled the glass from her hand, setting it down on the table in front of them. Anticipation thrummed through her body. He slid his hand into her hair and pressed his lips against hers, then pulled away, then did it again. Light, teasing kisses were placed on her lips and jaw and neck, and when she tried to pull him back to her lips he was already there. Soft lips roving over hers. His tongue was teasing, seeking permission, and her lips parted for him. Emma could still taste the minty sweetness of his drink on him.

His kisses were a heady thing, and she could feel heat pooling in her centre. He was being so gentle, but then he slanted his head and it built the kiss to a whole new connection. Deep, passionate, consuming. And she was falling. Her fingers were grabbing fistfuls of his hair. Nails scraping against his scalp.

Alex moaned against her lips. He pressed his body against hers, pushing her down into the couch cushions. His hand slid along her body and hitched her leg up. He was pressing his hardness against her sex, making her moan out his name. His kisses became hungrier. Fervent. Her breath was already coming in short pants, and they were still fully clothed.

'Tell me what you want, Emma,' Alex said as he trailed hard, lustful kisses down her neck.

'You. All of you. More...' she panted.

His hand travelled over her shoulder, down her side,

where he found the zip of her dress and slowly, maddeningly, pulled it down. Swathes of blue satin parted. A shiver trembled through her as his warm hand ran over her bare skin. He kissed her shoulder as he pulled the strap of her dress down and she wanted to be free of the constricting thing. All she wanted was to feel Alex's lips on every inch of her.

Sensing her need, he reared up, sliding the dress off her, uncovering her body and dropping it to the floor in a pool of fabric.

Emma watched him unbuckle her silver stilettos. First one, then the other. Both shoes hit the hardwood floor with a clatter. And then he was kissing her again. Moving his mouth up her leg, his nose brushing over her covered sex, lips caressing her belly, her breasts, before finally his hand slipped under her and unclasped her bra. A giggle escaped her as he tossed it over his shoulder, not caring where it landed.

His mouth closed over her nipple, and she drew in a harsh breath. It was as if a taut line tugged at her centre, and she knew he was only going to build her tension up more. Drive her mad until his name was all she could say all night.

Long, skilled fingers played with the band of her panties before dipping under, running through her slickness, and he groaned. Before she even registered what was happening, her panties were off and on the floor and Alex's mouth was on hers, demanding and desperate. No one had ever kissed Emma as he did. As if she was all that existed. As if she had been made to drive him wild. But drive him wild she did.

Alex reached out and picked an ice cube from the glass that sat on the coffee table. 'Open,' he instructed gruffly, bringing it to her lips.

She obeyed without hesitation, sucking the cold block. Her gasp broke the silence as he took back the cube, leaving a cold, wet path in its wake as he trailed it from her lips and down her chest and around her nipples, which hardened instantly. Goosebumps erupted over her skin. A shudder passed through her.

And then he was moving the cube lower and lower, until she squealed as it touched the apex of her thighs. But his hot mouth was instantly on her neck, and the sensation between hot and cold was setting every nerve-ending alight.

Alex's mouth continued its sensual assault on her senses, and he was about to drop the cube on the table when she pulled his hand to her mouth, wrapping her lips around the now substantially smaller block.

His eyes were intense and then his mouth was on hers. Tongues entwined until he pulled the cube into his own mouth with a grin. Her laugh rang out. Emma had wanted fun and now here it was, dressed up as the devastatingly handsome Alexander Hastings.

She kissed him with abandon. Her tongue searching his mouth for the hidden ice cube. She took it back, but not for long. Alex showed her the ice cube, held between his teeth. There was a twinkle in his eye as he crushed it. Loudly. Telling her that he had had enough of being teased.

He settled himself at the foot of the large couch, taking her hips in his hands.

'Alexander…' she breathed, watching his head dip down. Feeling his cold mouth on her sex.

As her pants and moans filled the air, as her chest rose and fell with the sweet torture of Alex's tongue, it seemed he was enjoying this. That it pleasured him to pleasure her. This man was so completely different from anyone who had come before. Emma had always been a little shy, but by no means was she a prude. She enjoyed sex just as much as the next person, but in her short and somewhat sporadic dating history no one had ever set her world alight like this.

Careful, a voice within her warned. *This is just fun. One night. He's a playboy and you don't do relationships.*

Emma shut the voice down and gave herself over to the explosive sensations that were making it hard to breathe. Higher and higher she flew. Her peak was in sight. He held her tight, watching her run her fingers through her hair as she came apart.

He stretched along the back of the couch, pulling Emma into his arms. Holding her until she was able to catch her breath.

'Shall we take this to the bedroom?' he asked, brushing her hair away from her face.

'Yes.' She nodded.

He scooped her up into his arms and marched, barefoot, down the passage to his room. A big, plush, warm space that overlooked the sea on one side and the city on the other.

On any other night it would have been a view to marvel at, but now the only view she craved was Alex above her, and below her, and losing control because of her.

He sat her at the foot of his bed and gave her a quick, hard kiss.

'This is hardly fair,' she complained. 'You're still clothed.'

'Then do something about it,' he whispered into her ear, making something in her belly unfurl. How was he able to do that to her with just his voice?

The thought occurred to her simply to rip his shirt apart, but it was probably very expensive, and she would feel guilty, so instead she slowly unbuttoned the shirt from the bottom up, hoping she would drive him as insane as he did her.

The shirt parted, revealing his impossibly toned body. He really must live by rules, because that body would not be a possibility without discipline. Control.

She kissed his taut, rippling belly and moved to push his

shirt off his shoulders, but he held his arm out with a smile tugging at the corner of his lips. First one cuff was undone, then the other. Then the white shirt fluttered to the floor and Emma's hands were already pulling off his trousers. Tugging off his boxer briefs, which he kicked aside. Emma hadn't even noticed when he'd lost his socks and shoes.

Alex was magnificent. Everything about him was perfect. From his chest, to his voice, to his kisses, to his impressive hardness.

Emma wanted to taste him. Kiss him everywhere. With a wicked gleam in her eye, she licked all of him. The groan he let out was deep, almost animalistic. Spurred on by his reaction, she gripped his length, passing her hands over it a few times before taking him in her mouth.

'Emma...'

It was a strangled sound that ignited her blood. She twirled her tongue around his tip, teasing him. His strain and pleasure could be seen on his face and tensed muscles. What was happening to her? She was never this playful in bed. She felt...unleashed.

'Emma, I'd like to make love to you.' His voice was hoarse, gravelly. 'This feels too good.'

She wanted that too, so she let him pull away from her. Allowed him to press her down onto the pillows before he reached over and pulled a foil packet from the bedside drawer.

Her eyes were drawn to his shoulder blade. The very proper, very handsome Alex had a tattoo. She drew herself up behind him, her fingers going to the amazing ink work. It was a globe. A map of the world held in a gyroscope. The contrast of the black ink on his light skin was stunning.

She placed a kiss on it. 'This is beautiful.'

Alex kissed her sweetly. 'You're beautiful.'

He tore at the foil pouch and rolled the latex on. The moment he did Emma was there, pushing him down on his back. Straddling him. She lowered herself on to him with exquisite slowness, heard his breath released in a hiss.

Something about the way Alex looked at her made her feel brazen. In control. Even though he was making her world spin off its axis tonight. He let *her* lead. Let her use *him* for her pleasure. It was exhilarating.

Being with Alex made her realise just how lacklustre her previous experiences had been. It wasn't as if he was blowing her mind into orbit. No. Every touch, every groan, the feeling of him being inside her, his eyes never leaving hers, the fact that he never once bothered hiding his pleasure was pinning Emma to the moment. Forcing her to absorb every drop of pleasure.

But when the rhythm of her hips faltered, he rolled her onto her back and took back control.

Alex had always had more than his fair share of female attention. He'd never really had to try very hard, and he'd never seen the point of doing so. It was just a physical release, and every one of those women had understood that it would be for only a night, even if they wanted more. He liked it that way. *He* never wanted more, never missed them when they left.

But now there was Emma. And suddenly he couldn't imagine feeling this for only one night. She was a drug, and he'd been hooked from that first kiss.

His hips sank deeply into her. Ecstasy flowed through his veins with every thrust. He couldn't remember sex ever feeling this good.

'You're so damned amazing,' he breathed into her ear, and felt goosebumps erupt on her skin.

He kissed her long and slow, until he felt a coiling at the base of his spine, the tension in every corner of his body, like a guitar string pulled tight. Alex could feel Emma was near her peak. Clenching around him. Holding on. Climbing towards her *jouissance*.

'Emma…' he groaned.

He heard his voice come out breathless and tight, and it seemed to push her over the edge. Her head was thrown back in rapture as she came apart, and then he did too, growling into her neck. His release was violent, explosive. Unlike anything he'd felt before.

When his senses returned, Alex felt delicate lips kissing his shoulder. Soft hands caressing his back. And he wanted more.

He eased out, settling alongside her and wrapping an arm around her shoulders, pulling her close. Pressing a kiss to her hair.

'That was incredible,' she said.

'I'm not so sure,' Alex teased. 'We might need to try it again.'

She playfully smacked his chest and he caught her wrist, running his thumb over the simple black outline of a cat that was there.

'Didn't think you were the only one with a tattoo, did you?' she said.

'Why a cat?' he asked.

'Because it's Lucky,' she said, and then, seeing the look of confusion on his face, continued. 'Lucky is my cat. I got this when I rescued him. He's actually my first pet. Though I think I'm his most of the time.' Emma laughed. 'What about you?'

'I've never had a pet,' Alex stated blandly.

'Never?'

'No. There's a couple of Airedale Terriers at the family manor, but I hardly ever go back there.'

Alex caught himself before he said any more. He didn't understand why he was volunteering information about things he would never talk about usually. Things he liked to keep buried. Things that hurt to think about.

'But that's enough about that,' he said with a smirk, before rolling over her and silencing her with a kiss.

CHAPTER FOUR

EMMA AWOKE WITH the sun streaming in through the glass wall. The rays warmed her back as she lay ensconced in the soft sheets of a large bed. It took her a moment to register that she wasn't at home, and she bolted upright. Then the night came flooding back to her, and she couldn't help squeezing her thighs at the memory.

Of all the beautiful women at the ball, Alex had picked her. Her. She could still scarcely believe it.

Then she looked at the empty space beside her.

Alex was already up. Running her hands over the cool sheets, she thought he must have been for a while. And it was time to face reality. It had been one night, and that night was done. Alex had had his fun and so had she. Now she had to go back to being plain old Emma. Alone in her bubble—just the way she liked it.

Emma clambered out of bed and looked around for her clothes, then remembered that they'd littered the living room floor. Mercifully, Alex's shirt, discarded the night before, still lay on the carpet. Emma buttoned it up as she made her way to the en suite bathroom to freshen up as best she could before what could potentially be an embarrassing ride home.

Alex was tinkering around at the kitchen counter when Emma walked in. The entire space had been transformed.

In the day, his apartment was bright and airy. It seemed as if the sun danced off every surface. He felt his mouth dry. Blood rushing south so fast his head swam.

Seeing her in his shirt made him want to take her back to bed. This woman had a power over him that he didn't quite understand. Attraction and lust were familiar concepts to him. But what he felt with Emma was on an entirely different plane. It had made no sense to him last night and it still didn't. Seeing her now, in the light of day in his apartment, and knowing that she would leave soon, made an ache grow in the depths of him.

He wanted more of her. No. He *needed* more.

Alex had always considered his home his sanctuary. Whether it was London or Melbourne. He never invited women there, choosing instead to take them to hotels or opting to go home with them. That was a reminder of how temporary their dalliance was. He had all the power over when he would leave, and there would be no reminder of them afterwards.

He was very aware that he'd broken that rule last night. Even more confusing was the fact that it didn't bother him in the slightest.

'I made you coffee,' Alex said, handing a mug to her.

'Thank you.' Emma relished the aroma before taking a small sip. 'Where's yours?'

'Right here,' he said, holding up a teacup.

She couldn't help the chuckle that escaped her, but it didn't seem to bother him. He pinned his blue gaze on her as he drank, and she was putty all over again.

What the hell, Emma? Get it together! she mentally chastised herself.

To give herself somewhere else to look, she located all her missing garments.

'You know, I actually come down to the beach here every weekend,' she said as she picked her shoes off the floor.

'You do?'

'Yeah, I like taking a walk in the morning and then getting a coffee.' Emma ran her fingers through her hair, hoping to smooth it out into something presentable.

'I might have to join you the next time you do that.'

'You're welcome to.'

Her phone buzzed on the marble countertop. There were a few texts from Hannah, making sure Emma was still alive and berating her for not texting back. Emma quickly responded with an apology, telling her best friend that she was fine and asking after her cat. Lucky would be fine, if a little angry with her.

Her phone beeped in her hand. The message that came through immediately got her hackles up.

'Breakfast?' Alex offered.

He made it sound like something sinful, but Emma was still scowling at her phone. It was a text from Lauren, summoning her to their parents' too large home in Toorak. It was by no means a difficulty for her to go...it was just a lot further than she was willing to go after such a spectacular night.

Picturing Lauren's face in her mind, not to mention her father's, she knew she would be walking into a berating because Alex had chosen her. It didn't matter what lies Lauren had told her father—the actual reason for her fury was that. Lauren believed that she deserved every special thing. Good things weren't meant for Emma.

Lauren's hatred of Emma had started early. She was older and had become used to being favoured. That was until they had started school. Quiet and studious, Emma had impressed every one of her teachers. Something Lauren had not done. Emma had continued to impress everyone as they'd grown older. And so the put-downs had begun, and had followed her right into the family business where Lauren would not have Emma upstaging her in front of outsiders.

She was the eldest. She was meant to take over from their father. Unfortunately Emma was still expected to give her all to the company. It was her duty as a Brown to ensure that the company prospered even if she would never be given a fair chance there.

But today Emma was riding a wave of absolute bliss and she was just not ready to crash. And that was exactly what would happen if she left.

She closed her eyes and took a deep breath. She felt calmer when she opened them. And then she thought, why shouldn't she spend a little more time with Alex? Last night had been an eye-opening experience. The sex had been unreal...

Alex was watching her with curiosity. He should have been trying to get her out through the door, but if he was honest with himself he really wasn't trying to get rid of Emma at all. If anything, he was picturing her laid out on all the various surfaces in his penthouse.

'You know what, Alexander? I'd love breakfast.'

His smile stole her breath, and she knew she'd made the right choice.

He took her clothes from her hand and dropped them to the floor. Her shoes clattered loudly in the silent space. Was it really silent? Because Alex clearly remembered switching on music, just as he did every morning. But he didn't hear it now. Emma was biting her lip, and that was all he could focus on.

'I really like the way you look in my shirt, but I think I like it off you more.'

Then his fingers were deftly undoing the buttons, pushing it off her shoulders. He brushed his mouth over the

smooth skin and heard her breath hitch. The shirt fluttered
to the floor and he lifted her up, placing her on the marble
countertop. A gasp left her lips as her warm skin made
contact with the cool surface, but his lips and hands were
already on her, to chase the chill away and make her burn.

He ran his tongue along her lips and felt her shiver.
Deepening the kiss, he pushed her down against the marble. Alex wanted to take his time with her. Enjoy this while
it lasted. Because in a few short hours she would be gone
from his life.

Except he couldn't take his time.

Laid out on the marble top, she made him hunger in a
primal way. He feasted on her, making her writhe and pant
until she was a mass of quivering need.

'So beautiful,' he said gruffly against her skin.

His praise made Emma feel as if she was flying. It was
easy to see why he was never short on female company.
She was just another conquest in a life full of them. The
thought burned like acid. Would she be forgettable to him?
Emma wanted fun. No strings. But she also wanted someone to think that she was special.

Emma pushed the thoughts away, focussing on how good
he made her feel. His mouth closed over her breast and
she didn't have to try very hard. Her fingers sank into his
soft dark hair, holding him in place. His tongue was sending bolts of pure pleasure right to her core. Alex covered
her hands with his, pulling them away and pinning them
against the counter before his lips sought hers once more.

'Alexander, please…' she whimpered. Whose voice was
that? It certainly wasn't hers.

'Please what?' he taunted.

She tried to press her body to his in any way she could.

His dark, teasing chuckle reached her ears and the sound
of ripping foil brought her back. She realised that he no

longer had her hands pinned down. She tried to push herself up on her elbows, but he put a hand on her shoulder to keep her down and slowly pushed into her. Her eyes fluttered closed and he stopped.

'Eyes on me,' Alex said breathlessly.

His blue eyes were so much darker. His pupils blown out. Emma felt the breath leave her. Then he began moving his hips.

His hand was moving up to her neck, his thumb caressing her lips. Emma pulled his thumb into her mouth, sucking it. Twirling her tongue around the digit. Making him groan her name. It was beyond erotic to watch what he was doing to her as he was setting her world alight.

She could feel herself drawing closer to the precipice. And then she was exploding around him, taking them both over the edge.

They needed more than just a few moments to catch their breaths.

'Screw breakfast,' Alex said, once they had.

She laughed as he led her back to his room. Being with him was drugging, and she just couldn't have enough of him.

CHAPTER FIVE

IT WAS QUITE a while before either of them was ready to surface for sustenance. But eventually, shirtless, with his trousers hanging off his hips in the most delicious way, Alex led the way to the kitchen.

Unfortunately, the fridge was mostly bare.

'Sorry, my housekeeper hasn't been in yet.' He closed the fridge door and turned around, drawing Emma into his arms. 'How about I take you up on your promise to show me around Melbourne?'

Emma wasn't sure she wanted to traipse around the city in her clothes from the ball. But she definitely didn't want to take Alex home with her, where Hannah would be waiting with a million questions. This was just a moment of pleasure. She should leave. The problem was that having his hands on her drove an insatiable hunger for him. And a bit of air would be good. Some space for them to collect themselves.

'I'd love to, but I can't exactly wear what I have here to go sightseeing.'

'That's easily fixed.' Alex pulled his phone out of his back pocket and after a series of rapid-fire taps slipped it back in. 'All taken care of.'

'Alexander...' she scolded.

'Emma...'

The way he said her name was a caress. Like silk over her skin.

'If you keep looking at me like that,' he said, 'I'm going to have to keep you here and we'll both starve.'

His words made her want to combust. The fact that she was affecting him like this made her feel seen in a way she hadn't ever been before. But, as much as she wanted to spend the day in his bed, she hadn't eaten anything at the ball and was well and truly ravenous.

'Why don't you go and take a shower and we'll get going soon?' he said.

'Okay.'

Emma stepped under the spray in Alex's ultra-large bathroom, a little disappointed that he hadn't chosen to join her. She could think of so many things he might do with the shower head that was hooked on the wall…

She shook her head. When had she become this person? Emma didn't date much. Her parents' marriage was more than enough of a warning against the entire institution, and when she had once found someone she genuinely liked he had chosen Lauren over her. Of course he was old news to both of them now. But the pain of that still stung. No one had ever chosen her over Lauren. Not until last night, that was.

Alex made her feel renewed. And if that made her a little greedy for his particular brand of sex, then she was all for it. She wasn't looking for love, and it was obvious that neither was he.

Emma turned the water off and pulled two fluffy towels off the rack, wrapping her hair in one and the other around her body. She padded out to the lounge, where she found him relaxing on the couch with his phone in his hand, looking far better than anyone had the right to in a pair of dark wash jeans and a Henley shirt. His aviator sunglasses were hanging off the neck of his top. His hair was still damp.

She would never understand how men were able to be ready in a few short minutes.

He looked up from his phone and his expression went from one of concentration to one of pure hunger. It made her squirm where she stood.

Then Alex picked up the bag beside him and walked over to her, dropping the handles into her hand. He smelled like shampoo and something woodsy. Spicy...

'Thank you,' she said. Her voice barely came out at all. She cleared her throat and tried again. 'I'll just get changed.'

She dashed back into his room, finding jeans, a shirt and sneakers in the bag. She dressed quickly and brushed out her damp hair in the bathroom, then rushed out so she wouldn't keep him waiting any longer.

'I don't know how you managed to get my size right.' She laughed.

His smile was wicked. 'I undressed you, remember?'

Her face burned. How could she forget?

'Shall we?'

She nodded and walked with him out of his apartment. When they entered the lift she stood away from him. His proximity was a danger to her libido. She saw his smile and knew that she was being glaringly obvious.

'This way,' he said, walking towards a pearlescent white Porsche SUV.

It looked faster than it had any right to, being so large. From the lip over the rear windscreen to the low tyres, with bright red peeking through black-spoked wheels, the whole thing screamed speed.

'So you're an SUV person?' Emma observed.

'I'm nothing if not practical.'

'Practical?' She laughed. 'Is that another rule? It can be big as long as it's fast?'

His grin was infectious. 'Almost right. It can be mine as long as it's fast.'

Emma barked out a laugh and it felt great. Being around Alex made her feel lighter. It also made it harder for her to breathe. Especially when he smiled like that and it lit up his face. Like the sun coming out on a cloudy day.

Alex, charming her with his chivalrous manners, opened the door for her—something no one had ever done for her before, not even her father. Although he would always show that courtesy to Lauren and Maddison.

She didn't know why it surprised her coming from Alex. Maybe it was because he had the air of a caged animal just waiting to be set free.

He eased the car out of the parking structure and onto the road. Emma kept shooting covert looks at him. His long fingers were gripping the steering wheel loosely. Those shades were hiding the eyes that had made her come apart this morning. Being in a car with him felt like being trapped in a stifling heat that she both wanted to escape and never leave.

He seemed so in control. He *always* seemed in control. Even when he let her take the lead in the bedroom. But Emma didn't mind, because his competence felt really damned good.

He looked over at her and a slow smile spread across his face. The air in the car became suddenly thicker. As if he could tell exactly how affected she was, his smile grew into a grin.

But before she knew it they were parked, and he had come round to her door holding it open for her.

'I thought Fed Square would be a good start,' he said.

Emma's fingers twitched towards him. She shoved them in the pockets of her jeans to stop herself reaching out. 'I agree.'

It was a place she had come to often. After a long day battling her family, it felt great just to be a nameless face in the crowd, sipping a cocktail while the sun disappeared behind the tall buildings.

She doubted today would be nearly as relaxing. Having Alex walking beside her, she felt hyper-aware of his presence. Of the space between them and how easy it would be to close it. But she couldn't. She didn't even know what she was doing here. Her night of fun had turned into a morning of fun, but at some point they would have to bid each other farewell and go their separate ways.

That was what should happen. But, heaven help her, that was not what she wanted.

Alex let her lead the way to a restaurant she liked. They were soon shown to a table and he sat down opposite her.

'So, what are we having?' he asked, picking up the menu.

Emma had no idea. She was struggling to have the words make any sense at all. When the waiter arrived, she randomly picked something and hoped it would at least taste good.

Looking for something to fill the silence in the waiter's absence, Emma spoke of all the attractions the city had to offer. It sounded like rambling to her own ears, though Alex seemed to be getting caught up in her passion for this city.

She was overjoyed when her phone beeped with a new message.

What do you think you're doing?! You were supposed to be here hours ago!

Lauren. The smile was wiped off Emma's face immediately. Hastily she shoved the phone into her back pocket and found Alex's intense blue gaze on hers. She plastered a bright smile on her face, but he wasn't fooled.

'Just my sister,' she said dismissively.

Alex had been cursing himself for suggesting they come out at all, because all he wanted was to be buried in Emma again—and that was a problem. He'd never had an issue sending a woman on her way after a night together. Yet he was craving Emma like a drug.

And right now he was still curious about the reaction she'd had to her sister at the ball, and again to her message that morning. He felt curiosity and another feeling he realised was a protective instinct. He'd noticed how her shoulders had sagged just a fraction when she'd read that text, and he wanted to put himself between her and whoever wanted to hurt her. Shield this beautiful, passionate woman.

It was an alien feeling that he pushed away with great difficulty, focussing on the curiosity. But Alex wouldn't ask her about it. As a rule, he never involved himself in the lives of the women he slept with. Never helped with their careers—even if he could. There was a solid line between business and pleasure. And an even thicker one between any kind of pleasure and actual feelings. He would not give them the wrong idea, and the last thing he needed was a relationship.

But what he did want was to enjoy Emma a little more, and if he was going to see this attraction out he needed to know more about her.

Being who he was, Alex was careful. 'So tell me, Emma, what do you do at Brown Hughs?' he asked.

Emma's momentary shock was covered by a small laugh. Of course he knew where she worked. He was rich and powerful. There was probably an entire background check on her already compiled.

'I'm a copywriter.' She said the words stiffly.

'Doesn't sound like you enjoy it.'

He was far too observant for Emma's liking.

'I feel like I can do so much more than I am, but my dad says I'm needed in copywriting so that's where I'll be. He's the boss.'

Unfortunately for Emma, having her father at the head of the table had not helped further her career, as it had for Lauren or Maddison. She could still hear his words, spoken so long ago. *'Everyone tells me you're intelligent, but I just don't see it.'*

Emma forced the memory away, not wanting it to spoil what was a pretty mind-blowing morning.

'If you want more, Emma, then take it,' Alex said.

'Spoken like a master of the universe. Is that what you're doing in Melbourne? Taking more?'

And running from ghosts.

He shut the thought down instantly.

He was done with London.

He wasn't going to think of his mother. Not now.

'Yes. Hastings International has a very long history. It started after the war, to rebuild, but in all those years its potential has never been maximised. No growth further than Europe.'

'And that's what you want to do? Grow it?' Emma asked.

'Yes. I want to see it on every continent.'

She smiled. 'Something tells me you'll do it.'

'Without doubt.'

Alex winked. His passion was contagious, Emma thought. Everything about him seemed so deliberate. So intense. It was as if he blotted out everyone else because he was the sun, and Emma ached to burn.

Alex leaned forward. 'Tell me...' he said. 'Why do your sister's texts get under your skin?'

Emma had hoped that she was being at least a little successful at hiding her irritation. Clearly she wasn't. She debated how she should answer. There was no way she was going to tell him how much she envied the love and attention Lauren received. Nor would she tell him how much Lauren detested her. In the end she settled for an edited truth.

'We have a bit of a love-hate relationship,' Emma said lightly. 'My mother should have dealt with it—I'm sure you know what that's like.'

She was certain that Lauren wouldn't have listened to her mother, though, and once she'd involved her father, her mother would have backed down anyway.

'Not really. I don't have a mother,' he replied.

Emma's cheeks flamed red. 'Oh! I'm sorry! I didn't mean to be insensitive.'

Alex seemed to realise what he'd just shared and brushed it off. 'Don't worry about it—really.'

Their meals were served and the awkward moment was quickly forgotten. Especially when Alex noticed a little drop of cream at the corner of her mouth. He wiped it off with his finger and she felt her heart stutter as he licked it clean. She could feel the burn in her cheeks.

'Was that good?' she asked, somewhat breathily.

'Yes,' he said. And then he leaned closer and whispered, 'But you taste better.'

A shudder passed through her. They needed to leave before they were arrested for public indecency.

Once they were finished Alex paid, despite Emma's protests. He knew there was still something he needed to make clear.

'Emma, I need to be honest with you. I don't do relationships. I do simple, and fun, and then it's over.'

He held his breath, waiting for an embarrassing explosion that never came. Alex firmly believed that love was for fools. It simply didn't exist. Lust was real. Tangible. Something that was irrefutable and then, once indulged, gone. A fleeting thing that made sense.

'That's good, because neither do I. I like simple. Simple is good,' she replied.

'In that case, Miss Brown, lead the way.'

They left the restaurant and Alex noticed Emma sliding her hands into her pockets again. He wanted to yank them out and place them around him. Wanted to wrap his arm around her as their feet swallowed up the ground underneath them.

He couldn't do that. She was affecting his sensibility. But that wasn't the person he was, and he wouldn't give her any hope that he could be. So he widened the gap between their bodies.

And immediately regretted it.

This was actual torment. He tried to seem laid-back, but felt his body pulled taut like a bowstring.

They went to watch the yachts and boats on the Yarra—or at least tried to. They stood so close together that he could feel Emma's heat. His arms ached to slide around her as they leaned on a concrete balustrade. But he couldn't touch her after what he'd just said to her. Not out here. Not when that would make it seem as if they were some sort of couple.

Emma couldn't know that his hands were clasped so firmly together so that he wouldn't be tempted to kiss her in front of all of Melbourne. Tempted to make her moan out his name with the city before them, making it theirs. He pushed off the rail. They had to keep moving. He had to get himself under control.

Alex pushed his sunglasses high up on the bridge of his nose, taking a last look at the river. It was a reminder of all the loves he'd found and indulged by himself. Alone. He was better off that way.

Emma took them on a walk through Alexandra Gardens and past the Arts Centre, but as they made their way back towards the city he was barely paying attention to where they were. All he could feel was Emma's presence, and all he wanted was to be back in his apartment, where his hands could be all over her.

He could bear it no more.

'Emma,' he said, pinning her against the wall in a spectacularly graffitied alley, where the walls were an ever-changing work of art. 'I have to tell you I really don't care about seeing the city. I just want to get you back in my bed.'

He could barely believe that he wanted to take her back home. Sending her on her way was the smarter plan. But how smart was it to deny himself? Emma knew the score. This wasn't about feelings or a relationship. It was just sex.

'Give me the weekend,' he said. 'I promise you won't regret it.'

He heard his voice, low and rough. He could see in her eyes that she knew just how aroused he was. And, with his body against hers, that she could feel it.

'I want that too,' she breathed.

'What I said before still stands. This doesn't change things.'

'I know that.' She grinned. 'I don't want it to.'

His lips crashed down on hers. The moment they were on her it was as if he was breathing again. Living again. Flying again. His hands were underneath her shirt, sliding under the waistband of her jeans. Squeezing her butt.

'These things have been driving me nuts all day,' he growled in her ear. And she laughed.

Voices grew closer and reluctantly Alex pulled away from her, not sure if that kiss had taken the edge off or made him thirst for her even more.

CHAPTER SIX

THEY BARELY MADE it into his apartment before their hands were all over each other and they were leaving a trail of shed clothes to his couch. Afterwards, they lay together, catching their breath and enjoying the feeling of being close.

In an unguarded moment, Alex wondered why such a vibrant woman didn't want a relationship. In his experience all women did. Even the ones who knew they would never get it from him but still hoped they might be the one to change his mind. His mind couldn't be changed. He had seen what the illusion of love could do to a person, and he had no intention of turning into his father.

With Emma it was different. But what could have happened to her for her to be as cynical as him?

The feeling of gentle fingers tracing patterns on his chest put an end to his thoughts. It felt as if her touch left a trail of fire on his skin.

Alex lifted her fingers to his lips, pressing a kiss to the soft pads. He opened his eyes and found her gaze on him. His heart stuttered. Her lips were rosy and full from his fevered kisses. The scent of his body still lingered on her skin. It surprised him how much he liked that. To have marked her as his to enjoy. The possessiveness alarmed him.

Alex pulled away to try to break the spell—only he couldn't leave. The electricity between them hauled him back.

Emma's fingers threaded through his hair, tugging him towards her. She kissed him, trapping his lip between her teeth. Giving him a little nip that walked the fine line between pleasure and pain.

'Witch,' he growled, and she laughed with wicked delight.

The ringing of his phone pierced through the moment, vibrating loudly on the glass table. Alex ignored it, sliding his tongue over hers. The phone wouldn't stop.

'You should get that,' said Emma.

'They can call back.' His voice was like gravel.

Still the phone kept going, until he picked it up with a frustrated sigh. He pressed the button on the side, silencing the device even as he registered the name on the screen. Feeling a niggle of guilt, he tossed it back onto the table, trying to remember a time when he had ever ignored his father's call.

Alex loved and admired his father, but Robert Hastings could hardly complain about being ignored. Not after the way Alex had grown up.

He dropped a steel shutter on those thoughts. He wasn't going there now. Not when he had a beautiful woman in his arms.

'Now, where were we…?'

Emma could see that the playful twinkle in his eye had been replaced by a harder look. A haunted one. She wanted to ask about it, but then it occurred to her that it really wasn't any of her business. Asking about his feelings wasn't keeping things simple. She doubted he would tell her anyway. Still, she wanted to make it better somehow, and there was one way she knew she could.

'Somewhere around here…' Her lips found his once more.

The sun had gone down and the bedcovers were carelessly tossed over Emma's bare back. Alex sat against the headboard, an arm draped over a raised knee, gazing down at her porcelain skin. Wanting to kiss every freckle.

What are you doing, Hastings? he asked himself.

He wanted to have another day with her tomorrow. And it didn't seem as if it would be enough.

Alex swung his legs off the bed, too much on edge to get any sleep. Work was always a welcome distraction. Pulling on his jeans and shrugging his shirt back on, he picked his phone off the nightstand and quietly left his room.

After pouring a measure of whisky into a glass, he replaced the stopper on the crystal decanter, setting it back on the bar, and stood by the large window overlooking the sea.

The shrill cry of his phone punctured the silence. He answered quickly, and the screen filled with his father's face.

'Dad.' Alex placed his glass down on the coffee table and eased himself onto the couch upon which, a few short hours before, he'd had Emma panting his name.

He shoved the image aside.

'Alex. How are you, son?' asked his father.

Judging by the dark wood bookshelves behind him, it looked as if he was in his study at the family manor Alex so rarely visited.

'I'm well. Looks like you've taken a trip.'

'A bit of country air does you a world of good.'

'So you always say.' Alex smiled.

'I do.' Robert chuckled. 'Besides, there was a soirée…' he rolled his eyes at the word '…that I just did not have the patience for. A bit of peace and quiet is what I need.'

Alex knew what that meant. His mother Catherine would have been there. That was the only reason his father would miss a society event that would have undoubtedly required his presence.

'We are the Hastings family. We have obligations we cannot turn our backs on,' he had said to Alex when he was growing up.

His mother was the only reason his father would have ignored such a commitment. But Robert would never want to speak of it, so neither would Alex.

'I know why you called,' he said. 'I've been looking through the reports. My projections for the Australian expansion are on track.'

'That's what I like to hear.'

Alex and his father had always had a cordial relationship, if a somewhat stiff one. It was just the two of them. A team. Even though as a child he'd sometimes felt like the benched teammate. That hadn't stopped him from growing into his power. He knew where his father's boundaries lay, and Robert trusted his son immensely. So much so that when Robert had stepped down, there was no question of who would take his place with the family legacy.

Even though he didn't need to, Alex liked keeping his father included in the running of Hastings International. It was a company that dealt with major construction, engineering and architecture amongst other things. A company meant to build, not tear down. He could tell Robert appreciated it, and discussing business felt good.

It was a bit of normality after being trapped in a lust-filled haze. And yet even though this was what he lived for, Alex wanted nothing more than to end the call, march back into his bedroom, strip the covers from Emma and take her again. Alex was always in control. Never ruled by his hormones. He valued logic over emotion, and it was driving him insane that when it came to Emma he seemed to be a slave to his baser urges.

Alex was about to end the call, but his father stopped him. 'Before you go…are you okay, Alex?'

'Fine. Why?'

'I get the feeling you have something on your mind,' his father said.

Alex ran a hand through his hair. 'There's a risky proposition on the table. I'm debating the merits of pursuing it,' he said.

He had no intention of explaining that the proposition was Emma.

'Son, the bigger the risk, the bigger the reward.'

'Not always,' he said under his breath.

His father clearly knew he was talking about something else.

'No, not always,' he said. 'And that's why it's a risk. But you're a lot more careful than I was at your age, Alex. Trust your gut. You'll figure it out.'

Alex ended the call and tossed his phone onto the couch cushions. He swallowed his whisky in one, relishing the burn at the back of his throat. He had to figure this out—because he wasn't going to end up being an old man sitting in his study, hiding.

No one would get the better of him. He wouldn't allow it.

Dawn was breaking. It was Monday, and still they hadn't had enough of each other. With each kiss the spark didn't die. It didn't even fizzle. It just kept burning brighter. But the weekend was over and the sun was rising on the end of their tryst.

A delicate kiss on Emma's neck had a smile curving her lips. Alex rolled her onto her back and kissed her slowly, completely. His hand ran down her arm and disappeared under the dark sheets. Teasingly, lightly, he moved it over the smooth skin of her belly and over her sex. She arched into the touch. Her fingers fisted in his hair as she moaned into his mouth.

His hands were such sweet torment. Pulling her apart and piecing her together. With her eyes closed and his lips everywhere, and the promise of blissful rapture dangling in front of her, Emma could barely breathe. She couldn't remember where she was. She didn't even remember her name. All she knew right now was Alex. His touch. His smell. His strong arms that felt far too safe for her sanity. She was trying to hold on to all of it. Every sensation. Commit it all to memory.

'Emma,' he whispered in her ear, 'let go.'

And she did. Shattering with a muffled sob.

His lips came to hers, kissing her until she came back to him. 'Hey…'

He smiled with that megawatt beam. It made her stomach flutter. With an intense look in his blue eyes, he brushed her hair away from her face.

Emma felt like the person she wanted to be when she was with him. Bold and strong. Feelings she often had to keep tethered. But she didn't need to with Alex. There were no expectations. No risk of her disappointing him because that wasn't what this was about.

This was a break from reality. From everything she was expected to be and couldn't live up to. But now it was over. So she would go back to being alone and having no one but Hannah and her cat.

'Emma,' Alex said evenly. 'I want more than a weekend. Nothing has changed. I just want more of you.'

That screamed danger to Emma. More time with Alex was beyond appealing. She hadn't ever experienced this chemistry with anyone on her short list of previous lovers. Looking back, it felt as if all those affairs were in black and white and now she was seeing in splendid Technicolor.

'Alexander…'

'Please.'

'I want more too,' she said, abandoning all good sense.

Why shouldn't she have a bit of fun? Emma always did the right thing. What was expected of her. What everyone else wanted. Well, now she wanted Alex, and the world would just have to continue without her because she was due some happiness.

The words had barely left her lips when Alex swooped down, claiming her. Branding her. His tongue slid over hers, dominating her. It wasn't a gentle kiss. It was a kiss of possession. Of pure want and desperate need. He swallowed Emma's moan and then had to tear his lips away from hers, smirking at her mewl of protest.

Alex kept his intent blue gaze fixed on Emma's as he brought his phone to his ear. She could only just make out a woman's voice on the other end.

'Reschedule my meetings,' he said, without a greeting.

Emma squirmed as his eyes darkened, pinning her in place.

'I don't care. The board can wait. Something's come up.' He ended the call and placed his phone down.

With limbs that felt like lead, Emma fired a text off to the only person she needed to—her manager, Greg. Emma was a Brown, and for once she was going to take advantage of the liberties her name brought her. To hell with what anyone thought. She was living for herself right now and it was liberating.

Her phone slipped through her fingers onto the bedding as Alex's fingers slid into her hair, tilting her face up to meet his.

'You're all mine.'

The words set her on fire.

CHAPTER SEVEN

EMMA WOKE TO find herself alone in bed. After Alex had shown her exactly how pleased he was that she'd agreed to spend a little more time with him, loose-limbed and fabulously exhausted, she had dozed off.

She could hear the shower running. Surprising Alex under the jets was too tempting to resist. She threw off the covers, but her phone buzzed against the bedside table. Emma had no intention of answering it, but then she caught the name on the screen. It was Maddison.

Where are you? Dad's fuming.

Emma didn't know why. There were no urgent meetings that required her to be there. Nothing at all going on that would make her father notice her presence. Or rather absence. He barely acknowledged her existence anyway. Everyone was well aware that, despite how hard Emma had worked earning her degrees, and the hours she put in at the office, she wasn't the daughter he intended for the C Suite. All his talk of her 'duty' was just to make sure she would do what he needed her to without question and would stay out of his hair. Because no matter what Emma did, her father would always make her feel like a burden.

Emma wasn't going to respond, but she saw the three little dots that told her Maddie was typing another message.

Actually, don't tell me where you are. Can't say anything if I don't know. Can't believe you ditched! Video call in ten. There's an announcement.

Emma groaned. There had been talk all week of this 'announcement', but no one in her family seemed to want to make it. Until now. Dread settled like lead in her belly.

Emma scooped up her clothes off the floor, quickly changing into her jeans and rushing out of the bedroom. Slipping into the other bathroom, she made sure she looked presentable before taking a seat at Alex's large dining table, which seated twelve. It was a quiet space that they hadn't once used. Idly she wondered if he had it there just to fill what would otherwise have been an empty space. But thoughts of Alex's social life were wiped from her mind the moment her phone began to ring.

Whatever they were going to say, Emma was determined not to react. Fixing in place the mask of indifference she often wore at work, she answered the call.

Her father sat at the head of his meeting table, with his business partner to his right and her mother to his left. Maddison sat beside her, with Lauren opposite and the head of HR taking the final occupied seat.

'Good day, everyone,' Emma greeted.

Anxiety bloomed in her chest. She could handle herself at work without batting an eyelid. It was what she'd spent so many years studying for. To prepare herself to one day lead the company in some way. The problem was that no matter how hard she tried to separate the two, her family life was inextricably woven in with her work life. She would never be able to escape that, and now, looking at her father, she felt her confidence waver.

'Emma,' her father said.

Peter Brown was a large man with greying temples and dark hair. He had cunning hazel eyes that, despite their colour, held little warmth. They simmered with anger now. A look she had often seen directed at her mother during their blazing rows. But the one thing his treatment of Emma had done was make her strong. So now she could hold her phone in her hand and appear to all that she was unaffected by him.

'We have an announcement to make, and we need you to stand beside your sisters tomorrow when we do.'

'Okay…' Emma said hesitantly, unsure of what was coming. She just knew she wouldn't like it.

Alex shut off the taps and left the en suite bathroom. He smiled inwardly at the disappointment of finding the bed empty. Shaking his head, he opened the closet door to get out a set of clean clothes. That was when he heard Emma's voice, and another. She was on a call, by the sounds of it. Nothing unusual about that, except something made his skin prickle.

Dressing quickly, he followed the sound of her voice to find her at the dining table. A little vertical line had formed on her forehead between her furrowed brows as she listened attentively, not noticing his presence in the doorway.

Alex knew he should be giving her a bit of privacy. After all, he never appreciated being eavesdropped on. But something about the way she sat, so stiffly, and the way her voice tried to show no emotion at all kept him in that doorway. Watching.

'We have taken the decision to move Lauren up to be VP of Services…'

Emma clenched her jaw as her father spoke, remaining silent.

'…and Maddison will be taking her place.'

'So Maddison is now my boss's boss?'

Emma hadn't meant for the words to sound as sharp as

they had. Especially when Maddison shot her an apologetic look. But it hurt. Again. Her younger sister, less qualified and less experienced, was now soaring far higher than her in the career stakes.

Part of her was happy that Maddison was getting some recognition for the work she'd put in, but the biggest part of her saw this for what it was. Evidence that her sisters would always be chosen over her, no matter what she did to prove herself to her father.

'Yes. Can we count on you to do your duty to this family?'

Hearing her father ask the question crushed her. After everything she had done, she'd hoped her commitment to her family, to the company, would never be in question. Seemed she was wrong.

'Of course. I will always do what the company needs me to. Tell me what to do and I'll do it,' Emma said. 'I just have one question. How did the vote go?'

'It was unanimous, darling,' her mother said.

Unanimous. She should have expected it. 'I see.'

Emma managed to keep her voice steady as she tried to quell the crushing disappointment that was ripping at her insides. That one word meant that even her mother, whom Emma had always been close to, had chosen Maddison.

It was no real surprise, if Emma was truly honest with herself. Internally, she was glad that for once she'd decided to do something that made her happy. Any tiny trace of the guilt she'd felt when she'd agreed to spend more time with Alex vanished.

'That's it. Your mother can give you the details.'

Her father was already closing his leather folder. Emma knew when she was being dismissed. She took no notice of the two people who were not her family as she bade them a cordial goodbye. At the table, though, her nails were leaving crescent-shaped marks in her palms. The pain of her clenched fists helped her keep the mask of professionalism in place.

As soon as the call was over, the mask slipped completely. She dropped the phone to the tabletop and ran her fingers through her hair. Closing her eyes, she willed herself to feel calmer.

It didn't last a moment.

Her phone rang almost immediately. It was her mother.

Emma hit the red button. She absolutely did not want to speak to her. Not when she had listened to Emma's frustrations, told her to hang in there, that her time was coming. Lies.

It rang again. This time it was Maddison. Her call met the same fate. Emma wasn't upset at Maddison. The only thing she was guilty of was being just a little spoilt, but she was the youngest. It was to be expected. And Emma was guilty of doting on her too. She just couldn't bear to speak to any of her family.

Why should I be upset? she asked herself.

She had known this was coming. That there would be a time when Lauren and Maddison would flourish from their parents' favour and she would languish in a little corner of the company where her father would never have to be bothered by her.

She couldn't leave either. Peter and Helen Brown both expected their daughters to work in the company. Leaving would be the ultimate slap in the face to her parents. There was still an expectation of her that she could never be free of.

'Emma?'

Her head snapped up at the sound of Alex's voice. 'Alexander... I hope you don't mind... I needed a quiet place to take a call.'

He strode towards her, taking a seat at the large table. His eyes were unreadable. 'What's wrong?'

'Nothing.' She forced a brittle smile.

'Emma,' he pushed. 'Talk to me.'

She looked into his eyes. They were intense. Unrelenting. And suddenly she wanted to tell him everything. Tell him about all the ways her family had hurt her. This was just sex, after all. She could say anything to him. Because at the end they were just going to walk away. Every secret would be safe because it would mean nothing to a stranger.

Emma closed her eyes and took a deep breath, feeling more in control when she opened them.

'It's just that I thought if I proved myself, studied hard and worked my way up, I could *be* someone in the company. I never once expected just to walk into a management job. I was prepared to work hard for it. But the same doesn't apply to my sisters. Lauren was pretty much gifted her position, and Maddison now has been too. Do you know how humiliating it is to constantly get passed over for promotion after promotion in your own father's company? I'm stuck as a copywriter because apparently that's where I'm needed and I should do it out of duty.'

'Duty' was just a nice word for the expectations forced upon all three of the Brown daughters. Lauren and Maddison relished their roles. Emma was alone in her feeling of being trapped. She had one shining light in her life with her charity work, but even that was frowned upon by her father. Money always came first.

'Duty doesn't fulfil you,' Alex said.

'No, it doesn't. But what choice do I have? I am who I am.'

Emma thought about the massive house her parents owned and the tiny flat that she'd bought and now shared with Hannah. She thought about the luxury cars her family had and the sporty little hatchback she owned. Who was she really? Yes, she was a Brown, but she had been trying to distance her life from her family for a long time. To escape the hate and the vitriol.

'Anyway, it doesn't matter. I knew it would come to this.'

'Why?'

Emma roughly pushed out her chair and stood by the window. With her back to him, she could hide the tortured expression on her face. Only Hannah truly knew what growing up had been like for her.

When she spoke her voice was even. Emotionless. She saw Alex frown. 'Because Lauren was always preferred over me. In every way. My father adores her. I tried to prove myself to him, but the only people I impressed were the ones who would never have any say in my life. Maybe I remind him too much of my mother. God knows, he hates her.'

She gazed out into the distance. The sea was so tranquil. Focussing on that made talking easier. She felt Alex move behind her, but he didn't touch her. He was waiting for her to finish what she had to say.

'My parents had Maddison to fix the cracks in their marriage. They were more like gaping chasms.' She laughed without mirth. 'My father was opposed to the idea initially, but when Maddie almost died during the birth, it changed his attitude. He'd almost lost her.' She finally turned around and looked into those intense blue eyes. 'So, you see, I can't compete with that. I'm not going to get a fair chance.'

'You don't have to deal with any of it. Leave. Do what makes you happy.'

'It's not that simple,' Emma said quietly.

Alex shook his head and took her face in his hands. 'Everything is simple. Life is a choice, Emma. People choose how to treat you. You choose whether or not to accept that. You can't make people stay if they have chosen to leave. You're worth more than that.'

Why did he have to be so kind? Why did this man, whom

she had known for such a short time, have to treat her with so much care? Make her feel seen? Say all the words she wanted to hear? Why did they have to come from the most temporary person in her life?

Emma looked away from his intense gaze. He was making her feel things, and that wasn't what she wanted. Especially not now, when she felt vulnerable.

When she let her eyes meet his again he lowered his lips towards hers, hovering above them, waiting for a sign to say she wanted this too. She closed the gap between them, ignoring any warning that his kiss might mean something more. She didn't need or want that. All she wanted was the distraction.

Alex pulled her against his body as he stepped backwards, reaching behind him for a chair that he dragged out. His lips left hers as he sat down. His eyes, though, were unwavering in their steely focus on her. She straddled his lap and his arm locked around her, the other brushing her hair back. He took her lip between his, gliding his tongue along it, and her breath left her in a sigh.

This was what she needed. To be so consumed that she had no room to think about anything else.

CHAPTER EIGHT

ALEX COULDN'T STOP thinking about what Emma had said. Every instinct had screamed at him not to get involved. Not to ask her what was wrong. But seeing her so deflated made something flare within him. A protective instinct he hadn't felt before for anyone other than his family and his company.

And that kiss afterwards. Another mistake. He was fully aware that he was breaking his own rules. The funny thing was that he couldn't bring himself to regret it. He'd wanted to kiss her and he wasn't going to deny himself any part of Emma. That was why he'd asked her for more time. Once their time was up there would be no reason to see any more of each other, so he was going to savour every kiss and touch he could with her.

That was why he had arranged this evening. Emma had had a trying day that he had done his best to make her forget. Now he was taking her out to dinner so that they could have a good time. It would be a good memory for her and it meant nothing more than that. He was convinced of it.

The dress that was laid out on his bed was there so that she would have something to wear, not to make her feel special.

Alex took a sip of the whisky in his hand, watching the lowering sun.

Emma stood by the bed, her fingers caressing the diaphanous fabric of the pale green dress. All Alex had told her was that they were going out for dinner tonight. By the looks of the garment on the bed she could only assume it was somewhere special. Apart from their brief adventure in the city, it would be the first time they were leaving the apartment in days.

The thought made her blush.

A small smile played on her lips. Whatever Alex had planned would be fun, and after all that had happened she needed it.

Not knowing what the next day would bring, Emma was determined to enjoy tonight. She picked the dress up and stood by the long mirror, gliding the smooth, silken fabric over her body. Fastening the straps behind her neck, Emma examined her appearance.

It was a beautiful dress, falling like a waterfall to the floor. It made her feel sexy and powerful and so very feminine. She buckled her strappy heels in place and was ready to go.

The breath was knocked out of her when she stepped into the lounge.

Alex slowly pivoted from the window, his searing gaze devouring her whole. In a suit several shades darker than his eyes, he looked like a builder of empires—or someone who could just as easily tear them down.

He extended a hand to her, and as if instinct alone drove her Emma crossed the room to take it. He pinned her hands behind her back, making her thrust her breasts out, her body pressed against his. Light as a feather, his lips trailed down her neck.

'Right now, I want to say screw dinner…but the car is waiting downstairs.'

His gravelly words had electricity firing in her core. He kissed her hard and quick, a promise for later, and with a warm hand on the small of her back led her out of his apartment.

The driver waited beside a black limo, opening the door the moment Alex and Emma appeared through the glass door.

'Pulling out all the stops, aren't you?' Emma laughed.

Alex simply shrugged with that smile she adored. He helped her in, then settled beside her, pulling her against his side with an arm wrapped around her.

The last time they had shared a back seat he'd wanted his hands all over her. It took a monumental effort to look away from her, so that he could control the temptation. Now it was different. Emma had agreed to be with him until they'd both had their fill of each other, which meant he could touch her to his heart's content.

'Where are we going?' Emma asked as the limo pulled away from the kerb.

'To dinner,' he said with that secret smile, and he pressed a button that had the privacy screen shut firmly in place.

'Yes, Alexander, but where?'

'You're not very patient, are you?' He draped her legs over his lap and whispered in her ear. 'Maybe I just need to occupy your mind with something else.'

He slipped his hand under her dress.

'Alexander...'

'Emma,' he mimicked.

His hand slid up her smooth leg, caressing her sex, pushing her lace panties aside as his fingers found her core, making her gasp loudly.

'You have to be quiet, Emma,' he whispered in her ear.

She was trying, she really was, but it was impossible with his fingers sliding into her. So he covered her mouth with his and swallowed her every gasp and moan as he thrust his fingers back and forth. Simultaneously pulling her apart and making her soar. And when she reached that pinnacle and shattered, she plummeted back down in a million pieces. But gravity wasn't pulling her to the ground, it was to Alex instead. His arms and his lips and his warmth. And when she finally opened her eyes, his were right there, ready to receive her.

'Welcome back,' he said with a wolfish grin. He righted her dress and pressed a kiss to her temple. 'We're here.'

Emma looked out of the window. They were in front of one of the tallest buildings in Melbourne. The setting sun was glinting off the mammoth glass and steel structure. Slowly, she moved her legs off Alex. They still felt a little shaky from his expert touch, but she didn't have time to recover.

The door was being held open, and he unfolded himself from the car with enviable grace and held out a hand to help her. Her face burned as he held her close, keeping her steady on her feet as they walked towards the entrance. Except she noticed that Alex wasn't leading her to the restaurant, but to a bright door next to it.

'But it's closed today,' she said with a frown.

'Not to me.'

Was there nothing beyond his reach? she wondered. Emma had enjoyed a very privileged upbringing, but at no point had she got to enjoy this kind of power. All Alex had to do was snap his fingers and he sent the world spinning in whichever way he wanted.

They walked through glass doors framed by bright yellow panels that bore the word 'Skydeck'. There was only one person waiting in the dimly lit foyer, who greeted them and pointed them in the direction of the elevator that would take them to the viewing platform.

Alex hit the button for the eighty-eighth floor, and almost instantly Emma felt the whoosh as the lift rocketed up through the floors. Her ears were popping a little as they ascended.

'Have you been here before?' he asked. She saw there was something like uncertainty in his eyes.

'I actually haven't. Feels like something you should experience with someone, and Hannah is terrified of heights.'

'So, a first?' Alex said.

The thought was mirrored in Emma's mind, but she shut it down. There was a first time for everything. That didn't have to make it some sort of revelation.

Faster than she had ever experienced, the lift came to a halt and the doors slid open.

'Shall we?'

Alex held out his arm and Emma linked hers through his as they stepped out into a wood-panelled passage that opened out to a wall of glass that beckoned her. Melbourne lay sprawling beneath her feet. The setting sun to her right cast everything as far as the eye could see in bright gold. And she could see so far.

She could see the ferry at the pier that seemed so massive from Alex's apartment. The mountains in the very distance. And the Yarra snaking through the city. Parts of it glistening like sequins, other parts in dark shadow. It was beautiful.

She had almost forgotten that Alex was standing beside her. She gave a slight start when he spoke in her ear.

'There's more to see.'

Of course there was. Her face split into a grin as she looked past him to a lit sign that said 'Edge'. It took more self-control than she had known she possessed to walk elegantly up a roped-off ramp. Another attendant waited there. After a warm welcome, he slid the door open on an entirely black antechamber.

Emma was buzzing with anticipation. This was something she had always wanted to do and now, thanks to Alex, the experience was hers. There wasn't another soul around. There was no rush. It was all theirs.

She stepped into an opaque glass cube, her heels clicking on the fine surface.

'Enjoy.' The attendant smiled before closing the door.

Emma stood at the rail as the cube began to move forward. She felt Alex stand behind her, his arms coming around her, caging her as he placed his hands beside hers on the silver rail.

'How long do we have?' she asked.

'As long as you want.'

It felt as if he was offering her the world on a platter. The inherent danger of the feeling was lost to her excitement. The cube had stopped moving. She stopped breathing. All at once the glass went clear, and everything was lit with the last rays of golden sunshine.

'Alexander...' she breathed. It was breathtaking. She wanted to take it all in at once, but there was so much to see.

'You wanted a view.'

And he had given it to her. Then she looked down through the glass floor and swayed. It was a daunting thing to look hundreds of metres straight down to the city below.

His arms wrapped tighter around her. 'I've got you.'

Emma leaned into his embrace, her eyes never once leaving the view. And that was how they stood, bodies pressed together, with nothing needing to be said as the sun sank below the horizon.

As the sky became inky, more and more lights began to twinkle below them. Suddenly the barely discernible streets became snaking paths of gold. The steel and glass structures around them weren't glowing but glittering, as a sea of lights reflected on their surfaces. Everywhere she looked, it was as if a new sequin came to life.

From up here everything seemed so small. Inconsequential. Her job, her family—none of it mattered. They were all just a blip in the tapestry of this city. Well, almost all of them.

Emma hazarded a glance behind her and saw Alex's gaze fixed on the distance. She had called him a master of the universe, and he had never looked more like it than right now. The world was his to do with as he pleased.

'Thank you, Alexander.'

In that moment, standing high above the dazzling city she loved so much, she felt every bit of the hurt and disappointment of earlier fade away as if it had never existed. All there was, was her and Alex and this amazing sight. A gift that only he could give her.

Turning in his arms, she held the lapels of his jacket, raised herself up and kissed him. He kissed her back. Claiming her just as much as she was claiming him. With all the fierceness she had in her…alight with passion and daring. Bold as she could be when she didn't have to hide.

Her fingers moved up to his dark hair, tangling in the soft strands as his hand travelled up to her neck. He kissed her deeper, making her burn before he broke the connection of their lips.

'Are you ready to go back?'

She took one last look behind her and nodded. Alex kept his eyes on her as he twirled his finger in the air and the cube began to slide back inside the building. When they walked back in, there was an attendant holding a tray with two glasses of champagne. Alex handed one to her, took the other in his hand.

She drew up to the large window with him beside her. 'This was perfect.'

She clinked her glass against his and took a sip of the cool bubbly, her eyes catching his, and she knew that he was reminded of the very first drink they'd shared, just as she was.

CHAPTER NINE

EMMA HAD BEEN to her fair share of fancy dinners. Every manner of restaurant openings and A-list events. It came with the territory. Brown Hughs was a large, well-respected PR and marketing company, and Emma's surname meant she was inevitably taken along for the ride. But even though she'd had all those experiences, none of them compared to sitting across the table from Alex, with the city far, far below them, admiring it through the floor-to-ceiling windows next to her with not another soul in the restaurant.

Somehow Alex had managed to book the entire place. An award-winning kitchen was at work just for them.

They didn't even bother with menus. They were enjoying a seven course dinner of the chef's finest food.

Alex sat back in his chair as the server cleared away their empty plates. His eyes were intense in the dimly lit restaurant. Light and shadow engaged in a battle over his sculpted face, making him look even more predatory than usual. Emma was fighting the urge to crawl over the table onto his lap, and almost as if he could read her mind he smiled at her.

A cheeseboard and the most artistic dessert Emma had ever seen were placed before them. Before she could even thank their server she was gone. Still, Alex didn't take his eyes off her.

Emma shook herself free of the spell he had placed her

under. Despite what their relationship was meant to be, she wanted to know so much more about him. What he had done for her tonight was something she would treasure always. But there was still so little she knew of him, and it didn't feel right to scour the internet for answers now that she knew him. She had a feeling that what she found wouldn't accurately reflect the man in any case. Every time he avoided saying something she would see the shutters falling in his eyes, and it made her want to know more.

'So tell me…in this arrangement of ours, am I permitted to get to know you better?' she asked.

Alex chuckled. 'What do you want to know?'

His eyes followed the movement of her lifting her spoon to her mouth, closing her lips around the silver, and for just a moment it looked as if his pupils had blown wide, and his throat bobbed.

'You mentioned that you don't often go to your family manor. Why is that?' Emma asked.

Alex kept silent. The heated look in his eyes cooled. She could see a muscle flicker in his jaw.

'Alexander? Am I not allowed to know the answer to that question?' she asked lightly, trying to keep the atmosphere between them upbeat.

He was quiet for so long that Emma thought he wouldn't answer at all.

'I've never really liked the manor. It's been in the family for generations. The first son and heir gets it, along with the title. That's how it became my grandfather's, then my father's, and one day—'

'Yours.'

'Yes.' Alex crossed his arms over his chest.

'But you don't like the place?'

'I don't like the expectation.'

Alex looked at her and she could see the pain he tried to cover up behind his eyes.

'It's beautiful enough—if a bit old and boring.' He chuckled. 'But once it's yours you're expected to be the master of the household—ensure you have an heir.'

'Be Earl Hastings.'

'Yes, and that pressure can make you make mistakes. Trust the wrong people. I would rather just be Alexander Hastings, brilliant CEO, than Earl in a place I barely visit. It's just another thing I don't need handed to me.'

Alex kept his eyes on hers, but his voice was more subdued than Emma had ever heard it.

'Is that why you said duty doesn't fulfil you?' Emma asked.

Alex didn't reply.

She fell silent, pondering his words, and placed her silverware down. 'Do you think that people think you've had everything handed to you?'

'I know they do, Emma.'

'Is that why you work so hard? Why you want to turn Hastings International worldwide?'

'Partly. It's not just because I have something to prove— it's also because I see potential that's never been exploited. I see the company for what it could be, not just what it is.'

'Alexander, I don't think anyone could accuse you of being entitled. You have nothing to prove.'

'If only that were true,' he said softly.

Emma wanted to reach out to him. To touch him. But the faraway look in his eyes made her hold back. There seemed to be so much weight on his shoulders. A weight that was a different kind of duty from what she had to bear. She understood that. Still, there was much he'd revealed without saying much at all. The one thing that really stuck with her was his comment about trusting the wrong people. It made her wonder if he had trusted someone he shouldn't have, or maybe his father had.

She wanted to ask about it, but he jumped in before she could utter a word.

'My turn.' He unfolded his arms and leaned forward, placing a perfectly cut piece of cheese on a cracker that he held to her lips. She crunched into it, and he took the remaining piece into his own mouth. 'I understand why you might not like your sister. I don't understand why she would dislike you.'

'All Lauren's ever known is being preferred over everyone else. That's her spot in the world and she likes it. On the few occasions when I had something she didn't, or received praise when she didn't, it irked her. It wasn't the natural order of things. It got worse at school, because I had a natural inclination towards academia and she didn't.'

Emma shrugged.

'I guess as we got older the prizes we competed for were greater, and she thought they should all be hers. I don't know why she bothers, to be honest. I'll never be a threat to her. If anything, today was proof of that.' Emma picked up her spoon again, twirling the silverware between her fingers. 'I asked how the vote went and my mother said it was unanimous, so I know I wasn't even considered. Not by anyone.'

That was what really hurt. Emma was well aware of how her mother felt about Maddison. She tended her more closely than anyone else, and Emma understood why. Nearly losing her had left a scar on Helen's soul, which was why she would always coddle her youngest daughter. But Emma had hoped that for once emotion wouldn't rule. That her work and dedication would speak for itself.

'Doesn't surprise me, though. You get used to knowing your place in the world.' Emma looked down at her food, concentrating extremely hard on the culinary art on her plate. Or rather, trying very hard to ignore the stinging in her eyes. 'I wanted to be close to Lauren for the longest time, but we only ever got close to that dynamic when I kept well away from all that was hers.'

Alex nodded. 'If you could leave, what would you do?' he asked, taking a sip of his wine.

'I help to run a small literacy charity. The work is amazing, Alexander!'

She smiled as she explained about the classes that were held a few times a week, where she taught people how to read. About all the colourful personalities she got to meet from different countries and impoverished neighbourhoods.

'I try to give as many weekends and afternoons as I can. We have a little team that carries most of the load. I do what I can.'

'Is that what you would like to do?'

'More than anything! Just doing it a few evenings doesn't feel like enough, but I can't get time off work to give more. As it is, my father hates it that I do it. "A waste of time" is what he calls it.'

Emma would never forget coming home from university and telling her parents that she'd decided to volunteer. Her father had told her that she'd proved that she wasn't one of them. That if she could waste time with schemes that made no money, then she had plenty of time to dedicate to the company. Money came before all else to Peter Brown, and Emma knew that would never change.

'Then do it, Emma,' Alex said.

'I can't, Alexander.'

'Why not?'

'Because I'm a Brown. There are expectations. I can't just go off on the charity path—it doesn't work like that.'

'Emma, life is too short to just do what's expected of you.'

Emma shrugged. 'Do you have any siblings?'

Alex huffed a laugh. 'No, the closest thing I have to a

brother is Matt, a friend of mine. It was just my father and I until I went to boarding school, and he was always busy.'

'That sounds lonely…' Emma thought that at least she'd had Maddison, and sometimes even her mother. She was suddenly struck by the image of a lost blue-eyed boy and her heart broke.

With a wave of his hand, Alex brushed the image aside. 'It's no easy thing for my father, being who he is.'

There was admiration in his words. Emma wondered what it must be like to admire one's father. As awful as she felt every time she thought it, she couldn't see a single decent thing about hers. And she knew why.

I never wanted you. You were just a mistake your mother refused to fix.'

Just a few words, callously tossed her way, had had her believing she was unworthy of love. But love didn't exist, so what did it matter?

A warm hand taking hers had her returning to the present. To the piece of pure perfection who was looking at her with so much warmth and heat that she wanted to lean into him. Because, as she was quickly realising, Alex was her favourite distraction from all things real and painful.

'Would you like to go?' he asked.

'I think we should.'

In barely any time at all they were back in the limousine and the door was shut. Emma didn't even notice that, and nor did she notice Alex holding her firmly against his side. A scene at the entrance to the residential tower was captivating her. A father was holding the hands of both his daughters, then he stopped and knelt to tie one of the girl's shoelaces. He gave her a little hug and the other little girl jumped onto his back. Smiling broadly, all three of them disappeared into the building.

She was still staring after them when the car began to move. How she had craved that kind of affection growing up, and never once received it. Watching that little family, she thought it seemed like such an easy thing to do. Be happy. Maybe it was. Maybe the problem was her. After all, it was only her that her father couldn't love.

Whatever it was, Emma was done with dwelling on it for now. She had just had the most amazing evening in a very long time after all.

Alex nuzzled Emma's neck, coaxing her back to him.

'Where have you gone?' he whispered in her ear.

'Nowhere I need to be.'

She turned around and kissed him with a savage intensity that had him rueing how quickly they were approaching his apartment. Not that it mattered. Even as the car slowed he didn't let her pull away. The only break in their connection came when the door was opened and he led her into the elevator. And then his lips were on hers once more.

When the doors dinged open, he scooped her into his arms and somehow managed to get them back into his penthouse. He only set her down once they stood in the middle of his apartment, taking her face in his hands.

'I don't know where you went to just now, Emma, but that's not where you belong.'

He had noticed the desolate look on her face and he didn't care to see it again. Not when there was so much life and passion in her.

A warning bell sounded in him, saying that he was starting to care for her more than he should, but he ignored it—because only a monster would not be moved by that expression. And, no matter what else Alex knew himself to be, cruel wasn't one of them. He knew cruelty, and he wouldn't wish it upon anyone.

Emma kissed him then. Soft and sweet and entirely soul-consuming.

CHAPTER TEN

IT SHOULD HAVE been concerning that he couldn't keep his hands off Emma. That every time he had her it never satiated his thirst for her. But now, having her back pressed against him, his lips on her nape, concern was the last thing on his mind.

It had angered him to see her hurt. He wanted to bring a smile back to her face. Needed to. He tried to convince himself that it was just because she was upset. Because he could see how lonely she had been and that was something he knew well.

The truth that he didn't want to face was that her happiness made his cold heart beat with joy.

He wanted to make Emma burn for him. For her to feel. To forget the thoughts that she wouldn't share with him.

They were done with talking. It was a pointless exercise when in a few days Emma and him would be done and she would move on. He felt a flare of bright hot rage at the thought of Emma with someone else. It caught him off guard and he almost shook his head at himself. Of course Emma would move on—however she chose to. It wasn't any of his business.

'Close your eyes.' His breath caressed her skin. He could already hear her breathing deepen.

Having his low voice so close, his warm hands on her bare shoulders, not being able to see anything, was making heat pool in her belly. Emma couldn't think because, as if he'd flipped a switch, Alex had sensation firing over every part of her.

He eased the zipper of her dress down, moving his hand to unclasp the straps around her neck. She felt the rush of cool air on her naked skin as the dress fell to her feet, exposing her breasts and the flimsy lacy scrap that covered her most intimate parts. He let out an appreciative sound at the sight of her. Then his hands were stroking her arms and her shoulders.

'Alexander…' she moaned.

Teeth nipped at her ear. 'Say it again,' he commanded. And she did.

Emma could feel the effect that she had on him through the fabric of his fine suit trousers, pressed against her back.

Alex guided her arms around his neck, making her thrust her chest out. 'Keep them there.'

Another instruction in that seductive accent.

Emma swallowed thickly. With her eyes closed and her arms raised behind her she was completely at his mercy. Yet it only made her feel alive. Every scrape of his stubble against her skin, the touch of his fingers as they glided down her arms, trailing over her stomach, made her feel electrified. As if she was buzzing with a current that came straight from him.

She shivered as his hands slid under the scrap of lace, guiding it over her hips, sliding it down her legs. And then one jacket-covered arm wrapped around her waist, holding her firmly, brushing against her already fevered skin. His other hand travelled down to her sex, and she let out a cry somewhere between a moan and a mewl.

He had to hold her tighter, because she was sure her legs would buckle if he didn't. And when he sucked on the juncture between her neck and her shoulder all she could do was feel. Feel him everywhere as she reached for her shattering climax, letting go completely in his arms as her breath hitched, then halted, then came in shuddering pants.

'Emma…' he whispered in her ear, but she couldn't form words to respond just yet, and she felt his chuckle reverberate through her.

Alex kept holding her, until she was finally able to turn around in his arms. He had a wild look burning in his blue eyes, and she shivered again because it felt as if a wolf had been unleashed upon her.

'I want to touch you,' she said.

Wordlessly, Alex stepped away from her, shrugging off his jacket and dropping it to the floor in a rumpled heap. His intent gaze fixed upon her, he went about divesting himself of his clothes. Every movement of his body was controlled.

He held out his arms—an invitation for her to touch him as much as she wanted.

Heels clicking on the wooden floor, Emma stepped out of her shed garments and into his embrace, running her hands over the contours of smooth muscle up to his neck and then standing on tiptoes to kiss him. Her hands didn't stop wandering until they tangled in his hair.

'More…' he breathed against her lips.

More. It was a simple word that did more than any praise ever could. It made her feel awakened. Emma was holding the key to his pleasure. She was powerful, and the realisation of that made her smile. Grin. Until a bubble of laughter broke out of her.

Alex had never had an issue with touch. It meant very little. People touched him all the time. The women he slept with, the people he worked with… But nothing had ever felt quite like Emma's touch. As if his skin was being branded. As if she was lighting a flame from the inside. It calmed his heart and had it racing all at once.

He pulled back to see a bright glint in her eyes. He could see her strength reflected in them. Despite everything she had against her. No. Not despite. *Because* of everything she had against her, she was stronger than anyone he knew. Stronger than even she realised.

This was Emma in all her glory.

He wanted to drop to his knees and worship at her feet, but that wasn't who he was. Alex didn't do softness, or all those other things that made one weak. He didn't do love. Was incapable of it. But what he could do was allow her to take a little control and feed the fire that he could see in her now.

He retrieved a foil packet from his wallet and tore it with his teeth, but Emma took it from him. Throwing his head back, Alex groaned as Emma rolled the protection onto his hard length.

'You're always prepared,' Emma teased.

'Being around you, I have to be. You're a siren, Emma.'

Using the tenuous hold he had on his control, he poured himself onto the couch, feet planted on the floor, back straight. He crooked his finger at her, beckoning her to come closer, and when she did he pulled her astride his lap and folded his arms behind his head.

'You wanted to touch…so touch.'

It was a challenge. He knew Emma recognised it for what it was. A gift. One that would let her exert her will in the way they'd both enjoy best.

She trapped her lip between her teeth, looking down at him as if he were a treat. A meal to be devoured. Maybe he was—but so was she. Alex curled his hands into fists. He felt his nails scraping against his scalp, and that helped him keep still when all he wanted to do was sink into her.

Emma felt slightly daunted. After all, there probably wasn't much that Alex hadn't experienced. What could she do that would blow his mind the way he constantly did hers? Then it occurred to her that it didn't matter—because so far he had found pleasure in everything. So she did the first thing that crossed her mind. She kissed him. Hard. In a clash of teeth and tongue as her hands travelled down his body.

He made a strangled sound as she gripped his hardness, guiding it into her as she lowered herself onto him until there was nothing between them. It was the most arousing sound she had ever heard.

Emma started to grind her hips against him and felt his every muscle tense beneath her like cords of steel. Ripping her lips away from his, she leaned against him as her breaths came in short pants. Then she reached around him, taking his hands and placing them on her breasts, shattering his control catastrophically.

Alex's arms moved around her, holding her back as his mouth closed on one nipple then the other.

'I wondered how long you'd last…' She laughed, never having seen his blue eyes quite so dark before.

He growled. 'What are you doing to me?' And then he was kissing her again, pulling her body against his as they rocked together, barrelling towards their release.

Emma pulled away from his kiss, tossing her head back. His arms tightened as her squeal turned into a whimper, and he groaned a guttural sound as he followed her into the clutches of rapture.

She slowly opened her eyes to find that he held her against his chest. The safe weight of his arms on her back was telling her that he had her. They were both covered in sweat. Chests still heaving. Emma crushed her lips against his, pouring everything she felt into the connection. It was past tears, or pain, or happiness, or elation.

She felt all of those things right now, but she also felt the shackles of them falling off her.

Alex couldn't understand why sex with Emma always felt so earth-shattering. And it was a dangerous thing, because how could he ever have enough? He had never grown dependent on anything—but this, with Emma, felt like an addiction. He knew right then that what he needed to do was get dressed and ask her to leave. Instead, he held her close, until her breathing evened out. She was so still that he wondered if she had fallen asleep. But she hadn't. She just couldn't bring herself to move away from him.

'I have to go to work tomorrow,' Emma said.

'And you're wondering how you're going to make it through the day without this?' Alex teased, even though he wasn't far off the mark. They had used up all of their time. It was back to the real world. 'Matt arrives tomorrow.'

'So it's just as well that I have to leave.'

'What are you talking about?' Alex shifted, forcing her to sit up and look at him.

'The weekend's over, Alexander. Today is over.'

'Emma, I said I wanted more of you. I didn't say it had to end tonight.'

'But if Matt arrives tomorrow, what does that mean?'

'It means that my friend will be in town and it might be nice to have a Melbournian to show us around. I do believe you offered your services as a tour guide.'

As he spoke, Alex could feel a prickle of unease telling him this was a bad idea. Flings weren't introduced to friends. This wasn't just breaking the rules. This was decimating them.

'I suppose I did.' She breathed out a chuckle. 'I just thought…'

'Emma, I want you here,' Alex said slowly. 'In fact, I'll

be fetching Matt from the airport tomorrow and I'd like it if you came over after work. Traffic is likely to be heavy, so I'll give you a key to get in.'

'Really?'

'Yes.' He kissed her chastely on the lips. 'It's settled,' he said, with an edge of finality in his voice.

The prospect of not having to end this for just a few more days was too tempting to resist.

CHAPTER ELEVEN

WHEN ALEX HAD said it was time for a drink, she'd thought he meant wine or coffee. Not the two bottles of water he was fetching from the fridge. Emma leaned against the counter on her elbows, admiring his sculpted muscular back and broad shoulders. He truly was the very embodiment of masculinity.

There had been a time when she would fantasise about someone like him. Unapologetic in his maleness. Strapping. Choosing her to love and be with. But that had been before her parents had eroded the very idea. Between their hateful bickering and her father's constant affairs, Emma had entirely given up on love. There was no such thing. And when she'd once thought she'd found someone to challenge that, just a little, Lauren had been right there to prove that Emma had it right the first time.

She hadn't given anyone her heart because there would never be a reason to. And now there was Alex, who believed the same. She had never had a connection to anyone as she did with him, and if even he believed that love was an imaginary construct, then it must be true.

Even if it wasn't, why would someone like him ever choose *her*? Emma had years of evidence that, given the choice, no one would choose her. If she thought about it, Alex had been careful to make sure there were barriers that weren't broken. In the overheard snippets of conversation on his phone and his driver in the limo, she'd heard them all call him Alex. Yet she didn't.

Emma didn't know why, but that thought stung.

'Alexander, can I ask you something?'

He turned around to look at her, sliding over the bottle of water. 'Of course.'

She wasn't looking at him. Instead, she ran her fingers along the patterns in the marble. 'Why do you let everyone call you Alex? Seems a bit familiar, given who you are.'

He placed his arms down on the counter, leaning in towards Emma. 'You mean why do I allow everyone to call me Alex but not you?'

He'd guessed her actual question. She didn't respond, trying not to show her hurt.

'Because, Emma, you're the only one who calls me Alexander.' He walked around the large island and pulled her to her feet, taking her face in his hands. 'And I love hearing the way you say it.'

'You do?'

He kissed her cheek.

'Mm-hmm. Especially when you're coming for me.' He kissed her neck. 'And when you think I'm being ridiculous.' He kissed her forehead. 'And when you're trying to get my attention.' He kissed her lips, slow and lingering. 'And when you want me to kiss you but you don't want to say it.'

He brushed his lips against hers once more and she was quivering with need all over again.

'But I'm really going to love hearing the way you say it when I show you your surprise.'

'A surprise?'

He nodded and pulled his trousers on, and draped his white shirt over her, fastening the buttons before placing a small kiss on her lips.

They went up the glass staircase and down a corridor she hadn't seen before. There were beautiful works of art lining the walls. From emotive photographs that captured a moment in breathtaking ways, to contemporary works in a myriad of colours. Emma looked at Alex, marvelling at the many sides of him and just how much of them he kept hidden.

'You ready?' he asked with a bright smile once they reached a closed door.

She nodded, her expression mirroring his. He held open the door and stood back to let her enter the cavernous room.

'Oh, Alexander!' she exclaimed on a breath.

It was a private library. There were shelves lining all the walls except for the one glass wall that during the day would bathe the room in light. Now, at night, it made the space feel cosier somehow.

Almost every shelf was filled to capacity with various books of different sizes and colours. Emma was drawn in. Stepping up to one of the bookshelves, she saw that some of the books looked extremely old. Probably first editions, she thought. She looked to her right and saw a ladder attached to a rail that would allow her to get a book from the very top shelf. She glanced behind her with barely contained excitement and saw Alex leaning against the back of a very comfortable-looking couch. There were so many places to sit. Lounge... Relax and forget reality.

'How—? You haven't even been in Melbourne all that long.'

Alex shrugged. 'I hope you didn't think that I'm just a pretty face.'

He pushed off the couch and moved to stand before her. Holding her shoulders, he spun her around and pressed his body against hers, making her step forward until she was right in front of the shelf. He held her hand in his and ran her fingers over several of the books' spines.

'While we're together,' he purred, his teeth grazing her

ear, 'whenever you want a little escape, you can come here and take what you need.'

Her heart was thrumming, chest heaving. How could he affect her so deeply? She turned around and crushed her lips against his. He didn't falter for a second, catching her instantly and kissing her back.

Alex felt buoyant, seeing how happy the library had made her. How happy it made him. He had shared something of himself with her and Emma seemed grateful for the surprise, perhaps thinking it was his generosity that had led to him sharing it with her because books and reading were so close to her heart. But it was more than that. This room was his sanctuary too.

Alex pushed her against the bookshelf, kissing her deeply, but his phone chose this most inopportune time to ring.

'Dammit,' he growled, pulling the device out of his pocket. 'I have to take this—it's my father.'

Emma handed his shirt back to him and wrapped a throw around herself as he left the library, answering the video call as he went to his study. Calls from his father were usually about work. It was the easiest common ground to find between them as they built and rebuilt their relationship over the years.

'Hello, Dad.'

Robert Hastings took one look at his son and asked, 'Are you busy?'

'I have company,' Alex said simply.

Alex knew it wasn't his dishevelled appearance that had struck his father—rather the way he was looking. Somewhere between relaxed and annoyed at being disturbed. His father would have seen that look on his face a hundred times while he grew up. When he'd been completely focussed on something he enjoyed and had been disturbed.

The thing was that even then he hadn't felt happy. Not like he did right now.

Alex wondered if his father had come to regret all the time he'd spent working. The time they had lost with Alex at boarding school, and then again when he had come home during the holidays and Robert had always been holed up in his study. It made Alex sometimes wonder how things would have been different if his father had been around more.

'How are you, son?' his father asked.

Alex frowned. 'Fine...' he said, feeling uncertain. 'I thought you were calling about work.'

'Can't a father enquire as to the state of his child?'

Alex laughed. 'Of course he can.'

'You have company, son. I don't want to interrupt. We can always talk tomorrow.'

'There's no need.' Alex jumped head-first into work and the two Hastings men talked business until they realised how late it had become.

When Alex had left the study Emma had stepped into the passage to better examine the art that was hung there. At first it seemed surprising that Alex would collect art at all, but as she looked at each piece the collection seemed to reflect him perfectly.

They weren't expensive pieces, bought as an investment. Nor were they a show of his wealth or status. They were parts of him—parts of a whole.

There were many paintings reflecting water. A river or an ocean. A lot of them seemed to feature blue prominently, which she guessed might be a colour he was partial to. The huge photographs were scenes from different places across the world, and she remembered what he'd said about wanting Hastings to truly be global.

Emma pulled herself away and went back into the library. It was so inviting, and now she knew it was there it was definitely going to be the place she spent the most time in.

Eager to see what sort of books Alex had in his collection, she started her examination of titles from the first bookshelf, reading the spines as she went.

She didn't get very far. A book she had loved for years caught her eye. Pulling the ladder over, she climbed up two rungs to reach the beautifully embossed hardcover book that was clearly a collector's edition. She ran her fingers over the gold letters on the cover: *The Time Machine*.

It fell open in her hand, to a page that had a magnetic bookmark attached to it. It was a fancy thing. Like something one would receive as a gift. It was leather, and etched in striking patterns with the initials *AJH*. It made her smile that he was reading the same book that had caught her attention.

Emma took it over to the couch, where she curled up with her feet on the cushions. Opening up the first page, she was lost to the fantasy…

After his call, Alex went straight back to the library. Remembering how passionately Emma had spoken of her literacy charity, he knew she wouldn't have left the room. Leaning against the door jamb, Alex watched Emma silently. Having her there fixed a piece of him in place that had been missing for so long, and he recognised how perilous a feeling that was because he just wasn't ready for something like that. It wasn't the way he was wired. But looking at her as he was now, seeing her wrapped in the luxurious throw, brought what he'd thought he knew about himself into doubt.

He noticed that the book she was reading was one of his favourites. One that he had recently started reading again.

'That's a good book,' he said from the doorway.

Emma looked up with a start. It was as if she had forgotten where she was.

'Sorry, I didn't mean to startle you.' He pushed off the doorframe and joined her on the couch.

'It's fine.' She laughed nervously. 'It's one of my favourites,' she said, turning to the cover.

'Mine too. Sorry I took so long.'

'It's okay. I've been entertained. What's the "J"?' she asked. She smiled at his obvious confusion and held up his bookmark, pointing at his initials.

'James.'

'Never would have guessed.'

'Really?' he asked with amusement.

She laughed, a teasing glint in her eye. 'I would have thought it would be some sort of haughty archaic name, passed down.'

He wasn't taking the bait. 'Sorry to disappoint.' He pulled her throw-covered legs over his lap, holding her against his body. 'I wanted to talk to you about tomorrow.'

'Work?' Emma asked, frowning.

'Work.'

Alex had been picking apart everything she had said to him over the past few days. A picture was beginning to paint itself, of exactly what she was facing. And the reality of the matter was that when Emma went back to the office she would be facing the wrath of her older sister. Unfair as it was, Lauren was, in effect, her boss. And the look he'd seen on her older sister's face at the masquerade—while amusing at the time—meant that Emma would be facing an untenable situation tomorrow. A situation Alex felt somewhat responsible for.

He never involved himself in the careers of the women he dated, that was true, but he also never got them fired. From what Emma had said of Lauren, it seemed she was waiting for an excuse to be rid forever of the smart younger sister who was very capable of upstaging her but never did.

Emma sighed heavily. 'I'm not going to stress about it, Alexander. Whatever happens, happens. I doubt Lauren is going to retaliate on the day her promotion is announced.'

'So you're just going to stand there and pretend you're happy for her? Even though you were overlooked again?' He could feel his anger rising.

'Yes, because I'm happy for Maddie. At least a part of me is.'

'The other part knows you deserve better.'

Emma shrugged. 'I don't know what I deserve,' she finally responded. 'Better than my family, but that's a low bar.'

He narrowed his eyes. How could she not know what she deserved? She was aware of how hard she worked. Knew what she wanted. Craved the opportunity to be given a chance. So how could she not know? Unless it wasn't so much not knowing what she deserved as it was not knowing her worth.

'Emma…' He made his voice low. Quiet. 'Why don't you think you're good enough?'

Emma didn't answer and looked away.

Alex wouldn't be ignored. He held her chin in a firm grasp, forcing her to look at him. 'What happened? You're not leaving here until you tell me.'

Why should she? a voice at the back of his mind asked him. The answer was simple. He wanted to know. Whether he needed to know was immaterial. And Alex always got what he wanted.

'It's nothing. Stupid, really.'

'Tell me anyway.' He knew he'd made it clear that he wasn't going to let it go.

She sighed. 'Not long after I had started working, I dated someone. I wasn't interested in anything serious, but he

said all the right things, and did all the right things, and
for a moment I contemplated what it would be like to have
something real with him. Then he met Lauren. Started ignoring my texts and calls. I found out he'd been seeing her.
He chose her. It had always been her. I was just a means
to an end.'

Fool. How anyone could choose Lauren over Emma was
baffling to him. She was by far the most stunning creature he had ever seen. He—Alex, master of control—could
barely control himself around her.

'Emma…'

'It's fine. It's in the past. But I should have expected it
because my father didn't ever want me either.'

'What do you mean?' Alex was having a hard time rein-
ing in his temper now.

'The reason my father hates me so much is because I
was—as he so delicately put it—"a mistake my mother refused to fix". He didn't want me.'

A growl left Alex's throat. His eyes turned to shards
of ice.

'You have to understand my father is someone who has
a plan and sticks to it. Anything outside of that isn't toler-
ated. Deviations are viciously and swiftly dealt with. He's
always been that way.'

Alex remembered what Emma had said about Maddison, and it just made him angrier. His hands were balling
into fists, ready to fight a person who wasn't there. 'He was
willing to lose you.'

'Yes.'

The matter-of-fact way Emma spoke of all this was even
more enraging, because she just accepted it and moved
on. As if it was normal. Remained in the family company
where she was committed to doing her best.

Once again Alex was moved by the sheer strength of
her. And she didn't think she was good enough? That was

laughable. He couldn't imagine a more ridiculous notion. If anything, it cemented his decision to walk away at the end of this, because Emma had it all backwards. She needed someone who was deserving of her—and that wasn't him. Could never be.

He moved the hand on her chin to cradle her face. When he spoke his voice was firm. Resolute. 'You don't need any of them. They don't deserve you. None of them do, Emma.'

He picked her up—throw and all—and walked out of the library.

'Where are you taking me?'

'To show you how a beautiful, strong woman should be treated.'

CHAPTER TWELVE

THE CONVERSATION WITH Emma had been playing on Alex's mind ever since they had left the library. Now he stood at the railing of his rooftop terrace, gazing out at the early-morning light with a cup in his hand. There had to be a way for him to help her. To get her out of a clearly unhappy situation. She was so vivacious, and it tore him apart to see her so downtrodden.

Pressuring her was the last thing he wanted to do, but he had to find a way to give her an out.

And then it occurred to him. Despite the early hour, he pulled out his phone and called in a favour.

The next day found Emma in her office. Her thoughts were constantly being pulled back to the time she'd spent with Alex. It had been perfect. So perfect that she was struggling to concentrate. It was completely unlike her, and she had to get it together, knowing she was being watched more closely than usual.

Her impromptu day off had in fact been noticed by most. But her father had said nothing to her. Well, not verbally. The look he had given her had said it all. It was official. She was now possibly more hated even than her mother.

The day had started with the announcement of Lauren's promotion. Emma had stood behind her sister, impeccably dressed, looking happy and supportive. Pictures had been taken for the company website, with others for the newsletter.

Emma had answered any and all questions aimed at her with grace and confidence. Playing the part of a Brown daughter perfectly. Even when she'd been asked how she felt now that both her sisters were in management positions while she was not, Emma had simply said that the right decisions had been made and that they all had a role to play at Brown Hughs.

She'd given no one any reason to have a gripe with her, and at the end had received the thanks of her mother and Maddison, who seemed to be in a constant state of apology. It wasn't her fault, and Emma was not upset with Maddison.

She found herself often saying, 'Don't worry about it, Maddie.'

After all, Maddison had a job to do, and she couldn't be feeling guilty all the time. They all had to move forward. And perhaps now Emma stood a chance of moving a little higher up the ladder.

It was a busy day, between meetings, approvals and the odd bit of hand-holding, and before Emma knew it she was staring down the barrel of yet another lunch break spent holed up in her office, working. Which was a pity, because it was such a beautiful day. All she wanted was just a little break to feel the sun on her face.

She looked up to see a small commotion outside, and wondered what was going on, but she was busy and had no time to indulge her curiosity. Until there was a knock on her office door.

Emma looked up to see Alex standing in her doorway, looking sinful in a tailored black suit with a white shirt and black tie. A silver tie clip was striking against the dark fabric, and as he dropped his hand a cufflink caught the light. He was perfect. It took her breath away every time he looked at her the way he was doing right now.

Her legs were already carrying her towards him. Magnetised. That was what they were. 'Alexander. What are you doing here?'

He kissed her. A quick but glaring show of his affection. *Mine!* was what it screamed. 'I'm taking you to lunch.'

'I'm swamped,' she said, deflated.

'Make time. You have a meeting,' he said, his voice low.

Her brows knitted together. Unsure of what he had planned, Emma was torn between what she wanted to do and what she had to do. But she did trust Alex, and if he had arranged something, it was worth checking out.

'Let me get my bag.'

Emma locked her computer and slung her handbag over her shoulder. He took her hand in his as they walked out, and she noticed everyone stood a little straighter around him, moving out of his way without him asking. He exuded a power that was *felt*, and she was reminded of the way everyone moved out of his path when they walked through the city.

The doors on the lift slid closed and the people around them kept shooting covert looks their way. It was something Alex seemed completely oblivious to. Perhaps it was something he'd learned to ignore. To Emma, it was new and a little uncomfortable.

She was grateful when they stepped out on the ground floor. Outside, in the bright sunshine, stood his car, parked in the bay just outside the doors.

Alex held the car door open for her and once she was safely inside, closed it and climbed in.

'You look incredible,' he said.

'We had Lauren and Maddison's announcement today,' she said, by way of explanation.

'I know. I saw it online.' He flicked the indicator and pulled out into the street.

'You did?'

'I had to look up the building address.'

'Right... I guess it makes sense that they put it out so quickly.' Emma looked around at the buildings that passed by them, trying to figure out where they were going. 'What's this meeting about?'

An enigmatic smile crept onto his face. 'Do you trust me?'

'Yes,' she said without hesitation. It surprised her how true it was. She trusted Alex.

'Then you'll see.'

Emma let it drop. There was a knot in her stomach that didn't seem to ease, and she knew he could sense it.

'It's worth it. I promise.'

She nodded and forced herself to relax. This would be the only quiet moment she had in her day, so she closed her eyes and enjoyed the feeling of the sun on her skin. It wasn't quite the walk she'd wanted, but it was better because it would be spent with Alex.

He brought the car to a stop in a roadside bay, then opened the door for her. Emma wasn't sure if she would ever get over his chivalry, but she hoped it would never stop. There was no telling when she would get to experience it again once things were over between them.

They walked into a high-end restaurant. The kind that garnered huge followings on social media. The kind you would have a meeting at if you were trying to woo someone. And suddenly she felt as if they were.

There was an immaculately dressed woman in a suit sitting at the table that they were being ushered to.

'Emma, I'd like you to meet Fiona Porter,' Alex said, making the introduction.

She shook the woman's hand. 'Emma Brown...nice to meet you.'

Alex pulled a chair out for Emma before taking his seat

beside her. 'Fiona is a director of one of the largest literacy charities in Australia.'

Suddenly it all became clear, and Emma's heart began to race. Alex must have seen the disbelief in her face, and he casually placed his arm around her shoulders. This was the most incredible thing anyone had ever done for her, and Emma was determined not to squander the opportunity.

'Alex tells me you're involved in charity work as well,' Fiona said.

'Yes, I am. I help run a small literacy charity here in Melbourne.' Emma smiled.

'A noble cause. Not a particularly easy one either.' Fiona nodded knowingly.

'No, it isn't. It's always a battle to secure donations. I have to say, I've followed the work of your organisation for a long time. It's what inspired me to get involved.'

'It pleases me greatly to hear that.'

A basket of breads and dips was placed on the table. They waited for the server to leave before continuing their conversation.

'So what does your organisation do, Emma?' Fiona asked.

'We offer classes to teach adults and children…hold book drives…try to collect school materials.'

Emma's heart was beating a frantic tattoo, but she felt the light touch of Alex's thumb caressing the back of her neck and tried to lean into the feeling. She spoke passionately of all that they did and the people she got to meet. How much she enjoyed the work and how they marketed themselves.

Despite the small size of Emma's little organisation, Fiona seemed impressed, and she had Alex to thank. Maybe this was his way of trying to make a difference. Trying to take her away from all the negativity she faced almost every day while still helping others. She'd been able to tell from the moment they met that he hid an enormous heart.

'You say you'd like to give more time to your charity work?' asked Fiona.

'That's right,' Emma replied.

'What do you do in your career?'

Emma launched into a description of her role at Brown Hughs and Fiona seemed more and more interested, asking questions about her academic background and strategic prowess. It was starting to feel a little like an interview.

A waitress came by to take their order. Emma barely registered what she said. She heard Alex's resonating voice. However, all she could concentrate on was the surreal experience she was having.

She was grateful for the fact that Alex had stayed there with her, and that he hadn't just set her up for this meeting, because she was struggling to be her usual composed self even though she tried not to show it.

He'd leaned back in his chair and fixed his intense gaze on Fiona. Something Emma realised he did whenever he was listening intently. People always seemed to respond to it. Now he was in full charm mode, and it gave Emma the time to pull herself together.

They chatted cordially through their meal. But once the coffees had come, Fiona wanted to get down to the matter at hand.

'Emma, as I'm sure you know, we have partnered with many smaller organisations in the past. Provided support where they needed it most. Based on what you've told me, I would love to meet with your colleagues so we can discuss a partnership of our own.'

'That would be amazing!' Emma breathed.

'Of course we would have to look into your organisation first. Can't be too careful.' Fiona smiled.

'Of course. I completely understand,' Emma answered, placing her cup down on the saucer with a clink.

Fiona fished a card out of her bag and handed it to her. 'Give me a call and we can set up a meeting.'

Emma handed one of her own cards over. 'Thank you, Fiona.'

She could scarcely believe her luck. Except it wasn't luck. It was the doing of the one person other than Hannah who wanted to see her happy.

'I hope you'll call soon. We don't want this opportunity to slip through our fingers,' Fiona cautioned.

Emma had already planned to contact the others as soon as she got back to the office. 'Absolutely not.'

'One thing, Fiona...' Alex started. 'These things usually take a while. Can we rush that along?'

Fiona narrowed her eyes at Alex. 'We can get going as soon as Emma is ready. Naturally, since you're here, Alex, I have to tell you how far having some international backing can go in organisations such as ours.'

'I'm well aware, and will have Hastings International's philanthropy division contact you.' Alex turned his attention back to Emma. 'Does that work for you?'

It was a simple question. She recognised it as his way of telling her that she was still the one in control. She could walk away if she wanted, or pursue it, and he would support her. It was her decision to make. His company would be dealing with Fiona's, not hers. There was no pressure on her. And no permanent link to him.

'Yes, definitely.'

The drive back to her office was quiet. There was a lot for Emma to think on. Excitement was thrumming in her, but so was apprehension. Was she good enough to seize this opportunity? And what would happen if she did? How would her family react if she was involved more heavily with the charity than she already was?

She didn't even realise they had arrived back until Alex opened her door.

'One step at a time,' he said softly.

'Yeah. Just a lot to think about.'

Fiona could change everything. All the projects the charity wanted to get off the ground, all the people they could help—all of it would become easier.

'You can do this, Emma.'

He walked her back to her office.

To her horror, it seemed that news of Alex's presence had reached Lauren. The employees on her floor were all trying to look everywhere except at the tall blonde who had been waiting for her sister. To Emma's relief, her mother arrived just in the nick of time. Helen would be able to ensure that no scene was made.

'Alexander, how nice to see you again,' Lauren said sweetly.

Emma rolled her eyes. *When will you stop?* she thought to herself. They were at work. And they were professionals.

'It's good to see you too, Lauren,' he said politely. 'And, please, it's Alex.'

Alex was curious to see what sort of game Lauren would play. After all, everyone working on this floor would have either seen or heard that he had kissed Emma. Part of him smiled inwardly at the possessiveness of it all...another part was screaming warnings at him.

'Well, Alex,' she purred, 'it's a surprise to see you here. Wouldn't you rather come up to *my* office? We have a much better meeting space up there.'

Alex wanted to laugh. He heard Emma huff beside him, and wrapped his arm around her waist. 'Oh, I'm not here on business. I just came to drop Emma off after lunch.'

He pressed a kiss to her hair and Lauren's jaw twitched.

'Oh, that's lovely!' Helen said, stepping forward. 'I'm Helen—Emma's mother.'

She extended her hand to him, which he shook warmly. Honestly, he didn't need to be told who she was. Looking into Helen's eyes was almost like looking into Emma's. Like a mirror.

'It's nice to finally meet you, Helen. And I don't mean to be rude, but I do need to rush.' He turned his back on the two women, keeping Emma beside him, and walked her to her office.

For the first time Alex was able to take it in. The space was perfectly neat and orderly. There wasn't a single thing in it that was unnecessary or sentimental. No photos on her desk or pictures on her wall, save for a framed degree which was fixed behind her. The other thing he noticed was how small it was. It would fit into his own office four times at least.

'I expect to see you tonight. I'll text you the code to get in.'

'I'll come straight over after work.'

'Good.' He leaned down to kiss Emma, and she was already meeting his lips halfway. He kissed her long and slow, but pulled away before either of them really wanted to. 'I'll see you later.'

'Alexander?' she called once he was out through the door.

'Yes?'

'Thank you for today.'

He smiled back at her, then left.

CHAPTER THIRTEEN

THE DRIVE TO the airport took longer than Alex would have liked, but he knew it would be nothing compared to when he was driving back, so he tried his best to remain patient. It would have been easy to send a driver, or have Matt rent a car or use a ride-share, but he had missed his friend. He was probably his only true friend, and Alex wanted to spend as much time with him as he could. They would have time to talk, and Matt would question his sanity.

One morning. That was all the time he'd spent away from Emma, and he could hardly believe how much he craved her touch. After lunch he had been distracted in his meetings. With thoughts of Emma constantly breaking through his normally laser-sharp focus.

Alex checked the time on his watch. He would have to wait only a few minutes for Matt to come through. He parked in the closest available bay to the airport structure. Still dressed in his suit, Alex shrugged off his jacket, depositing it on the back seat, and rolled up his shirtsleeves. Making sure he had the parking ticket, he walked to the pick-up point, keeping an eye out for the tall blond form of his friend.

First class always had its perks, and before the large wave of people disembarking from Economy could pass through, a much smaller number were already exiting the building. That was when Alex saw him. Standing a head taller than most, it was impossible to miss Matt. With the physique of a rugby player, which he'd never lost despite not having played since leaving university, Matt cut an imposing figure. That was before he smiled. He had always had a magnetic personality and people seemed to gravitate towards him. It was easy to be around him.

Matt grinned as soon as he saw Alex, making a beeline for him. 'Alex!'

They hugged and slapped backs.

'It's good to see you, mate.'

Alex had always attracted attention, and he did well to ignore it most of the time, but whenever he and Matt were together it seemed there were ten times as many people looking their way.

The two of them walked back to the car, and Alex stowed his friend's single piece of luggage in the boot. In no time they were back on the road.

Alex had looked forward to Matt's arrival, but what he hadn't counted on was the calm seeing his friend would bring. Between work and his relationship with Emma, Alex had been in a vortex of powerful feelings. It was refreshing to have back the tranquillity that always came from being around Matt.

'What's on the itinerary for tonight?' Matt asked.

'Don't have one. We'll go back to my place and decide from there,' Alex said.

'Sounds good. Just us?'

Alex looked over at his friend and caught the knowing look on his face. It annoyed him sometimes, just how well Matt knew him. 'Emma's coming over.'

Matt didn't comment. Alex knew it was more than a little unusual for him to invite a woman along when standard procedure dictated that they'd cruise the social scene as unattached eternal bachelors. An introduction meant something. Alex knew it would make Matt curious to see what Emma was like for himself. Alex also wanted to see how she got along with Matt. Which meant he was in bigger trouble than he'd realised.

Traffic had come to a crawl and it was already sunset. Alex wondered if Emma was at his flat yet, but he didn't linger on the thought as Matt caught him up on everything going on back in London.

Emma parked in the second empty bay assigned to Alex and carefully picked up the box of cakes she had purchased on her way over.

With a beep, her car was locked, and she made her way to the elevator which was waiting. She pulled out the key to Alex's apartment, still surprised that he had given it to her. It might only be for one night, but it felt as if there was more to the gesture. She hoped she wasn't reading too much into it.

You are, a snide voice at the back of her mind commented.

She slid the key into the lock, opening up the door, and stepped into the apartment.

'Alexander?' she called, but there was no response.

Glancing at the time, she figured he would be on his way back. Her heels click-clacked on the wooden floors as she walked through to the kitchen to deposit the sweet treats on the counter. The apartment was eerily quiet. Then she realised there was no music playing. The only time it had been this quiet was when she'd first come over after the masquerade, and then she hadn't really noticed because Alex had seemed to fill the space they were in.

She looked around for something to do, fingers drumming on the countertop. Nothing appealed to her more than making another trip to the library. There she found the book she had been reading, still placed on the couch. Except there was a long copper-coloured bookmark between the pages she had stopped at.

Emma settled in and fell into the story once more. It was at least an hour before she heard voices coming from downstairs, and Alex and Matt finally arrived at the apartment.

Emma flew down the stairs, and the first thing she saw was Alex moving towards her. It had become the most natural thing in the world for them to gravitate towards each other. As if the world had tilted on a different axis.

He kissed her ardently. As if they were being reunited after a great time apart.

'Have you been waiting long?' Alex asked.

'A little over an hour.'

'Sorry, traffic was a nightmare,' he apologised.

She waved it off and he held her against his side.

That was when she saw the man standing with a large black suitcase next to him. As tall as Alex, but much broader, he was an imposing figure with kind green eyes, a handsome face, and a shock of blond hair. Emma thought that these two friends together would set hearts alight wherever they went.

'Emma Brown, this is Matthew Taylor,' Alex said.

'Just Matt.'

Emma smiled.

'It's nice to meet you, Matt.'

'And you, Emma.'

'Before I forget, Alexander, I went to the patisserie. There's a box on the kitchen counter.'

'I like her already.' Matt grinned.

She watched the two men head to the kitchen and inspect the contents of the box. It was a treat to watch Alex like this. She had already seen so many sides to him, and watching him now, with Matt, he seemed younger. More relaxed.

Alex fiddled with his tablet and music came alive overhead.

'You have that on even when you're working?' Matt asked.

'Yeah,' Alex answered.

'Some things never change,' Matt commented, and went back to selecting a cake.

Emma watched the two men keenly. There was something about this evening that niggled at her. It almost felt as though it was some sort of test. That Alex was watching how well she got along with Matt. It didn't make any sense to her that he should want them to get along. Matt seemed very important to him, and Emma was only ever going to be a moment in his life.

A little bit of hope and fear bloomed in her chest that maybe it meant he wanted more time with her. But she closed her eyes and tried to push the feeling away. He had been honest with her, and had never once said this would develop any further. Emma forced herself to remember that. To remember what she wanted too. Fun. No strings. No toxic relationship to follow her around for the rest of her life.

'Emma? Are you okay?' Alex asked.

'Hmm? Oh, yeah. Just thinking about work,' she lied.

She hadn't realised Alex had been watching her, and wasn't sure if he bought the flimsy lie. But he didn't push and for that she was grateful.

Alex presented Matt with the opportunity to talk to Emma alone after dinner, when he was about to make coffee. Throughout the meal, Matt had been watching him with Emma. When they touched, or shared a look or a smile. As if he could tell that whatever was going on between the two of them was different from anything Alex had experienced before.

A loud buzz echoed against the counter. Picking up his phone, Alex frowned as he read through an email.

'I have to take care of something,' he said.

Alex caught Emma's eye and winked. She felt her cheeks turn red, which made his smile grow as he walked away to the study, leaving Matt alone with her. She finished making the coffees, handing a cup to Matt, who took it to the living room.

'So, Emma, you're involved in charity work?' he said.

'Yes. A small charity. I'm hoping we can partner with a larger organisation, thanks to Alexander.'

She sat cross-legged on the couch opposite him, getting comfortable. She'd had a feeling that he would want to talk to her at some point. After all, friends looked out for each other. She wished sisters did too.

'Oh?'

'Yeah... Alexander has introduced me to the director of a large literacy charity. They seem to like what we do and how we operate.' Emma held the coffee cup in her hands, enjoying its warmth.

'Wow...' Matt said, as if to himself. 'Alex would normally never do that.'

'Help someone out?' she asked sceptically. She was starting to wonder how well Matt knew Alex at all.

'No. He's always willing to help. He's just...disciplined. He has these rules he lives by, and one of those is to never mix business with pleasure. If he got you that meeting he pulled in a favour, and that's not something he would ordinarily do.'

'I've noticed.'

'It means you're different, Emma. I've known Alex for a very long time, and all of this,' he said, gesturing towards her, 'is new. He obviously has strong feelings for you.'

Emma looked at Matt, then dropped her gaze to her cup. Unsure what to say or how much to say.

'I'm going to take a stab and say you do too. You don't have to say it. I can see it. I'm sure Alex does have feelings, but if you're waiting for him to say the words, they're not going to come.'

Emma already knew that. Knew there was going to be an end. It splinteeed a part of her every time she thought about it, because this was the most alive she had ever felt. Awakened. The fear that she would lose that once he walked out was real. And she wasn't ready to say goodbye to him just yet. But when it did happen she would thank him for helping her find herself. For being *him*. Every moment they'd spent together would be a treasured memory that she would tuck away as she moved on with her life.

Emma cleared her throat, not quite trusting her voice. 'I just want him to be happy. I can see there's things he carries that he doesn't want to talk about. I wish I knew how to help him.'

'Get in line,' Matt said, looking out of the window. There was an unseeing look in his eye. As if he were deep in thought. And then his features set. As if he was resolved in some kind of decision. 'How much have you read about Alex?'

'Actually, nothing since we met at a masquerade. And before that just what was in the news. I didn't want to invade his privacy.'

Matt smiled. It was a soft expression. 'Do you know about his father?'

Emma shook her head. 'He's an earl, and that's as far as I know.'

'And his mother?'

'Just that he doesn't have one.'

'Well, that's half true... Robert Hastings married a woman named Catherine Evans and they had Alex. Robert needed an heir, but Catherine was indifferent. When Alex was born she hated being a mother, had no maternal feelings or even any love for him, and one day she just left.'

Emma listened, horrified that his mother could have done that. It was common knowledge that her mother favoured Maddison, but at least she had been there for Emma in the past, and in a lot of ways still was.

'The thing is, she never left high society. She likes the life. Robert had a reputation as a difficult man in the business world, and Catherine perpetuated rumours that he was the same, if not worse, in private. It was easily believed, so she wasn't cast out. But it isn't the truth. Robert is a hard man to please because of who he is, but he is a good man. So Alex has grown up knowing who his mother is, but she's a complete stranger to him. He's never actually met her.'

'Oh, my God!' Emma covered her mouth. 'That's awful. And cruel.' She uncrossed her legs and got off the couch, moving to stand at the massive window. 'Everything he's said makes so much sense now.'

'What did he say?' Matt asked.

Emma turned around and leaned her back against the large pane of glass. 'He told me he doesn't want the title. He said it leads you to make mistakes and trust the wrong people.'

'That sounds like him. He doesn't ever trust people.'

'But he trusted me,' Emma said softly.

He had shown her as much when he'd spoken to her about his reluctance to accept the legacy that awaited him, and when he'd brought her to his home. The key in her pocket suddenly became an immensely heavy weight.

'He did. Make sure you don't lose that trust. You'll never get it back.'

Matt picked up his coffee and took a long sip. Emma was silent. Reeling from his revelations. It was a clear warning from Matt, but Emma was determined to be what Alex needed, just as he had been for her, for as long as she could.

She couldn't stop thinking about everything Matt had said. It played over and over in her mind like a broken record and, despite wanting to spend another night with Alex, she knew she shouldn't let herself forget exactly what this relationship was. Spending the night here with Matt around would feel like a lot more than either of them wanted. So she stole a moment alone with Alex just as he was about to leave his study.

She pushed him back in and closed the door behind her. He clearly knew what she was after. Pressing her back against the door, his hands on either side of her head, Alex kissed her with a ferocity that promised so much pleasure. The air was sucked out from around them and all that was left was a vacuum, thick with desire.

When she plunged her hands under his shirt Alex groaned, pressing his hardness against her. Making her whimper. But Emma broke the kiss.

'I have to go.'

'Tease.'

The smile she gave him was nothing short of wicked.

Alex let her leave, cursing himself as he did so, because all he really wanted right now was to take her to bed. He stood at the rail of his rooftop terrace, with the sea air cooling his overheated face and helping him find some sort of equilibrium after that kiss.

Matt came up beside him, leaning on his elbows, taking in the spectacular sight of night-time in Melbourne at the water's edge. 'What's going on, Alex?'

'With what?'

'You and Emma.'

Alex snapped his gaze to his friend, but Matt's face was a blank mask. There was neither hope nor judgement. It was just a simple question from the person who knew him better than anyone else.

'Nothing is going on. We've agreed to have some fun.'

'Alex, you know I love you, right? But you're an idiot.'

Alex couldn't help the smile that broke through. He'd missed Matt's particular brand of caring.

'Bloody hell, mate… You feel something for her.'

Alex couldn't lie to Matt. He did care for Emma. But that didn't mean he would change the course of his life for her. He had made it perfectly clear what he was looking for, and he felt no guilt because Emma wanted the same. It was possible that she was as jaded as he was—except he wasn't going to tell Matt that. Emma's secrets were his to keep.

'I'm not in it for the long haul, Matt.'

'Then what are you doing? She's not the only one growing attached. You are too. Have you considered that maybe you wouldn't fare as badly as your father?'

Matt never pulled any punches. Not with Alex. For their entire lives they had been totally honest with each other. A difficult conversation was never avoided for fear of how the other would react.

'I know I won't, because I'm not going to commit.'

'That's a lie and you know it. You have a title to think about,' Matt pushed.

'I don't know what to tell you. We're having fun, and when it's done we'll go our separate ways. She knows the score.'

'I know you're lying to yourself.' Matt shook his head, his tone softening. 'Whether you want to or not, one day you will have to accept everything you're trying to push away right now, Alex.'

Maybe Matt was right, but his legacy didn't mean as much to Alex as it did to everyone else. So what if he never had a family? The manor, the title—they meant very little to him. How could he set any store by them when it couldn't keep his family together? When that burden caused nothing but pain. Alex refused to put himself through that. There was no room for love in his life and there wouldn't ever be. Of that he was certain. Alex enjoyed his life as it was right now.

Right now, you have Emma, said a voice within him. He stubbornly ignored it.

'We're going out,' Alex said to Matt.

He needed to get away from his apartment to clear his head. Because everything in it made him think of Emma.

CHAPTER FOURTEEN

EVEN WITH MATT spending the next two weeks at Alex's apartment, Emma found time to be with him. She had tried to keep her distance, but after just two days neither she nor Alex had been able to resist the urge to be with each other.

She still knew it was time that Alex needed with his friend, and that being around the two of them felt too much as if their relationship could be something more, so Emma kept away as much as she could—even though it often felt as if she couldn't breathe for missing Alex. That worried her more than anything.

So when Matt suggested the three of them go out, Emma invited Hannah along as a buffer. But Matt was so taken with Hannah that Alex and Emma were soon forgotten, allowing them to slip away. They were so desperate for each other that his lips were on hers before she could even get out of the car.

When it finally came time for Matt to leave, everyone was sorry to see him go.

Emma went to shake his hand, but he pulled her in for a hug, and once she got over the surprise she found the familiarity endearing. It was a kind of warmth she had never truly encountered in her own family, and even though Matt was just a friend, by Alex's own admission he was as good as a brother.

'Take care of him,' Matt whispered in her ear.

Emma managed to contain her shock. She had been certain he knew that she and Alex had an expiration date, despite what he had told her.

All she said in reply was, 'Take care of yourself, Matt.'

Alex was next to embrace his friend, and once they'd bade each other farewell he led Emma away, giving Matt a private moment with Hannah.

'I want you to stay with me tonight,' he told her.

'Are you trying to make up for lost time?' Emma laughed.

'Yes.'

There was an intensity in his eyes that drew her in. She was lost in the sea of them.

'I'll be there.'

And she was—as soon as she was done with her evening's commitments to the charity.

Alex immediately took her to bed, making love to her over and over again until they were both utterly spent.

When she woke he wasn't in bed with her—as she had come to expect. She readied herself for work and then went searching for him in the large apartment. He was in the gym, and she had to stop herself from salivating at the sight of him. A towel hung around his neck, and his shirtless torso was drenched in sweat. He pushed away the hair sticking to his forehead as he placed large weights on a metal rack.

Catching sight of her in the mirror, he smiled.

'I hope I didn't interrupt,' she said.

Alex was tapping the screen of his fitness watch. 'No, I've just finished up.'

Emma stepped over the threshold of the room, walking towards him. Her delicate finger traced a line along his glistening pectoral. A gentle touch. He closed his eyes.

'Emma, we have to talk,' he said softly.

'I know what you're going to say, Alexander.'

The past two weeks didn't mean anything. It couldn't.

They had simply had a good time. Emma wouldn't let herself believe anything other than that.

She looked around at all the workout equipment. This room was better equipped than some professional gyms. 'Why do you work yourself so hard?'

'For control. I need it in every aspect of my life,' he said, watching her. Her hands were still on him.

'Is it because you want to control who enters and leaves your life? How you feel about it? How you respond to it?'

'Emma…'

He had never said her name like that. She knew it was a warning to drop the subject. He wasn't going to discuss his mother with her.

'It might not be so bad to let someone into your heart,' she said, holding his gaze. It was careful. Guarded. No emotion to be seen. No weakness for her to read.

'I don't have one,' he said flatly.

It was a statement. And suddenly there was a buzzing in her ears from the rage she felt for a woman she had never met. Emma didn't push. She didn't have a right to. But she hated that shut-off expression on his face.

Her hands travelled around his neck and into his hair, tugging his face down to hers. The moment their lips connected she felt the steel-like stiffness leave his body as his tongue plundered her mouth, making her moan. And then he took her up against the mirror.

Alex couldn't remember the last time he had enjoyed himself so much. Having Emma around just felt right. He'd wanted to see how she would fit into his life, and so far he was running out of reasons to push her away. Not that he wanted to. But he *had* to.

Confusion wasn't a feeling he often felt, and it was not one he was enjoying. He couldn't forget the conversation he had with Matt, and was scared that all the time they were spending together would start meaning something more to Emma. That the fact he craved her touch meant something more.

He sat in his office, tossing a little ball in the air as he pondered through all the thoughts in his head. Sorting through work and home and Emma.

He had a ball like it in all his workspaces, but it was placed back on the desk as he figured out the solution to a work problem. Just as his fingers reached the keys of his laptop, his phone rang.

'Alexander Hastings,' he answered.

'Good evening, Mr Hastings. This is Dr Bernard from the Fairmont Hospital.'

Alex's blood ran cold. 'What's happened?'

'Your father has had a heart attack.'

Alex was already on his feet, storming out through the door.

'He is stable, but he will have to remain in our care for a few days.'

He bashed the elevator button. It was taking too long to come up. Just as he moved towards the stairs, the ding informed him that the car had arrived. He rushed in, hitting the button for the car park.

'Okay, thank you. Keep me informed of everything. I'll be there as soon as I can. Probably very early in the morning.'

Alex barely heard what was said after that. He shoved his phone in his pocket and threw open the car door. He hurriedly climbed in and shut it, much harder than he meant to. Much harder than he should. He ran his fingers through his hair and punched the steering wheel. He felt as if his lungs were being squeezed as he fought to keep the dread at bay.

With squealing tyres, his car left the space.

Barely an hour had passed since Alex had received the call from the doctor, but he was already at Essendon Airport, climbing aboard the Hastings International private jet with single-minded determination. He had to leave. Right now.

And he kept up a mantra in his head of what he had to do. Alex could think of nothing else.

Operating on autopilot, Alex was silent. He said nothing to the pilot, or even to his cabin crew when they came through offering refreshments. Fear had a stranglehold on him. It was a vice around his lungs, squeezing the air out.

It was an unbearably long flight and despite arriving in the early hours of the morning, Matt was there to meet him.

He drove straight to the hospital and before he could bring the car to a complete stop, Alex was already getting out. His heart was hammering in his chest, terrified of what he would find.

Practically running, he went up to the private ward. The doctor was waiting, ready to talk to him before he could enter his father's room.

'Dr Bernard?' Alex asked. He hadn't slept at all on the flight, and it felt as if he was staying awake through sheer will.

She nodded. 'Mr Hastings,' she said in greeting.

'How is my father?' Though Alex seemed in control, the only tell that he was afraid to hear the answer was the clenched fist at his side.

'Tired. He's had what we call a non-ST elevation myocardial infarction—or a mild heart attack. There should be no lasting damage, but he will need a change in diet and lifestyle. A good exercise regime. And he must avoid stress. But all in all I think he will be fine. He will need to take it easy for the next few weeks while he recovers.'

Alex's shoulders sagged in relief. 'And his treatment?'

'I will be prescribing a list of medications. I think he should be out of here in a day or two, but he'll need to have constant follow-ups with his cardiologist.'

'He doesn't have one. Hasn't needed one before. Since you've treated him, I'd like him to be seeing you,' Alex said, instantly feeling more like himself. 'And if you give me the prescription, I will have it filled. May I see him now?'

'You can go ahead—but don't wake him.'

Alex walked into a room that was beautifully decorated. Had it not been for the medical equipment, it would have rivalled a luxury hotel. He'd expected darkness. For his father to be asleep. But the bedside light was on and he was reading something on his phone. It took a moment for him to notice his son at the door.

'Alex?' he said with surprise, putting his phone down.

'Dad.' With relief coursing through him, Alex showed more emotion than he ever had in his life. He walked straight to his father and engulfed him in a hug.

'What are you doing here?' he asked.

'Seriously? You gave me a scare!' Alex seemed to be caught somewhere between anger and hysterical laughter.

Robert Hastings took his son's hand in his. 'I'm so happy to see you, but you didn't need to come all this way.'

'Of course I did.' Alex sank into the armchair beside the bed.

'Did you speak to the doctor?'

'I did,' Alex said. 'And we'll be making some changes.'

His father rolled his eyes and Alex narrowed his. 'Don't give me that look. It's time you completely stepped back from the company.'

Walking into this room, he'd felt as if he'd let out a breath he had been holding in for nearly a day. Now Alex almost felt light-headed. The moment he'd received the news all he'd been able to think about was how he wasn't ready to lose his father. His only real family. He had prayed—actually prayed…something he hadn't ever done—to anyone who might hear him for his father to be okay. Alex would have done anything. And now that he was here changes would be made whether his father approved or not.

'Alex—'

'I don't want to hear it, Dad. You need to remove all the stress from your life. You're going to take some time out

at the manor. You can come back to London for your follow-ups. And we're getting someone to help you recover.'

'You want me to get a nurse?'

'Yes.'

'Alex, I have things to do...'

'I can take care of all of that.'

The two Hastings men stared each other down, but it
was Robert who gave in first. His son's stubborn streak
surpassed even his.

'Fine. There's a charity dinner the day after tomorrow.
You can start with that.'

'I'll attend in your stead, and when you're discharged
I'll take you to the country myself.'

'Alex, you do realise that I'm your father?'

'Yes—and I only have one of those, so I'm going to make
sure he takes care of himself and outlives me out of spite.'

It was the first smile Alex had cracked in over a day.
The terror was gone, the fear had left his eyes, and he was
himself once again.

'Son, you need to calm down.'

'Like hell I do.' Alex took a breath as his father's fingers
tightened around his. 'I think I need to let you get some
sleep. I take it the dinner invitation is at the house?'

'Yes, in my study.'

'Okay. Would you like me to bring you anything tomorrow?' Alex asked as he stood.

'Now that you mention it—'

'I mean books...that sort of thing.'

'Anything, son.'

'Get some sleep, Dad.'

Alex kissed his father's head then left. Happy to see the
light go out in the room as he walked away.

Alex fell into bed that night completely exhausted. Not a
single thought was spared for the fact that he was in his

London apartment after months of being away. It could have been a tiny room in the middle of nowhere for all he cared. Nothing in his life had prepared him for the feeling seeing his father in that hospital bed had brought. Knowing that Robert would be fine was a small comfort, but he was being confronted with his mortality, and everything Alex had been denying all these years suddenly loomed so large in front of him he could barely breathe.

Earl Hastings. He wasn't ready.

With a knot in his gut that wouldn't let up, he fell into a fitful sleep.

CHAPTER FIFTEEN

Two days.

It had been two days since Emma had heard from Alex. No calls. No messages. No promises of the pleasure that awaited her. This must be it. What she had been dreading for weeks. The inevitable end.

There had been no promises of long goodbyes when they'd started this. All it was meant to be was a release. Exploring their chemistry. And then it would be over. That was the promise Alex had made to her. Nothing more.

Emma walked to her office in a daze. Not willing to admit it, having their relationship end so abruptly hurt. She wasn't upset with Alex. He'd kept his word after all. All she wished was that he had told her instead of just disappearing. Especially after all that they'd shared. All that he had awakened in her.

Despite everything, a tiny part of Emma wondered what it would have been like if she and Alex were different people. If they could have had more than just a few mind-blowing nights. If life hadn't ripped their hearts to shreds, could they have had a future?

She flopped into her chair with a huff. Those thoughts wouldn't help her, or fill the hole that was growing in her chest because she missed him. Maybe a part of her always would.

There was a small blossom of hope that maybe she would

get to see him again. After all, he had promised Fiona that Hastings International would provide her charity with financial support through their philanthropy programme.

But even if she saw him it wouldn't be the same. The passionate kisses, the explosive chemistry would be gone. It was over.

Throwing herself into work, Emma refused even to look at her phone for the rest of the day. Keeping busy was the way she would deal with this, because whatever she'd shared with Alex wouldn't bow her or break her, it had only built her up.

It was late in the afternoon and the office had mostly emptied. There were only two lights on in the entire floor— hers and her manager's. Emma was exhausted. She tried not to think of Alex, but he kept creeping into her thoughts. Stealing away her concentration with memories of their time together. The night at the Skydeck would be one she would treasure to her last breath.

The phone that she had been ignoring all day sprang to life, and when she saw the caller she was caught between concern and confusion.

'Hi, Matt,' she answered.

'Emma, something's happened.'

She tried to suppress a sob, her heart breaking for Alex as Matt quickly told her all that had happened. An image of his father, the man he so greatly admired lying in a hospital bed filled her mind. *It was just my father and I,'* he had said to her.

And then guilt ripped through her. She'd thought he was done with her. That they were at an end. When he probably hadn't even thought about her at all. He would have been consumed with terror. He needed her. That was why Matt had called her, she realised.

'I'll be on the next flight out.'

Emma rushed to Greg's office, convincing him to give her time off. It was an emergency, after all.

And the moment he agreed, she was running for the elevator.

The flight took an agonisingly long time. It was more than enough time for her to question if she was doing the right thing.

Would Alex want her there? They weren't in a relationship.

Then she realised it didn't matter. Because he *needed* her. She was going to be with him. To help him carry this load, however heavy it turned out to be.

She could do that for him.

Alex entered the bright banqueting hall. It was spectacular. With red and gold carpets and carved wooden walls, it was like stepping back in time. The rows of hanging chandeliers cast a golden glow over everything, making it seem like a scene out of a fairy tale.

There were people everywhere in stunning outfits and expensive jewellery. He didn't care. He was numb to all of it. The ridiculousness of having to be at a party full of rich sycophants while his father lay in a hospital bed sickened him.

This wasn't his scene. It never had been.

It wasn't like the wild parties that he and Matt had enjoyed. Two bachelors without a care in the world. Where his title didn't matter. Where he didn't have to worry about a casual hook-up thinking there might be something more.

From where he stood now, even those held little appeal. All he wanted to do was drive to the hospital and sit in that chair beside his father. But he couldn't. Atlas. That was who he felt like. With the obligation of his family title bearing down on him like the weight of the world on his shoulders. But for his father, he would endure it.

Alex walked through the sea of bodies, not seeing hide nor hair of Matt. He made his way to the bar, still fighting that empty feeling he carried since leaving Melbourne.

After ordering a drink, he leaned against the bar—and then the world was tugged out from under him.

Emma.

There she was, standing at the entrance.

An absolute vision.

Alex thought he had to be hallucinating, but then his feet were carrying him towards her. That emptiness in him was closing a little more with each step and he knew she was really there.

She walked up to him with that smile that dimmed everything around her. 'Hello, Alexander,' she said softly.

He didn't answer. All he did was take her face in his hands and kiss her with desperation and longing. She had come all this way for him, and he realised right then just how much he had needed her. From the moment he'd got that call, every thought had been about getting to his father. He felt like a fool, because now that he had Emma in his arms he felt centred again.

Resting his forehead against hers, he said, 'You're here.'

'Of course I am.' Her hands came to his chest. 'I'm so sorry about your father…but I'm here now. We'll get through it together.'

'Emma…' he breathed.

It was all he could say. No one had ever stopped their world spinning just to be there for him. He had always accomplished everything alone. It was why he was so single-minded at times. Having Emma drop everything to support him at a time like this made him want to weep.

He suddenly realised that people were staring, so he offered her his arm and then saw Matt and his sister

Sarah entering. He offered his friend a smile. Matt simply winked back in response.

Despite her upbringing, Emma felt like an interloper amongst these people. Still, she held her head high and wouldn't let anyone shake her confidence. Especially after Alex had walked towards her with an expression that had morphed from a scowl to disbelief to...happiness?

Emma couldn't deny it any longer. She was there to support the man she loved.

Loved.

When she'd stepped into his embrace, every head had turned to look at them. Emma didn't care. And when she looped her arm in his it felt right. As if this was where she belonged. Even the warning she usually kept close, telling herself she shouldn't entertain these thoughts, was cast aside. None of it mattered. Not right now.

She was dressed in a long-sleeved blood-red velvet dress that hugged her body and flared out below her hips, falling like a curtain to the floor. The deep V neck exposed her long neck and fair chest, but still remained entirely demure. Her hair was swept back and straight, and silver and diamond drops hung from her ears. She knew she stood out from the crowd.

'Ravishing,' Alex said looking down at her.

But to Emma he looked just as good. In a black tux, he made all the words she wanted to say die on her tongue. Instead, she ran her fingers over the stubble on his cheek and pressed a kiss to his jaw.

Wanting her closer, Alex moved to wrap his arm around her waist. He was afraid she might disappear, as if this was all a trick of his overstressed mind, and he wasn't going to let her go. Even when Matt and his sister approached them and made the necessary introductions.

Emma thanked Sarah, who had lent her the dress, and then the four of them seated themselves at one of the many round tables spaced out around the floor. A section had been cleared as a dance floor, before a small stage with musicians playing various string instruments sitting upon it.

An auction was held, during which Alex paid an exorbitant amount of money for a piece of art that would likely be left behind in his flat in London when they went back to Melbourne. He didn't mind. As much as he hated these events, he always approved of the fundraising.

During dinner he paid little attention to everyone around them. Emma was with him, and he hadn't realised until now how much he needed her. Scarcely believing that he hadn't once thought to call her, Alex held her hand tightly now, not wanting to let go for even a second.

'What is it?' Emma asked as she caught him staring at her for what must have been the hundredth time that evening.

'You look beautiful,' he said, but it wasn't what he wanted to say.

He wanted to say how grateful he was that she was here. How hollow he had been feeling. How she made him not care even a little about who else was in this room tonight. He just couldn't get the words out.

Once all the plates had been cleared, and the mingling had begun in earnest, Sarah insisted on introducing Emma to some of the other ladies.

A group of the most elegant women Emma had ever seen stood near a window, each with a flute of champagne in her hand. Sarah was busy giving Emma a crash course on who each woman was, and any titbit of information that would help her fit in. Emma was grateful. Sarah made her feel welcome in this world, and it was nice to have found someone so friendly.

The two of them approached the group, who welcomed them with smiles. That was until Emma saw a beautiful tall blonde woman, who reminded her very much of Lauren in the way she held herself.

'Catherine,' Sarah said.

Catherine? Emma thought to herself. *Could it be?*

When she saw the smile on Sarah's face falter, she knew it was Alex's mother. Emma was suddenly consumed with a red-hot rage that she tried to bottle up. Alex was just a few meters away, and yet here was his mother who didn't even care.

'I heard you weren't coming tonight,' Sarah said sweetly, quickly recovering.

'Where else would I be, dear?'

Sarah didn't answer. Instead, she looped her arm through Emma's. 'This is Emma. She's visiting from Melbourne.'

Everyone welcomed her. Each had a different question to ask, and she happily answered all of them without missing a beat. Remembering her fine manners, it was easy to slip into conversation with them, but once the dance floor opened up one by one they left to join their partners, until it was just Catherine, Sarah and Emma.

'We should get back too, Emma.'

Sarah tried to turn them around, but Catherine had different ideas.

'So you're Alexander's date,' Catherine said, in a haughty way.

'Yes, I am,' Emma replied.

Sarah exchanged a look with her, telling her that unfortunately they couldn't just walk away. Making a scene was out of the question.

'Just his latest conquest then,' she said snidely. 'Someone should warn you: the apple didn't fall very far from the tree, I'm afraid.'

'It would seem that you aren't very familiar with Alexander at all,' Emma said pleasantly. She looked over her shoulder and saw him staring at them. His eyes were like ice. 'I have to get back to my date. Have a good evening.'

The two of them walked away, with Sarah grumbling under her breath, 'I hate that woman.'

'Matt told me a little about her. She didn't want to be a mother.'

'Oh, she's remarried now,' Sarah said. Seeing the look on Emma's face, she continued. 'Society at large may now be open-minded and progressive, but you have to keep up appearances in these circles. Her husband doesn't care what she does, and she feels the same, as long as they appear together when they need to.'

Emma didn't like the sound of that at all, but they had arrived at the group surrounding Matt and Alex and the two women split apart.

Alex's lips came down to her ear. His arm wrapped around her possessively. 'What did Catherine say to you?'

Emma shook her head. 'Nothing important.'

Alex studied her face. But whatever he was thinking about was pushed aside as he asked her to dance with him. With her hand in his, Alex swept her onto the dance floor. The sweet melody drifted over them and he pulled her close, leading in his effortless way. Swaying to the music, wrapped in a bubble… This was where Emma wanted to be. In his arms.

'Emma?' he said, in a voice that caressed her like smooth velvet.

'Yes?'

'I'm happy you're here.'

She beamed up at him and then tucked her head into his shoulder. There was a part of her that had worried that he didn't actually need her. Seeing him now, hearing his words, made every second spent travelling so very worth it.

'Would you like to leave?' he asked.

'Can we?'

He kissed her forehead. 'Of course. I can't wait to get you home.'

CHAPTER SIXTEEN

THE NEXT DAY Alex took Emma to the hospital so he could fetch his father and drive him to the family manor. Robert had flat-out refused to be wheeled out to the black Range Rover that his son had arrived in, already loaded with bags and the exercise equipment Alex had procured to assist in his recovery, and Emma waited patiently while Alex fussed, making sure his father was properly buckled in before he walked her to his low, sleek Porsche and handed over his key.

'It's fast. Be careful,' he instructed.

'It will be fine, Alexander. Relax. I have the satnav already set and I'll follow right behind you, I promise.'

He knew he was being a little obsessive; it was just that he needed Emma to be safe. There would be no relaxing until they all arrived at Greenfield House. Alex kissed her sweetly, then opened the door for her. Once she was in, he closed it. Emma started the car with a throaty roar and gave him a thumbs-up.

Alex climbed into the large SUV and pulled out of the parking area, checking his mirrors to ensure Emma was following.

It took them a little under two hours to reach the long gravel driveway of the manor, which crunched under his tyres. Despite the icy weather, the place looked beautiful. Tall trees lined the long drive, hiding the dwelling from sight. But as he rolled forward, the immense redbrick house was gradually revealed. Its Georgian architecture was beautiful, with white accents on the windows and pillars popping brightly against the red background and green scenery.

Emma was absolutely captivated by the house. She brought Alex's car to a stop, and when she got out revelled in the tranquillity. In front of the house, Alex and a member of staff were already pulling the bags out of the back of the Range Rover and carrying them up the steps into the house.

When Emma entered, she thought she had gone back in time. The walls were panelled in dark wood and a grand, carved staircase took centre stage in the hall. The only word she could think of to describe the place was regal. It had an old-world glamour that she only ever experienced when she'd travelled or read about it. There was so much history here. These walls must hold generations of memories.

She followed Alex upstairs. He had deposited his father's bags in a large master suite that had its own sitting area and now he led her to his own, situated on the same floor, but at the far corner of the house and overlooking the grounds.

He grinned at her as he put the bags down. 'Gives us a bit of privacy.'

She giggled at his flirty wink. Following him out and along the many corridors, it started to dawn on Emma exactly who Alex was. What his life was meant to be. The large portraits of his ancestors didn't help the anxiety blooming in her. He wasn't ordinary, and suddenly their life in Melbourne seemed like make-believe. More evidence of why this could never be anything but a temporary fixation.

All of a sudden he seemed further from reach than he ever had, and she was even more determined to make the most of this while she could. And when she was old and grey, alone with her cats, she would have memories to keep her heart warm.

The melancholy was hard to push away.

Alex left her when they went downstairs, and went to the room where the nurse he had hired had already set up a gym. The cook was there, listening carefully to the nurse's instructions as she handed her a list of ingredients that were permitted and those that were now forbidden.

Emma was deep in conversation with his father when Alex came back into the living room.

'Emma, shall we go for a walk?' he asked. 'You'll need your coat,' he said from the door.

'Enjoy it,' his father called as they left the room.

Alex already had his heavy charcoal pea coat on, and waited at the front door as she ran upstairs to fetch a puffy jacket.

'Ready?' he asked, watching her jog down the stairs.

'Yup.'

He held the door open and out she stepped. The cold bit at her cheeks. They trudged down the steps onto the gravel, then Alex stopped. Curling his lip over his teeth, he whistled loudly and waited. From around the side of the house two large fluffy dogs bounded towards them. Tails wagging frantically, they jumped up, trying to get as close to Alex as possible.

'Hey guys!' He patted their heads and scratched their chins. 'Okay, that's enough. Sit!' he commanded, and instantly they listened. 'Good boys.' He looked at Emma. 'This is Clifford and Gatsby.'

Emma remembered the Airedale Terriers he had told her about and she had wished she could meet them. Now she was.

Holding her hand out to them, she let both dogs sniff, and once again their tails began to wag. 'They're beautiful!'

He grasped her hand in his and turned to walk away. 'Clifford, Gatsby—let's go.'

The dogs were at their side as they followed the path that crunched beneath their feet, through a copse of trees.

'It's so lovely here,' Emma said, looking out over an empty paddock. 'Horses?'

'Yes. To both.'

'But you don't like coming here?' Emma looked at Alex, who was watching the dogs run ahead.

'Not particularly. When I was young and Matt would come, it was fun. There was plenty of mischief to get up to.' He smiled fondly at the memory. 'But there's a lot I don't like being reminded of here.'

'I understand. Especially after meeting Catherine.'

'What did she say to you?' he asked.

His feelings were masked but his eyes spoke volumes. Emma could see hurt and anger burning in them.

'She just made a snide comment,' Emma said.

Alex let go of her hand and stuck his in his jacket pockets. Emma followed suit.

'Which was?'

'I don't want to upset you, Alexander.'

'*You* won't.'

Emma sighed, and told him exactly what Catherine had said. Saying the words to him now made her just as angry as she'd been on hearing them the night before. Catherine was cruel, and Emma could only imagine how it must have made Alex feel to see her.

You understand what it's like. You can help him, that inner voice said.

Alex pulled on her sleeve, forcing her to stop. 'You know that's not true.'

'I know. I told her she doesn't know you at all.'

'And you know who she is?'

'I do. Although when you said you didn't have a mother I assumed…'

'She was dead?' he said, without the tiniest hint of emotion.

'Yes.'

Alex moved to the paddock, folding his arms on the high white fence. His gaze was far off. 'Dead or alive, it makes no difference.'

Emma climbed onto the fence, sitting on top of it to face Alex. 'Would you like to talk about it?'

She could tell his teeth were clenched behind his lips. That would be a no, then. 'Whatever she says is a lie anyway. But I think your dad is amazing. And so are you.'

Alex still wasn't looking at her.

'You know, growing up, I wished that I had a father like yours,' she told him. 'I would read story books about earls and dukes and pretend the characters were my family. I'm not proud of it, but sometimes I wished that my dad would just go away. But then I'd realise what that would mean and I'd feel guilty.'

She watched the dogs run around and chase each other, oblivious to the cold.

'It's hard when you have to deal with parents like mine. And, of course, you can never say anything bad about it— not that you'd want to anyway. Everyone sees what you have—a big house and money—but they never see what you don't have,' she said sadly.

Alex was watching her carefully now. Silent.

'And the biggest of that is faith. Faith that things will work out and be okay. For as long as I can remember my parents were at each other's throats. They would bicker constantly. Sometimes I would put a pillow over my head to block them out, and then I asked to move my bedroom. It was quieter in the new room, even though it was the

smallest room in the house. After that the affairs started.
My father didn't even bother trying to hide it. And I swore
that would never be me.'

She looked at Alex, who held so much warmth and love
in his eyes. And she wanted him to stop looking at her like
that because he couldn't ever be hers. But she wanted to
get lost in those blue pools anyway.

She looked away. It was easier just to keep talking. And
the rolling hills were a beautiful distraction.

'It got a little better when Maddison was young, but
we're right back where we were again now. At least she
has me. Lauren doesn't seem to care as long as she and
my father get their way. It's a pretty sad way to live, don't
you think?'

Alex moved to stand between her legs. Holding on to her, he
set her on her feet and pulled her against his body. Hugged
her tightly. For a moment the place he stood in didn't feel
like a prison. For the first time it felt like home.

After the terror of his father's heart attack, and days of
constant worry, Alex didn't have the strength in that moment to push Emma away. For just this one time he wanted
to feel peace. It was as if his lifestyle of beautiful women
and doing what he wanted when he wanted to, always the
armour to protect himself, meant nothing. Could be cast
away.

'I'm sorry.'

It was all Alex could say, because it was true. He was
sorry that she'd had to endure all that for so long. Sorry he
hadn't met her earlier. Sorry that she had to be strong out
of necessity. Sorry that they couldn't be more to each other.

'You deserve better.'

'So do you,' Emma said, her voice muffled by his coat.
'We should probably start making our way back.'

'Yeah, we should.'

He whistled to the dogs, who walked beside the couple as Alex showed Emma around the estate. Through the stables, past the enormous garage, along the garden paths. She was delighted to see the maze and Alex walked her through it, having long ago figured out all the ways out.

When they got back to the house the dogs made a bee-line for the fireplace, settling in front of the hearth. His father was seated in an armchair, waiting for their arrival.

'Alex, I want you to go back to London,' he said, when the two of them had settled down. 'I appreciate all you're doing, son, and I'm willing to do as you ask. But for me to relax, I need you to be close to the company.'

'Dad...'

'I already know everything you're going to say, but I'm being well taken care of here.'

'Robert, we just want to make sure your recovery goes well,' Emma said.

'My dear, I know that. But I also know my son hates it here. He needs the city, and the company needs him there. If you want me to be stress-free, you'll go back.'

Alex laughed. He knew there was no point arguing with the man. 'We'll leave tomorrow—but we will be back before we return to Melbourne.'

'Lovely.'

'And remember, everyone is reporting to me...so I'll know what's going on here,' Alex said sternly.

'I'd expect nothing less, son.'

Emma and Alex spent all the time they could with his father that evening. Stories were told of what their lives had been like over the years, and Emma found out that Robert had always been a stern and imposing man, but had loosened up considerably when Alex took the reins at the company.

Despite what they said, Emma could see how much Robert loved his son. Watching them, she couldn't help but smile. It was sweet to see how much Alex cared for his father. He was, after all, the only family Alex really had.

Alex caught her eye, and she stopped breathing at the look he gave her. Moments later they were up in his room, with Alex creating a new memory for this house to hold.

CHAPTER SEVENTEEN

ALEX AND EMMA didn't leave for London until late the next day. For the first time Alex felt the manor wasn't an imposing prison for his soul, waiting for him like an over-eager jailer. The sun beamed down over the rolling hills, and even though it didn't warm them, Alex wanted to enjoy it for just a little while.

Soon enough the life in this manor would claim him, and the freedom he craved would be gone. When that happened he would at least have these two days to think on. A small reminder that once upon a time, these walls had held laughter and that three-letter word he yearned for. Fun.

When they arrived back in London, Alex realised how well his father knew him. He had been right. Alex *did* need the city. As soon as he stepped into his flat he felt the tension that had pulled him so taut ebb away.

Alex didn't show Emma around his flat that night. He simply took her to bed. And that was where they stayed until he blearily opened his eyes and needed a moment to figure out where he was. Then everything came rushing back and he was suddenly wide awake.

He ran a hand through his tousled hair. The room was still dark, and after finding the control pad on his side table he pressed the button that would raise the blinds. The sky beyond the large window looked like steel. He missed the sunshine.

Taking a moment before he looked over at the sleeping woman beside him, Alex still couldn't quite believe that Emma had flown all this way to be with him and expected nothing in return. Her hair fanned over the pillow. Light was falling over the curve of her breasts, the sheet only just hiding her nipples from view. This woman—this tremendously beautiful woman—had him stirring without even trying.

Emma was still fast asleep. He rolled onto his side with his head propped up on his arm. She looked so peaceful that he didn't want to wake her. But need coursed through him so painfully that he couldn't bear not to.

'Emma,' he said softly, brushing her hair away from her face.

Her brows knitted together as she slowly woke, blinking away the sleep from her eyes. 'Morning…'

She bathed him in a glorious smile and he felt his heart clench. Still stroking her hair, for a moment he wondered how he would ever walk away from her. Why he would want to. Their attraction showed no sign of dissipating. Frustrating. That was what it was. Because it seemed ridiculous that he should deny himself. But what if this attraction never died? Then what? He didn't care for strings. For relationships. For love.

Emma leaned into his touch, her eyes closed. His hand slid from her hair, grazing her cheek as his thumb traced the line of her lips. Slowly, she opened her blue-grey eyes wide. The embodiment of winter. Those eyes would haunt him for the rest of his life.

Something shifted in them, as if she'd suddenly realised that for once he was there with her in bed. Alex had been so careful. Even at the manor he had always woken before she had. Broken boundaries. That was what this was. And he was the one who'd done it.

Idiot, he chastised himself.

Surprise flickered in her gaze, but then her eyes turned molten. Reflecting what she must see in his.

'Shower first?' His voice was rough.

She agreed. Another broken boundary.

Jets of hot water spurted overhead as the two of them climbed into the large glass cubicle. He pulled her under the water, pressed her body against his and claimed her lips in a fierce kiss. He'd wanted to see how she would fit into his life, and now he knew. Wanted it despite himself. A life with Emma. A terrifying thought. He wanted it, but he could never have it.

'Thank you for being here,' he said, looking down into the depths of her eyes.

'I wouldn't be anywhere else, Alexander.'

Emma kissed him once more. Sensing that there was some sort of vicious battle raging inside him, she wanted to lighten the atmosphere. To take him back to having a good time and taking over the world. Carry his burden. That was why she was here. Because he needed her. What he didn't need was being needled for information. To talk about things he didn't want to.

With the water falling around them like rain, running down their bodies and pitter-pattering, on the tiled floor, Emma kissed a line down his torso as she went to her knees. His sky-blue eyes clouded over with lust, pupils dilating as he watched her lick his length.

Emma took him in her mouth and he groaned, low and deep. He was like steel encased in velvet in her hands. Teasing him with her tongue and her fingers and her warm, wet mouth, she watched him coming apart at the seams. One of his hands gently rested on the back of her head, the other was braced against the wet tiled wall as his hips began moving of their own accord.

Emma felt more alive than she ever had. Control and

power ran through her veins, along with an arousal so strong it seared through her. *She* was making Alex come apart. This man that Aphrodite herself could have carved.

'Emma…' he said.

A breathless warning. One she wouldn't heed. Emma sucked deeper and his hips stilled, his body becoming rigid as he found his release. He pulled her up and kissed her thoroughly.

Laughter bubbled up, filling the space between them. Because *that* had been fun and overwhelming and consuming. Then, still breathing raggedly, and with a roguish smile, Alex returned the favour.

The breakfast that Alex had ordered was delivered soon after they got out of the shower, and Emma chose to finish her coffee out on the high-up balcony overlooking the river below. This apartment was so different from his other one. Just as luxurious. Filled with light and glass. But more masculine, with dark wood and brooding colours. The view was incredible too. There was no questioning which city she was in, with all the beautiful landmarks she could see.

'Penny for your thoughts?' Alex asked as he joined her.

Rain was starting to sprinkle overhead, and Emma tried her best to warm her hands on the coffee cup. Shivers racked her body.

'I was just thinking this place is so different from what I was expecting.'

He moved to stand behind her. Wrapping his arms around her waist. Drawing her into his warmth. 'And what was that?'

'A fancy high-tech townhouse in Mayfair or something.'

Alex laughed. 'I like being close to the water. And I can watch the boat race from up here.'

'The Regatta?' Emma asked.

'Mm-hmm.'

'Isn't rowing a bit slow for you?'

She couldn't imagine him doing anything that didn't involve wild amounts of speed. Rowing somehow seemed too tame a sport for Alex.

She knew he was rolling his eyes, even though she couldn't see it.

'I used to be on the team at university,' he said.

'That's impressive. It explains all the water-related art you have.'

'You noticed?'

Of course she had. There wasn't much Emma missed. Considering how she'd grown up, being observant had served her well. Noticing when to make herself scarce, when to give up something to Lauren, when to shield Maddison.

Alex tightened his hold on her. 'I sail now.'

'You do?'

'I have a sixty-footer.'

He pulled out his phone. She could hear him tapping the screen.

'Unfortunately, the weather is not ideal so we can't take her out.'

'That's okay.'

He frowned at the disappointment curdling in him. He didn't share his sailing with anyone apart from family and friends. But how wonderful it would have been to have her all to himself, with nothing but ocean around them, as he made her scream out his name over and over again.

'How long do I have you before I have to return you to the world?' Alex asked in a low voice, teeth nipping at her ear.

'Two weeks. I didn't know what I was walking into or how long you'd need me when I asked for leave,' she explained.

Two weeks. He liked the sound of that.

With rogue thoughts still clouding his usually sound judgement, Alex decided they needed to get out. He'd take Emma on a tour of the city. Show her everything she would never have seen during past visits to London. It would be London as he knew it. No locked doors and even fewer rules.

They still had most of the two weeks ahead of them, and he resolved to enjoy it as much as possible.

He took her somewhere new each day.

That was when they weren't exploring each other in his bed or couch or kitchen.

They spent virtually every minute together.

It made them both forget, just for a little while, the end.

They visited Robert one more time, as promised, even though Alex video-called his father every day.

Buoyed by how much better he looked, they were at ease with leaving for Melbourne.

Alex's private jet stood on the tarmac, gleaming in the weak sunshine. He followed her up the stairs. Emma had grown up with money. There wasn't a thing on earth she couldn't buy. But this life that Alex led was on a different level. She didn't care to reflect on it. Not when Alex was leading her to one of the cream-coloured seats and buckling her in.

'You know, I'm perfectly capable of doing up my own belt.'

'I do know, but I'm enjoying getting to tie you down.'

She felt the colour rise up her neck as he ran his nose along her jaw, then seated himself across from her. She wondered what it would be like to be bound to his bed, with him having his way with her. Showing her pleasure as only he could. The look on his face told her that he had a direct line to her thoughts.

Once the plane had levelled off, a stewardess placed artful plates containing their lunch on the table between them. Throughout it, Emma kept casting longing glances at Alex, until she knew he couldn't take it any more.

Calling for two glasses of champagne, he handed one to Emma, then took her hand and led her to the bedroom at the back of the plane, where they crossed off another first...

Alex lay tangled in sheets that had damp patches on them, from where the champagne had run off Emma's body and collected in the fabric. With their chests heaving and sweat glistening on her skin, she drew abstract patterns on his hard torso, and he curled his arm under his head as he watched her fingers dance.

'Everything okay?' he asked, when at last she came down from her high and Emma was able to reply to the email that had pinged on her phone.

'Fiona wants a meeting as soon as I'm back. She says she wants to get going on things as quickly as possible.'

Emma propped her head up on her arm and looked down at Alex, who tucked the curtain of her hair behind her ear.

'She told me she wants to make the transition as smooth as possible and keep everyone on board. We're all volunteers anyway.'

Emma laughed to herself. A small sound that he knew held very little humour.

'I don't know how my family is going to react.'

'What are you going to tell them?'

'No idea. But I couldn't possibly disappoint them any more than I do already.'

She tried to cover up the sadness in her eyes, but he still saw it.

'Emma...' he whispered, and pulled her down into a kiss, wrapping his arms around her as her head came to rest on his chest. 'It hurts when your own blood doesn't acknowledge you, but you don't need them. They're just people. People who don't even really know you. Just be proud of yourself. You have achieved this without anyone.'

'That's not true. I've achieved this because of you, Alexander,' she said softly. 'I would never have met Fiona if it wasn't for you.'

'You would have found a way. I have no doubt.'

Maybe, she thought to herself.

But those words could have been said to him just as much as to her. It did hurt when family abandoned you. And no one would understand that more than Alex. A little boy abandoned first by his selfish mother and then by his father, when he chose to throw himself into his work.

She rested her chin on her hands as she turned to look at him. 'How do you do it?'

Strong fingers stroked through her hair. 'Do what?'

'Deal with it? Your mother was at that ball. I saw how angry you were. But you acted like she wasn't even there. Most of the time…' she tacked on at the end, remembering the look on his face when she had spoken to Emma.

'I told you. I don't have a mother.'

While his fingers still caressed her, and his arm still held her to him, his eyes wore that empty look that appeared whenever he shut his feelings away. A simple message. *Back off.* But Emma didn't want to. That woman had hurt him over and over again since he was a child.

'Except you do. She may not want to be, and you may not want her to be, but the fact is, she is.'

'Emma…' It was a warning.

'It's okay to be angry at her, Alexander. You're entitled to your feelings. But don't let that woman rule your life… destroy any happiness you could have in the future.'

Finally, those fingers stilled. He opened his mouth, but Emma cut him off before he could say anything unkind. She knew it would just be a defence mechanism. 'I'm not saying that happiness should be with me, or that you should find it any time soon. I'm just saying don't let her take away more from you than she already has. You're amazing, Alexander. You deserve more.'

She lifted her lips to his and kissed him. Kissed him until there was only heat scorching them. Until she felt weightless. Until the chill left his eyes. Until neither of them could breathe.

Alex rolled them over, lifted his head, and bathed her in that crooked smile that stopped her heart.

CHAPTER EIGHTEEN

THE FIRST DAY back at work was torture. Emma could barely concentrate. London was still fresh in her mind. All she wanted was to be back there, in that apartment above the river. What they'd shared had been pure pleasure, and even her family's ire at her leaving for two weeks couldn't dampen her spirits. But it could make the day unbearably long.

Sitting in her office, Emma was taking a moment to gather her thoughts when there was a knock on the door.

'Fiona,' she said, getting to her feet, pleased that the morning had gone by. 'Please, take a seat.'

'Busy day?' Fiona asked as she sat down, elegantly crossing her legs.

'Like you wouldn't believe.' Emma looked at the closed glass door and the minimal privacy it provided. Everyone could see in, which meant her family would easily find out about Fiona's visit. 'Would you like to move to one of our meeting rooms?'

'Oh, there's no need. I'll be quick.'

Emma sat back in her chair. Butterflies had been unleashed in her stomach. Years of charity work had come to this point. She knew what Fiona wanted to talk about. Her small charity was finally going to soar as she'd always wanted it to. Excitement and trepidation in equal measure coursed through her.

'Everything is on track with the merger?' she asked.

'Yes, but that's not why I'm here.'

The serious look on Fiona's face had Emma's stomach plummeting. Had something gone wrong? Had her family interfered in some way? Did Fiona want the charity but not her? It wouldn't be the first time she hadn't been good enough, but she had done a great job so far. At least she thought so.

In the time it took Fiona to pull out a document from her bag, Emma considered every possibility that could have gone wrong. When Fiona slid the papers over, Emma had to make a gargantuan effort to keep from shaking.

'Relax, Emma,' Fiona said, clearly sensing her worry. 'Just take a moment to read this.'

Emma gave her a wary look but picked up the document. She read the top of the page and almost dropped it. Her eyes snapped to meet Fiona's.

'I'm not here for the charity, Emma. I'm here for you.'

The words *Offer of Employment* stared at her. Three times. She read it three times but still couldn't believe it. This was her dream.

'I thought you wanted to keep me on as a volunteer,' Emma finally managed to get out.

'I do. But you're too valuable an asset for me to overlook, Emma. You would be coming into a management role with us. I understand if this comes as a shock. After all, you do have other options.' Fiona looked around the small office. 'But, to be frank, I think you're wasted here.'

Emma scanned each line of the offer, falling more and more in love with the role. *'Do what makes you happy.'* That was what Alex had said. Heaven knew she wanted to. But, having been told over and over again since she was young what was expected of her, Emma didn't know how to do that when she was supposed to be here. In this tiny office. Until she was called upon.

'You don't have to decide immediately. Give it a day, think it over and then call me.' Fiona leaned forward in her chair, taking Emma's hand. 'There are many successful careers with us, Emma. I think this would only be the beginning for you.' Fiona stood and Emma followed her to the door. 'I really hope you say yes.'

'Thank you, Fiona.'

That was all Emma could manage. She watched her leave, then shut the door and dropped into her chair, reading through the offer again. This was what she had always wanted. Possibilities of a very different future ran through her mind then. Each one of them so much brighter than the path she was currently on.

She let herself imagine what it would be like. Not to have to be here every day. Not to feel like the spare daughter who wasn't wanted or needed. In front of her now was the opportunity to do something special. Words she wouldn't ever use to describe her job at Brown Hughs. Right now she was waiting. Waiting to be needed. Waiting for her life to start.

Emma wanted to make a difference. She knew she could do it. The only thing holding her back from immediately saying yes was her family. And, while she knew they wouldn't support her, she felt she owed them a chance to discuss her future. Or at the very least an explanation of why she wanted to leave.

The bravery to follow her dreams was what she needed now. Looking back on the past few weeks, she realised she had been braver than ever before. Exploring her sensuality with Alex, allowing him to see how her family affected her instead of always shoving the feelings away, letting him comfort her, flying to London to be with him. All those things had taken bravery.

Her phone was in her hand before she had even realised. Alex answered on the very first ring.

'Come out for a drink with me tonight? I have good news.'

'Where am I picking you up?' he asked, without even a moment's hesitation.

'My office.'

The floor was completely deserted. Emma's office was the only one occupied. If anyone walked by they would think that she was pulling long hours yet again. Nothing unusual.

Except she was obsessively rereading the offer.

'Stare any harder and you might set the paper on fire.'

She jumped at the voice and Alex laughed as he strode in. Heart leaping in her throat, she rose to step into his arms. His lips came down to meet hers in a gentle kiss that had her feeling giddy. Would she ever tire of this man?

'What's this good news?' he asked, keeping her pressed against his body.

Emma plucked the letter off the table and handed it to him. He stepped away from her, pacing as he read it. 'Tell me you've accepted.'

'Fiona told me to take a day to think it over.'

'You don't need one.'

Emma smiled. 'No, I don't.'

As conflicted as she felt, and having gone over every scenario a million times, there was one thing she kept coming back to: this was her dream. Surely she should be allowed to pursue that. There was nothing she did at Brown Hughs that someone else couldn't. No matter what happened after this, with her family or Alex, she would have one thing that made her truly happy.

The letter fell with a smack against the table as Alex dropped it, coming around her desk and yanking her to him. He kissed her hard and quick.

'This is the best news I've had all day. Let's go and celebrate,' he said, rubbing his nose along hers.

'Let's.'

Sipping the most delicious champagne she had ever tasted, in the most spectacular bar in Melbourne, Emma couldn't help but feel grateful for the man sitting beside her. Ever since she'd bumped into him her life had become so full. And now, as she stared out over her favourite city in the world, with Alex's lips on her neck and goosebumps racing along her arms, she understood that, despite her better judgement, she was irretrievably in love with him.

What a stupid, *stupid* thing to have let happen.

She wouldn't tell him. No. This was still a no-strings exploration of their off-the-charts chemistry. Nothing more.

'Do you want to go home?' he asked.

As if she was conditioned to respond instantly to him, Emma felt moisture pool in her core. The purr of his voice promised an unforgettable night.

'I want to go for a walk,' she said.

Telling him she loved him was off the table, but maybe she could share something of herself with him. Maybe he'd treasure it.

'Where are you taking me?' Alex asked.

'Somewhere special.' She smiled. 'My favourite place in the city. It may not seem like much to most, but I love it.'

Unlike the last time they'd walked through the streets and alleys, this time they couldn't bear not to touch. Alex laced his fingers in hers, holding tightly. It was such an innocent thing, holding hands. With them it didn't feel like it. It was the craving of having the other's skin on theirs. Feeling their heat and knowing they were one tug or pull away from losing all control.

If anyone had told Emma in the past that holding hands

could feel like a sensual experience, she would have laughed at them. Now she knew the strength in those magic fingers. The safety of his touch. Felt the memories of each time he'd made her come apart.

'I'm going to tell my family tomorrow, after work,' she said, just to fill the silence that was burning through her so much that she'd almost given up on their walk altogether.

'Will you be okay?'

He looked down at her. Concern was what she saw in his eyes.

Emma shrugged her shoulders. 'I think so. Doesn't matter, though. It needs to be done. I'm following my dream, Alexander. Doing what makes me happy.'

'I'm glad to hear you say it.'

'Which means I can't see you.'

'Good thing we have tonight.'

'We're here,' Emma said in a quiet voice. 'This is it.'

Emma looked around her, feeling the same wonder she'd felt the first time she'd seen it.

They stood at an intersection, with buildings on all four corners. Glorious sand-coloured, weathered pieces of art. They stood golden in the streetlights. Their black, shadowed crevices only making them more breathtaking. And rising from each corner was a tall tree. Rough bark and smooth emerald leaves alike shared the golden illumination cast upon them.

'It's beautiful,' Alex said as he came up behind her, wrapping his arms around her waist. 'I can see why you like it so much.'

'I thought you would appreciate the Victorian architecture.'

'I do,' he said softly. 'Thank you for sharing this with me.'

Emma turned around in his arms. 'Thank you for appreciating it.'

She felt the apprehension leaving her body as he drew her to him, his gaze pulling her in. He took her face in his hands and pressed his lips to hers. Long and slow. Tongues entwining. Drowning in each other. It was a miracle they were still on their feet. She had never felt such a primal need to be with someone as she did right now.

He was like a beacon in the darkness. She could kiss him forever. She wanted to. And the fact that he was kissing her here, in her favourite place, broke and mended and shattered something within her.

CHAPTER NINETEEN

ALEX SAT IN his office. He had a morning of back-to-back meetings and a slew of issues that he'd normally tackle head-on. Not today. He was distracted. In fact, he'd cut the last meeting short because he hadn't been able to handle being in that room when his every thought was of Emma.

Last night, he'd thought that a day apart from her was exactly what he needed. He'd felt so off balance since they had returned. Emma was starting to make him question why he lived his life the way he did. The way he always had. It was something he wasn't willing to accept. He'd thought a tiny bit of space would do them both a world of good, even as his chest had tightened at the prospect. As if his body had physically rejected the idea.

When had he ever worried about anyone like this? Or at all? Somehow she had found a way under his skin and he cared now. More than he should. Because he still intended to walk away.

Convincing himself that leaving had always been the best course of action, Alex figured that when the time came, walking away would be the greatest show of his caring. There was no happy future with him.

Emma needed someone capable of love. Not someone who hadn't been good enough for a mother who had abandoned him or a father who had left him to his loneliness. That same blood flowed through his veins, and he was damned if he would ever do that to anyone. Or allow them to do it to him. When their attraction was gone, Emma would leave, and he wasn't going to risk becoming like his father, no matter how brilliant the man was.

His thoughts didn't stop him from picking up the phone and calling her. When she answered, her voice was like a warm caress over his skin.

'Alexander.'

'Ripped off the Band-Aid yet?'

Her musical laugh came through, wrapping around his spine with a tingle.

'Not yet. I was just about to call my mother.'

'Good luck.' Alex paused. He wanted to offer to be there with her. Protect her. But he knew it wasn't his place.

'Emma…'

'Alex…'

They spoke at the same time and laughed.

'You first,' he said.

'Thank you for checking in,' Emma said.

Alex held the phone to his ear, picturing what she looked like now and how she would feel later. 'Remember why you're doing this,' he said.

'I will.'

She sighed, and he had the strangest feeling she was trying not to say something.

'I'll talk to you later.'

Emma placed her phone on the table. She had been putting off calling her mother all day, but speaking to Alex had given her the little shove she needed.

Lifting the receiver of her desk phone, Emma called her mother's extension. 'Hi, Mom, I need a favour.'

'What is it, Emma?' Helen Brown's distracted voice came through.

'I need to talk to all of you tonight. Do you think you

can make that happen?' Emma asked. Her heart was pounding in her chest.

'Sure, darling. Shall we have a family dinner? Is Alex coming?'

Family dinners were torture. The thought of having to sit through a meal after she gave them the news was too much to bear. Maybe if she spoke to them after the meal? That was sure to be unpleasant, and there was no way they would allow her to make them wait when she had called for everyone to be present.

'No. I won't be long, and Alex is working.'

'Okay. What time will you come over?'

'Straight after work. Six?'

'That's fine. See you later, Em.'

Emma hung up and scrunched her fingers in her hair. It was ridiculous that she should feel scared. This was her flesh and blood. They had raised her. For better or worse, they would be in her life forever.

The problem was she was certain tonight would be for worse...

Emma drove through the city and eventually came to the tree-lined roads of Toorak. The houses were as big as the bank accounts around here, and that was exactly what her family liked.

She pulled up to the gates of her family home and pressed the button on the little remote that lived in her car. She waited for the gates to swing open and then rolled the car to a spot on the driveway where she always parked when she wanted a quick exit.

Emma eyed the behemoth of a house, with its towering walls and smooth pillars. It was a stately mansion, and ordinarily she would have appreciated it. Except she had grown up within its walls, and there was nothing she coveted more than the small sanctuary she now called home.

Emma took a deep breath at the front door. Her palms were already sweaty. She straightened her dress and walked in.

'Mom?' she called.

A round table stood in the middle of the hall, with an obnoxiously large flower arrangement in its centre. Two sweeping staircases clung to the wall, beckoning her in as if the house itself offered a welcoming hug. But even shiny polished banisters couldn't help the cold that lived within.

'Emma?' Her mother's head poked out from the doorway.

'Hi, Mom.' Emma hugged her mother.

'You look nervous. Everything okay?'

Emma nodded.

'Okay, well…everyone's here.'

Her mother walked back the way she'd come and Emma followed her into the dining room, where everyone had taken their usual seats. Emma decided sitting was probably better than standing. It wouldn't seem as if she was impatient to flee, even though she was.

'What's this about, Emma?' asked her father as she took her seat at the opposite end of the table. As far as possible from him.

You can do this, she told herself.

'I have an announcement to make, and I want to tell you all in person—not drop a surprise on you at the office.'

It was the truth. If there was a scene to be made, she would rather they dealt with it in private than have an audience. No doubt that would cause all sorts of rumours to spread like wildfire throughout the company, the way gossip often did. She didn't want that for Brown Hughs.

Lauren narrowed her eyes. 'Have you done something?'

Emma smiled. A full, beaming, megawatt smile. 'Yes, something good. As you all know, a few years back I joined a small literacy charity as a volunteer.'

'Ugh, that charity again?' Lauren scoffed.

'Yes, the charity, Lauren.' Emma forced herself to remain calm. She wasn't going to get upset or angry. It wouldn't help her. 'Recently I've had a few meetings with a large national charity, and they were so impressed with us that they've decided to merge our organisation into theirs.'

'That's wonderful news, honey,' said her mother.

'It is. Now we'll be well funded, and we can reach so many more people. But that's not why I'm here.' Emma took a deep breath. 'I have been offered a management position in the organisation and I've decided to accept.'

She looked at everyone, waiting for the explosion. They were all silent.

Maddison was the first to show any response at all. She grabbed Emma's hands with her own, a broad smile on her face. 'You're going to be amazing!' she said, elated.

Their mother, on the other hand, looked worried. But the sight that really burst her bubble was the delighted sneer on Lauren's face and her father turning what could only be called puce.

'Charity!'

Emma froze in shock. It had been years since she'd been yelled at by her father, and of all the reactions she'd thought of, this wasn't one of them.

'Do I need to remind you of who you are, Emma? Being a Brown means you have a responsibility. Each one of us has to grow this family's standing and our wealth for the next generation—and you want to abandon that duty?'

Emma's hands curled into fists. 'Abandon my duty?' Her voice rose, but she didn't care that she was addressing her father. 'How could anything increase a family's standing more than doing charity work, Dad? And I didn't say I was leaving the company tomorrow. I'm prepared to do what's expected of me. I always have been. But what's the point of me sitting in that shoebox of an office with all the potential I have and doing nothing with it? You won't even give me a chance.'

'Your *potential*?' he said scornfully.

'Peter. That's enough,' her mother said firmly, and for once he listened. 'Emma, I'm so proud of you for following your dreams, sweetheart, but this isn't the most appropriate path for you.'

'Why not?' Emma was struggling to get her words out now. She refused to cry in front of her family. Her throat burned from unshed tears.

'Because we're not people who can do as we please,' said Lauren. 'There are expectations of us. That's how we got to where we are. You can't walk around with your head in the clouds.'

Their father clapped her on the shoulder. Such a blatant show of where his approval lay. And Lauren's smug expression was clear to everyone.

Emma shook her head. One person. Only one person at this table was happy for her. But there wouldn't be a thing Maddison could say that the others would listen to.

Hurt beyond words, Emma stood up. 'I wanted to tell you, and I have.' Emma placed a folded glossy brochure on the table, so her family could see what she had managed to make happen. 'I'll see you at work,' she croaked.

She turned to go but her father stopped her.

'If you go ahead with this, that's it. You will be cut off,' he said.

Emma spun around. 'Would you like me to pay back my trust fund as well?' she spat.

Helen bolted between father and daughter. 'Peter. Emma. Stop it. That money was to set you up for life and we wouldn't ever take it back.'

'Of course you *would* defend her!' Peter shouted at his wife. 'She was a mistake from the beginning, and now she's an accident that is costing us, and it's your fault.' He turned his cold hazel gaze to Emma. 'You do this and you are no longer my daughter.'

Emma staggered back at his words. It was like a dagger plunged into her chest. Even Lauren had the good grace to look shocked.

'Was I ever?' she asked in a small voice.

'You can cut her off, Peter, but I will not have you attack my daughter like that,' her mother fired at her husband. 'Emma—'

She went to hug her daughter, but Emma recoiled from her touch. With one last look at everyone, she fled.

CHAPTER TWENTY

EMMA RAN TO her car and started it up in a daze. She drove away from the large house completely numb. As if she was completely detached from her body. She barely noticed the rain starting to fall, or the roads she took. Not even the numbers she pressed to gain access to the car park in Alex's building.

It was only when she was at his door that she realised where it was she had driven to. She stared at the key in her hand. The key Alex hadn't taken back. She was breaking, and he would make her feel whole again. But then what?

Right now, she didn't care. Emma just wanted to feel.

She slid the key into the lock and pushed at the large swivel door. The apartment was bathed in bright golden light. Soft music floated overhead, drowning out the raindrops battering the windows. She closed the door behind her, and with the sound of her heels and the snap of the door she knew Alex would have heard her enter.

He walked out with a folder in his hand that he dropped to the table the instant he saw her, and the numbness ebbed away, only to be replaced by a torrent of emotions washing over her. It was overwhelming.

Alex took one look at her face and she knew he'd see that it had gone badly with her family.

Closing the distance between them, he pulled her into a protective hug. 'Do you want to talk about it?' he asked.

Did she? Part of her did. Part of her wanted to wail. But maybe forgetting would be better.

And as she sorted through all the thoughts occurring to her at once, the only thing she was certain of was that she didn't want to let go of him just yet. So she stayed in his arms.

'What's that?' she asked, staring at the manila folder on the table.

It wasn't work, because she had come to learn that everything in his office had the company logo. Every document was logged.

Still keeping his arms around her, he pulled back to see what she was looking at. 'The results from my yearly medical check-up.'

'Healthy as a horse?' she teased. But her voice wasn't bright or cheery.

'Yeah, all clear. I wasn't expecting you tonight,' he said.

She didn't respond. It was true—so what was she doing here? She should have gone home to Hannah and Lucky.

'I know.' A heavy sigh escaped her lips. 'I should go.'

Emma huffed a laugh, feeling a little silly. This wasn't a normal relationship. It had never been. And she had fully expected her family to react badly. She'd been prepared for that.

Alex frowned. 'Come with me.'

He led her to the one place in his home that he knew made her happy. From the moment he'd shown it to her Emma had felt that the library was a safe space. She would often curl up on the couch with whatever book she was reading whenever he had to take a call he just couldn't ignore.

Pulling her down to the couch, Alex draped her legs over his. 'Talk to me, Emma.'

Blinking away tears, she bit her lip. Still not feeling entirely composed, somehow she managed to tell him exactly what had happened when she went to her parents' home. As she spoke, Alex's eyes became more and more glacial.

'I'm sorry, Emma. But you don't need them. You don't need their approval. You're nothing like them.'

'It still hurts.'

'I know it does.'

Alex ran his hand up her arm and over her shoulder, caressing her neck with a protective touch. Her hand came to rest on his cheek. Fingertips stroking the stubble she found there. She kissed his jaw, shifting so his lips could come down to hers. It was the softest brush. He was watching her, waiting for a sign of what she needed, but he didn't have to wait.

Emma closed her eyes and leaned in, wanting more. Opening up for him. He sucked her bottom lip into his mouth and her hand moved to the back of his neck, pulling him closer. His scent wrapped around her and she got exactly what she wanted. His tongue dancing with hers, growing the need between them. Heat building within her. A heat that she could focus on. That would distract her from the swirling thoughts of inadequacy.

And then her lips were urgent on his. Desperate. As if he was a life raft she was clinging to. His arms locked so tightly around her that he might as well have been. And then her lips were gone from his. Kissing his sharp jaw, his strong neck.

Alex cursed. 'Emma,' he said, in a rough, strangled way. 'I'm out of protection.'

She wasn't meant to come over tonight after all.

Emma pulled away to look into his eyes, which were darkened with need. 'I don't care. I want you, Alexander.'

Cradling her head in his large hands, he gazed at her intensely. 'Are you sure?'

'Yes. I promise.'

'I trust you,' he said, and kissed her once more.

Picking her up bridal-style, Alex carried her to his bedroom and laid her down on the king-size bed. Holding himself up over her, he kissed her softly.

'I'm going to ask you again. Are you sure about this?' Alex whispered.

'Yes,' she replied, wanting him heart and soul, and in that very moment she couldn't think of anything else.

His fingers went to the ties on her blue wrap dress. Pulled on it slowly. It unravelled, the fabric falling away slightly. His lips moved to the exposed skin of her side while his hands pushed the rest of the fabric away. Trailing open-mouthed kisses across her stomach to her hip, and then up her body and over her shoulder, he peeled the dress away. She never took her eyes off him.

Alex helped her out of her dress and tossed it aside.

Her bra was next.

He sucked her clavicle, teeth nipping at her earlobe.

'You're so damn beautiful,' Alex said on a breath, and her heart stuttered.

He kissed her neck.

'Intelligent...'

He sucked her nipple into his mouth and drew a moan from deep within her.

'Kind...'

A kiss above her belly button.

'Determined...'

His mouth came to her sex. He traced his tongue slowly through her slickness.

'Perfect.'

'Alexander...'

It was part moan, part sob. He wanted to hear her say it again. It made him feel like Icarus, flying too close to the sun. And she had become the sun. The centre of his world.

With his tongue and his hands, he worshipped her. He was focused on her. On being in this moment. On getting to love her in this intimate way that slightly terrified him—because what if he could never let go after tonight?

Her fingers sank into his hair as her hips bucked beneath him, but he didn't slow down. He kept going until his name was an incantation on her lips as she came apart. Waves of pleasure rolling through her.

The apartment became silent.

Emma's eyes were tightly shut, her chest rising and falling rapidly. He kissed her everywhere. Along her thighs, over her belly, on her neck. Until she caught her breath. Then Alex could wait no more.

He pulled away, standing at the foot of the bed. Grasping the front of his shirt, he ripped it in opposite directions, sending buttons popping off and clattering to the floor in a shower. He divested himself of the rest of his clothes and then he was hovering over her, holding himself up on his arms.

Their gazes locked together. Alex leaned his forehead on Emma's and slowly sank into her. His moan was guttural. Being careful, disciplined, was who Alex was, so he had never done this before. What they had was so powerful, what was one more first between them?

'You feel amazing...'

Alex had never felt this connected to a soul in his life. He wanted to savour every moment of the feeling. He took his time. Moving slowly, languorously.

He was always in control, but she was making him lose it. Dissolving all the strings that kept him so rigidly in place. Making him question why he'd ever thought he could live without this. This wasn't sex. It wasn't fun. It was love. And he was drowning in it.

Alex could feel Emma climbing. She was bearing down on him. Her gasps coming in quick, almost musical pants. And then her body arched and she shattered around him, moaning incoherently. Unable to breathe and completely overwhelmed.

Alex kissed her hard as he rode her through her release and into his own as it crashed into him. His moan was quiet. Ragged. Vulnerable. Their lips were still connected. He pushed all the way into her silken depths, unable to disconnect himself from her.

Looking down at Emma, he saw tears run down the sides of her face. He brushed them away but said nothing.

Because he felt it too.

They had been irrevocably changed.

CHAPTER TWENTY-ONE

THE SKY WAS only just lightening to a deep blue when Emma woke. After a few sleepy blinks she felt her brain catch up, and remembered the events of the night before. Every night with Alex was great, but last night had been soul-consuming. She knew he'd felt what she had—it had been clear in his eyes.

So when she looked over and saw that his side of the bed was empty, she got an uneasy feeling in the pit of her stomach. He had woken up with her every day they'd spent in London. In that little fantasy bubble.

Emma dressed hurriedly in the clothes she'd worn the day before. She would have to leave soon, if she had any chance of going home to change and still getting to work on time. Not that she was keen to. The confrontation with her family was still fresh in her mind.

She found her shoes in the library and slipped them on before rushing downstairs, where she found Alex.

'There you are.'

He placed a mug of coffee on the counter for her and she took a grateful sip before kissing him. It didn't feel right.

Emma gathered her things. There was a message from Hannah on her phone.

Lucky is fed. Heading out early.

Emma chuckled at her phone. Her cat would no doubt be upset that she had spent another night away. But it was nothing he wouldn't forgive with a few tasty treats.

She noticed Alex was being unusually quiet.

'Alexander? Are you okay?' she asked, holding the mug in her hand.

'Of course. Why?'

'Well, you've only said three words to me. Usually…'

Usually he wouldn't be able to keep his hands off her.

Usually he had a flirty smile for her, or a naughty wink.

'Emma.'

She didn't like his tone.

'Can we talk before I leave for work?'

'What do you want to talk about?' he asked. She could smell his tea from the other side of the counter.

'Last night was…' Words failed him.

'Yes, it was,' she said quietly.

She looked up and he was studying her. She held his gaze until he walked around the kitchen counter and stood before her. Putting her cup down, she took his hands in hers.

'Alexander, you pieced me back together last night.'

He caressed her cheek, but he looked so composed. Too composed. 'You should never have been broken in the first place,' he said.

Emma shrugged. The feeling that something was amiss just would not leave her. 'What's wrong?' she insisted.

'Nothing,' he said forcefully.

'Really? Because for the first time since I met you I don't believe you,' she said testily, brushing his hand away.

'I don't know what to tell you, Emma…'

She shook her head, anger quickly heating her blood. 'I don't believe this. We have a real connection, and your next move is to shut me out.'

'I'm not shutting you out.'

'What do you call this? What you're doing right now?'

She took a breath, and turned around to get her coat, but he caught her wrist, drawing her back.

'I told you from the beginning that I can't change. I was honest with you. And I was honest with you last night.'

'But you're not being honest this morning. I didn't ask you to change. Not once. Not...'

Emma had opened her mouth to yell at him, but she stopped. Instead, she closed her eyes and took a deep breath, and when she opened them she was calm. The shutters had come down on her feelings. She knew she was falling into the abyss now, but no one would see.

It made Alex snap. 'For God's sake, Emma, stop doing that! Feel what you feel! If you're angry, show me, dammit!'

It was the most out-of-control she had ever seen him.

'Not when you became the most important person to me. Not when I fell in love with you,' she said softly. Her eyes welled up. She was damned if she would let the tears fall. 'I love you, Alexander.'

She loved him.

She watched the words fall on him like a blade. All he could do was shake his head.

'I don't do love, Emma! I don't know how to.'

There was desperation and agony and no small amount of sorrow on his face.

She stepped closer and cupped his cheek. 'It breaks my heart that you think that. Because you love harder than anyone I know. Maybe one day you'll figure it out.'

Alex dropped his head and pulled her hand away from his face. 'Emma, I can't change—even if I want the same things. You're better off with someone else,' he said.

'Goodbye, Alex.'

She placed his apartment key on the counter, picked up her things and left. Her heart breaking. This was never meant to last. And she knew she would never love again. Not like this.

She felt as if she had to fight for every breath. She had always known this day would come, and yet she still felt woefully unprepared. Climbing into her car, she slammed her head against the headrest, fighting the tears that she didn't want to shed.

'Keep it together!' she told herself.

Her phone sprang into life, Alex's face flashing on the caller ID. But she rejected the call and threw her phone onto the passenger seat. There was nothing he could say now. She knew what they'd shared. What he wasn't ready for.

The car tore out of the parking bay and she rushed home. Not even once glancing back at his building. She was a vortex of grief and anger. Within the course of one night she had lost the one bright light in her life and lost most of her family. And neither because she had done anything wrong.

It didn't matter. Emma felt resolved. She knew what she had to do.

Hannah had already left when Emma arrived home. Lucky, her beautiful black cat, had a full bowl of food and obstinately ignored her, angry that she hadn't been home. She pulled out a couple of his favourite treats, bribing him for his forgiveness, before she readied herself for work and rushed out through the door.

Emma clocked in with minutes to spare. Normally the friendliest person on the floor, this morning she barely greeted anyone. Everyone who saw her simply moved aside to let her pass. She was immediately reminded of Alex, and she felt as if she was suffocating.

She shut the door to her office with a rattle. She was done. Done with all the people in her life, done with this company, done with living in hope.

Her laptop was fired up and she typed a resignation letter, printed it in her office. The next thing she did was save all her personal files on a thumb drive and wipe them from the hard drive. There wasn't much, but it felt final.

She knew the correct protocol was to hand her resignation letter to her manager, but she was a Brown, and she wanted to look at the glee on her father's face when she gave it to him.

Snatching up the letter, she took the elevator up to the executive floor and barged into her father's office. She didn't even acknowledge her mother or Lauren, who were with him.

Her father opened his mouth to yell at her. Not willing to give him the opportunity to say anything, she slapped her letter down on the table.

'What's this?' he asked, irritated by her interruption.

'I'm leaving, if you recall,' Emma said. Her voice was hard. 'But I will work out my notice period.'

His eyes scanned the page. 'If you want to leave, you should go.'

'Are you firing me?' she asked in a steely tone.

Her father stared her down, but for once, Emma was not moved. She stood straighter. Unintimidated.

'Dad, are you firing me?' she repeated.

'Yes.'

'Peter!' her mother exclaimed.

'Fine.'

It was exactly the outcome she'd wanted. It wasn't about the pay-out she'd receive—rather that everyone would know that Peter Brown had fired his hardest working daughter, and she silently wished him luck in sorting that mess out.

Initially she'd wanted to save the image of the company. Now she didn't care. Now she would be able to walk into her dream job without having to wait.

Emma was almost through the door when she turned around. There was something she had to get off her chest.

'I know you don't approve of my passion for charity

work, and you don't have to, but just know that I was the one who ignored every dream to be what this company needed, and now I'm doing this for me. I don't need you.'

She closed the door behind her and went back down to her office to gather her things. Glad that she wasn't the sentimental type, and there wasn't much to take apart from the framed degree that hung behind her. Placing it carefully on the desk, Emma looked around at the tiny office and realised that, as much as she'd enjoyed working with the people here, she would not miss the place.

A knock at the door made her jump and spin around to see Greg in the doorway.

'Can I see you in my office?' he asked.

Emma picked up her framed degree and her bag, and without a backward glance followed her manager who gestured for her to take a seat in front of his desk.

He sat heavily in his chair. 'Where do we start, Emma? I can't believe you were fired.'

She lifted her shoulders nonchalantly, an action completely at odds with how she felt inside. 'It was going to happen sooner or later.'

'I know. But it's unbelievable. I just want you to know it's been a pleasure to work with you and you'll always have friends here.'

'Thank you, Greg.'

'And if there's ever anything you need, just call.'

She gave him a hug, and had to fight tears she hadn't expected from leaving Brown Hughs. Then she picked up her belongings and headed out to her car.

She idly wondered how long it would be before her name was removed from her parking space. Driving out, she glimpsed the handyman in her mirror. He was walking to her spot and she knew.

A song wafted through the speakers in her car as she joined the road but Emma turned it off. She couldn't bear any more music. Her heart couldn't take it. There were too many good memories of Alex. And one soul-crushing one. She felt like an idiot for ever thinking she could hold on to those memories when the last memory tainted all the others.

Her phone rang again. This time it was Hannah. She pressed a little button on her steering wheel and her best friend's voice came through loudly in the car.

'How are you holding up, Em? I heard.'

'That was quick. How?'

'Maddison called me. She sounded genuinely concerned,' said Hannah's disembodied voice. 'She said your dad said some harsh things.'

No doubt Lauren would have filled Maddison in the moment Emma was out the door. 'I don't really know what to say,' she told Hannah.

'That makes two of us. And I can tell that's not the only thing. What's going on?'

Emma huffed a laugh. Of course Hannah would be perceptive. She knew Emma better than anyone.

'Emma?'

'Alex and I broke up.'

And they were the words that broke the dam.

'Oh, Em, I'm so sorry! I can take the rest of the day off?' Hannah offered.

'No. I just want to be alone.'

There was nothing anyone could say or do that would help her now. She knew that what she and Alex had shared was temporary. He'd always been honest with her. Emotions didn't follow logic, though, and she felt as if there was a rip right through her soul.

'I understand. Call me if you need anything. Okay? Anything.'

'Thanks, Han. I'll see you later.'

Emma hung up just as she reached her building. With heavy steps, she made her way up to her apartment. Lucky was still ignoring her. She dropped her things on the small dining table and flopped onto the couch, where she curled up and let the tears fall. With arms wrapped around herself she sobbed, feeling completely bereft.

Lucky jumped off his perch and pounced on the cushions, pushing his way between her arms. She scratched his head, but nothing could stem the flow.

CHAPTER TWENTY-TWO

'Goodbye, Alex.'

Alex. That had crushed him.

All he'd been able to do was watch her leave and feel a part of him fracture.

He'd felt like raging. He'd wanted to break something. Tear his apartment apart. But he'd done none of that. He'd controlled his shattering heart, standing inhumanly still.

He'd stood rooted to the spot as he'd heard the door close behind her. The silence had been deafening. All he'd been able to feel was his lungs expanding and contracting. Everything else had fallen away. He was hollow.

'What did I just do?' he asked himself now.

A voice at the back of his mind told him it was the right thing, but it didn't feel like it. He was sure Emma hated him now, and that felt worse than any torture he could imagine. Hadn't he wondered what a life with her would be like? Except he'd told her to find someone else. He didn't want to picture that. It hurt beyond words.

He'd called her, wanting to apologise, to ask her back, but his call had been rejected.

He ran his fingers through his hair, as if somehow that was going to fix all the broken pieces inside him. It did make him move. Back to his room, where he looked at the bed. His cruel mind replayed images of Emma stretched out over it, calling his name. Of him watching her sleep last night after she'd toppled his world.

Alex backed away from the piece of furniture as if it were a dangerous animal. He showered and dressed robotically. What he needed was work. Something to stop him feeling as if the walls were crumbling.

He walked into his study and was assaulted by the memory of kissing Emma against the door. A heavy sigh escaped him. She was going to haunt him.

Sending a message to the office to say that he would be working from home, Alex sat at his desk and forced himself to concentrate. He ignored the beauty of the sunrise outside his window. He ignored every intruding thought of her. Even though he knew ignoring everything around him wasn't going to fix the gnawing void within.

No music played this morning. When he was younger, music had filled the stifling silence. Being an only child, with no mother and a father lost to his grief, had made for a silent childhood. Emma had said it sounded lonely. She had no idea. Music had made the space feel less empty, and as he'd matured he had grown so used to it that it had become one of those things he didn't think about. Just the norm.

Now he couldn't bear the thought of it. Any music would just set his teeth on edge.

For a few hours he worked through the list of tasks he had set for himself, but the ringing of the phone on his laptop brought that to a halt. He accepted the call, and Matt's concerned face filled his screen.

'Are you okay?' Matt asked.

'How did you…?'

'Hannah just told me. What happened, mate?'

And Alex told him the edited version of events.

'Alex, I could punch you right now.'

'I know I hurt her,' Alex said.

'You didn't just hurt her, mate. When are you going to

see that you're punishing yourself for a mistake that wasn't even yours? You know you love her. I saw it. I'm sure everyone else did too!'

Alex saw Matt look away, his eyes unfocussed, as if he was deep in thought. 'You keep saying that you can't change, but you're lying to yourself.'

'I'm not ready for that, Matt.'

'That's another lie. You're gutted, mate. It's not too late. You can fix this.'

'I don't think I can,' Alex said, propping his elbows on the table and running his hands over his face.

'I've known you for ever, Alex. I don't believe that for a second. You deserve to be happy, mate.'

Alex appreciated the words. He just didn't know if he could believe them just yet.

Matt ended the call and Alex stared at the ceiling, wondering if he'd done the right thing.

By the time the evening came round, he felt more like a shell than ever. He poured a measure of whisky into a cut-glass tumbler and sought the sanctuary of his library. Yes, it would remind him of Emma, but it was also the room with the best distractions.

When Alex entered the room, he knew exactly which book he wanted, but the one on the table was what caught his eye. It was Emma's favourite. His favourite. He picked it up and lifted the cover. Her bookmark fell out.

Snapping it shut, he raised his arm to hurl it across the room, but couldn't. Instead, he sank into a plush chair and started reading.

He felt as if his heart was tearing itself apart and then stitching itself together and tearing apart again, like some sort of Promethean torment. And he felt as if he deserved an eternity of it.

Lucky sat at Emma's bedroom door and, as usual, she picked him up and took him to her bed, where he curled up on the pillow next to hers. Emma was restless. Her family were silent. The person she wanted was an impossibility. Hannah was working late. There was only one person she could call.

The phone rang for an age before her mother answered. 'Emma?'

'Hey, Mom,' she greeted her as she climbed under the covers.

'How are you, sweetheart?'

'I'm okay,' she said tiredly.

Emma wanted to tell her mother everything. She wanted her to come over and hug her and tell her it would be okay. That she was wrong and would love again.

'Darling, is this important? I'd love to chat, but Maddie is here,' her mother said.

Pure mirthless laughter bubbled up in Emma's throat. She choked it down. Why had she thought she would find solace in her parent? She wasn't Maddie or Lauren. Her mother might have tried to defend her to her father, but that didn't seem to mean all that much. Alex had been right about one thing: she didn't need them.

'No, Mom, don't worry about it. I'll talk to you later.' Emma hung up before her mother could say anything more. 'Well, Lucky,' she said, turning over to face her cat. 'Looks like it's just you and I.'

The black cat chirped and continued licking his paws while Emma watched. At least she had one love that would never leave her...

CHAPTER TWENTY-THREE

WHEN ALEX SAW his father's name flash on his phone, he was instantly filled with guilt. He hadn't called to make sure his father was okay for two days. Hadn't checked on his progress.

'What's happened, son?' his father asked.

'Nothing. I'm sorry I haven't called.' He looked at the time and realised how late it was in the UK. 'You should be asleep, Dad. You know what the cardiologist said.'

'Alex, I feel fine. My recovery is going well, and it was just a minor heart attack. Now, tell me what's happened, so your old man doesn't stress.'

Alex sighed and looked away, debating what he should tell his father. When he was growing up, it had seemed as if the man had always known when he was hiding something. Alex had quickly learned to tell the whole truth and own up to his actions. If he didn't tell his father what was wrong, he had no doubt he would figure it out anyway.

So he told him everything. Even what he'd left out with Matt.

He didn't know why he was letting everything out like this—he never shared emotional stuff with anyone. He was stronger than that. But it all poured out of him and he knew he couldn't stop it if he tried.

'Son, you are not me, and Emma is not Catherine,' his father told him when Alex stopped talking. 'You love each other in a way we never did. At times I was a little too domineering, but that isn't who you are. Emma isn't going to leave you a broken man, like I was when your mother left. You're broken because you left her.'

'Dad—' Alex started, but a look from his father made him stop.

'That's what you are afraid of and that's what's made you run now. She's the only person you've dated that you've brought home.'

'She's the only person I've actually dated, Dad.' He had had encounters in the past. Purely physical releases. Emma had been different from the very beginning.

His father shut his eyes tightly. 'That's my fault,' he said sadly.

'What do you mean?' Alex frowned. He'd never blamed his father. He was his hero. Just as much a victim of his mother as he had been until he'd decided he wouldn't be.

'Over the years, every time you asked about your mother and didn't get the answers you wanted, you retreated into yourself a little more. I didn't know how to handle it. I was so caught up in my own loss. I really did love your mother, but I didn't show it. And then it was too late.'

'It was too late because you wanted an heir,' Alex said simply.

'No, Alex, I wanted a child. I didn't care about the title; my brother could have had it. Maybe then you would have had cousins. It doesn't change the fact that I should have been there for you. You would have been so much happier. But I wasn't, and I'm sorry.'

Alex's lips pressed into a thin line. 'Dad, you were there. You were the only one who was.'

Robert shook his head. 'Not enough. But I will tell you now what I should have then. Your mother leaving was not your fault, son. And it wasn't mine either. It was her own decision. She wasn't capable of giving you the love you needed.'

Alex felt something inside him crumble. 'Dad...' He barely got the word out.

'I'm proud of the man you've become, Alex, and that man doesn't run when it gets tough.'

'But I did.' Alex dropped his gaze and said softly, 'I miss her.'

'Then get her back. She makes you happy, son, and that's all a parent ever wants for their child.'

Alex pinched the bridge of his nose. As usual, his father was right. But he was scared. And that was hard to admit to himself.

'Go, son. Don't waste any more time.'

Alex listened. He hung up and shoved his phone in his pocket, then slipped on the jacket of his blue three-piece suit. Picking up his keys, he hurried to his car and rushed over to Brown Hughs. When he arrived at her office with a racing heart he found it empty. There was no sign of her. Not even her degree on the wall.

He went to the office of her manager, who was walking around his desk, going back to his chair.

'Where's Emma?' Alex asked.

'You don't know?' Greg's brow furrowed.

'Know what?' Alex growled.

'You should speak to her family.' He threw the file he was holding onto the table, clearly upset.

Alex was already on the move. He had no idea how they could have made life any worse for her, but being on edge and emotional had his temper simmering just below the surface.

The elevator doors slid open on the C Suite floor, and as luck would have it he ran into Lauren.

'Alex!' she said, surprised.

'Where's your father?'

His tone was sharp and low. Lauren clearly recognised the edge in it and had him follow her to her father's office. She walked in behind Alex and silently closed the door.

'Alexander Hastings!'

Peter Brown greeted him warmly, but his eyes were cold. Cruel.

'This is a surprise. How can I help you?'

'Where's Emma?' Alex stared the man down. He was not in the mood for pretences.

'As of two days ago she no longer works here,' Peter said.

'What did you do?' Alex clenched his fists at his sides.

'What did *I* do? You dare barge into my office and question *me*?' Peter was incensed. 'I fired her, and it was about time too. I don't have time for anyone who abandons their duty to their family for frivolous pursuits.'

Alex had to fight every urge to punch the man in front of him. 'You fired your daughter?' he said slowly. Disbelief turning into blazing fury.

Helen rushed into the office. Out the corner of his eye, Alex saw her enter, but he didn't acknowledge her. Not even when she called his name.

'It's none of your business,' Peter spat.

Alex brought his palms down onto the glossy wooden desk, leaning over this man he hated with a passion. 'Oh, it's very much my business. Every time you hurt Emma, it's my business,' Alex snarled, his pulse pounding in his ears. 'Let me tell you right now, if by some miracle she ever lets you back into her life, and you cause her even the slightest bit of distress, I will have no problem coming after you with everything I've got. You've been warned.'

'You think you can threaten m—?' Seeing the look in Alex's eyes, Peter let the words die on his tongue.

Alex brushed past the two women. He had had enough of the Browns for one day. All he wanted was to find Emma.

'She's at home.'

It was the last thing he heard. He didn't thank Helen.

Emma had her feet curled up on the couch. Lucky lay against her, happily dozing, while Emma watched whatever was on the flatscreen TV. She didn't care. She felt empty. Grief-stricken. There was plenty to mourn—her job, her family, a relationship that had been doomed from the start.

The laptop she'd been working on stood open on the coffee table. Words she couldn't concentrate on stared back at her. Judging her. She'd allowed herself these two days. A lot had happened, but tomorrow would be the start of a new journey. A new Emma. The Emma she was some of the time. Except now she could be her all of the time. She no longer had a family who could make her feel as if she needed to withdraw. Tomorrow she would be liberated, but today she was sad.

There was a knock at her door, which she figured must be the takeout she had ordered. With her hair up in a messy bun, her feet bare and wearing an oversized T-shirt, Emma went to answer the door, knowing the pizza guy wouldn't care that she looked like a slob.

She pulled the door open, but it definitely wasn't the pizza guy.

'What do you want, Alexander?' she asked. She'd slipped up. Saying his name made her heart skip a beat.

'Can we talk?' he asked hopefully.

Lucky had heard his voice and jumped off the couch to rub himself around Alex's legs.

'Traitor,' Emma mumbled, at her usually aloof cat.

She stood aside, and he picked the cat up as he entered. She went to the couch to get the remote, switching the television off before she faced him.

She wrapped her arms around herself. 'Before you say anything, I want to tell you that you don't need to check up on me. I'm fine. You owe me no explanations. I knew what this was before we started. We're all good. I'm sure you must be very busy, so you don't have to waste any time here.'

'Can I speak?' Alex asked, and laughed in a defeated way. He put Lucky down on the cushions and took a step towards Emma, but then stopped. 'I do owe you an explanation, Emma, and an apology. I'm here to ask you to forgive me.'

'You're forgiven. You can go now.' She needed him to leave. It was too painful to see him.

'Emma...'

The tormented way he said her name cut right through her.

'Please listen to me, and after that if you still want me to go, I will.'

Emma nodded, and he felt a small amount of relief that she wasn't kicking him out. He still felt as if he was holding in a breath, though. He ran his fingers through his hair, piecing together what he wanted to say.

'I was scared, and I reacted badly.'

A sad smile curved Emma's lips. 'Alex, you don't have to apologise. You told me what you wanted from the start.'

'Please stop calling me Alex,' he begged. 'I do have to apologise—but that's not the only thing. I'm here to tell you I love you.'

'What?' Emma's eyes widened in shock.

'I love you, and I think I have since the first time I met you. I knew you were special then, and I've been scared since that first kiss. I've always had my life ordered just the way I like. You were right. I was always in control because I needed to make sure that *I* was the one who decided who was allowed to enter and leave my life. I could never allow the chaos of love in my life—how could I when I was convinced that I was unlovable?'

Alex closed his eyes and swallowed thickly. Emma could see how hard this was for him.

'Alexander,' she said, reaching for him, and he smiled fleetingly, taking her hand and placing it on his stubbled cheek. 'You could never be unlovable.'

'Of course I could. Why else would a mother leave her

child? Why would she know who I am, be in the same room as me, and never once reach out? I wasn't worthy.'

Emma's eyes welled up. 'That's not true. Her decisions don't reflect on who you are.'

'I realise that now, but it made me foolish. It made me hurt you. And I'm so sorry, Emma.' He cradled her face in his hands. 'I didn't want to be falling in love, but I did it anyway. I didn't want to make my father's mistakes and be a broken man when you left, as I was convinced you would.'

Emma couldn't stop the tears that were rolling down her cheeks.

'And when I saw how perfectly you fitted into my life I was terrified, because for the first time I wanted that more than anything. I do want that, Emma. I want to go to sleep with you beside me and wake up with you in my arms. I want to share everything I have, everything I am, with you.'

'Alexander…' she breathed in broken sobs. 'But how do I know you won't get scared again?'

He leaned his forehead against hers, taking a ragged breath. 'I guess you don't. But I promise you I will work every day for the rest of my life to prove myself worthy of you.'

'Worthy of me?'

'Yes! You are the most incredible, courageous, beautiful, intoxicating woman I have ever met. The question is: will you accept me?'

'I love you, Alexander, so much. Of course I accept you! All I want is you.'

'You have me, baby. For the rest of our lives.'

Alex kissed her as he never had before. With desperation and fervency and so much love that neither of them could breathe.

'I have one more thing to ask of you,' he said against her lips. 'Will you and Lucky move in with me?'

Emma laughed brightly, giddy with joy. 'Let's go.'

EPILOGUE

Two years later

THE SKY OVERHEAD was a vibrant blue. Fluffy white clouds drifted over in the gentle breeze that offered some relief from the unusual summer heat. It was a beautiful day. Serene. Even the horses in the paddock seemed to be enjoying the sun.

Emma sat on the red-and-white-checked blanket that was laid on the grass, her back against the trunk of a tree. Fingers stroking through Alex's black hair as he lay with his head in her lap. The sunlight was catching his blue eyes, making them even more vivid than normal. Almost otherworldly.

Emma still couldn't believe that this amazing specimen of a man was hers. He had been for a little over two and a half years now, and in that time so much had changed.

There was no fear of love, nor feelings of inadequacy.

They'd left Melbourne, but travelled back often enough. In fact they travelled extensively, as Alex grew Hastings International. Their most frequent trip was back here, to Greenfield House. A place that Alex had grown to love.

They had come here when he'd proposed to her, in the middle of the maze, when he had set up a scavenger hunt that had ended with him in the centre, waiting on a bended knee. They had come back again when they'd got married in the gardens. And now they were back here for a few days, and intended to stay for a few more.

Alex kissed Emma's swollen belly. He couldn't wait to meet his baby. It had been Emma's idea that they—including Lucky—should spend the pregnancy and the year afterwards in London. She wanted his father to be as close to his grandchild as possible, and Alex had gratefully agreed.

His father had, after all, accepted Emma as the daughter he'd never had, and she'd got the father she always wanted.

Having been back for a few months already, those plans had morphed. They had decided to stay in London permanently. Alex was finally embracing every part of his life. Being heir to an earldom no longer felt like a shackle, and he'd helped Emma set up a British branch of the literacy charity, taking the organisation international—much to Fiona's excitement.

Emma moved the hand that had been in Alex's to her belly. 'Did you feel that?' she asked, and smiled.

Alex beamed. Felt his face lighting up. 'Yes! I can't wait to meet you...' he said, turning over with his lips inches from her belly. 'Take you to your first concert. Teach you how to drive really fast...'

He whispered the last two words, making Emma laugh.

'He's going to be a rower—just like his dad,' she said, kissing her husband on the head.

'He?'

She shrugged. 'I just know. I have a feeling.'

Alex sat up, taking her face in his hands, and kissed her slowly, lovingly. Roving his lips over hers. He couldn't imagine that it was possible to love her any more than he did right now, but he'd thought that the day before, and the day before that. He knew his love for her would only grow. That no matter how much time he had with her it would never be nearly enough.

'I love you, Emma Hastings,' he breathed against her lips.

'I love you too, Alexander.'

* * * * *

COMING SOON!

We really hope you enjoyed reading this book.
If you're looking for more romance, be sure to
head to the shops when new books are
available on

Thursday 27th October

To see which titles are coming soon, please visit

millsandboon.co.uk/nextmonth

MILLS & BOON®

Coming next month

HER CHRISTMAS BABY CONFESSION
Sharon Kendrick

His words were as emotionless as his expression and Bianca couldn't deny a twist of pain as their coldness washed over her.

But what else had she expected? Joy? Excitement? Surely she hadn't anticipated Xanthos would behave in the way would-be fathers were supposed to behave. Get real, Bianca.

"You're not suggesting I planned this?"

"I have no idea," he drawled, dark eyebrows shooting upwards. "Did you?"

"Please don't insult me!"

He nodded, as if her anger and indignation were in some way reassuring. His gaze rested upon her face. "What do you intend to do?"

"I'm k-keeping my baby, of course!"

"Good."

The word took the wind right out of her sails and she blinked at him in confusion, before reminding herself that she didn't need his approval. But that didn't prevent the sliver of hope which shot through her, like sunlight breaking through a dark cloud. "I know you never intended to be a father—"

"No, you're right, I didn't." His words effectively killed off that brief flash of optimism. "So what do you want from me, Bianca?"

Continue reading
HER CHRISTMAS BABY CONFESSION
Sharon Kendrick

Available next month
www.millsandboon.co.uk

LET'S TALK
Romance

For exclusive extracts, competitions
and special offers, find us online:

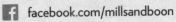 facebook.com/millsandboon

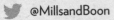 @MillsandBoon

@MillsandBoonUK

Get in touch on 01413 063232

For all the latest titles coming soon, visit
millsandboon.co.uk/nextmonth